TWILIGHT MAN

TWILIGHT MAN

A Novel

Lenore DeKoven

iUniverse, Inc.
New York Lincoln Shanghai

Twilight Man
A Novel

iUniverse, Inc.

For information address:
iUniverse, Inc.
2021 Pine Lake Road, Suite 100
Lincoln, NE 68512
www.iuniverse.com

ISBN: 0-595-30009-X (pbk)
ISBN: 0-595-75170-9 (cloth)

Printed in the United States of America

CHAPTER 1

1967 Thurgood Marshall First Black Appointed to Supreme Court

"Next!"

The word hung in the dense grey air. It was late in the day and the two men and one woman who sat at the long pockmarked oak table on the hard wooden ice cream parlor chairs were weary. The room was dark and chilly like a basement after a hard rain and they'd been at it since ten a.m., captive in that inhospitable space. Nobody moved for a moment. They were intently focused on the small empty platform in front of them as though by some mystical vibration of group will they could cause a vision to materialize and end their ordeal. The table was speckled with the crumbs of their take-out lunch and littered with paper cups which once held coffee and coke and were now filled with soggy cigarette butts. A few small spotlights mounted on pipes stretching across the ceiling provided the only light. Funereal black velour drapes hung across the wall behind the small stage.

"We're never going to get this play done unless we start thinking about some kind of compromise."

It was Adam who spoke, not looking at Len, the small, wiry black man on his left. Then he scratched his hand and sighed. Karen had watched the hand scratching all day and wondered whether it was an invisible rash or a nervous tic.

The room was strangely silent. Len smiled secretly as if he had just told himself a clever private joke. Karen had watched him do that during all the auditions as actors filed in one after the other. Today it annoyed the hell out of her.

Throughout the last two days, Len had smiled his smile and spoken in monosyllables like 'no' or 'well.' Occasionally there had been a 'possible' with a shrug. He looked so fragile. Karen wondered if he ate enough. She watched him hunch over his knees and withdraw into himself. He looked more like one of those tortured Munch paintings than a playwright. Karen stifled a yawn. God, this is not fun! Who do you have to fuck to get out of this job? An audible giggle escaped her throat before she could control it. The two men looked at her questioningly.

"What the hell is funny? asked Adam.

"Nothing. I'm just getting jumpy."

Karen knew that she had to be careful. She mustn't make too many cracks or jokes or be too smart, too obtrusive. She had to be on her best behaviour because the producer was her husband and they were sure to think that's why she got this job.They might even suspect that he'd placed her here as some kind of spy. Oh, well. Assistant to the Director was a credit of sorts. At least it was a start.

"How many left out there? asked Adam. He stood and shook out his legs. He was a thin-boned man with a head that seemed a little small for his body and arms that were unusually long. His blonde hair had deserted the front of his scalp and what remained was flecked with gray, but his face was unlined. It was a boyish look reinforced by horn-rimmed glasses and white sneakers.

Karen consulted her list. "There are three. Two men and a beautiful blonde"

"A blonde? What's she doing here?"

"Understudy. I saved her for last. I figured by this time you'd both appreciate a change." She grinned at them. "Do you want to see John Castle next?"

"Yeh. Bring in the blonde too. Let them read together." Adam yawned. "God, I'm exhausted."

Karen grabbed a Salem out of the almost decimated pack of cigarettes in front of her.

"We're all out of matches" whispered Len. He rarely used full voice.

Karen rose and stretched. Her jeans were sticking to her thighs. She hated rooms without windows. Her limbs felt stiff from sitting for so long and she had a dull headache. She'd been imprisoned with these two men for a solid week. Whoever said that the theatre was a glamorous life? Adam had no sense of humor, Len was a stone wall and the days were getting longer and longer. She prayed that the next actor would be the perfect solution. In her mind's eye she saw herself in a tub full of bubble bath finishing that Dorothy Sayers mystery with the radio playing her favorite Mahler Symphony in the background.

There were only two men left. One of them had to be it or it would mean another endless day of this.

Adam casually contemplated Karen's figure and scratched his hand again. He wasn't usually attracted to curly-headed brunettes but her five and a half foot voluptuous, well proportioned body was pleasing to the eye. "Tell the last actor and the blonde to look at page 27."

"Okay." Karen's leather heels clicked on the tile floor as she walked a few steps down the narrow hall and stuck her head into the small adjoining room.

A stocky broad-shouldered young black man wearing jeans, T shirt and an Afro sat on a bench poring over the script. He was mouthing the words as though trying to memorize them. The slender beautiful woman sitting next to him had her script closed on her lap and, lids lowered, seemed to be dozing. She wore a simple figure hugging black dress that was printed with tiny pink flowers and had buttons all the way down the front. It was the third person in the room that grabbed Karen's attention. He was a tall man, more than six feet, with dark curly hair and a strong, chiseled jaw-line. Bone structure was one of the things that Karen noticed first. Some people went right to the eyes and others looked at mouths first, but with Karen it was definitely bone structure. This man had the sexiest jaw she'd ever seen. Stunning, but a white man. Did he get sent to the wrong audition by his agent?

He had been pacing like an animal testing the perameters of his cage, when Karen entered the room. He stopped in mid-pace, staring at her with dark, piercing eyes.

Karen was startled by the sudden feeling of warmth that crept into her cheeks. She held out the unlit cigarette in her hand. "Uh, anybody got a light?"

He came toward her, extending the one he'd been smoking. He offered his pinky finger, hooking it into hers to steady the linkage of the two as she drew deeply to ignite the tobacco. As their fingers touched Karen felt him tremble. It was a quiver not visible to the eye but seeming to come from somewhere deep inside him, more nerves than emotion.

"Thanks." She looked up at him. "Your name is…?'

"Conrad Taylor. I had a five o'clock appointment." There was accusation in the statement. It was well past that now.

"Oh…yes." Karen recalled her conversation with Scanlon, the agent who had sent him. But what did he have in mind? Karen had given him a detailed breakdown of the character, told him exactly what they were looking for. "Umm, I think there may have been some mistake. Have you had a chance to look at the script?"

"Yes. There's no mistake." Conrad's nostrils flared slightly.

He was like a wired thoroughbred racehorse about to fly down the track. Karen half expected the man to prick up his ears and paw the ground. There was a feeling of intense energy, contained but in danger of exploding any moment.

She tried to sound reassuring. "Well, it'll just be another few minutes. Would you look at the scene starting on twenty seven?" She turned to the two actors on the bench. "Will you both come with me please?" As she turned to leave she felt Conrad's eyes on her back.

Karen ushered the two actors in, referring to the 8X10 photos on her clipboard. "This is Cynthia Carter."

"Hi. I'm very happy to meet you, Mr. Adler." Cynthia flashed a toothpaste ad smile at the director. She knew Adam's reputation as one of the better and busier directors on the east coast. "Hi, Len", she nodded at the writer. They had worked together on a benefit. That might or might not be an advantage.

"And this is John Castle," continued Karen. "John, this is our director, Adam Adler, and our playwright, Len Sutton."

"Hi." John shook hands with the two men.

"Sorry to have kept you waiting." said Adam as he glanced at the resumes on the backs of the pictures Karen had handed to him. "I see you've done your share of PORGY AND BESS tours, John"

"Yep." The actor nodded and grinned. He knew that Adam understood. That show was one of the few that could keep Negro actors working. He turned to the playwright. "This is a wonderful play, man. What a rare opportunity for an actor!"

Len nodded, whispered "Thanks" and did an imitation of a turtle.

"Can we try the scene that starts on 27? Just take your time and make yourselves comfortable." Adam was trying to be gracious and patient but he wanted desperately to go home and have several large shots of Scotch.

As the actors stepped onto the platform Karen scribbled a note and shoved it toward Adam. He read it then glanced at Karen with raised eyebrow before turning his attention to the actors before him.

"Okay folks. Whenever you're ready." Adam wondered if the pretty blonde knew that they'd already cast the part of the leading woman and they were only looking at understudies. Watching the two actors as they struggled through the scene, he knew immediately that she was capable and he was hopeless, but he waited patiently until they'd finished.

"Thank you, John. That was very nice. We'll let you know. Cynthia, can you do us a big favor and read with the next actor? Thanks a lot."

Cynthia nodded delightedly. She hoped the next guy would give her more to work with.

Adam looked at Karen's note again while he was waiting for John to make his exit. "Okay. Send in the Polynesian," muttered Adam as the door closed behind him.

"Who?" The turtle head shot out of its shell. During this last reading, Len, lids lowered, had curled up in his chair in the fetal position. He straightened suddenly, eyes wide open.

Karen winked at him "You'll see." She knew how important the casting of this role was. The character was clearly the writer's voice and he had allowed the character to express thoughts and feelings that Len could never reveal in life. The actor playing this role had to be unmistakeably black and charismatic enough to make the audience care about him and feel for him. Karen had enormous respect for the courage it must have taken for Len to reveal his innermost self in all its nakedness. She felt pity for the anxious actor waiting outside. She was sure he'd spent time studying the script and preparing for this appointment. She wondered why agents had to be so indifferent and uncaring. It was obvious that Scanlon hadn't read the play or even the character breakdown. And in any case, where did this particular actor fit? You'd have to create a new category: beige actors. The giggle threatened to escape again.

"Mr. Taylor, would you come in please?" Karen called through the door.

As the actor moved into the room, Karen was again aware of his commanding physical presence. The jeans and sweat shirt he wore accentuated the athletic solidity of his body. His nose was straight and long, rather Roman or Egyptian. His bone structure reminded Karen of the statues she'd seen at the Museum in Athens on her honeymoon trip. His dark hair was silken-curly. He really was a mix, a gorgeous mix.

"Hi. Conrad. Conrad Taylor." He reached forward to shake Adam's hand. "Hi, Len." He grinned at the writer.

"Con, for God's sake, what are you doing here? How the hell are you?" cooed Len, suddenly standing to grasp Conrad's hand.

Karen was amazed. She hadn't seen Len react like that to anyone all week.

The voice was low and soft. "What do you think I'm doing here, man? I'm reading for this part in your play." He was still smiling but the charm had taken on an edge.

"I haven't seen you in a long time. What have you been up to?"

"I have my own theatre group uptown. And the bread jobs…you know."

Conrad wished they'd get past the small talk. His gaze covered the rest of the room and rested on the beautiful blonde actress for a moment. He knew why she was still there and her presence pleased him. He'd been admiring her beauty in the waiting room. Now he wondered how good an actress she was and how she would respond to him. Sometimes the partner in a reading could make or break the audition. In any case, it was a lot better than having to work with some stage manager type who might deliver flat monotonous cues and make him look bad.

Conrad's gaze turned to Adam. It was a stare of scrutiny and discovery, like a child's. Yet he stood before them with the kind of physical ease and grace expected of an adult accustomed to being on display, with one knee bent slightly and the toe of that leg turned in. He carried a baseball jacket slung over one shoulder and his stance was ready and alert, like a pitcher on the mound ready to throw a strike. Karen noticed that his ankles seemed thick and fat, as though he were wearing several layers of heavy wool socks. The sneakers were very professional looking. Had he been a pro-athlete? Karen wondered what he'd be like in bed, then, startled at the sudden intrusion of that thought, busied herself with the pile of head shots on the table in front of her.

Conrad was still talking quietly to Len. "The word on the street is that this is a terrific play and a terrific part."

Len laughed. "I'll bet you say that at all your auditions."

Conrad laughed along with him, but the edge of impatience was still there. "Yeh." His nerves were beginning to tighten. Why were they stalling?

"Conrad, do you know Cynthia? I've asked her to read with you." Adam had surrendered. It was obvious to him that this actor was wrong for the part, but what the hell, might as well hear him read. He's been waiting out there for a long time. Adam never forgot his own early days as an actor. Remembrance of that pain tended to make him more gentle with actors than most directors.

"Yep. We met outside." Conrad nodded at the actress. He moved to the raised platform. "Hi," he said softly as he took her offered hand.

Karen suspected that it was the odd combination of sensitivity and macho that she found so sexy. The actors began slowly at first, testing one another like two dogs sniffing each other out. It was a difficult scene because of the deeply emotional states of the two characters at this point in the play. Conrad studied the actress, stalking her. Gradually his connection with her became more and more intense, so that he drew her in almost against her will. Cynthia began to look more at Conrad and less at the script. He threw his script to the floor and grabbed her shoulders as if to shake her into surrender. As she attempted to escape he stopped her with a voice so loving and gentle only a stone could have resisted.

Karen was blown away. She knew nobody had given this much. He was making something happen. It was without a doubt the best reading they'd had. What a pity that he looked so wrong for the part!

The scene ended with Cynthia in Conrad's arms. Both actors were sweating.

"Con, come here." Len sprang to his feet. As Conrad moved toward him Len hung his arm around Conrad's shoulders and in a mock whisper said "Confidentially, that's by far the best reading of that scene we've had to date". Conrad started to speak but Len pressed on. "But I have to tell you that you're totally wrong for this part. You're marvelous, man. Only he's got to <u>look</u> like a black man or there's no point to this whole damn play."

Adam breathed an inaudible sigh of relief. He would not have had the nerve to say what all three of them had been thinking: Good as he is, the man is too light-skinned to play this role. It was really a shame. No wonder Harry Belafonte became a singer.

Conrad faced the three of them squarely. "Just what does a black man look like?" The nostrils flared again.

Although his voice was low and controlled, Karen could tell that he was seething inside. She saw his hands shake with the effort to contain himself. She suspected that he could be dangerous if sufficiently provoked.

Cynthia stood anxiously on the platform waiting to be told what to do next.

"Thanks very much dear. We'll let you know as soon as possible," Adam called to her.

It was very clear that all the attention was now on Conrad and Cynthia knew a delicate moment when she saw one. Best to remove herself gracefully and let her agent take it from here "Thank <u>you.</u> I really enjoyed reading with you Conrad. Good luck."

"Yeh…me too." His smile lasted a quick second and he turned back to the business at hand. As Cynthia closed the door behind her, he repeated the question. "Just what does a black man look like?"

There was a silence as Adam searched for appropriate words and Len withdrew into himself again. Karen couldn't help thinking that this scene had more drama in it than most of those in the play.

"<u>I am a black man.</u> This is what a black man looks like sometimes. We're not all Amos and Andy!"

From the way the words erupted from between tightly pressed lips, Karen sensed that Conrad had been through this many times before and that his patience had reached its limit. He was right, of course. They were all thinking in stereotypes. Black women were supposed to be very round and jolly and look like the face on the pancake box, and black men were supposed to have very dark skin, flat noses and kinky hair. Even Len had fallen into the trap.

"Look Conrad," Adam was struggling with the moment, trying to decide how to handle it. "You've given us a lot to think about. You read that scene beautifully, without question. You're a fine actor. But we have to have time to think this over and weigh the pros and cons. No pun intended," he grinned, in a futile attempt to lighten things up a bit. "I'm really happy to have met you. Can't imagine how it is that we haven't crossed paths before." Adam extended his hand.

"Well, there hasn't been much to audition for. I don't sing or dance. There goes another myth." Conrad grinned at them. He would rather have hung by his thumbs than have to go through this again. He knew that one day he'd lose it altogether and punch someone in the mouth. He told himself to stay cool. There might still be a sliver of a chance. Better not alienate them altogether. "Later, Len. Good luck."

"Listen, Con. Let me think about this. That was a helluva reading," whispered Len. His head sank deeper into his collar.

"Thanks." Conrad headed toward the door, then turned suddenly with a parting shot. "There's always Texas Dirt." He winked at them and disappeared.

Adam turned to Len and Karen. "What the hell is Texas Dirt?"

Karen shrugged. Len shriveled into his chair as he whispered. "It's some kind of dark makeup base. I think they use it in westerns to make all those white actors look like Indians."

The room seemed suddenly very quiet. Somewhere in the building a band had started to rehearse and the steady percussion beat filtered into the room like the ticking of some huge clock. Adam glanced at his watch. It was almost seven. No wonder his stomach felt so empty. He wanted to go home. He wondered what the hell he was doing here anyway. He was supposed to be one of the big hotshot directors on the east coast, and here he was frying his brains over a glorified Off-Broadway production that might not have a chance of going anywhere. He wondered who in the world would want to see a play about an interracial relationship and what he was thinking about when he agreed to do this. Five months without a decent script, that's what. And Len was a damn good writer. Another time, another place, this could be a powerhouse of a production. But right now they were in trouble and couldn't cast one of the most important roles.

Len reached for another cigarette, then remembered that there were no matches left. His thoughts suddenly flipped back to his high school prom. How he had yearned for that beautiful girl in his math. class! He had finally collected enough courage to ask her and she'd said yes, she'd go with him. He had been euphoric, hardly daring to believe his luck. Then the axe fell. He could still hear her apologetic, halting explanation. Her father had forbidden it. Len was too dark-skinned and therefore an unsuitable escort for that proud family's beautiful light-skinned daughter. He learned then that you can't win. Either too dark or too light. Who made these rules?

Karen couldn't recall ever having had such a strong physical reaction to a man, including her husband who had grown on her gradually. It's the stuff that makes stars, that magnetism or whatever you call it. Charisma? She wondered what the right makeup might be able to accomplish.

Adam rose and began to pace. "That was some reading. Damn! What a shame."

"He's a very talented guy," Len said softly. He gave Adam one of his large-eyed penetrating stares.

"Where does he come from?" asked Karen.

"135th Street and Lenox Ave. ah reckon," Len mocked. "Where do you think?"

"No, I meant…Oh, forget it."

Adam studied the resume that the agent had sent over. "He's studied with Paul Mann and his assistant, Lloyd Richards, it says here."

"See, there aren't many teachers who take Negro actors, and even if they do, it doesn't work out because there's no trust on either side," said Len. "Con said he has his own group now. The ones who are lucky enough to get some good training try to pass it along to each other."

"I think we've seen every black actor between the ages of twenty and forty. We need somebody with training, intelligence, emotional depth and he also has to be the right age and the right color." Adam threw his hands up. "I give up!"

Len stiffened. "What are you saying? That it's impossible to cast?"

"No, Len. I'm not saying that. But we re going to have to make some compromises. Big ones." Adam was pacing again.

Karen knew how her husband would react if he were here. Daniel would want someone who looked the part, someone attractive, charismatic and unmistakably Negroid. To hell with the rest. They'd had so many fights about art versus commerce. Daniel didn't know much about the art of the theatre. His kick was the challenge of putting the whole thing together, wheedling the money out of resistant backers, competing with whatever else was on the street for media space, presiding over the hundreds of lunches, dinners and backers auditions that were the by-product of the effort to launch. Daniel didn't even want to do this play when they first discussed it. It was payback to Karen for the years of devoted service. All those times when she did the dirty work and he got the glory. She thanked God that he was in Boston at this moment. If he were here they'd be listening to Daniel's lecture number forty two on What Sells.

"Look." Len startled them with his commanding tone. "I think we've got to make a decision. I'd like to go with Conrad."

Karen couldn't believe her ears. This careful, introverted writer had actually taken a stand.

"Tell me what you know about him." Adam threw himself down on a chair.

"Well, he used to make his living as a model. You know…EBONY, JET, the black magazines. And the publisher who owns them all runs fashion shows. Conrad was popular because he looks white. And he's got 'good hair.'" Len grinned wryly at them. "Good hair means not kinky like this," he pointed to his head. "I've seen him work. He looks great in clothes and the women adore him. Uptown he's a celebrity. They ask for his autograph when they see him on the street. Unfortunately, not many folks from uptown go to the theatre downtown."

"I thought RAISIN IN THE SUN changed all that. They've been playing to very mixed audiences, I'm told."

"That was an all black play about black people. So the uptown folks had characters they could identify with. There was only one white character and he was a bit. Most unusual." Len paused for a moment. "What are we going to do?"

"But damnitall, Len, the guy looks white!"

"So what about makeup, man? White actors use blackface! Why can't he makeup darker?"

"I need time to think about this."

"We don't have time, I'm afraid," said Karen. "Daniel said he needed a decision by tomorrow, negotiations and all."

Actually they should have finished casting long before this. Everything else was filled. Ann Chandler was coming in from the west coast to play 'Sally' and

Jim Copeland was set for 'Bernie'. Both these actors, although not really in the star category, were established and somewhat familiar theatre and film names, and would be an asset to the production. But this last was the most important, and now it was turning out to be the most impossible. It had been a calculated risk. It was Karen who had been drawn to this story of an interracial relationship, Karen who introduced the writer to her husband. She pushed him into having a trial backers' audition in Westport at the home of her friend from college. The liberals had been caught at a sufficiently guilty moment. They had coughed up enough support at that reading to make Daniel feel that maybe they had something workable as a project after all. Maybe its time had come. So he went ahead slowly, always with Karen urging him forward. Now they were only days ahead of the designated start date without a decision on the key role. Daniel had been in Boston the past few days and expected it all to be settled when he returned. Now he would surely have a fit.

Aloud she said, "I think we have to make a decision in the next forty-eight hours, and from what we've seen…unless you know some agent or other source I've overlooked."

"We've looked everywhere but London and Canada. Oh, and the West Indies. They all have the wrong accents," shrugged Len.

Once again they shuffled through the 8x10's of the actors they'd seen during the week. One by one they were discussed and rejected. One was immensely talented but had a speech impediment. Another was good but much too short for Ann, who was already signed. One was the perfect type but moved like a stick of wood. And they came to the end of the pile.

"When is Ann's plane due?"

"She gets in at 8:30 tomorrow night," said Karen.

Adam paced. "There is absolutely no air in this room. I can't think straight anymore." He turned to face them. "Shall we put it to a vote? No, forget it. I've always said that the theatre must be a fascist state with the director as dictator." He smiled bleakly.

"I'd vote for Conrad," said Len.

"Tell you what I'm going to do." The dictator was assuming command. "I'm going to call him in again and have him read with Ann. Sunday if necessary. As soon as possible. Let's see how she reacts. That will help me make the decision." He turned to Karen. "Tell Daniel."

"How do you know we can get Conrad in to read on Sunday?"

"If he wants it, he'll do it," said Adam. "If not, then we'll just have to go with Clifford and that's that. We'll give him five inch lifts and teach him stilt-walking." He was putting on his jacket. "I'm going home. I can't stand this place another minute. Make it one o'clock. At my place. That way Daniel won't have to pay rent for another day. Thanks." He patted Karen on the shoulder and left.

"He didn't ask me if I could make it," whispered Len. He chuckled. "I'll bet you ten dollars he's running to CHARLIE'S for a nice stiff drink."

"Or two or three. I could stand one myself. This has been a day and a half," sighed Karen as she gathered up the debris and swept the pile of photos into her briefcase.

"C'mon. I'll buy."

Karen was startled. That was the first gesture of friendship or even warmth from Len. She wanted very much to take advantage of the crack in the door but Daniel was due soon and she wanted to call Conrad and set up Sunday before he got back.

"I'll take a raincheck, Len. Thanks, but I've got to get home."

"Okay," he shrugged.

Karen knew he felt rejected. She hoped he didn't think that she…why was it so complicated just because he's…. Why was he so damn sensitive? And why was she even thinking about it? Damn!

"Well, I'll see you on Sunday at Adam's. Unless you call me to the contrary," said Len as he prepared to leave. "Bye."

"Goodnight." Karen was sure she heard the hurt in his voice. She wondered when she was going to be able to get rid of this awkwardness with him, always choosing words, afraid to say what came into her head for fear it would offend or be misunderstood. She looked at her watch. Perhaps Conrad was home by now. She looked at his address on the sheet and knew that it was uptown. Harlem? Would a woman answer? She wondered if he was married.

The early fall evening was the color of lavender as Karen walked down the tree-lined upper west side street toward her building. She felt her body begin to relax as it always did in the presence of trees. She loved living off Central Park, loved the brownstones that dotted her block with their shuttered windows and five step stoops. This stretch between the subway and her house never failed to give her a sense of well-being, of belonging to a kind of community. Although she had always been a city kid, there was a part of her that craved a more rural life surrounded by trees and flowers and small picturesque houses. Her building was the only pre-war apartment building on the block. Seventeen stories of one, two and three bedroom spaces. Karen was grateful for the trees that dared survive the city stresses and lined the areas in the back yards behind her building. They provided a park-like view out of every window of their rear-facing rooms. It was one of the features that made her want to grab this apartment when they found it. Daniel had wanted to hold out for something more up-scale on the East side but Karen couldn't visualize herself living on that alien turf. Everyone in the theatre lived on the west side. She had lived there since her teen days in high school and, scrungy or not, it was close to the best subway. It was probably that last fact that won the argument and brought Daniel around, since he was always in a hurry and they couldn't afford to take cabs all the time. That and the fact that the building sported a uniformed doorman.

"Hi, Joe, how're you doing?" Karen felt sorry for the stoop-shouldered wizened old Irishman who had held down this job for almost as many years as she'd been alive.

"Evenin' Mrs. Stoner." Joe held the door open for her.

"Thanks. Goodnight." Karen always felt just a little uncomfortable when these old guys waited on her. It was bad enough to need help carrying a heavy suitcase or package, which they could scarcely manage, but to have a man twice her age have to stand there and hold a door for her was something she could never stomach. When she started high school and she and her parents left Queens and moved to Central Park West there was a self-service elevator and a doorman, but the doorman just stood there nodding as people came and went. More like a security guard.

The phone was ringing as Karen entered her apartment and she dashed to grab the nearest extension which was on the hall wall leading into the kitchen. It was Daniel calling from Boston. As usual, the airport was completely fogged in and nothing was flying. It was either take a Greyhound bus or rent a car if he wanted to get home tonight.

"Why don't you stay over," Karen suggested. "You can get the first plane out in the morning." She was so tired, she would welcome a quiet evening to herself with no demand to discuss the production or tend or cook or listen.

Daniel agreed that it would be easier to wait over and asked to be filled in on the events of the last twenty four hours.

"I think I'll go to Adam's on Sunday," he said when Karen had finished.

Oh, oh, Karen mouthed to herself. "See you tomorrow darling. Take care."

"You too. I'm gonna go have a lobster."

"Yum. Have some for me. 'Bye." Karen headed for the den and dropped her purse and clipboard on the desk. The den was really the second bedroom with small half bath that Daniel was always hinting about filling with a crib and bathinette. But they had agreed that until such time as Karen got pregnant, and in view of the fact that Daniel had his law office as his work space, this would be a place for Karen's work. So they called it the den and Karen was able to keep her rolltop desk and file cabinet there instead of giving them to the Salvation Army. She even managed to put a few of her show posters and production pictures up on the wall, alongside Daniel's. The plum colored Saarinen chair that they'd found at a Knoll warehouse sale and the single bed with cover and bolsters made to look like a couch were recent additions. Daniel hadn't wanted the chair but Karen had pleaded for it. She loved the feel of it when she curled up in it with a play or a book. It seemed to envelop her like a womb.

Conrad's number was at the top of the clipboard. She stared at his picture as she dialed, hoping he would be home so she could give him the news that he was still in the running. She loved it when she could give an actor good news. It was such a rare occurence and the joy in the response was as warming as a caress.

"Hello?" It was a woman s voice, low and husky.

"Is this Conrad Taylor's home?"

"Yes?" It was a question rather than a reply.

"Is he in?"

"No." Nothing volunteered.

"Could you ask him to call 472 0380 as soon as he comes in please? It's about the audition he had this afternoon," she added, making her tone as reassuring as possible.

"Oh yes, of course. I'll be sure and tell him the minute he comes in. This is Mrs. Taylor. 472 0380? Right." The mood had shifted and the accent suddenly sounded almost British.

"Thanks a lot."

Karen kicked off her shoes and padded into the living room, turning on lights as she went. The days were getting shorter, she thought. She would miss the sunlight streaming in through the trees and dappling the parquet floor. During fall and winter the sun seemed to move around to another place and its light became more indirect. Daniel had won the fight about the charcoal gray walls, protesting that she could have as much color as she wanted in the upholstery and throw pillows of the couch and chairs. But with the dark walls and the shining ebony of the large grand piano dominating the room, the more light she could provide, natural or electric, the better she liked it. She poured herself a generous scotch from the decanter on the rolling tea cart that doubled as a bar and found some stray ice cubes left in the freezer, making a mental note that the thing needed defrosting. She headed towards the bedroom sipping the cool sharp liquid that seemed to turn hot as it hit her throat, unbuttoning her dress as she went. When she was comfortably settled in the Saarinen chair in her velour bathrobe, Scotch in hand, she thought about the Conrad call. She had sensed the woman's initial hostility over the phone. So he was married. With a man who looked like that she guessed a wife would have to beat women off with a stick.

Karen didn't think she would ever have that problem with Daniel. Not that he wasn't reasonably attractive, with big eyes and curly brown hair. His round face and soft body gave him a kind of teddy bear look. But he was always so driven, so single-minded, so self-involved. She wondered if he would ever have time to fool around. They had met in college, she the undergraduate drama major, he the second year law student. She had been flattered by his attention and touched by his willingness to wait until she was good and ready to surrender her virginity. He was so unlike the eager, panting and usually clumsy undergrads she had been pushing away, or the hard-eyed older war vets who had returned to school too demanding and experienced to take no for an answer.

Danny's sense of humor was his most appealing trait. Fast one-liners punctuated his dialogue. He was completely stage-struck, hanging around the Dramatic Club and its members and lounging around in the theatre whenever he had free time. It was inevitable that he would choose entertainment law as his specialty. He would, Karen had thought, become the perfect complement to Karen' s career as an actress. They'd been extrmely lucky. Dan had risen quickly, using his wit and wits together with Karen's theatre contacts to establish himself as one of the brightest of the younger deal-makers on the Broadway scene. It was a time-consuming effort and Karen soon discovered that their entire social life revolved around Dan's career. It had been just as well because at the time, Karen' s career had been less than successful. After several years of making rounds, interviewing, auditioning and doing all the things that young actresses were supposed to do, she was forced to accept the fact that she was not a 'commercial type'. She had thought about getting a nose job. She had tried straightening her hair, but couldn't bear the smell of the chemicals, so gave it up and let her hair surrender to its natural kink. Finally she had said to hell with it. They'll either take me as I am or I'll do something else.

The something else became playing the role of the terrific wife, always there for Daniel at the dinner parties, always an ear when he needed one, always ready with advice when he sought it. During the long and ever more frequent periods when he was busy or out of town, she would take short term jobs in production on a play or movie. It had been an amiable, considerate and uneventful relationship. Their sex life was pleasant and reliable and as much a part of their lives as their morning coffee. Routine. They had quickly become financially comfortable and Karen had enjoyed the luxury of being able to buy whatever she saw that she liked and wanted to own. Her collection of Claire McCardell dresses grew and although she didn't care much about owning precious gems, Daniel was generous at birthdays and Christmas and her jewelry box contained some beautiful pieces. It was a nice life. For a time.

Frustration replaced tranquility when her desire to be something more than Mrs. Daniel Stoner, to have an identity of her own, began to gnaw at her. Daniel, during one of their increasingly irritable discussions, suggested she have a baby.

"That's a good way to shut me up," Karen had answered. "Just find something to keep me busy. What a great reason to have a baby! I can see it now. Daddy's off to work and lunches and dinners and out of town trips while Mommy's busy in the sand-box. I don't think I'm ready for that!"

After that she took very good care of her diaphragm and began reading articles about this new thing called 'the pill'. She'd be damned if she'd make the same mistake she'd watched her friend Leslie make. Leslie had fallen right into the trap, and now the baby was two and she was stuck and miserable.

A rumble in her stomach like the purring of a kitten reminded Karen that she was starved and she reluctantly pulled herself out of the womb chair and headed for the kitchen. While she heated up a can of vegetable soup her thoughts suddenly flipped back to Daniel's first venture as a producer. She had been the silent co-producer, and as a reward he had gotten her a small part in the show. It had been a disaster. They fought all the way through it and the critics pulverized it. It was the second show that was the big hit. Karen had found the play and brought it to Daniel. Playwright and husband were now doing magnificently, thank you, but she was still the ever-humble, ever-silent assistant.

She slammed her soup plate down on the counter with unexpected force. "Damn, damn, damn!" The plate had cracked neatly into two pieces. It was a Russell Wright bowl that was part of her favorite set. A decision as to whether to chuck it in the garbage or try to salvage it was delayed by the insistent ringing of the phone.

"Hello!," she barked.

"Hi," said the voice on the other end. It was low and soft. "Conrad Taylor returning your call?" There was a hesitation in the question, as though he knew instinctively that he had picked a bad moment.

"Oh, hi. Yes, Conrad, I'm glad to hear from you. How are you?" That was dumb, thought Karen. I just saw him a few hours ago. I must sound like a jerk.

"I'm fine. What's happening?" he prompted. He knew this was going to be a yes or no, so let's have it.

"Well, Conrad, the director would like to hear you read with the actress playing 'Sally'. Uh…we were all extremely impressed with you, but it's a question of balance."

He chuckled softly into her ear. "You mean it's a question of color, don't you?"

Karen was silent for a moment while her mind quickly selected and rejected several responses to that.

"Look, I honestly think they want you, but they're grappling with the decision. If it were up to me…," she hastened to add, "I'd have hired you on the spot. It was a fantastic reading." She bit her lip. She knew she shouldn't have said that. What was she doing?

"Who's playing 'Sally'? Is she as attractive as that girl I read with? I thought she was sensational." His voice dropped to a very low key. "So are you."

No wonder his wife is nervous. Make like you didn't hear it. "It's Ann Chandler. She's coming in from L.A. tomorrow night. Can you make it Sunday at one o'clock?"

Now the silence was on his end.

"Hello?" said Karen.

"I play softball on Sunday. The Broadway Show League."

"Len told us you play ball on Saturday."

Conrad laughed. "That's basketball. Sorry."

Karen felt herself losing patience. "Can't you skip it this one time?"

"I'm the pitcher," he explained patiently.

"But this is a possible job. I'm sure the Show League will understand."

There was another silence.

"Can't you make it at five instead?"

She couldn't believe this guy. Instead of jumping at a chance that might come to him once in a decade…

"Can you?" He was insistent now. "Make it at five?"

"I don't know. I'll have to talk to Adam and get back to you." Karen swore silently. Who needed this? Now she would have to spend the evening on the phone. She felt like hanging up on him.

"Five or anytime after that. See what you can do, would you? I'd appreciate your help. I'll be home the rest of the evening." Pause. "I'm sorry." He listened to her breathing for a moment. "Hey, are you okay?" he asked softly.

Karen wondered if he could see her through the phone with some weird e.s.p. He seemed to be able to read her mind. "I'm fine, thanks. I'll give it a try. Talk to you later."

It wasn't easy but she worked it out. Adam was furious at first. The temerity of an actor to whom he might be presenting the wonderful gift of a job! But he relented finally. Karen had handled him well, pointing out that Ann would probably appreciate a chance to sleep off her jet lag and read the SUNDAY TIMES. She had simply left a message on Len's answering service.

Conrad allowed the phone to ring only once before answering it. Karen guessed he'd been sitting right next to it, waiting for her call.

"Hi, it's Karen Stoner."

"Are you feeling better?"

There was that hint of intimacy again. "I'm fine, really. It's all arranged. Five o'clock at 114 West 71st Street, Apartment 3A. It's Adam's place."

He repeated the address. "That's great. I want this, you know. Sorry to give you a hard time. Couldn't let the whole team down."

"You mean if you don't pitch, they'll lose?"

He laughed. "Well, of course. I'm invaluable. Or so I'd like to think."

"Well, it's okay. I wish you luck."

"Thanks for being in my corner. See you Sunday." He added as an after-thought, "You will be there, won't you?"

"I'll be there."

"Good. Take care," he said softly and hung up.

Karen placed the receiver carefully in its cradle and stared at the phone for a long minute. All sorts of conflicting feelings invaded her consciousness and she couldn't make sense of them. But something told her that the weekend would go by very slowly.

CHAPTER 2

Adam lived on the third floor of an upper west side brownstone. It was a medium-sized one-bedroom apartment but it created the impression of opulence with its deep lushly upholstered furniture and hand-hooked Rya rugs. The walls and shelves were filled with books, original art and sculpture. Large exotic plants filled the corners of the rooms and the sills of the windows, each pampered with its own eternal flourescent light. One wall was entirely built in with shelves containing various awards, memorabilia, brass and copper objects and expensive looking hi-fi equipment. The total impression of luxury upon entrance was startling after the three flight climb up dimly lit dark wooden stairs.

The group around the coffee table looked more like a social gathering than a casting session. Ann Chandler had responded with a mixture of astonishment and amusement when given the background on the reason for this meeting. She had been apprehensive about the whole project, and particularly about who she'd be saddled with as co-star. A love scene with a Negro actor was risky business and might get her blacklisted. On the other hand this was New York not L.A., and the gamble was worth it if it got her back into the press which had lately acted like she'd died. Her nitwit agent had forgotten to push for cast approval. He was so glad to get her off his back he was willing to settle for anything and Ann had made a mental note to fire him as soon as she had reclaimed some visibility. She arrived looking stunning in a coffee colored silk pantsuit, gold hoop earrings and brown alligator heels. Anyone in her immediate vicinity was treated to an intense whiff of JOY cologne which it pleased her to use rather lavishly. The men were in various versions of comfortable but chic Sunday leisure dress all studiously casual but thoughtfully chosen. Daniel and Len both wore jackets, perhaps in deference to the star. Daniel's was butterscotch suede and Len's a modest corduroy. Karen had dressed carefully for this meeting, wanting to look pretty, sexy, but not too jazzy. She had finally chosen her best fitting black pants and a black and red print sweater that showed off her figure.

Conrad arrived in a grey sweat suit, navy baseball jacket and Mets cap.

"Well," murmured Ann to Karen who was seated next to her. "Certainly different."

Conrad seemed ill-at-ease, sitting quietly while his gaze wandered over the contents of the room during the initial small talk. His eyes rested for a while on the large quantity of books and records on the shelves. It occurred to Karen that he might be intimidated by these surroundings. He seemed to behave very differently on what must have felt like alien turf. There was a charm about his shy awkwardness and the females immediately responded to it, in spite of his tendency to mumble almost inaudibly when he spoke.

But once the two actors began to read the scene, Conrad's talent took over, and the result was again dynamic and compelling. They sat together on the couch facing the others and tried, in that difficult physical circumstance, to create the necessary intimacy. After the first few lines, Ann's eyes narrowed and she stared at Conrad with renewed interest. Soon she forgot to watch him and began to work. The intensity built until the room, on this brisk fall day, suddenly felt warm and close. There was a surge of electricity between the actors that made the scene immediate and telling. The small group sitting across from them was motionless, infected by their emotional heat. As they finished the scene, there was no doubt in anyone's mind that Ann had been completely won over.

Ann opened her eyes wide. "My God, you're terrific!" she said. We must have him!" Without waiting for response, she swept up her things and declared she was totally jet-lagged and simply had to get some rest and could she drop Conrad somewhere?

"Thanks, but I think I go in the other direction." He smiled. "It was a pleasure meeting you." Conrad began to relax. He knew he had just assured himself another vote.

"Don't be so formal, darling," she cooed. "We're going to be spending a lot of time together, I'm sure." And she winked reassuringly at him.

Karen wondered if he knew what Ann had in mind.

As Adam returned from seeing Ann out he exchanged looks with Daniel. "She was very impressed with you, Conrad." It was tossed off. Adam wanted it known that he would take little stock of what Ann thought. Under no circumstances would he surrender his authority to a mere actress.

"Well....?" Conrad stood up. He was getting impatient. The question was unmistakeably a confrontation. He wasn't going to let them beat around the bush much longer. This place made him feel uncomfortable. Everywhere he looked said money, success, education, the privilege of the white world. He keenly resented feeling like one of the disadvantaged in the presence of all this luxury.

"Anyone want a drink?" asked Adam, moving toward the small bar in the corner of the room. "I do."

"Thanks, but I have to go. Is there a verdict?" Conrad's dark piercing eyes rested on Karen, as if she might supply some clue.

She met his gaze, trying silently to signal him, to tell him to let it rest. Let them chew over it. She knew that the more men like Adam and Daniel felt they were being pressured into something, the more they would back off.

Daniel made the definitive move. Crossing over to the couch, he offered his hand to Conrad in a gesture that was at once congratulatory and dismissive. "You're a fine actor. That's very clear. We need a little more time on this. Can you give us another twenty-four hours?"

"Sure. Why not?" Take twenty four days. And meanwhile I starve. It isn't as if I have four other parts waiting for me. Conrad grabbed his jacket and started to go, then stopped and turned to them. "Look, I know the problem. But I can <u>do</u> this part and I <u>want</u> it." This last went straight to Len who had not said more than two words since his arrival. He stared at Karen for a moment as though trying to say 'can you help me?' Then with a nod and a sigh he smiled, said "thanks for your time folks" and left.

Len broke the silence that followed. "I can use that drink, Adam."

Slowly, tentatively, they began to discuss the issue. Adam had been stimulated by what had just occurred, and the reading had given him some new ideas. He realized that Conrad might be the one to bring a more complex reality to the character. And he ruefully acknowledged to himself that they would need all the help they could get. It was Daniel who kept resisting. Karen couldn't tell whether his refusal was based on commercial concerns, her outspoken support of Conrad, or just pure stubbornness. That streak in the man had generated many problems in their relationship. Sometimes it seemed to Karen that it boiled down to a question of control, rather than any rational or carefully considered choice.

"Let me sleep on it," he said finally. "I'll call you first thing in the morning."

The discussion continued on the way home.

"Why couldn't you settle it?" asked Karen as they walked the few blocks to their apartment. "Must you always play devil's advocate?"

"I'm not going to be railroaded into a catastrophe," answered Daniel. "It's bad enough to be taking the risk of doing this project. Why should I stick my neck in the noose?"

"What noose? What are you talking about? He's obviously the best actor we've seen."

"The guy looks white! Somebody's bound to accuse us of racist casting…A white actor for a black role. Do you know what that will start? Controversy. Bad press. Maybe even pickets. Use your damn head for a change."

"Why must you always get abusive when we have a discussion about work?"

"Oh, here we go."

"No, it's true. The very fact of my having an opinion of my own seems to drive you nuts."

"Aren't you overstating it a bit, my dear?"

Karen didn't want to lose her temper. She was too tired. The whole damn week had been a killer. They walked the rest of the way home in silence.

The several drinks downed by Daniel while Karen prepared dinner served to rekindle the embers.

"Are you sure you're not being influenced by the fact that this guy is so good-looking?" he smirked as she served him his chicken breast.

"Oh, give me a break. Can't you ever give me credit for some taste and intelligence? After all, I'm the actor here. I know a little more about casting and talent than you do."

"Perhaps. But what you know about business I could write on the head of a pin in large letters. And this is a business we're talking about, not some artsy fartsy ode to bleeding heart liberals. I don't know why I let you talk me into this fucking project in the first place!"

"Bleeding heart liberal?" Karen threw down her fork. "You sound like some damn McCarthyite. When did you change horses?"

Daniel responded with a snort and became totally involved with his food.

Karen knew that Daniel would shut down when they reached a certain point. They could never really have a full-blown fight where both sides came out punching, because Daniel always closed off and clammed up. So all the really important issues between them lay underneath the surface, festering, never given the opportunity for release that a really good fight might provide. "I'm so sick and tired of being treated like the hired help. I'm not supposed to know enough to <u>have</u> an opinion, much less offer one. And God forbid you should ever take my suggestions. I think you only do it when you want an out—someone to blame if things go sour." She was trying desperately to provoke him into a response.

Daniel's reply was a raised eyebrow and a disgusted look. He rose from the table to get a cigarette.

Cumulative fatigue and the anger of the moment wore down Karen's control. Her throat began to constrict and ache in a prelude to tears and she rushed into the bedroom, slamming the door behind her.

When Daniel climbed into bed later that evening, Karen was already curled up under the covers, knees almost touching her head. As he reached over for her she turned away face to the wall, muttered "G'night" and feigned sleep.

In the morning, Daniel made the call. It wasn't so much capitulation as it was practicality. They needed to move ahead and there seemed to be little choice. With Conrad in the part they were ready to go. They would be able to meet the rehearsal start date for a week from that day. The schedule for the first public performance and opening night could be met, promotion could proceed as planned, the theatre booking would not have to be adjusted. All was right in Daniel's orderly world.

Karen knew that his need to have the wheels turn smoothly had triumphed, not her insistence. But she didn't care. She was looking forward to this production. And she was beginning to feel more alive than she had in a long time.

The next few weeks were hectic. Daniel had suddenly become involved in a major litigation, forcing him to be in court most of the time and move Karen from her spot as assistant to the director to that of surrogate producer. He left her up to her ears with the details of mounting a show, promising her associate producer billing as the carrot for doing the hard work that lay ahead. There were budget meetings, meetings with the press person, meetings with the designers, meetings with the box office staff. The weather suddenly changed. Fall took on a bite that forecasted winter and there was as yet no heat in the rehearsal hall. She had to deal with the theatre owner, a slimy character who kept pawing her. And the advance sale became something of a concern when the staff member assigned to that matter had to go to California for a funeral. Karen was dealing with everything but her real interest—the play, and more specifically, the actors. She came home every night with just enough strength left to eat something and fall into bed exhausted. She and Daniel passed like ships in the night, living more like roommates than husband and wife. In a paranoid moment she had caught herself wondering if Daniel had actually conspired to keep her away from rehearsals.

The only contact she'd had with the cast had been at the first reading to which everyone was traditionally invited. Karen had looked around the long wooden table in the bare, white-walled rehearsal hall that morning. The flourescent light made everyone look a bit pasty and the emptiness of the room created a slight echo when someone spoke. Karen had had butterflies in her stomach as she always did at the start of a new venture, and she remembered thinking giddily as she stared at these people lining the long table and intently staring at their scripts that the scene reminded her of The Last Supper.

There were the five actors: Ann, Conrad, Jim Copeland, Shirley who was playing Jim's girl and covering Ann, and the character woman, Louise.

Adam sat at the head of the table with Len at his side. On his other side was the stage manager, a tall, extremely thin dark fellow everyone called Mac, and next to him in order were the set, costume and lighting designers. There was the young, cute production assistant Emily, who had been scurrying around serving coffee to everyone, and Daniel and Karen herself. The two understudies would not come in for another two weeks.

Sixteen people, Karen had thought, all working on this black play by a black writer. Only two out of the group were black. And one of those was hardly what you would call visibly black. Her memory had flipped back to the first time she'd heard that phrase 'visibly black' used. It was at a meeting of the Dramatic Club at college as names were being offered in nomination for membership. The President had said "in view of the shifting climate, I think we should make an effort to find a visibly black candidate." And Karen had thought at the time that it was an absurd thing to say. It was like describing someone as 'visibly naked'. She was ignorant about a lot of things in those days. Conrad, personification of invisible blacks, was getting a lot of sidelong glances from the other members of the cast. Karen knew that they had expected something quite different.

The reading went well. As always on the first day, everyone congratulated themselves and each other at the end, assuring themselves that they had a smash hit and happy to be the chosen few who were working this month. The actors always tried to look their best on this day, wore good clothes, put their best feet forward, gave it their best shot. It was important to make a good first impression. They were always aware of the five day clause, the contractual agreement in the Equity contract that allowed either party to change his mind within the first five days. It was after this that they would let their hair down, put on the jeans, dig in and go to work.

Conrad had seemed nervous and preoccupied. As Karen watched him her earlier impression had been confirmed. He became much more introverted in unfamiliar surroundings. But the cast was very intrigued by his talent and his obvious attractiveness.

The days flew by with terrifying speed. Daniel, always concerned with more pressing matters, kept throwing more and more responsibility Karen's way. The more she did, the more annoyed he was with way she did it. They were in constant conflict.

One day as they were both in the kitchen grabbing their respective choices of breakfast, Daniel began to itemize his list of complaints. Karen slammed the Silex drip carafe down on the counter hard. "If you feel that way, why don't you do it yourself?" she demanded.

"I haven't got time, damn it! Must I do everything?" he snapped.

Two weeks into rehearsal and they were barely speaking. It really didn't matter. Karen wondered fleetingly if Daniel was having an affair and using their fights as a way to assuage his guilt. Even as the thought entered her head she shrugged it off, amazed at how little she cared. She promised herself she would give the whole question of their relationship some serious in-depth consideration after the opening.

Rehearsals had moved into the 299 seat theatre and things were not going well. The theatre itself was part of the problem. It was an old Greenwich Village building, full of charm and historic signifigance which was meant to compensate for sadly outdated insulation and plumbing. This gave the actors something to moan about on a daily basis. It was chilly, the bathroom was stopped up, the dressing rooms leaked when it rained.

"This is insufferable," said Ann one morning. "Maybe kids just out of school will put up with this, but after all, we're professionals! I think we should all go to Equity." She was annoyed that Conrad was proving to be a more difficult conquest then she had planned, and for some unknown reason she took an instant dislike to Jim, campaigning to have him replaced. Fortunately, it was Jim who had been voted union representative and he wasn't about to bother Equity with what he knew to be par for the course in off-Broadway theatres.

Louise, who was playing a bag lady, so immersed herself in the role that she was becoming an eccentric herself. She came in every day with garbage which she called 'the life', and insisted on throwing the clutter around the room which was her set. In addition, she managed to catch the flu and for an entire week only a laryngial croak could be heard from her.

Adam went from depression to hysteria to elation and back to depression in a single days' work, trying to fulfill his position as father, psychiatrist, teacher, advisor, friend, taskmaster, as any good director would, but asking himself every night how in the world he ever allowed himself to get stuck in such a mess.

And last but not least was the problem of Conrad. It was clear that something had to be done to make his character more understandable. As good an actor as he was, his own instincts seemed to be very much the opposite of what the script implied. One day, in the middle of a scene, he walked down to the front of the stage and confronted Adam. "I can't find the truth in this. Why is he begging her to come back? Why doesn't he tell her to go to hell?"

"Because he loves her," answered Len. He was curled up on the seat next to Adam's, nested in an over-sized looseknit cardigan sweater.

"Yeh, but why is he allowing this white woman to wipe the floor with him? If it were me I'd..." Conrad showed them his clenched fist. He heard a gasp behind him. "In a manner of speaking, of course," he added quickly. Hold your temper man, this is a big chance so don't blow it, he cautioned himself. He'd been holding himself in so much lately that he was getting stomach aches. He didn't know how much more he could take of this before he punched this Ann bitch in the mouth. She was a spoiled, self-centered, nasty female. Perfect for the part, Conrad had observed wryly. He'd known there was going to be trouble when he hadn't responded to her obvious ploys to get him into the sack. So he never let his guard down for a moment, even though he knew that it might affect the work.

Karen tried to spend more time at rehearsals, delegating more of her work to the assistants. She loved watching the director, loved hanging out with the actors. This is where she felt happiest, where she felt she belonged. It was fascinating to watch the play take shape and come to life. With all their anxieties, hostilities, tensions, they were a professional and hardworking company and watching them was an education. So she'd tiptoe quietly into the theatre and slip into a seat in the last row. And, although there was little opportunity for contact, she knew that Conrad was as aware of her presence as she was of his.

At the end of a long day in the third week of rehearsal, Karen deliberately timed it so she would be in front of the theatre when Conrad came out. He emerged as though shot from a cannon, but stopped short when he saw Karen. He studied her face for a moment.

"Are you all right?," he asked. No preamble, just right to the point. As though continuing a conversation already begun.

"Why do you ask?"

"You've been looking very troubled lately."

"That's funny. I thought I was covering beautifully. Actually, I was concerned about you. Ann's been giving you such a hard time." Karen sank deeper into the collar of her coat. The late fall wind made her eyes tear.

"Are you worried about the show?"

"No, no. Not at all."

"Can I help?" Again he stared at her directly, searching.

She laughed, shrugging it off and said "Thanks, but I'm okay. Really. Listen, I've got the car. Can I give you a lift?"

"I'm going uptown."

"So am I. The car's just down the block."

"Great."

They walked down the village street lined with curious small craft and objets d'arts shops. One store whose window was filled with odd exotic looking musical instruments drew Conrad's attention and he stopped in front of it for a moment.

"Do you play something?" asked Karen.

"Just drums. I collect them when I've got some bread. These are beauties." He looked longingly at a pair of oddly sculptured pieces.

"What are they?"

"Dumbeks. They're middle Eastern. I'd love to get them, but they probably want an arm and a leg. Especially in this clip joint."

"Well, maybe if we're a hit…" Karen grinned at him.

"Yeh." They walked on in silence, broken once by a chuckle from both of them as they passed one of the more picturesque village characters. He wandered by them reciting poetry aloud for an unseen but apparently admiring audience.

"What make is this?" he asked, as Karen approached the passenger side door of a small red foreign car.

Karen chuckled. "It's called a Daf." Conrad wedged himself into the seat, trying to tuck his legs in. "It's for people my size, really." She glanced over at him. "You look like you're wearing it."

They both laughed.

"Daf? Is that short for Daffy?"

"No, Daffodil, I think. It's Dutch. There aren't many of them in this country. Daniel saw it at the auto show. It was the only foreign car with automatic transmission. We thought it was a great idea until we discovered that you have to go to the end of Brooklyn to get it serviced." She chuckled again, remembering Daniel's face when he found out.

"It's a very…red car." Conrad said solemnly, and was delighted when Karen laughed out loud. "You know, you're very beautiful when you're happy." He said it very softly, as though afraid he might be heard.

Karen was startled to find herself blushing. She used the traffic's demands to buy time. "What makes you think I'm happy?", she said finally.

He hesitated for a moment. "Do you want to talk? Could we maybe park somewhere for a few minutes?"

They were at a red light and Karen turned to look at him, trying to read his eyes. She couldn't get used to the way he skipped over the usual amenities. He was always throwing her off balance. Was he the shy, private man he appeared to be at rehearsals or this direct, persistent and surprisingly perceptive man at her side? She knew she was attracted to him. Should she risk it? It would be a chance to get to know him better. But where to go? She wondered if she should suggest they stop for coffee or a drink. Or if she should just pull in somewhere. She knew that either way, she'd have to find a parking space and that wouldn't be easy at this hour.

They were both silent as they wound through the Eighth Avenue traffic moving towards Central Park.

"We can go through the Park," she said suddenly. Maybe we'll see someplace where we can stop for a few minutes."

"Good."

Karen liked the challenge of New York traffic. In a strange way it relaxed her because it took all her concentration. She knew she was good at holding her own in a maze of cabs, buses, trucks and New Jersey drivers. They could kill you if you weren't careful.

"You're a good driver," Conrad said after a bit.

"Do you drive?"

He laughed. "Nope. There are two things you don't learn when you grow up in Harlem. You don't learn to drive and you don't learn to swim."

"Then you'd better stay out of California," Karen laughed. So, he grew up in Harlem, she thought. She sighed as they entered the Park. "How beautiful it is. I've been so involved with the show, I've missed the changing of the leaves this year."

"Missed the changing of the leaves? Is that an important event?"

"Beauty is my life!" Karen retorted. She knew he was teasing her. "Seriously, I love the Park. I've lived next to it or near it most of my life."

"How lucky for you."

There it was again. That constant reminder of the difference between them. The same feeling she had with Len, of having to watch her words so as not to offend. It was true that the Park had always been an integral part of her life. Her parents had moved to Central Park West when she was a child and the Park had been her playground. During her high school years she had played tennis, gone riding, picnicked, roller skated and—the times she loved best—strolled with friends sharing confidences about boyfriends or sat on a bench with Dad talking about life. She suddenly flashed on the evening before she left to go away to College. Dad had suggested they go for a walk after dinner. They were sitting on their favorite bench watching the shadows gather and the leaves form intricate patterns on the sidewalk. He had turned to her unexpectedly and declared that he and mother had both been virgins when they married and that he was sure this had enriched their relationship. It had something to do with the joy of mutual discovery, it seemed. She had known what he was trying to tell her and she had been both amused and touched by this odd effort at a "facts of life" speech.

She'd spent so many nights gazing out of her bedroom window, watching the planes flying over the park on their way to or from LaGuardia Airport, the dog-walkers and lovers entering or leaving the Park, the designs made by the headlights of the cars winding their way through the park road, the life on the street. The Park had always been her connection to what she loved about the country and had been denied as a city child; the trees, grass, flowers in their constantly changing seasonal colors were a source of refreshment and gave her a sense of contentment and security.

"Hello? Where did you go?" Conrad had been watching her.

"Oh! I'm sorry. I was just thinking about how quiet and peaceful it is in the Park. Such a relief!"

"Yeh, peaceful sometimes. It depends on your frame of reference, I guess."

"What do you mean?"

"Oh, I was just thinking about something that happened the other evening. It was hilarious in a macabre sort of way. I was taking a short-cut through the Park to get to my mother's place—she lives in the projects all the way over on the east side—when this guy jumps me from behind and shoves a blade against my throat."

"Oh my God!" exclaimed Karen.

"He says, 'gimme your wallet', and I knew the voice because it's a peculiar one. So I swing around to face him and he yells 'mother fucker, it's Con! How are ya man? Hey, sorry, I didn't know it was you!' It was a kid I went to school with."

"You're kidding."

Conrad laughed. "He practically escorted me the rest of the way. Eighty percent of the guys I went to school with are either dead or in jail."

"Where did you go to school?"

"Countee Cullen High." Karen shook her head. Although an inveterate New Yorker she'd never heard of that school. "In Harlem", he explained. "Say look, what about that parking place over there?"

Karen swung the little car into a small parking area in front of a grove of glowing maples and cut the ignition. She stretched and took a deep breath. The air always smelled better and felt better in her lungs when there were trees around. There were only a few cars parked in the space and they were empty. It was suddenly quiet and peaceful and if you looked straight ahead you could pretend you were in the country. The leaves had turned to Karen's favorite colors: russet, amber, gold, burgundy. There was something about the fall palette that struck a visceral chord in Karen's innards. "Isn't it beautiful!" She whispered the words as though fearful that any sound might cause the whole setting to vanish.

Conrad turned to face her. "Yeh. Beautiful."

"I was talking about the fall leaves. You're not even looking at them."

"You look where you want to look, and I'll look where I want to look," he said, his eyes never leaving her face.

Karen was suddenly aware that the parking area was deserted and that she was with a man she hardly knew. She wondered what had possessed her to take this kind of chance and what she would do if he actually tried to make a pass. She dismissed the thought. She was sure he just wanted to talk about rehearsals and was dealing with her as the producer's wife. She tried to pick a safe topic. "Tell me something, Conrad. Are you really a model?"

"Yup. Why do you ask?"

"I don't know. I just wondered."

He snorted. "A male model is probably queer, right? No, I am not queer."

"I didn't think that at all," she protested. "Why are you so defensive?"

"That's usually what I get. People make assumptions when they don't know anything. Actually, it pays very well, and I've had the chance to go to places I never would have seen, like South America, Hawaii…"

"You mean you actually go on tour?"

Conrad proceeded to explain that there are people all over the world who do not see their image in WOMENS WEAR DAILY or VOGUE and that there was a huge group of middle and upperclass black people who attended the touring fashion shows put on exclusively for them. He asked her if she had ever looked at magazines like EBONY and JET. "I do some print work for them," he shrugged. "Terrific clothes and sometimes I can buy them at a big discount." He paused for a moment. "We do what we have to do to make a living, right?" He patted the script in his lap. "Of course I'd rather be doing this all the time, but the parts are few and far between."

"Is your wife an actress?" asked Karen.

His expression changed. Karen couldn't read it.

"No, she's a princess," Conrad said wryly and shifted in his seat. "We're having some problems."

So are we. Karen almost blurted it out. The impulse startled her. Aloud she said, "it's awfully hard to keep a stable relationship in our business."

"What do you mean?" he asked.

"Well, it's such a crazy business. So insecure. You never know from one day to the next whether you're going to eat or pay the rent. Then when you finally reach some degree of achievement, you're terrified that it will end any minute and you have to spend all your time holding on to it. That puts an enormous amount of pressure on a relationship."

Conrad nodded. "You're right. That's something that my wife doesn't seem to be able to handle. See, she married 'a star', or so she thought. Uptown, I'm something of a celebrity…only because my face is all over the place, not because I've <u>done</u> anything," he hastened to add, "and she insists on behaving as though I'm making a star's salary. She's an obssesive shopper. Has to have everything she sees in the magazines. She has this image of herself as a debutante. You know the other day when I lost my cool at rehearsal? I found out that morning that Lou had run up a five hundred dollar tab on her Bloomingdale's charge account. And here I am doing an off-Broadway play and making fifty a week rehearsal pay!"

"Wow," said Karen. Funny, it had never ocurred to her that residents of Harlem might have charge accounts at Bloomingdale's. But then, she had never given it much thought. One didn't see too many Negroes around the elite department stores. Karen realized with a shock how little she knew about black people and how bigoted she was. There were few if any black people in the schools she went to. Her main contact had been the women her mother had hired to work in the household. She suddenly remembered her beloved Bessie, a huge amply breasted chocolate colored woman who was their housekeeper when Karen was about eleven. Bessie loved to bake and would make Karen a special cake for every holiday. She never forgot the amazing work of art with the green cocoanut nest holding muticolored eggs that Bessie solemnly presented to her for Easter. Her reformed Jewish family thought it was hilarious and it became an inside joke for years after. But Karen had hugged Bessie with all her might and basked in the warmth of the loving gesture. And after that Bessie was like a grandma to her.

Conrad was still talking. "We're up to our ass in debt. Doing this show at this salary is a big financial sacrifice and it's going to put me deeper in the hole. That female is completely out of touch with reality!" He paused and grinned at her. "There. Now I've spilled my gut. It's your turn."

Five hundred dollars. Daniel would have had her head on a platter if she had spent that much without consulting him. "Well, to tell you the truth, we've been having some problems too. But I thought we were being pretty discreet, at least where the cast was concerned. Does it show?" she asked anxiously.

He patted her hand. "Only if someone is watching closely. I've been watching."

"It usually happens when there's work involved. But it's getting worse, I think. Maybe it's my frustration at always having to take a back seat. But a lot of the time, Daniel doesn't know I'm alive, except to give me orders. He doesn't have any concern for my opinions, my feelings, or even my self respect. And yet he wants me to be there for him a hundred percent, dancing attendance, taking care of his creature comforts and doing his bidding. It makes me feel like shit." Karen was suddenly horrified at what she had revealed to a stranger. "I'm very embarrassed", she said aloud. "I haven't talked about Dan with anyone, and I have no idea why I'm telling you all this now."

"It's because you know I have a sympathetic ear. Maybe your husband and my wife should get together. You know, they might make a good pair." They laughed. "I have this theory. There are two kinds of people, the givers and the takers. You and I are givers and we both married takers. Maybe that makes us kindred spirits."

Karen turned to him. "How do you know I'm a giver?"

"I told you. I've been watching you."

Although she thought about making a glib reply, Karen remained silent.

Dusk was turning into darkness and the air, clear and sweet with the oxygen from the great trees surrounding them, swirled around and through the little car. It was somehow serene in this small cul-de-sac and they seemed completely separate from the rest of the world. The place had its own reality and everything outside of it suddenly seemed very distant. A strong gust of wind invaded the mood. Karen shivered and rolled up the window on the driver's side.

"Brrr. It's getting chilly," said Karen.

"The hawk is on his way." Conrad buttoned up his jacket. He moved to put a protective arm around her shoulders but thought better of it and left it casually draped across the back of the seat.

"The hawk?" Karen was acutely aware of the nearness of him.

"Yeh. That's what we call the bitter winter wind." He paused for a moment. "Do you think the show will go? There's a lot riding on this for me."

Karen sighed. "How can I tell? I'm too close to it to be objective. The acting is good. I know that. The script still has some problems. We both know that! A lot depends on who reviews it for THE TIMES. That's the money review."

"You mean my whole future is in the hands of one guy?"

"It's Las Vegas time."

"What do you mean by that?"

"It's a throw of the dice. A gamble. It's always like that."

Conrad clutched his head with his hands in mock despair. "Oi vey," he moaned.

The Yiddish expression was so incongruous coming from him that Karen burst out laughing.

Conrad grinned at her. Then he suddenly moved away. "We'd better go. I've got to get home."

They drove the rest of the way uptown in silence. The respite in the Park had been strangely relaxing and Karen felt somehow refreshed. But at the same time she was uneasy about how suddenly close they had become and how much she had wanted him to put his arms around her. Had they stayed another few minutes…

"Turn here," said Conrad shortly after they left the northern end of the Park. They went down a side street lined with tenements in varying stages of neglect. Although the buildings had an air of past respectability, clearly there had been no thought of urban renewal here. Karen noticed that some of the broken windows had been covered with tin-foil. Groups of men and children hung about the stoops. Garbage cans overflowing with refuse dotted the street at each end. An old Malcolm X poster hung on a street lamp. Conrad pointed to a dark stone four story building in the middle of the block. A bearded black man was draped across the top step smoking a joint.

"This is my castle. Thanks a lot. See you tomorrow." Before she could reply, Conrad had jumped out of the car and was disappearing from view.

It was very dark by the time Karen found a place to park and headed for her building. The tree-lined street looked oddly different to her after her visit uptown. It was as if it were a place in another country.

"Hi, Joe," she said to the doorman who had jumped up from his seat to admit her. "Thank you."

"Gettin' cold, isnt it missus?"

"Sure is," she replied dutifully. As the elevator carried her to her floor, Karen found herself recalling the image of Conrad's profile: the aquiline and ever-so-slightly hooked nose, the graceful jaw-line, the tiny black curls that traveled around his ear to the nape of his neck. What blending of parentage produced such good looks, she wondered.

CHAPTER 3

1967 Black Power Conference in Newark, New Jersey

The week prior to the first preview, Actors Equity allowed a twelve hour rehearsal each day with breaks for lunch and dinner. Whenever possible, Karen worked it out so she could have dinner with several members of the cast at the small Italian restaurant across the street from the theatre. She enjoyed the sense of community that takes place among actors who, for the period of the run at least, become a family in the closeness of their working hours and the shared knowledge that their careers were at equal risk.

And she enjoyed the continued contact with Conrad. At first he refused to join them, but Karen had urged him and he finally agreed to come along. She soon discovered that he had backed off because he knew he couldn't afford the price of dinner in a restaurant. He would protest that he really wasn't hungry, but once Karen caught on she would offer him 'tastes' of her order. A couple of times she insisted he let her lend him enough cash to pay for his own meal.

"I'm just trying to squeak through until we open. Then I'll have my days free to make some money," he apologized.

"Forget it," she said. "It's for the good of the show. We can't have you fainting from starvation."

Although they were always in the company of others, Karen and Conrad learned about each other through the banter that was part of the meal.

"Who gets your vote as the sexiest male star today?" asked Conrad one evening. He was addressing Louise and Ann but watching Karen out of the corner of his eye.

"Tony Quinn," Karen answered quickly as the other two thought over the question. "And Brando, of course. That goes without saying."

Conrad nodded approval as though she had passed an important test.

Karen learned that Conrad's mother was a white lady from Washington, D.C. and his father was a West Indian from Antigua. He talked little about himself, but someone had asked him where his family was from, and he had answered with a knowing smile, fully aware of what they were really asking.

One evening the group got on the subject of age. It was revealed finally that, among those present, all were under the age of thirty except Karen who had reached that age a few months back. Conrad, after some prodding, confessed that he was twenty-eight.

He whispered to Karen, "Between you and me, Lou is thirty-one. She'd kill me if she knew I'd told you."

"Why do you put so much salt on your food?" Karen asked on another occasion as she watched Conrad pouring from the salt shaker as though it were a water pitcher. "That can't be good for you."

"It's my heritage." He winked at her. "No, you see nothing seems to have any taste. I like my food spicy."

"Oh, my God!" she gasped later when he offered her some of his pasta. "What have you done to this!" She grabbed for some water. "You must have a mouth made of leather."

"It's the hot pepper. I love it."

There were always discussions about current or future productions on and off-Broadway. It was generally agreed that WHO'S AFRAID OF VIRGINIA WOOLF would get the Tony Award for best play and Uta Hagen would get it for best actress.

"What did you think of it?" Karen asked Conrad.

He shrugged. "I haven't seen it."

Karen was startled. Everyone in the theatre had flocked to see this original and highly touted production. "How come?" she asked.

"We don't get downtown much." His reply was a taunt, as if it had somehow become important to remind everyone of his identity.

But Karen realized that Conrad probably couldn't afford to go to the Broadway theatre and was sorry she had a brought it up in the presence of the others.

When they privately compared notes on movies, it seemed as though their tastes were identical. They liked the same things and loathed the same things. They even had the same favorite actors, with one major exception.

"Sam Jaffe in GUNGA DIN? We would call that the epitome of Uncle Tom. Are you kidding?" Conrad snorted in disgust.

"But he's a wonderful actor. You can't blame him for the script!" It was one of the few times that they'd had a difference of opinion about the work.

When they were with the group, Conrad was more guarded, keeping his opinions to himself unless he was asked, and listening to, more than participating in, the conversation. The one topic that was never addressed at mealtime was the show they were all rehearsing. That was too much like touching tongue to sore tooth since all were anxious about the outcome. It was, after all, their meal ticket—or not.

Karen began to bring the car to the theatre every evening so that she could drive Conrad home after rehearsal. The stop in the little parking space in Central Park became part of the ride.

One night Conrad began talking about his mother and father. "He was a night watchman and she would run into him every evening on her way home from work. She was young and inexperienced and he was much older and full of stories about the islands. I don't think she'd ever been out on a date even. She was very withdrawn and shy. She still is, as a matter of fact. And her two sisters were always beating on her. So having this cat pay so much attention to her all of a sudden must have been overwhelming."

Karen nodded. The night was cold and she shivered a bit.

Conrad saw it. "Are you cold? Maybe we should head home."

"No, no. Tell me more, please. I'm fine." she protested.

"You realize," he went on, "that in those days consorting with a NEGRO...," he gave the word special emphasis "well, it was unheard of. So she kept it from her sisters. And one day she ran off with him and they got married. I think she may even have been pregnant by then."

"With you."

"No, with my brother."

Karen was surprised. He had never mentioned that he had a brother until this moment. She gathered that they were not very close and wondered why.

"You have a brother?" she asked. "Does he live here? Will he be coming to the opening?"

"No, he's dead."

"Oh Con, I'm sorry."

"No, see I never knew him. My father took my mother to the islands to wait out the pregnancy and they came back to the city just in time for her to have the baby at good old Harlem Hospital. That's where he died."

"You mean at birth?"

"No, he was a fine healthy baby. Something apparently went wrong with the circumcision. I've never been able to get the whole story. But the bottom line is that the hospital screwed up, as they do so often with poor people in a city hospital," he added wryly. "So the baby died. And here's the capper: they insisted he be buried in a place set aside for 'Negroes Only', somewhere way the hell out on Long Island."

"I can't believe it! Here? In New York? I mean, I know in the South…but here?"

Conrad reached for his wallet and drew out a creased and worn piece of paper. "Here's the certificate, or whatever they call it. I don't know why I carry it around with me."

Karen could hardly make out the faded writing in the darkness of the car. The words 'Baby Taylor' and 'Colored Only' were visible, along with 'died Feb. 12, 1930'.

She shook her head. "I can't believe this. My God, it's shocking. To think that something like this could happen. I mean, you read about this kind of thing happening in Mississippi or some place like that, but…"

"But it has no reality? You don't know the half of it."

"But your mother is white. How could they?" Karen drew her coat around her. She was really cold now. And she had an urgent desire to touch Conrad, to put her arms around him, to somehow make up for the pain others had inflicted. He seemed to sense her thoughts, because he moved closer to her and put his arm around her shoulders.

"Do you know that when they went to the movies together, my mother had to sit downstairs while my father had to sit upstairs? They couldn't sit together!" He chuckled. "My mother must have been some strong chick to put up with all that shit."

"Well, thank God we've come a long way since those days," sighed Karen.

"Have we really?"

The tone of his voice was a warning bell to Karen. For the most part, she had felt more comfortable with Conrad than she had ever felt with a Negro before. More able to say whatever came into her head, without worrying about how it would sound. But every once in a while she was jarred into the realization that their perceptions of the life around them were very different.

"So where were you born?" asked Karen.

"That same old Harlem Hospital. Only this time my mother wouldn't let them come near me." He grinned at her. "So, I remain as I was at birth." He patted her shoulder. "This has been a lop-sided conversation. I tell you about me, but you never talk about you."

"Your story is much more…interesting."

Conrad laughed. "You mean more colorful?" he teased.

Karen responded with a playful jab to his ribs. She took a moment to think of how to begin and how much to tell him, then started with the fact that she'd been born in New York and lived there all her life except when she went away to college.

"Went to college, huh? Lucky," Conrad interjected.

She explained that among the middle class Jewish intelligentsia, it was expected that the children would go to college, even if the parents had to scrimp and sacrifice to make it possible. "Education is everything to the Jews. I guess it's related to the fact that the truly orthodox spend so much time studying the Torah."

"What's a Torah?" he asked.

"Well, it's sort of like the scriptures. It's the most holy writings. Actually, you're making me realize that I don't really know what it is. I'm Jewish as a fact of birth, but I'm not religious at all, so I'm the last person to ask about any of that stuff."

"Where I come from, a Jew is someone whose religion is making money."

"Well, that's a pretty bigoted, anti-semitic generalization," protested Karen.

"Yeh, but you've got to remember that all the slumlords in Harlem are Jews," he retorted.

Karen felt herself getting angry and defensive. It drove her crazy when people lumped her into a group. Especially one over which she had no control. Must she take responsibility for a couple of evil Jews whose behaviour gives all of us a bad name? She fell silent.

As Conrad watched her, she shrugged. "My feet are getting numb. I'm afraid winter is upon us," she said lightly, trying to change the mood as she started the tiny car.

"You're mad at me." He seemed amused.

She turned to look him in the eye. "I just hate it when I'm made to feel defensive about something over which I have no control. We're not all alike, you know."

He took her hand in his. "Look, there are lousy black people and there are lousy Jews. Present company is <u>always</u> excepted in our comments of course. It's obvious that we're perfect." He laughed. "Tell me more about yourself."

"I really am freezing," she said as she stepped on the accelerator. "Let's save it for next time." She couldn't dispel the uneasiness she felt everytime he hit a nerve with his frankness. It occurred to her that they were actually both bigots.

With the increasing demand on her time as they got closer to opening night, Karen didn't have a chance to be alone with Conrad during the next few days. Because most of her concerns were with the box office, the house staffs and the promotion of the show, Karen found herself inventing reasons to go backstage so she could get a glimpse of him. She became acutely aware that she missed him and that she was thinking about him a good deal of the time. Their contact was reduced to a fast 'hello, how are you?' in a whispered exchange in the darkness of the wings during a run-through. She could sense his mounting anxiety and tension, assuming that it was his concern for the future of the play and the usual actor's insecurity about his performance.

Karen made it a point to clear her schedule so she could watch the whole run-through the night before the dress rehearsal. The show looked pretty good to her, but there were weaknesses in the script that were still evident and the second act really seemed to sag. Karen couldn't tell whether her opinion was a detached observation or a reflection of her interest in Conrad who had much less to do in the second act. For the first time, in the protective darkness of the theatre, she allowed herself to acknowledge the strong chemistry between them. The sexual attraction was overpowering, and it was a new experience for Karen. She had always taken sexual need as a matter of course, but had never permitted it to rule her. Now it was becoming so pervasive, it was all she could think about.

It was very late, almost midnight, by the time they left the theatre and the blustery weather held the promise of snow. Although it was against her better judgment, Karen welcomed the opportunity to drive Conrad home that night.

"The Daf doesn't have snow tires and now I'll never have time to deal with it. Damn! I'll probably have to go all the way to Brooklyn. What a pain a car is in the city," moaned Karen.

The streets were almost empty as they drove through midtown on their way to the Park. The theatre crowd had already headed for the warmth of home.

"Can I help you in any way?," asked Conrad.

"It's sweet of you to offer. But remember, you don't drive," she teased him. "I guess I'll have to teach you."

"That would be fantastic." He paused for a moment. Then softly he added, "You realize, if it hadn't been for this car, we wouldn't have had a chance to know each other."

Karen's pulse quickened and she knew that they were treading on dangerous ground. "Maybe we should go straight up tonight. It looks like it's going to do something any minute. And you must be exhausted. I know I am."

"Let's just stop for a minute or two. I want to tell you something." Conrad's voice was low, but there was an urgency under the words. He added, "And you haven't said a word about the run-through tonight."

They had stopped for a red light. Karen studied his face. "What's up?'

"When we get there. I want your full attention."

"Is it about the show"? she asked anxiously. She certainly didn't want any surprises at this stage.

He shook his head.

"You were really good tonight," she said quickly.

"Well! Finally! You had me worried." He grinned at her. "Seriously, any notes?"

"No, really, I loved what you did. But then, I usually do…I mean…" Karen was startled to feel herself blushing.

"Go on."

"Well, there was just one spot where I couldn't understand you."

"Underprojected, you mean?"

"No, just unclear. I'm not sure you know how to respond there. So it comes out sort of mumbled. It's in the first act right after she tells you about getting the new job."

"Oh, yeah. You're absolutely right. I really don't know what I'm doing there. I'm not sure whether he's happy that she's doing what she wants to do, or threatened by it. So I guess I've been trying to play both and muddying it up."

"Well, what does Adam say?"

"He hasn't been much help, I'm afraid. He just says to take it moment to moment and see how I feel when it comes up." He snorted. "He's so busy trying to get our darling star together, he hasn't had much time for the rest of us."

Karen knew that the tension between Conrad and Ann was escalating and that it was getting harder for Conrad to contain his anger. She was an utterly selfish actress, and to make matters worse, was still defending her own inadequacies by attacking every one else. That made Conrad's task in the play all the more difficult.

"Well," replied Karen thoughtfully, "it seems to me that your natural instinct, if you were in conflict, would be to withdraw, but you don't want her to see what you're feeling so you might try to cover up by bending over backwards, you know, making a big deal about congratulating her...still keeping the anxiety there, but underneath."

He stared at her for a moment. "I'll try it. It's a good idea. Thanks."

As they pulled into their usual spot in the Park he said, "I'll bet you're a terrific actress. Why aren't you out there doing it?"

"Well, that's a long story," answered Karen as she yawned and stretched back against the seat. "If I get started on me, we'll be out here all night."

"You know, you always put me off when I ask you to tell me about yourself. Why?"

Karen knew it was true. Although she loved people and their behaviour fascinated her, she had always been a private person unwilling to share her past or her innermost thoughts with others. It had distanced her from her friends, and especially from her roommates and classmates at college who sat around spilling their guts to each other by the hour. She had often been called 'aloof' and that distressed her but she couldn't help herself. She just couldn't seem to open up the way the others did. In a way, she supposed it was a lack of trust. Her mind flashed back to something that happened when she was in high school.

Karen turned to Conrad. "You're right. But I don't know why. I do that with everyone, I guess. I hate to talk about myself. I'd much rather listen to what others have to say. But when you asked me just now, I remembered something that happened a long time ago. I had a very close friend when I was in high school. I guess we were sophomores or juniors, I can't quite recall. Anyway, we were as tight as girlfriends can be. We spent hours telling each other everything. You can imagine the phone bills! Well, Evie—that was her nickname—was crazy about this very handsome boy in our homeroom class. And they started going around together. He was a nice kid, very bright and outgoing, a real flirt actually, and I liked him a lot. But I always thought of him as Evie's man, so I was very careful to keep him at arm's length. One day, without any warning, Evie snubbed me cold as we were taking off our coats in the locker room. I tried to find out what was the matter but she wouldn't talk to me. I spent the whole day in pain, wondering what in the world had happened. I couldn't concentrate on anything, and finally I cornered her after our last class. Even now I remember that we were standing on the landing of a staircase with everybody going up and down between classes, when I grabbed her and demanded to know what the hell was going on. She accused me of trying to steal her boy friend and swore that she was never going to speak to me again since this was no way for a 'true friend' to behave. She wouldn't even let me defend myself. And that was the end of that. It wasn't until much later that I found out that the boy had been taunting her rather cruelly, for reasons I can't imagine, and let it drop that he thought I was the sexiest girl in the home room class. I cried for days over the loss of the friendship and the injustice of being accused of something I didn't do. It hurt me so much that she was quick to believe him and not me. After that, I kept my distance and only trusted friendships but so far." Karen paused for a moment, then laughed. "Everything is so intense when you're in your teens! You know, it's amazing. I haven't thought about this in years. And I've never told this story to anyone."

"I'm flattered." Conrad smiled at her. "Lie down and tell me more." He indicated his shoulder and put his arm around her as she let her head rest against his arm.

She giggled. "Okay, herr doktor." She felt relaxed and warm and protected with his arm around her. She was just about to tell him that when a patrol car slid up alongside the Daf and a beam of light shone through the window, momentarily blinding them.

"Oh, oh," whispered Conrad under his breath. Karen could feel his body go taut.

"Something wrong, officer?" said Karen straightening up in her seat. She was furious.

"The Park is closed folks," said a voice from within the patrol car. "There's no parking in this area after twelve." The two cops leaned forward, casing them.

"Oh goodness, I had no idea it was so late." Karen flashed what she hoped was a charming smile and turned the ignition key to start the Daf's motor as the patrol car at first lingered, then backed out and drove off. She let the engine idle until she was sure they'd gone. She had no intention of letting cops spoil the mood.

Conrad put his hand on her arm. 'Let's get out of here."

"But we weren't doing anything wrong," she protested. "You'd think they'd have enough to do chasing criminals. Why do they have to hassle us? It's only a few minutes after twelve."

"Listen, two nights before opening is no time to look for trouble. I know these guys. Where I come from they act first and ask questions later."

Karen heard and was surprised at the fear in his voice. Funny, she thought, this big strong man makes me feel so safe and protected but he's threatened by a couple of cops. Cops to her were simply public servants. She had never had anything to do with them and pretty much took them for granted, except when one needed directions in a strange neighborhood or when there was a traffic problem. She remembered her father swearing about how they're never around when you need them, when some wild driver swerved in front of him on the highway. Karen wondered if Conrad had ever had a run-in with the law.

He was trying to make a joke out of it. "Don't mess wif de f-u-u-u-zz," he said. "There are two powers you learn to respect in Harlem: cops and large dogs. They are always right, regardless. Let's go."

Karen obeyed with regret. Even though it was threatening snow, they were so close to the wire with the show, she didn't know when they'd have another chance for a few minutes alone together. So often relationships formed during the course of a project, which seemed so intense at the time, dissolved into a dew once the show opened and each went his own way. And since she wasn't even in the cast, there would be no excuse for her presence every night. Karen had no idea if this show would have any longevity, but she did know that she wished the rehearsal period would never end.

Again it was as though Conrad had read her thoughts. "Once we open, will you still be around?" he asked.

"Oh, sure," she said softly.

As they headed north he turned to her. "Tell me, honestly. Do we have a chance? What do you think? Do you think we'll get good reviews?"

Karen sighed. "To tell you the truth, I've always felt it was a crapshoot. How can you predict what a critic is going to think? Sometimes it just depends on whether he had a good dinner or not. I've seen them sleep through an entire show and then give it a rave. It has nothing to do with whether it's good or bad, really. Most of them don't know much about the theatre, they just have an emotional reaction. The reactionary papers like the NEWS will probably hate it just because it's about an interracial relationship."

Conrad shook his head impatiently. "Those bastards have my life or death in their hands," he growled.

"Well," Karen laughed, "That's putting it a little dramatically, don't you think? You'll survive, no matter what, and you know it." She pulled the car up in front of his building.

"Maybe." He turned to confront her. "But will we?"

"Oh yes," she smiled at him. "I think I can survive this too."

His eyes were like an animal's, almost opaque their gaze was so intense. "No, I mean <u>you and me.</u> How would we keep on seeing each other if…That's what I wanted to talk to you about. I'm in love with you, you know."

It was simply stated and it sent little shivers traveling along the length of Karen's spine. Conrad pulled her to him gently and kissed her. It was a soft, searching kiss but it surged through Karen's body as though warm butter had been injected into her veins.

In a swift motion, he opened the door of the car. "Later," he said. Before Karen could reply, the car door had closed and he was gone.

CHAPTER 4

And now the opening night was upon them and Karen had the familiar churning in the pit of her stomach all day. It was always that way. It had started when she made her first public appearance as an actress in her teens. And, like Pavlov's dog, the feeling returned whenever she had anything to do with an opening. It didn't seem to matter what position she held, the knots were there.

She had given a lot of thought to what she was going to wear. The aim was to look good but, as part of the producing team, not too flashy. It wouldn't do to appear to be attempting to upstage the performance. But she also wanted to look sexy, show off her figure and be appropriately dressed for the gala cast party after the show. She finally chose a black matte jersey which hugged her body to the hip and then flared gracefully around her legs. As she stared at her image in the floor-length mirror she could hear her mother's whisper in her ear: "black doesn't do anything for you, dear, you need bright colors." But she knew Conrad liked her in black and she confessed to her mirror image that perhaps that was what had influenced her choice. One day she had come to rehearsal wearing a black skirt and sweater and Conrad had given her a low, long whistle, whispering "faaaanntastic." She added the pearl drop earrings and necklace that Daniel had given her last Christmas and surveyed the effect. Her mirror said sexy but elegant. Just the effect she wanted. Karen stared at the pearls for a moment. Daniel and she had hardly spoken in the past few weeks. Karen wondered what was going to happen to their marriage.

"Let's think about that tomorrow, Scarlett," she said to the face in the mirror.

Daniel had announced he was going on ahead so he could have a few words with the General Manager and Karen was actually relieved that there wouldn't be any opportunity for discussion. She wasn't in the mood for a fight right now, which was the direction in which all their recent discussions seemed to be headed.

She got to the theatre at half-hour so she could wish everyone backstage good luck. She knew the audience would be trickling in even though it was early. So as not to run into anybody she knew before the show, she ducked into the alley and entered through the back loading dock. The lights were down on the stage but everything was set up for the first act and there was an aura of expectation about the set as though it were waiting for guests to arrive at a party.

The wings and the dressing rooms were alive with activity, however. Lights were being checked, the stage manager and his assistant were going over their scripts, the actors were pacing, dressing, vocalizing and generally trying to work off their opening night nerves. As was often the case in Off-Broadway theatres, there were only the two large rooms, one for the men, the other for the women, each lined with mirrors. They were divided by a seven foot high partition so that, while separate, men and women could converse with one another without having to yell too loudly. In each room there was a long rack holding the costumes which were carefully marked with each actor's name and the act in which it would be worn. The tables in front of the mirrors were filled with all kinds of makeup, in pots and sticks and jars. Brushes of every size, powder puffs, kleenex, cans of Albolene and other forms of makeup remover fought for space with flowers, telegrams and all sorts of good luck talismans. Some of the actors were very neat and organized and had everything laid out carefully in rows. Others just let things fall where they might. It was all part of the individual ritual with which each actor hoped to guarantee success on this special and most difficult night.

Daniel and Karen had sent each actor a bottle of champagne with a personal note, so as Karen moved between the two rooms there was much exchanging of thank you's and good luck wishes. In the midst of everything, there was a moment of panic when Shirley realized she had forgotten to bring the special pair of black panties they had decided she needed to wear under one of her costumes. The assistant stage manager was immediately dispatched to her apartment (which fortunately was not too far from the theatre) to hunt up the all-important undies and reassure the frantic actress.

Karen saved Conrad for last. They hadn't had a chance to exchange more than a few words since that startling moment of intimacy. Karen had been up to her ears in last minute production detail and Conrad had made himself scarce. As she came up behind him their eyes locked in the mirror, exchanging volumes. She noticed Conrad's hands were trembling slightly. She bent to kiss him lightly on the cheek as she had done with the other actors and whispered "Don't worry. You're going to be great."

"Sure, sure." He made a face at her in the mirror. "Will I see you at the party?" He sounded anxious.

"Of course."

"Lou is coming. Unfortunately." He whispered the last under his breath.

"Break a leg. See you later." She tried to sound nonchalant, using the actors' 'code' for good luck. But she actually felt her pulse throbbing in her neck.

Going around to the front of the house, she saw that the theatre was beginning to fill up and the buzz of expectation was growing in volume. The theatre, a long time fixture of the Village with its 299 noisily creaking plush red seats and curtained proscenium, was something of a landmark to the true theatre buff who preferred to make discoveries of new talent by frequenting the off-Broadway venues. This particular house had a history of successful productions that in some cases made their way to larger and more lucrative Broadway theatres, and booking it had been a major coup for Daniel in spite of its intimacy and modest decor. Opening night audiences were mainly friends, relatives and loyal fans who were determined to impress the critics with their appreciation of the offering. So their reactions were rarely to be trusted as a true prediction of the outcome of the evening. But it was reassuring to know that they were going to laugh at all the jokes and be effusive with their applause. The critics were unimpressionable, of course. If they hated it, nothing would dissuade them from writing a lousy review. But it was nice for the actors to have an enthusiastic response, even if only for this first night.

Karen looked for Daniel and found him finally in a corner of the lobby talking to one of the backers.

"Everything seems to be under control backstage, darling." She was hoping they could carry this night off without the bickering and unpleasantness so inevitable lately. "Hello Mr. Osborne." She smiled at the backer who was one of their most loyal participants. He believed in putting money in anything that had a positive message, particularly about race relations. He was the CEO of a company that imported cigarette paper and had made a fortune. He was in his fifties with a slight southern drawl that had stuck long after he left Georgia and which often took the edge off a certain feistiness in his approach to people. Karen supposed that the stress of being both an authority figure in the business world and a southern liberal had produced his somewhat confrontational manner. But he was their chief angel and this time he had even offered his apartment for the opening night party.

"Nate's been kind enough to supply his own caterer for tonight," said Daniel. "It's going to be a feast."

"How wonderful of you. Thanks so much!"

"Hey, I'm lookin' forward to this. It better play as good as it read." Nate Osborne could afford to lose the whole bundle but he hated being anything but a winner.

Daniel silently raised crossed fingers. "Better check the house. See you later." He slipped away speedily.

Karen knew he was deliberately sticking her with the task of chatting with Osborne and hated him for it. "Are your seats okay? Is Mrs. Osborne here yet?"

"Yeh, she went to the ladies'. I haven't looked at the seats yet. I'll go and do that now." He departed abruptly.

Karen breathed a sigh of relief. She never knew how to talk to those people, never felt comfortable with them. The business world was a foreign country.

"Curtain going up. Please take your seats." The usher moved through the crowd.

As the lights dimmed, Karen's heart began to thump in her chest and her mouth went dry. Was she nervous for the play or for Conrad? She had to admit to herself that it was some of both but probably more the latter.

The performance went well, with only one minor mishap in a late lighting cue. Karen could tell that Conrad was very tense but she didn't think it affected the work or that anybody else could see it. The audience was attentive and there was no coughing until that sag in the second act. Karen had deliberately avoided contact with anyone during the intermission, slipping out before it began and walking a few blocks south to smoke a cigarette. She hated to put people on the spot if they didn't have anything good to say. When it was over there were four curtain calls and the applause sounded sincere. Karen knew that the relatives always kept it going, but it gave her hope nevertheless. One could never read the faces of the critics as they dashed out to make their respective deadlines. Tomorrow night the second string papers and the magazines would come, but these guys would have to write their immediate reactions within the next hour. Karen's mother and father came over and hugged her and wished her luck and Daniel's mother did her usual "my Daniel knows how to pick 'em" routine. Karen tried to identify Conrad's wife Lou, without success, and soon she was surrounded by the loyal crowd of friends who had always supported Daniel and Karen's efforts. Their comments were many and varied. "Very moving" said one. "Tough play." murmured another. "Talented writer…I was never bored." "I loved it darling!" Karen hated these one liners that could mean they really liked it or they couldn't think of anything else to say with honesty.

Daniel had joined the group and whispered to Karen, "We've got to shake some of these people and get to the Osborne place."

She had pleaded with Daniel to have the party someplace where they could invite family and friends, but he'd resisted saying that it should be confined to cast, crew, backers and Osborne's friends. Karen hoped he hadn't heard her best girlfriend Amy's remark: "Where did you find that gorgeous guy? He's not really black, is he?"

"Of course he's black. He's just very light skinned." Karen had retorted. "Let's talk tomorrow. I've got to get backstage."

As Karen ducked into the alley and entered the backstage area she could feel the mood of exhilaration that always seemed to permeate dressing rooms right after an opening. There was that wonderful feeling of accomplishment and release, like having successfully climbed a mountain or taken a race horse over a high hurdle. The euphoria usually lasted until the reviews came out. Then it was either manic elation or the doom and gloom of dashed hopes.

"Thanks everybody for a wonderful show. You were all great!" Karen called out so both dressing rooms could hear. "See you all at the party."

Karen knew that the actors were rushing to dress and see the friends and relatives who were waiting for them in the lobby. These small off-Broadway theatres didn't accomodate visitors backstage. So she thought it best not to linger. They'd get the critiquing soon enough.

Daniel was waiting impatiently for her at the front of the theatre. Although they had been operating independently for the most part in the past few weeks, it was clear that he wanted them to be together when they made their entrance at the Osborne apartment.

It was an incredibly luxurious apartment overlooking Central Park. The size of it quite took Karen's breath away. Nate Osborne greeted them warmly, clapping Daniel on the back with congratulations. Karen grinned with relief. He must have liked the show or he would have let them know immediately that he was pissed off over having dumped money 'into the toilet' as he would say. That had happened once before. In fact Karen was surprised that he'd agreed to come in on it this time. As he ushered them around the apartment, introducing them to his friends, Karen took in the habitat of this wealthy liberal. The walls were paneled in a wood that looked like mahogany and the ceilings were wood beamed. The furniture was expensive modern, desgned by Saarinan and Wright and Noguchi and upholstered in lush earth tone suedes. Windows lined the entire Park side and the view of the Fifth Avenue skyline and beyond was magnificent. Glass doors opened at each end of the living room onto small landscaped terraces overlooking the park. Huge bookcases were built into the opposite wall and Karen imagined there must be a thousand books living on their shelves. As they moved into the adjoining dining room, Karen saw the mammoth table laden with food: roast beef, turkey, trays laden with hot and cold hors d'oevres, trays laden with cold vegetables, sliced breads.

"Oh, what a wonderful spread," she exclaimed. "The actors will be so happy. I'm sure they're starving."

"Actors are always starving." Daniel had come up behind her. "Well, if nothing else, at least we'll all get a good meal out of this," he whispered in Karen's ear.

"I just love your optimism, dear." Karen knew he expected the worst. He'd been hanging crepe for the past week.

Most of the guests who had already arrived were grouped around the bar in the corner of the room. It was manned by a young black bartender whom Karen suspected was an actor because he was making such an effort to be ingratiating. Karen edged her way toward him.

"And what can I get for you?" he purred to Karen.

"Scotch on the rocks please. Not too much ice."

"Coming right up. And good luck tonight," he added as he handed her the drink. Now she knew he was an actor. He had thought to find out who the producers were.

The decibel level rose as more people arrived. Although there was much laughter and a general tone of gaiety, there was an undercurrent of tension. For the most part, everyone avoided discussion of the play. Nobody wanted to commit to a reaction until the reviewers had had their say. As the actors began to arrive there were shouts of congratulations and the applause that was mandatory at these events. Karen kept watching for Conrad and his wife and finally they arrived.

Lou was a handsome, tall coffee colored woman with an ample figure that could be described as just short of hefty. She wore a tight fitting maroon velvet dress that was cut low enough to reveal her generous bosom. Her hair was done up in an elaborate french knot and the general effect was striking. If Karen hadn't heard Conrad's stories about how neurotic Lou was, she'd have been very impressed with her dignity and charm. As it was, Karen admired the performance. After the introductions and a brief exchange of niceties, Conrad steered Lou away from her and towards the food. Karen knew that he was deliberately keeping his distance. She was startled an hour later when Conrad suddenly appeared at her side.

"Lou has a headache and I'm taking her home. I'll come right back. When do the reviews come in?" he whispered anxiously.

Karen consulted her watch. "Should be another half hour or so. Are you sure you can get away?"

"I'll be right back," he said grimly. "She's always pulling this headache routine. I'm not going to miss this. Don't start without me." He tried to make it playful, but Karen knew what a toll the strain was taking.

He got back just as the press agent for the show was hearing the TIMES review read over the phone. He pulled Karen out on the terrace as they waited to hear the results of the call.

"Thank God Lou went home." Conrad took her hand. "I'm so glad we can be together for a little bit. Where's Daniel?"

"He's with Nate Osborne. He's all set to do what he always calls 'damage control' in case the reviews say anything negative. Daniel's head is already in his next project. Gotta hang on to the main backer. At all costs." Karen made a wry face.

"He should be with you at a time like this."

Karen looked up at him. "Well, you're here." She grabbed his hand. "Come on, let's get the word."

As they moved inside Karen sensed the change in the mood of the place. The raucous laughter had subsided and the occasional drunken shriek was replaced by Adam's shrill proclamation—it was a register Karen had never heard him use before.

"Brace yourself, darlings, here it comes," he cried gayly. And Karen knew they were in for it.

As the review was read aloud the room gradually became totally silent. The press agent tried to read dispassionately, without comment or inflection, but it became quickly clear that the TIMES critic hated the play. He found it self-pitying and unbelievable, although he did identify both writer and actors as talented and full of potential. It was not an out and out disaster, but it was clearly not a 'money review'. The final blow came in the last paragraph when the critic expressed his dismay that a black character had been cast with a white actor. When Conrad heard that, he turned on his heel and went out on the terrace, fuming. Both Len and Karen followed him as the rest of those present quietly headed for the bar. Len was very drunk.

"The mother fucker said he didn't believe it," growled Len. Then he turned to Karen. "Sorry. But it's my fucking life. What does that asshole know?"

"Steady, man." Conrad grabbed Len's arm to keep him from falling.

"And he wondered why your part was played by a white man! Can you believe it? Where's the fucking bathroom. I'm about to throw up." Len reeled away from them into the room.

"Wait here for me. I'll be right back. He needs help." And Conrad followed Len, putting his arm around the suffering writer to help guide him.

Karen leaned against the stone wall, gazing out at the skyline. Tears blurred her vision as the reality began to sink in. Well, that was that. It was a swell ride, but now it was clearly over. She knew how Daniel would react. The TIMES was just about the whole story. They didn't expect much from the NEWS or the TRIB, both of which were pretty reactionary papers that would hardly be expected to encourage a new and intelligent black playwright. The POST might be better, but didn't usually have enough pull to keep a show running. And if it lost any more money, Daniel would close it in the twinkling of an eye. Karen wondered what that would do to the friendship with Conrad. Would she ever see him again once the show closed? If so, they would have to be planned meetings. Did either of them want to pursue the relationship in view of their respective marriages? And how did she really feel about him? Was it just the convenience of having someone to talk to who shared the experience? Or was it much more? Karen knew that she would sorely miss the rides to the park and the quiet talks.

Conrad reappeared on the terrace and stood quietly alongside Karen. He was silent for a while, then sighed deeply. "What will happen now?" he asked.

"We'll have to see what the others are like. We might be able to pull something out for the ads. You never know. Sometimes word of mouth picks up a whole audience. I'll have to see if I can talk Daniel into keeping it open long enough to let it build."

"You're very sweet. Trying to let me down easy. But I can see the handwriting on the wall. All you have to do is walk through that room in there to get the picture," said Conrad grimly.

"I've got to talk to Daniel," Karen replied as she started to move indoors.

"Len is in very bad shape. Do you think we should take him home?" Conrad asked anxiously.

Karen knew what he was up to. It was a perfect excuse for the two of them to leave together and have some time alone. She also knew she was traveling on dangerous ground, allowing herself to get more and more involved with a man who was to all intents and purposes off-limits. But the magnetic pull was irresistible. Aloud she said "Let me talk to Daniel. I'll suggest it, then instead of coming back here, you can take me home."

"Good." Conrad understood that she had received his message without more being stated. They were beginning to get close enough to talk in shorthand. That was a good sign.

Daniel was more than willing to let Karen take care of another mess. He had never allowed himself to get that familiar with Len and he wanted him out of the Osborne apartment before there was an emotional scene. Daniel couldn't bear emotional scenes. He patted Karen's arm and told her to go on ahead, take Len home, go home herself and he'd meet her there. "I just want to try to do a little damage control." he said wryly.

"How bad is it?" asked Karen. "Is there any hope?"

"It's pretty bad. They just weren't ready for this subject matter. Ahead of its time, maybe. And it looks like all three biggies resented the casting. I hate to say I told you so, but Conrad was a big mistake. I'm going to put up the closing notice to cover ourselves. We can always take it down if things improve. But I doubt if they will."

"You never know." Karen was grateful that Daniel was being so stoic about the failure. She suspected that the small triumph of 'being right' was making up for the loss. "See you later then."

"I won't be too long." Daniel's attention had already shifted to the press agent who was on the phone again.

Karen and Conrad collected Len and finally managed to maneuver him into a cab. At which point he refused to allow them to accompany him to his destination. "Wouldn't hear of it." he said thickly. "I'm okay. Really, really am okay. Yeh…I can survive those mother fuckers. Sorry, sorry Karen…Sorry."

"Please let us come with you, Len," pleaded Karen.

"What's your address?" asked Conrad.

Len leaned over and muttered into the driver's ear. "120 West 12th Street." He turned to them and reached for the cab door. "I'm awright folks. Thanks, See ya." Slamming the door, he yelled "go!" to the driver and they sped away.

They stood together on the quiet avenue, aware of the doorman ever watchful behind them. "Let's walk," said Conrad and he took Karen's hand. It was late and the traffic was thin. Across the avenue the trees of Central Park swayed gently in the fall breeze making wooshing sounds. The streets were almost deserted except for an occasional uniformed guardian of the well-to-do emerging to check things out. They walked silently hand in hand for a while.

"If it had been a white man with a black woman, we might have gotten away with it," Conrad suddenly said, as though thinking out loud.

"What makes you think that?" Karen stopped to look at his face.

"More acceptable. The old plantation custom." They walked on.

"So what happens now I wonder?" asked Karen.

"We starve." Conrad sucked in his cheeks and made a comical starving face.

"No, I didn't mean…"

"I know."

When they reached her street Karen stopped. "Listen, let's go up to my place. I'll make us some coffee. Daniel won't be home for a while, I'm sure."

"I'd have to carry a package to get in," Conrad replied after a moment.

"What on earth for?"

"So the doorman would think I was making a delivery. Otherwise he wouldn't let me in." Conrad grinned at her.

Karen chuckled. He was always doing that. Always reminding her of what lay between them. "Not Angel" she retorted. "He's very broadminded. Besides, you've got to face it now. Everyone thinks you're white!"

But as they neared her building, Conrad suddenly stopped and let go of her hand. He looked searchingly in her eyes for a moment as though trying to find the answers there. Then softly he said, "What are we going to do about us?"

"I don't know." Karen was shocked to discover that her eyes were filling with tears. There was so much unsaid, yet so much understood by them both. It was almost as though they had been able to completely transfer thoughts to one another without the need of verbal communication.

"We have to give ourselves some time to think. And I have to figure out what I'm going to do next," said Conrad. "How long do you think we'll be able to run?"

Karen found it difficult to speak. "No way of knowing yet," she whispered.

Conrad suddenly put his arms around her and kissed her, lightly at first and then deeply, holding her so tightly that they could feel one another's heart beats. Then, pulling away, he said "Go home. I'll see you at the theatre." And he hurried off into the night leaving Karen too breathless to protest.

While waiting for Daniel to come home with the rest of the news about reviews, Karen undressed, made herself a cup of coffee and curled up in the Saarinen chair. As the hot, soothing liquid slid down her throat she let her mind wander over the past few weeks, Conrad, her marriage and then, almost as an afterthought, her career, or lack of one. Conrad had made her feel alive and beautiful and capable of doing anything she wanted to do. She realized that she had been in denial for a long time, refusing to acknowledge her feelings, not wanting to confront the realities of her relationship with Daniel.

With the careful reticence of one testing the viability of a sprained ankle, Karen allowed herself to wonder what would happen if she left Daniel. Would he continue to support her financially? If not, what could she do to earn a living while she attempted to resurrect a career? The theatre was certainly not a life that offered security. Would she have to leave this apartment? Where would she go? Would Daniel be furious enough to put her out on the street? Karen's stomach knotted suddenly at the thought of being forced to move in with her parents. She had turned into a pampered princess, she realized ruefully.

And what about Conrad? Would this intense chemistry developing between them grow into something more? What about his wife? She really didn't know where he stood in regard to his marriage. And what were the pitfalls of an interracial relationship? Would they have to hide like his parents did? Had society advanced sufficiently to allow them a normal existence? There were still some states in the U.S. where miscegenation was against the law, actually considered a crime! The stories Conrad had told her about his mother and father were pretty daunting. But that was a generation ago. Surely it was different now. How would her friends react? Well, she could pretty much guess at who would disappear and who would stick by her side. The disappearing ones weren't worth much anyway, mainly acquaintances who were originally Daniel's friends.

And Daniel. What about him? Karen wondered how he wold react to the suggestion of a trial separation. One thing was certain. Whether Conrad had entered the picture or not, she would have wanted out of this marriage. It had been going downhill for a long time and neither of them had the guts to acknowledge it. They were growing farther and farther apart. Best to do something now while they could still end it reasonably and perhaps even salvage a friendship.

Karen looked at the clock on top of the bookcase and wondered when Daniel would get home. She almost dreaded having to face his inevitable 'I told you so'. She would have to fight to try to keep the show open so it could find its audience. She knew it would be an uphill battle but she still believed in it enough to want to make the effort. And then, she admitted to herself finally, the longer it ran the more time she would have to figure out the situation with Conrad without making any hasty and potentially dangerous choices.

Some time later Karen finally heard Daniel's key in the lock. His face and his breath told her they weren't going to have any discussion that night.

"They're all pretty much the same. The critics agree on this one," was his response to her questioning look. "Phew! What a night! Can we talk tomorrow? I'm exhausted." Daniel threw off his coat and tie and dropped onto their king-sized bed.

As Karen crawled under the covers she nudged him. "Get undressed Dan." The only response was a snore.

Two weeks later the show closed. Karen had tried every possible trick and wile to try to keep it open, but to no avail. Although some of the reviews were more favorable than the TIMES had been, Daniel had wanted to end it right away. He grimly agreed to a second week against his better judgment. But with no money spent on advertising the audiences began to dwindle until one night there were only twelve people buying tickets. He put his foot down.

"Are you nuts?" he exclaimed when Karen protested. "We've got more people on the stage than in the house!"

During this period Conrad and Karen saw very little of each other. Karen had no real excuse to hang around the theatre and Conrad seemed to have crawled into a shell. They both needed time to sort out their lives and decide what to do next. There was no closing night party. The actors, who had devoted six weeks of their lives to the project were too depressed to want one and Daniel, only too aware of the financial loss already incurred, wasn't about to throw one.

The striking of the set took place right after the last performance so as to avoid paying any additional rent on the theatre. It was always a sad event watching something so carefully put together and so creative being so ruthlessly torn down. Sad too, to watch the actors pack up their belongings and drift out one by one in civilian clothes carrying totes and knapsacks, murmuring goodbyes and promises to 'get together real soon'. They had been a tight little family for this short intense period of time. Now each would go his separate way and they might not see one another again for years, if ever. It was one of the unique facts of life in this business that one formed deep close relationships during the period of creation and performance, lived like a family for a time, and then saw it all dissolve at the end of the run.

Karen stood in the back of the house watching the stage hands tear flats apart on the bare stage as Conrad approached.

"Hi." he said softly. "I left the suit on the rack to go back to the costumer's. Okay?"

"Yeh, that's fine." Karen didn't know what to say to him. There was so much she wanted to tell him, but not now. "I'm so sorry, Con."

He shrugged. "A throw of the dice." He stared at her intently, dropping his voice. "Are you okay?

"Sure."

"Will I see you?"

"Of course." Karen tried to make it sound casual, but her voice betrayed her.

"I'll call you." And he was gone.

CHAPTER 5

Daniel had agreed to a separation almost too readily and had even offered to be the one to move out of the apartment, which he did almost immediately. His attitude convinced Karen that Daniel was involved with someone else. Just as well. How little it mattered! There was some feeling of regret and even of failure, but no real pain. Years down the drain? Not really, Karen reassured herself. She'd been very young when she plunged into marriage. There had been a few very good years, a lot of experiences, a lot of maturing.

Quite suddenly Karen found herself single and alone. But it was as though she had lost a roommate, rather than a husband. There was a kind of relief, a welcoming of privacy and a discovery of personal time. The feeling of freedom when she remembered that she didn't have to be home at any particular time reminded her of how she felt as a young girl at the 3:00 p.m. exodus from school.

Weeks had gone by and there had been no word from Conrad. Karen longed to call him but didn't dare. She missed him terribly and spent the hours before sleep imagining converations with him, wondering what he was doing and why he hadn't contacted her. Was it just one of those run-of-the-play friendships? Had he also confronted the problems that might arise were they to get any closer? Perhaps he'd simply straightened things out with his wife. Or was he just being flirtatious to stay on the good side of the producer's wife? Why didn't he call?

Friends from Karen's past suddenly began to surface as word filtered out that she and Daniel had split. Amy, one of her best friends from high school, with whom she made it a point to have a three hour lunch at least twice a year to catch up and who loyally saw any production Karen was involved in, admitted that she had never really liked Daniel. She insisted that she would drive in from Westchester for an immediate celebratory lunch. There were other surprises.

They were at their usual biannual meeting place, a charming little middle-priced bistro in the east sixties called Cafe Trois which they both liked because the tables were small and discreetly spaced and one could talk about intimate things without being overheard. Amy asked the inevitable question.

"Well, are you dating?" Amy speared a crouton. She always had Caesar salad and a big gooey desert.

"No. I don't have any desire to do that," replied Karen. She paused for a moment, then added shyly, "But there is somebody."

"Wonderful, darling. Who? Tell me all!"

"He's an actor. He was in the play."

"Really? Which one?"

"The one you thought was gorgeous."

"No! Not the one who played the black character? The one who looked like some mid-eastern prince?"

"He _is_ black, Amy."

Amy put her fork down carefully and stared at Karen for a moment. "Karen, you can't be serious. A black man? Are you out of your mind?"

"He's wonderful, Amy. He's caring and sensitive and he makes me feel beautiful and important," retorted Karen. "But I don't know why we're even discussing it. A, I haven't heard from him in weeks and B, he's married."

"Karen, drop it, I beg of you. It's just an infatuation because you're particularly vulnerable right now. It can't be anything but trouble. A black man! Do you have any idea what you'd be getting into?" Amy's voice rose to such a pitch that the couple at the next table turned to look at them.

"Why are you getting so emotional about it? I had no idea you were so prejudiced."

"I am not prejudiced! It has nothing to do with that. It has to do with reality and my concern for you. The world is what it is and you're not going to change it overnight."

Karen hastened to reassure Amy by explaining that little or nothing had come of her 'infatuation', that she hadn't heard from Conrad and that the whole thing would probably fizzle out before it got started. Then she quickly changed the subject to Amy's impending trip to Europe and they got through the rest of the lunch without further mishap. There was just one more difficult moment as they said their goodbyes at the parking lot.

Amy put her arms around Karen. "Darling, please be careful. This thing with this man. You know how they are. They can be <u>dangerous</u>!"

Karen thought wryly that the 'they' might be men, actors or black people the way it was put, but she knew damn well what Amy meant and she hated learning this about her friend.

The call finally came on a rainy Saturday afternoon just as Karen was curling up in the beloved Saarinen chair with a new paperback edition of a Dorothy Sayers mystery she had somehow missed reading.

Conrad had been having a rough time. The first thing he had to deal with when the show closed was the fact that he was behind in the rent, had a mountain of bills to pay and was losing his patience with Lou's constant whining.

"It's so close in here, Con. I have such a headache," she'd moan. "When are we gonna be able to move out of this hole?"

"Not right now, Lou," Conrad would reply, teeth clentched. "Not right now."

"Flora and Stan just got a swell apartment on 97th Street in that new complex. Why can't we go look there?"

"For God's sake, Lou, think! I don't know where I'm going to get this month's rent here and you're saying we should look at something where the rent is double? Shit!"

"Well, why shouldn't I get as good as Flora gets?" Lou shouted. "She hasn't got my looks or my brains."

Conrad stared at her. She'd been a great beauty when he married her, but she'd so let herself go that he no longer found her physically appealing. "Well, why don't you take your looks and brains and get a job instead of sitting around watching soaps and doing your nails all day," he shouted back. Lou flounced away with a toss of her head.

"I need twenty five dollars," she announced one morning.

"What? What for?" Conrad had been down to his last few dollars and had taken a job loading trucks in the garment center. The time taken for the play had cost him several modeling jobs.

"I have an appointment to get my hair done," Lou replied haughtily.

"Where? Saks Fifth Avenue? Are you out of your mind? Twenty five dollars!" He knew that was the top downtown price. Leave it to her to find the most expensive place. "I don't have it."

"Well what am I suposed to do? I have an appointment at two o'clock!" she shrieked.

"Fuck the appointment." Conrad stormed out slamming the door behind him. He hated how she made him feel: guilty, inadequate, less of a man.

Lou's response to these scenes was always in terms of a physical malady. In addition to the headaches there was a hip joint ailment, a strained ankle, a burned hand, a sinus attack. Conrad was certain that these ills were merely ploys for attention. Noone could have so many things go wrong in such rapid succession.

One night Lou put on her black see-through nightie right after dinner. "Waddya say we go to bed early tonight Con?" she whispered seductively into his ear.

"Yeh. Sure, Lou," he grinned back. It was the least he could do. He was still her husband, but it was getting more and more difficult to respond to her occasional need when she no longer aroused him sexually at all. He supposed it was because she'd worn him down to the point of desperation and he felt so much anger towards her. So he managed to perform by thinking about Karen as he lay on top of Lou.

He longed to see her, to hold her and make love to her and the intensity of his need startled the hell out of him. He didn't understand why the chemistry between them was so potent and undeniable. It wasn't the first time he'd been attracted to a white woman. He'd actually had a couple of brief affairs with white models on the few occasions when photographers' parties had enabled him to meet other members of the modeling community. But he'd always walked away with no difficulty and for the most part he'd tried to stay clear of that kind of involvement. It meant nothing but trouble. All he had to do was look at his mother and father to appreciate the enormity of the inevitable pitfalls. He threw himself into the task of finding work and since no acting or modeling jobs immediately presented themselves, the only alternative seemed to be physical labor. It was fairly easy to pick up temporary day jobs in the garment center. In a way, it was a good thing, because he worked long days and came home so exhausted that all he could do was eat and flop on the bed too tired to argue or think.

But on this particular rainy Saturday he was deliciously relaxed after a long hot bath followed by watching the Knicks win a game with the Celtics and polishing off a couple of beers. His resistance weakened and he grabbed the phone.

"Hello." Karen got to it on the third ring. She hoped it wasn't business. She really didn't feel like dealing with anything today.

"Hi. I'm glad you're home." Conrad's tone was so low it sounded conspiratorial.

"Conrad? Hi! Oh, It's great to hear from you. I was wondering what happened to you."

"How are you? Are you okay?" Conrad asked anxiously.

"Sure. Don't I sound okay?"

"You sound different."

Karen chuckled. "Do I? Well, maybe it's because I'm a single lady now. Daniel and I are separated. He's living somewhere else."

"Wow." Conrad paused to digest this news. "Was it rough?"

"No. It was surprisingly easy. He's going to Juarez in a couple of weeks to get one of those quickie Mexican divorces and phhht!, it's over."

There was another silence, a bit longer this time.

"Can I see you?" Conrad asked.

"Where's Lou?"

"She went to visit her rich aunt in Jamaica."

"Jamaica, Long Island?"

"No, Jamaica, West Indies."

Karen laughed. "Oh. Lucky her."

"Yeh." He waited. "Well, when can I see you?"

"How about tomorrow? Lunch maybe?"

Conrad thought for a moment. Lunch would mean little privacy and an outlay of cash he didn't have at the moment. "Do you still have the car?" he asked.

"Yup. Daniel's been very generous. He's leaving me practically everything but his clothes and books. I guess he's really relieved to get rid of me."

"Sounds more like guilt to me. Why don't we just go for a drive. We need to talk."

"Okay. When and where?" Karen's pulse quickened at the thought of seeing him.

"I'll meet you at the Central Park West corner of your block at 12:30. How's that?"

"Why not come here?"

"No, meet me on the corner."

Karen understood. He was proceeding with caution. "Okay. See you tomorrow."

"Karen, I've missed you," he whispered.

"Me too."

"Later." He hung up swiftly, as though afraid of what he might say next. And Karen knew that the day and night that lay ahead woud be interminable and filled with fantasies about what the future might hold for them both.

The next weeks seemed to fly by with the speed of light. Conrad revealed to Karen, much to her horror, that he'd been loading trucks in the garment center to pay some of his debts.

"What a waste of talent," she'd cried in protest. "Why won't you let me lend you some money? Daniel's taking care of my basic financial needs, and I've been doing a lot of free-lance script reading and stuff."

"It's against my religion," he'd replied grimly.

They tried to see one another every day, or at the least, talk on the phone. But Conrad was very careful to keep their meetings out of the public eye and the car became their nest, a place for quiet talks, touching bodies and long searching kisses. He refused to come to the apartment. Then one night, after Karen had picked him up after work and they had driven to their park spot, Conrad announced that Lou was returning home from Jamaica.

"Oh." Karen was very still for a moment. "What happens now?"

Conrad turned to look her full in the face, his eyes burning with intensity. "I've been working my tail off to get enough money to be able to leave Lou. I want to get a divorce, marry you and pack us off to L.A. where the work is. What do you think?"

Karen's heart pounded in her ears. What did she think? She'd been lying awake nights thinking about what it would be like to be able to really make love to Conrad, to sleep with him every night, to live with him, share her life with him. When his arms were around her his strength made her feel so completely safe, so protected. Together they seemed invincible, as though nothing harmful could touch them. And now, as he did so often, he jumped right to the end of the dream, the part where they go off to seek their fortune and live happily ever after. No mention of all the details, the obstacles that lay in their path. Just cut to the chase.

"What do you think?" he repeated insistently.

"You take my breath away she said coyly," she answered after a moment's silence, then bit her lip. It sounded flippant and she didn't mean it to. Should she tell him that it was what she'd been dreaming about?

"You know I love you." he whispered urgently. "I've never wanted or needed anything so much in my life."

"Not even a career? Stardom?" Karen blurted it out.

"I know what you're saying. You think our being together might hurt us? That they won't hire either of us because we're a mixed couple? Look I've been fighting those barriers all my life. I've still got plenty of fight left." Conrad clentched his fists and his jaw tightened.

Karen put her arms around him. "I love you too," she said into his ear. "But I need time to think about this. What about your parents? What are they going to say?"

"I'm a grown man. Aren't you really thinking about <u>your</u> parents?" Conrad held her at arms length to study her face again.

"I'm thinking about all of it. And what about Lou? How's she going to let you go?"

"She needs to find a duke or a count to support her. I've had it. I can't stand it any more." Conrad's jaw tightened again. "There's nothing but hostility between us. She thinks I failed her because I'm not a rich celebrity. I guess we both married for all the wrong reasons. We were too young. I've been hoping she'd meet somebody in Jamaica and stay there."

"Let's give ourselves time to think about this carefully, darling," Karen said gently.

"There'll be plenty of time. None of this can happen overnight you know." Conrad grinned at her. "Take a week."

It took months, which seemed like years to Karen. But the time was well spent as they saw more and more of each other. What began as merely an intense, passionate physical attraction gradually became a much more mean-ingful, closer and deeper relationship. As time passed, Karen's divorce came through and Conrad weathered the storm of Lou's wrath once he revealed his intention to divorce her. They allowed themselves to be a little freer and more open when they were together. And they began to learn each other's culture, background, likes and dislikes, in the way two people do when they share the intimacy of daily living. But Conrad persisted in his refusal to enter Karen's apartment. They always met at some pre-arranged spot and usually said good-bye on the corner, when Karen wasn't dropping Conrad off someplace with the car.

One Saturday Conrad announced that he wanted to take Karen uptown and show her his 'roots'.

"Great." Karen knew he meant Harlem and amongst her friends that was always considered off limits for casual strolling, but she was never afraid of anything when she was with Conrad. He was her protective blanket. They took the subway up to 125th Street and the minute they emerged into the light

Karen felt as though she had stepped into another country. As they walked down the wide Avenue she saw every shade and description of black person. The only white living thing was a small dog. And she could see that she was an object of curiosity by the stares of passersby. She instinctively reached for Conrad's hand.

"No, It's best to walk side by side here," Conrad said gently in a low voice. "Just hang loose." The street was lined on either side with low grey stone buildings that looked like they'd been there since the turn of the century. They housed small shops selling a myriad variety of items: discount clothes, incense, records, shoes, drugs, all familiar items but with an unfamiliar look, very different from downtown. There was a beauty shop advertising a process for straightening hair with pictures of brown beauties attesting to its merits. An empty storefront was filled with posters announcing a coming rally about something called SNCC. When Karen asked Conrad what that was, he tersely explained that 'Snick', as he pronounced it, was the Southern Negro Christian Conference, an activist group. Conrad pointed to a large, elegant movie theatre across the street that reminded Karen of some of the LOEW'S she'd gone to in her childhood. It had an ornate rococo facade which showed signs of neglect and the marquee announcing ZORBA THE GREEK read ORBA THE G EEK.

"There's the Apollo Theatre," he announced with pride. It's where I spent most of my adolescence, when I wasn't playing ball."

The avenue was dense with traffic, making the street crossing difficult, but finally they managed to get to the front of the theatre. Karen studied the posters and three-sheets. She recognized Ella Fitzgerald and Louis Armstrong, but the others were unknown to her.

"That's that terrific new comic, Richard Pryor." Conrad stopped in front of a photo of a slim young black man with large eyes. "He's brilliant. I'm going to bring you up here to see him one day."

As they walked on, Karen realized that some of the stares she was getting were not just curious, they were openly hostile. She had dressed very carefully for this adventure. Low key, no jewelry, just jeans, sweater and jacket. She had wanted to be careful not to call attention to her middle class status. But now she realized that it wasn't just the fact of her presence that provoked insolent and mean looks. It was the fact of who she walked with that was the issue. As they turned a corner two chunky dark black men fell in behind them and followed close tailing them, or so it seemed to Karen. Oh, oh, she thought as her pulse quickened.

Conrad, as always sensing Karen's thoughts before they were expressed, tried to distract her. "Over there is the birthplace of Conrad Taylor." He pointed to a rust colored four story building with fire escapes decorating the facade on a block lined with tenements. "My humble origins," he announced bowing with a flourish.

Karen laughed. "Listen, I've got to be honest with you. I'd be scared shitless to live up here."

"I don't blame you. If you ever have to walk alone in a neighborhood like this, always keep one hand in your pocket."

"Why?" asked Karen.

"The folks will assume you're a cop with one hand on your gun and they'll leave you alone." He proceeded to walk Karen's feet off, pointing out the landmarks: "That's the Hotel Theresa. Faded glory. Used to be quite something in the old days." It was a massive building in the classic style of twenties' elegance and it dominated the corner on Seventh Avenue. Walking further he pointed out Small's Paradise, the famous cabaret. It was a black and white low building with a modest front. "I've had some great times here."

"Listening to music?" asked Karen.

"And dancing. Did you know I'm a great dancer?"

"Oh, I love to dance!" Karen exclaimed. "And I hardly ever get the chance."

"Well, what do you do at parties?"

"Talk mostly. And eat and drink."

Conrad shook his head. "You white people are so strange. You just don't know how to live! One of these days I'm going to take you to a rent party."

"What's a rent party?"

Conrad explained that a rent party was one of the support systems of the community. When someone was in financial trouble and couldn't make their rent, they threw a rent party and invited all their friends, each of whom was expected to chip in towards the rent payment in return for some fried chicken, dancing and a good time. "I might need one soon," he said ruefully.

"You could move in with me, you know," said Karen softly.

Conrad suddenly turned left, saying "I'm going to introduce you to the best soul food in America." He led her to a small, unobtrusive low red brick building on 126th Street. There was no sign. If one didn't know it contained a restaurant, it could easily have been overlooked. Delicious smells wafted out onto the sidewalk and intensified when they entered the tiny dining room. There were only about eight small tables and six of them were occupied. There was little that could be described as decor. The walls were a pale rosy color and there were a few photographs hung haphazardly here and there. Karen guessed they were well known black performers but she didn't recognize any of them. One large shaded ceiling fixture provided most of the light assisted by several small wall lamps with pink paper shades. Once again, Karen was the only white person in the place. Plaid oilcloth squares served as tablecloths. A tall dark-skinned woman wearing what seemed to be a floor length dashiki and matching head wrap greeted them.

"Hey, baby, what's happenin'? Where you been?" she demanded, giving Conrad a hug.

"This is Karen, Sylvia," he replied, almost as if in answer to the question. "Karen, this is Sylvia, the woman who makes the best food in the city. Can we get some greens and sweet potato pie?"

"Happy to meet you, Sylvia." Karen was getting that 'alien in another country' feeling again, so she tried to give the woman her warmest smile. It was not returned.

"What is this?" she asked Conrad when the food arrived. It smelled pungent and marvelous, but it was definitely strange to her.

"Collard greens." Conrad was already devouring them hungrily.

"What's this meat?"

"Ham hocks. You're going to have to learn how to make this if you want to keep me happy." He grinned at her. "It's wonderful, nourishing poor peoples' food. When I lived in the projects with my folks I smelled greens cooking all day long. You cook them for hours and the smell gets in the walls and stays there."

Karen loved the greens which seemed to her something like exotic spinach, but the ham hocks were much too salty for her taste. "I can see why you love this. All the salt," she teased.

"Hey, I'm sorry. Is ham a bad thing for you? I wasn't even thinking," Conrad asked anxiously. He hadn't made any reference to the fact that Karen was Jewish in a long time.

"No, not at all. I'm not orthodox, or even observant. You might say I'm Jewish by nationality, not by religion."

"Nationality?" Conrad looked puzzled.

"Well, I'm Jewish by birth, and Israel is a nation."

The discussion was tabled by the arrival of the sweet potato pie. It was warm and tasted like sweet potatoes with ginger and cinnamon added and it had a huge dollop of whipped cream on top. "Oh!" exclaimed Karen. "I've never tasted anything so good. I <u>have</u> to have the recipe for this."

Conrad laughed. "I'm going to buy you *Princess Pamela's Soul Food Cook Book.*"

In spite of the undercurrent on the streets it was a wonderful day. After lunch they strolled down several blocks and Conrad showed Karen Mount Morris Park and all the beautiful elegant old brownstones on the adjacent tree-lined side streets.

"I had no idea there were such lovely houses here." observed Karen.

"Harlem isn't all slums, you know. And there are some very wealthy black people, quiet as it's kept. Doctors, lawyers, business men. Next time I'll show you Sugar Hill. Have you ever been to the Schomburg?"

Karen was surprised to discover how little she knew about the black community. And she had always thought of herself as a hip liberal. "No. And what's Sugar Hill?"

"The Schomburg is a Collection, like a library or museum, of all that's a part of black culture. They tend to overlook us elsewhere," he added wryly, "so we have our own. And Sugar Hill is just a section of Harlem that the wealthy niggers inhabit."

"I hate that word, Con."

"What, nigger? Yeah, well, you should. When we use it, it's a term of endearment. When white people use it, it's an insult."

There it was again, just when Karen was beginning to feel more relaxed. The difference lay between them like some sleeping monster and emerged when least expected. "But we don't call ourselves 'kikes' as a term of endearment. I don't get it."

Conrad shrugged. "It's different. Let's not get into it now, okay?" Karen let it drop. As they walked on Conrad pointed to a small corner building at the south edge of the park. "That's a black Synogogue. One of the oldest I think."

Karen's mouth dropped open in amazement. "Black Jews? I didn't know there were any."

"The Jews take over everywhere." Conrad said it jokingly but Karen had a momentary pang of doubt. Was he subconsciously anti-Semitic as so many Negroes were? The day had gone too well, and Karen didn't want anything to spoil it, so she buried the thought. But she made a quick mental note that if the relationship really had a future, at some point they were going to have to air their innermost thoughts about things like this.

That night as they emerged from the subway at Karen's stop she turned to Conrad and, as usual, pleaded with him to come up to the apartment. "Come on, please. I'll make us some drinks and we can put our feet up."

"Okay." He put his arm around her shoulders.

"Okay? Great!" Finally, she thought. He'd taken her by surprise. She wondered whether this day had been some kind of test for him. Oh well, whatever it was she must have passed it, and that was certainly cause for celebration.

They were silent in the elevator. This would be the first time they'd be alone together in sheltered privacy. Karen felt as though the very air throbbed with anticipation.

As they entered the dark apartment, she reached for the light switch, but Conrad held her arm. "Wait," he whispered and drew her to him, pressing her body close to his. Karen dropped her purse and stretched against him. They kissed long and deeply.

Coming up for air Conrad gasped "I've been waiting for this for such a long time."

"Me, too." They kissed again, the flame growing.

"Do you realize that this is the first time I've been able to hold your entire body? I've been wanting this since the first time I laid eyes on you," said Conrad into her ear.

"Oh Con, I...." Conrad silenced her with another kiss as he removed her coat. Their hands moved down each others' bodies and they continued to kiss as they undressed each other in the darkness of the foyer, as though afraid to let go of one another even for a moment. Sweaters, skirt, pants, bra dropped to the floor and when they were almost naked, Conrad lifted Karen up in his arms and moved forward in the darkness.

"Where am I going?" he said softly.

"Turn right," Karen breathed into his ear and they managed to make it into the bedroom somehow without falling.

They made love like people who have been lost in the desert drink water.

"It's been so long," Conrad gasped when they finally came up for air. "Forgive me."

"For what, my darling?"

"I wanted it to last forever."

Karen clung to him. "It will. The memory of it will. I never knew how beautiful it could be."

"Did I please you?"

Karen giggled. "Please is such a lame word for what you just did." She snuggled against him. She'd never felt so utterly relaxed and content. The throbbing in her body still echoed gently sending delicious little shivers throughout her nerve endings.

Conrad pressed his lips against her hair. "I love you, Karen," he breathed. He wrapped himself around her and exhaled deeply as though for the first time he could really let himself go.

"I love you, Conrad." And they nestled in each others arms and fell asleep.

Karen awoke first and, propped up on one arm, studied Conrad's sleeping face and the six foot long muscular perfect body that lay on top of the quilt. He reminded her of those Greek statues at the Met Museum, especially when he was in repose. He was a beautiful man, no doubt about it. Was that what made her passion for him so intense? Was she really that superficial? Or was it that rare combination of gentleness and strength, of light humor and depth, of so many opposites that intrigued her. Or was it his beigeness? He was such a wonderful color! Karen stifled a giggle at the absurdity of that last thought. Just then Conrad threw his arm across her, grabbing her to him and nibbling on her ear.

"You tease!" Karen protested. "I thought you were sound asleep."

"Where am I?" said Conrad in mock panic.

"So...the myth is true."

"What myth?" he asked.

"That all black men are great in bed." Karen grinned at him.

Conrad grinned back. "As true as the one that says all Jewish girls are promiscuous and suck dick."

Karen responded by throwing a pillow at him which he promptly threw back at her. They started to tousle and before they knew it, they were making love again.

CHAPTER 6

The weeks that followed were filled with discoveries for both Karen and Conrad. Karen's entrance into the black community as Conrad's friend together with the ever growing closeness of their relationship were experiences filled with revelation. They began to learn about each other on a more intimate level. As time went on, they managed to see one another more and more frequently, until finally Conrad revealed one day, as they were walking through Central Park after a snowfall, that he and his wife had separated.

"Why didn't you tell me?" Karen asked.

"I'm telling you now" Conrad said impatiently. "I didn't want you to feel in any way responsible."

Karen bent down and picked up a handful of fresh snow.

"Why would I feel responsible? You didn't feel that way about my divorce, did you?"

Conrad shrugged. "No comment."

"Well then, we're partners in crime. Let's wash away the guilt!" And she washed his face with the snow in her hands precipitating an all out snowball fight which left them breathless as they rolled in the snow like a pair of three year olds. It was one of those special New York winter nights: crisp, bright and freezing. Wet and shivering, they hugged and kissed and ran back to Karen's apartment to warm themselves with scotch and lovemaking.

That night they ordered Chinese food and curled up on the couch in front of the TV set with their trays piled high. They were watching a news documentary when clips of black leaders appeared against the voice-over of Martin Luther King's "I Have A Dream" speech. Conrad identified them as they appeared in rapid succession: Stokely Carmichael, Rap Brown, Eldridge

Cleaver followed by shots of a throng marching and singing "We Shall Overcome."

"I can't overcome these damn things!" exclaimed Conrad as he struggled with the chopsticks Karen had given him. "Can I have a fork please?"

Karen giggled at his distress and dutifully went to the kitchen for a fork. She was always impressed with Conrad's complete candor and lack of pretense. The people she'd hung out with would have never admitted they couldn't use chopsticks with Chinese food. But he had no patience with window dressing. He made no bones about what was right for him, never worrying about whether he appeared unsophisticated or lacking in polish. He made up his own rules and, as he kept reminding her at every step of the way, they were often the rules of the jungle in which he lived and spent most of his time. It was a place very different from 'the white world' and Karen discovered she would not only have to learn a whole new set of rules, but also a new language. For example, right now they were 'scarfing' Chinese food—wolfing it down, that is.

As she settled back onto the couch with her tray, Martin Luther King appeared on the TV.

"No matter how many times I see that man, he always moves me," she observed as she popped a large clump of Lo Mein into her mouth.

"'That Man' is going to get himself shot."

"Oh Con, how can you be so cynical?" protested Karen.

"Baby, the man wants change. And he's a leader. The white world doesn't want change and they don't like leaders who might be a threat to the status quo. And in fact, the only time there's any real chance for change is when somebody starts shooting. So that's what has to happen."

"I don't agree with that! Nothing good can come from violence. There's no way to justify it."

Conrad patted her knee. "You've been so sheltered. You don't understand that there's a kind of war going on."

"Don't patronize me!" Karen was silent for a moment. "You know, you sound like one of those Black Muslims or Black Panthers." She turned to see his face. "Have you been involved with those groups?"

"Would it make a difference for us if I was?" he asked softly.

"I don't know. They frighten me."

"Well, I'm not a joiner of movements. And I'm certainly not going to grow an Afro, that's for damn sure. The brothers have been torturing me about my 'good hair' all my life. But if I were to join anything I'd have hooked up with Malcolm. He's brilliant."

Karen put her tray down on the end table with a bang. "Malcolm X? He really frightens me!"

"That's because you only know what the establishment tells you." Karen started to protest but Conrad interrupted her. "Don't worry, Karen. I'm not a joiner, I'm a loner. Always been too 'bright' to belong."

"Too smart? I don't understand."

"Bright means light-skinned," he explained.

"But Malcolm is light-skinned."

"Yes, and so is Cleaver and so is Angela Davis and on and on…You see, the likes of us have to become leaders to be accepted."

"I see," said Karen thoughtfully, "the lighter the skin the more militant one has to be to gain acceptance? I'd call that overcompensating."

"Don't start psychoanalyzing us." There was an implicit warning in Conrad's tone even though he seemed to shrug off the topic. As he rose to change the channel on the TV Karen sensed danger in continuing this discussion. Although their relationship had grown in intimacy there were many lines she was still not allowed to cross. She was still a white woman and he was still a black man.

This grappling with the differences between them and the chasms created by outside circumstances was reinforced by the constant reminders confronting them as they began to travel about as a couple. Karen couldn't help but notice the stares they got as they walked down a street or sat in the subway or in a restaurant. It was ironic, thought Karen that the world thought he was a white man playing a black character on stage, but when they became a couple the whole perception changed.

They didn't eat out much, but when they did Conrad preferred the Indian restaurant on 110th Street or any one of the Chinese restaurants downtown because they weren't as likely to get stuck in the back near the kitchen. One evening as they were walking home from seeing a movie on Broadway a young black man approached them and spat at Karen's feet. Karen, startled, let out a little yelp and Conrad lunged at the man as he quickly turned and raced across the street away from them. Conrad started to chase after him but Karen clutched at his sleeve and begged him not to make it worse than it was. She finally prevailed but she could feel Conrad steaming with pent up emotion the rest of the way home. When they were almost there he finally spoke.

"I once broke a guy's jaw" he said grimly.

"Why? What did he do to you?"

"He was playing the dozens on me," Conrad replied. Karen looked at him questioningly. She had no idea what that was. "He was insulting my mother. You know, the white lady." Conrad atttempted to grin at her but it came out more like a grimace. "I just reacted. Don't know my own strength when I'm mad. Had to pay his doctor bills."

"What's the dozens?"

"It's like a curse. Sometimes it's just: 'Your momma'. Or 'your momma goes up on the roof with Polacks', or something equally charming."

One Friday Karen brought home her favorite bread because she knew Conrad would be coming over and she was determined to cook dinner for him. His taste for food was so different from hers. He liked things like sausage sandwiches with onions and peppers which she pretended to like but could hardly get down, and she liked things like bagels and cream cheese and lox which he had little desire to eat. But this bread was so good Karen was sure he would go for it. As she fussed over the pork chops which were one thing she was sure he would eat, Conrad examined the cellophane wrapping on the bread.

"What's this?" he asked. "Challah? Never heard of it."

Karen doubled over with laughter.

"What's so funny?" demanded Conrad.

Karen tried to control herself. He had pronounced it as though it were 'chill-<u>aah</u>' with the accent on the second syllable. "It's pronounced <u>chhha</u>la." She couldn't stop giggling. "The 'ch' sound is in the throat." She demonstrated. "Chhhhh. Like that. And the accent is on the first syllable."

"Sounds like you're spitting up," he observed solemnly. But he did dig the bread.

Karen was constantly learning new vocabulary. 'Dig' meant like. 'Sky' meant hat. 'Scarf' meant eat ravenously. 'Split' meant leave. Conrad would tease Karen about her college education and the multi-syllabled words she would use sometimes to describe something.

"Never say something with one word when you can use three, right?" he would observe thoughtfully.

With anyone else Karen would've taken offense, but she knew he yearned for that education and wanted to learn everything he could about anything that was new to him. He read voraciously and was constantly suggesting books and authors that Karen should read. She began making a list, although she knew it would take half a lifetime to cover the world that he was revealing to her.

And then there was the rent party. Karen had been looking forward to it all week with a mixture of anticipation and apprehension. It was the first time they were actually going public with their relationship and the first time she was going to get a chance to meet some of Conrad's uptown friends. She knew that it was going to be unfamiliar territory and perhaps even a test of sorts. Would she be able to handle herself well? Would they accept her? What should she wear? She wondered if Conrad had asked himself these questions when she took him to a dinner party that one of her friends threw on the upper west side. There had really only been one awkward moment when Shirley, who moments before had whispered to Karen about how 'gorgeous' Conrad was, sidled up to him and batting her eyelashes asked loudly enough for the room to hear "Where did you get that beeyootiful tan?"

"From my father," Conrad had replied as he bestowed a charming smile on her.

Karen asked Conrad what he thought she should wear to this party.

"Just be yourself" he replied. "Sexy and beautiful."

So she decided on a simple burnt orange wool jersey dress that was figure revealing but not too dressy.

They could hear the party blocks before they reached the brownstone on 116th street where the Jacksons lived. Aretha Franklin's throaty, sobbing voice was up full blast and filled the street, drifting out of the open windows which faced the front of the building. As they climbed the two flights of stairs leading up to the apartment a host of unfamiliar smells hit Karen's nostrils.

Conrad, always sensitive to her every reaction, patted Karen on the back and muttered "Years of cooking ham hocks and greens. Like I told you, the smell gets into the walls and stays there. And then there's the incense."

Conrad pushed open the door to the apartment and entered a small, dark and very crowded room filled with people who were dancing, drinking, eating, talking, swaying. The whole room seemed to be moving to the beat. Men, women, short, tall, fat, thin, but, as Karen quickly observed, all black. That is, not really, thought Karen. Some were brown, some very dark almost purple, some tan and some very light like Conrad, but clearly she was the only white person in the place. In one of those sudden revelations that sometimes occur when least expected, Karen flashed back to a memory of an acting class she was in. There was one black actor who disappeared after the first couple of weeks. Now she understood what he must have felt and what had to be overcome.

It was a small apartment but it probably seemed smaller than it actually was because it contained a lifetime of belongings. The walls were covered with posters of every variety: bullfights, musicals, political rallies, and art gallery exhibits, a truly eclectic display of Cleve and Helen's interests. The light bulbs in the three small table lamps were pink or red, giving the room a warm, dark glow. What appeared to be a large rug had been rolled up and lay against one wall revealing a black hardwood floor. The furniture was vintage Salvation Army; a highbacked black wood chair that looked like it came right out of a stage set, a two seater sofa upholstered in a rough material with a strange beige floral pattern and a small round table with two small chairs that looked like garden furniture. A beaded curtain covered the entrance to a tiny hallway which led to the bathroom and bedroom where Conrad led Karen. They piled their coats on a queen sized bed laden with outer clothing. The walls of the bedroom were covered with pictures of friends and several large African masks. Dark brown drapes covered the windows. There was a large colorful pottery bowl sitting on top of the only chest of drawers in the room and Karen thought it was an odd place for it until she saw Conrad drop several bills into it.

"Here, let me," she said reaching into her purse.

"You don't have to."

"I want to."

"The price one has to pay for being an artist," said Conrad grimly.

"What do they do?"

"He's a playwright and she's a poet. They starve a lot of the time."

As they made their way back to the living room Karen noticed the tiny kitchenette behind what seemed to be a bar loaded with bowls of food and bottles of wine and beer.

Conrad steered Karen through the crowd to the bar. "Want you to meet Helen, baby. The best cook in Harlem."

Karen smiled at the short, round, cherub-faced woman behind the counter. "Hi. It smells wonderful."

Helen Jackson wore a brightly colored African achbada, long dangling gold earrings and was sweating profusely from the heat of the stove.

She reached out a hand to Karen. "Nice to meetcha. Dig in honey. With these folks around, it won't last long."

Helen turned back to stir what seemed to be a huge pot of chili. It was a polite enough greeting, but Karen caught the quick up and down survey in the woman's glance. The look was one of measure and appraisal rather than greeting. Karen had immediately felt the curiosity in the stares of the men in the room but she wasn't prepared for the hostile undercurrent in the vibes she was getting from the women.

Conrad offered her a paper plate, took one for himself and proceeded to serve them from bowls of chili, greens and fried chicken wings.

"Want a glass of wine?" he asked as he loaded Karen's plate.

"Whoa! We just got here. Shouldn't we mingle a little before we start stuffing ourselves?"

"You heard what the woman said. It"ll all be gone before you know it so get it while you can. Besides, I'm starving."

"Mmmm, this is good. Do you think Helen'll give me the recipe for the greens?"

Just then two women approached them. One, the taller of the two, seemed a little unsteady on her feet. The other was as wide as she was tall. Both were wearing black décolleté mini length cocktail dresses. They greeted Conrad like a long lost lover with hugs and kisses while Karen stood by awkwardly. Finally they turned to confront her.

"Hey Connie. Introduce me to Miss Anne." The tall one's speech was just a little slurred.

Karen saw Conrad stiffen. "Karen this is Cheri and this is Diana. Meet Karen. Karen Stoner."

Cheri put on a fake British accent. "Oh, how do you do. Honored I'm sure." And the two women giggled uncontrollably.

Conrad put his arm around Karen. "I think you two better get something to eat." He moved Karen away. "Don't pay any attention to her. She's stoned. C'mon. Let's dance."

"What about all this food?"

"Just put it down. Our stomachs can wait a minute."

Karen knew he was trying to protect her. "Con…I don't think I want to make a spectacle of myself. Look at those people. I can't keep up with that."

There was indeed some superior movement going on. The range of style went from Katherine Dunham to Pearl Primus to Donald McKayle and some were inventing altogether new moves and embellishing the Watusi, the fish and the frug. These people really knew how to dance freely and joyously, thought Karen. The parties her friends threw were so uptight by comparison. And usually everyone just stood or sat around talking and drinking. They almost never got up to dance. And if they had, it sure wouldn't look like this. An alarm bell went off in her head. Listen to me, she realized grimly. 'These people'. I sound like a honky. No wonder they call me Miss Anne.

"C'mon baby, Just relax and be yourself. Just do whatever you feel like doing." Conrad grabbed her waist and spun her around.

Conrad was a wonderful dancer and he had a style all his own. It had the rhythmic grace of black-African-disco combined with the slick elegance of the latino. Like his heritage, it was a happy mixture. Everything moved, sensuously but subtly. Karen began tentatively, self conscious and not wanting to take a chance on doing something that would disgrace him. But she could feel all eyes on them, and her dance training and performer's instinct kicked in and gradually loosened her up until she began throwing caution to the winds and giving her hips to the beat. 'What you want?' demanded Aretha in her high soul voice as their feet stomped and their hips swayed. "Work out!" "Do it!" the men yelled as they watched. It was a rite of passage for Karen. She had somehow crossed over and been accepted, at least by the men in the room. So then she danced with Clinton, a wiry young man with rubber in his legs and Tommy, a chubby middle aged man who sweated profusely and David who kept staring at her pelvis and shouting "Whooee!".

The women were more reluctant to make contact with this invader of their territory and Karen wasn't going to push it. While she was busy dancing with one after the other of Conrad's male friends, she noticed that he was constantly surrounded by two or more women, and they all treated him like a former lover, with one even sitting casually on his lap. But she also noticed that he wasn't taking his eyes off her and his stare was like a protective hug. Breathless and thirsty finally, Karen sat down with her replenished paper plate and a glass of wine and struck up a conversation with Louise, a very light skinned reddish haired woman who seemed to be a little friendlier than the others.

"I've known Conrad for a lot of years and I haven't seen him this relaxed in a long time." Karen knew that Louise was paying her a compliment.

"Really? Mmm, this food is fantastic. Can you let me in on how to make this stuff?" Karen wasn't about to get into a personal exchange yet.

"You mean the ham hocks and greens? Oh, honey that's so simple. You get about six ham hocks and about three pounds of collards and three pounds of mustard greens or whatever and you cover them with boiling water in a big pot with an onion or two and a couple of red pepper pods and a clove of garlic and you throw in some pepper and salt and boil them for a couple of hours and that's all!"

"Wow," marveled Karen. "And they come out tasting this good?"

"Well, there is a little trick, honey." Louise lowered her voice as though she was giving away a secret code. "The trick is in the vinegar."

"Vinegar?"

"Yeh. After the first half hour you add a tablespoon or two of vinegar."

Again, Karen felt as though this sharing of the 'trick' was some subtle form of acceptance into the club. "Thanks so much Louise. I have so much to learn."

"Ever eaten at Princess Pamela's downtown?" asked Louise.

"No, I haven't."

"Well, you oughta get her book. Princess Pamela's Soul Food Cookbook."

"Yeh, Conrad's mentioned that. I'll pick it up. And I'm grateful to you." Karen reached for her hand.

Louise wasn't ready to go that far yet, at least not in full sight of the crowd. So she rose with a smile saying "Just remember to invite me over when you get good at it."

Karen noticed that while everyone was very polite and some even seemed to go out of their way to make contact, there was a definite difference between the way they related to one another and the way they related to her. And to Conrad, she suddenly realized. Yes, the women were attentive, but more like bees around honey than like good friends. And the men, for the most part, were guarded with him, mostly talking basketball and making forced guy jokes. There was only one man who she really felt Conrad was close to and that was Cleve, Helen's husband, the one who had invited them. They seemed to have some kind of bond, quietly unspoken. Karen wondered if it had anything to do with the fact that Cleve was also very lightskinned and a struggling playwright, which would give them much in common in their daily struggles.

"You're very quiet all of a sudden. Let's have one more dance before we pack it in." Conrad had suddenly appeared and Karen realized that even across the room he could read her thoughts. She was grateful for his unerring ability to read her mind, understand her moods. It was one of the things that made him so special.

They stayed another two hours, dancing and drinking and laughing together and Karen gradually forgot to feel strange or different and had a wonderful time.

As they emerged from the building in the wee hours of the morning, the streets were deserted. Had Karen been with anyone but Conrad she would have been terrified at the prospect of walking the uptown streets at that hour. But she felt so happy and free that even the bite of the winter wind gnawing at her face didn't bother her.

"Whoooeee! That was great!" Karen gave Conrad a hug. They were both high on wine and pot liquor and the knowledge that their baptism as a couple had gone well. The pot liquor, juice from the cooking of the greens, was a real discovery. Not only was it delicious, it had a kick to it.

"Whooooee? You startin' to sound black, girl." Conrad teased as they walked towards the subway.

"I haven't danced like that since...never!"

"You be dancin' like a black woman. Now I gotta teach you to walk that walk and talk that talk." He stopped and faced her. "Now what do you say when a hood on the street comes up to you?"

"I dunno. What?" Karen giggled uncontrollably.

"Repeat after me." Conrad wrinkled his brow and gave her a menacing stare. "Watchoo want, mutha fucka?"

The giggling burst into laughter. "Con, you know I can't even bring myself to say 'fuck' in public."

"C,mon, try it."

"What you want, mother fucker." Karen couldn't keep a straight face.

"No, no, lissen. You gotta get down! Watch me." He shoved his face up close to hers. "Wachoo want, mutha fucka!" Karen giggled hysterically. "Try it!" he urged.

Screwing up her face to look as fierce as she could, she spat it out. "Wachoo want, mutha fucka."

"By George, you've got it!" said Conrad in his best MY FAIR LADY accent and then he cracked up and they both roared and hugged, laughing all the way to the subway.

The next night after dinner at the apartment Conrad relaxed in the big leather chair in the living room and Karen stretched out on the couch. They talked about the party and Karen shared some of her feelings about the obvious hostility of the women. Conrad pointed out that the women were reacting to the fact that these days many black men seemed to be seeking relationships with white women, in their quest for acceptance and affirmation after years of denigration.

Conrad explained it carefully. "You must understand that what we have had here is a matriarchal society. Negro women could get work, Negro men could not. The women have cleaned houses, taken care of white children, brought home the bread. The men are feared by white society, represent more of a threat apparently, are hired less, and therefore are emasculated. So a liaison with a white woman is an affirmation, a badge of success. But the black woman becomes a 'Bertha', the authority figure, the boss of the family and that makes her even less desirable. The women feel rejected, hate their color, hate their

kinky hair, hate the white women who are claiming their men, and are generally angry females. And that's what you were sensing."

"Am I your badge of success?" asked Karen. She went over and sat on his lap,
wrapping herself around him.

He gently held her at arms length so he could look straight into her eyes.
"Don't you see? They don't think of me as one of them. I'm somewhere in
between because I could pass for white. I'm much more acceptable than most
to the white world. I can get hired. I can be a token 'out' for the guilty liberals.
Once I got my picture in the paper because I got hired by American Airlines.
The first Negro. The only Negro. 'The spook that sits by the door'. You know,
out in front for all the world to see. So there's envy and jealousy and all kinds of
complicated feelings to deal with."

"When did you work for American Airlines?"

Conrad shrugged. "Some years back. Lasted a couple of months. I couldn't
stand what I was seeing happen around me. I knew if I stayed I'd hit someone
eventually."

As the weeks passed and Conrad grew more and more comfortable in
Karen's environment she finally pressed the idea of his moving in with her. He
had moved back to his parents' apartment in the projects temporarily while
waiting for his divorce and it was less than an ideal arrangement, so he agreed
to this further test of their relationship. They'd been spending so much time
together that it was hardly an adjustment, but Conrad was getting more and
more worried about money and being able to shoulder responsibility for their
daily expenses. In between the temporary jobs he went to auditions but there
was little work to be had and what there was did not hold opportunity for the
likes of him. Karen kept reassuring him that she had enough saved to see them
through any slow period, but his pride would not accept that. More and more
he began to talk about a move to the west coast which everyone said was the
center of the entertainment industry and the place one had to be if one wanted
to work. Karen always sidestepped these conversations, not wanting to deal
with a momentous decision to relocate just yet.

One morning Karen was brushing her teeth when Conrad appeared in the
doorway.

"Honey, do you have a pick? This looks like hell," he said pointing to his
hair.

"A pick? What's a pick?"

Conrad snorted. "See that? I'm beginning to think of you as a black woman. Of course you don't have a pick. It's kind of a forked comb that looks a little like a trident. It's great for getting the kinks out of a 'fro."

"A 'fro? Oh, an afro you mean. But you don't need that. Your hair is silky and you always use a comb."

Conrad grinned. "Yeh, but sometimes when my coils get too coily a pick is useful." He wrapped his arms around Karen and stared at her in the mirror. "How come you look so beautiful in the morning?"

Karen smiled at his reflexion. "Because I've spent the night with you, darling."

As he walked back into the bedroom he called "I've got to pick something up at the folks' place tonight. How would you like to come with me?"

He didn't see the triumphant gleam in Karen's eye as she replied "Sure, I'd love to." Neither had met the other's parents. Since they were both only children there was no other family involvement for either of them. She had been waiting for a cue from him, not wanting to push anything. He had finally come around. He'd talked very little about them after those early days during rehearsals. Aside from her natural curiosity, Karen was anxious to see how they would respond to her. She wondered if they even knew of her existence. Conrad could be very closemouthed when he wanted to be.

What Conrad always referred to as 'the projects' turned out to be a large group of buildings on east 112th Street built within the previous decade. They must have been part of the city wide mushrooming of chicken-coop apartments designed to relieve the crowded ghettos and offer families an escape to something more habitable. The trouble was they were built cheaply with cost rather than comfort in mind and rapidly disintegrated into taller and more formidable ghettos. Even though it was after 8 o'clock, the grounds in front of the building were filled with black and hispanic kids of every size and shape playing in the snow that had recently fallen. The lobby was dark and more like a vestibule with cream colored walls that reminded Karen of her old elementary school. The elevator was self service and groaned and creaked in a way that made Karen wonder if they were going to make it to the fourth floor. When they got to the Taylor apartment there was a sign on the door that said 'bell out of order, please knock.' Conrad used his key, but knocked at the same time calling "Mom? Pop? We're here!"

The opened door revealed a compact three room apartment very modestly but neatly furnished much like what Karen might have expected to find in a suburb of Topeka, Kansas. The light brown two seater sofa and club chair had lace doilies on their arms and backs. The end tables were covered with lace mats and small picture frames. The two table lamps had old fashioned ecru colored silk shades in odd octagonal shapes. There was actually a 'Home Sweet Home' Sampler on the wall near the kitchenette. Several still life oil paintings of flowers adorned the living room walls. The windows were covered with white glass curtains. The floor was covered with a beige looped cotton rug. Karen hadn't known what to expect, but what she saw seemed utterly incongruous with the outer setting. But totally appropriate, she thought as Conrad's mother appeared, welcoming them with outstretched hand.

"Hi," she said shyly, "I'm Faith." She turned toward the closed bedroom. "Walter" she called. "They're here. Would you like some tea? Please sit down."

Faith Taylor looked like a little librarian from a suburb of Topeka, thought Karen. She was a small, portly woman with very white skin and piercing blue eyes. Her round face was soft and carried several chins offering a sweet frame to a cherubic smile. Her hair was almost white, parted in the center and combed straight back into a neat bun at the nape of her neck.

"It's very cold out isn't it? I've turned up the heat but we're not getting much. I'll make some tea." She turned to hug Conrad. "How are you doing dear? She stared anxiously into his face as if the answer lay there.

"Hi mom. Relax, we're okay. This is Karen."

"Poppa will want some." Faith bustled into the ktichenette as Walter emerged from the bedroom.

Walter Taylor was a small, slight, cinnamon colored man with large dark eyes, high cheekbones and, Karen noted, the beautiful jawline that made Conrad the Adonis that he was.

"Why is it so damn cold in here?" The West Indian lilt sang out. Walter strode over to the radiator and banged on it with a hammer that lay close by. He turned to Karen. "Sorry. They never send up enough."

"Pop, this is Karen. Karen, my father."

"I'm very glad to meet you Mr. Taylor." Karen rose to shake his hand.

"Sit, sit. Conrad, help your mother. Let's all have some tea." And with that he sat in the club chair and gave Karen the once over. Then he chuckled and said "My son knows how to pick 'em, don't he?"

Karen laughed. "I think that's a compliment, so thanks."

It was a strange hour. For a while they sat drinking tea and exchanging pleasantries about the weather, the coming holidays, and other safe topics. Conrad and his father got into a discussion about football and Faith took the opportunity to show Karen pictures of Conrad when he was a baby. Mention of his previous wife and the divorce were studiously avoided.

"Would you like some more tea?" asked Faith when there was a lull in the conversation.

"No thanks." replied Karen. "We should be going soon."

"I think you're both daft is what I think!" blurted Walter finally. You want to know what you're in for? Ask her." He nodded at his wife.

"They're thinking about going to California. Maybe it's easier there." said Faith quietly.

Walter suddenly rose and went to a closet. He pulled out a baseball bat and held it up. "You remember this Connie?

Conrad chuckled. "Yeh Pop."

When Karen looked at him questioningly Conrad explained that once some creep had hassled his mother in the supermarket around the corner from where they lived. She'd run home pretty shook up. When she told her husband about it he went after the man with a bat. He ran all over the neighborhood looking for him but he never found him. And from then on all his cronies in the 'hood called him 'Bat Walt'.

"You know, instead of 'Bad Walt.'" Conrad added with a grin and a secret wink at Karen.

Faith looked embarrassed and folded her hands primly in her lap, not saying a word.

"Well, mon, you didn't listen to me when you were a boy and I told you not to smoke, so why would you listen to me now?" Walter shrugged. "Tell you what though. If you go ahead with this foolishness, you'd better have this thing," he said shaking the bat at them, "cause you're damn well going to need it!"

CHAPTER 7

1968   Civil Rights Bill Becomes Law

Weeks went by and turned into months as Karen and Conrad planned their move to California. There was a lot to deal with and every night was spent in discussion of strategies. The days were filled with trying to make enough money to support the move. Conrad took every odd job that came along. Karen began to sell off belongings. They had decided that it would be wiser to go with a minimum of baggage because moving vans were incredibly expensive for a cross country trip. So Karen bit the bullet and sold off as much as she could, agreeing to put the things she absolutely couldn't bear to part with in storage until they got their bearings and were sufficiently settled to send for them. There was never any question about keeping the piano. But she got such a good offer for the Saarinen chair that she couldn't resist it, although it pained her mightily to part with it. It was hard to let go of the paintings, too, but they brought a good sum and Karen comforted herself with the thought that they would be so successful in Hollywood that they'd be able to start a new art collection. The dishes and silver and books and memorabilia all went into storage with the piano.

It was a difficult time, filled with elation and doubt, anxieties and anticipation, euphoria and depression. But through it all was the wonderful joy of their new relationship. They made the decision to marry before they left for California, at Conrad's urging. He felt their chance for social acceptance would be improved if they were more than just living together. Karen was so in love that she would have jumped off a cliff if he had suggested it. Spring was around the corner and as they grew closer and more intimate it seemed as though they were strong enough together to handle anything. They could lick the world.

Their passion was limitless and made them feel invincible, even though all around them racism was festering like a boil and people were getting shot for being the wrong color or for fighting for the rights of those who were the wrong color. It was as though they had woven a protective cocoon around themselves, spun by their love, that nothing in the outside world could penetrate. Or so they thought.

They had decided to get married at City Hall. It would be fast, simple and cheap. Karen drove out to the shore one Saturday to break the news of their plans to her parents. They'd met Conrad and found him a charming novelty. The Nathansons played an active part in the liberal intelligentsia's myriad menu of causes, thereby acquiring a colorful and varied group of friends and acquaintances. Since they didn't take the relationship too seriously, regarding it as part of the transition of divorce, they hadn't paid much attention to it. But Karen felt obliged to tell them before rather than after the fact expecting, in view of their political stance, a shrug, a kiss and a hug.

It was a mild day and Karen's mother Sarah suggested they have lunch on the patio. The Nathansons lived in a Manhattan apartment but spent a good deal of their time in this ranch house on the south shore of Long Island. When David, Karen's father, retired they planned to live here full time and give up the New York apartment. Karen loved the house which was surrounded by trees and had a view of the ocean, but it was hard for her to spend time here. As much as she loved her parents, she couldn't stand being with them for any length of time. One had to conform to their program, agree with their opinions, be willing to fight their philosophical fights or be in for a dialectic battle that was frustrating and exhausting. Karen never could figure out how it was they that they seemed to think as one. She often wondered whether one had capitulated to the other or whether their total agreement had formed the basis for the relationship initially.

Karen waited until they were sipping their coffee to make the announcement. She was stunned at the reaction. Sara leaped up and started to clear the dishes. She seemed to be on the verge of tears.

"Sara, sit. We have to discuss this," ordered David. He turned to Karen with a grim look on his face. "Now."

"Well Dad, there's really nothing to discuss," Karen responded hastily. "We love each other. We've made up our minds. There's nothing to discuss."

Sara jumped in. "Look dear. It's lovely that you have this relationship. And you know I've always been colorblind. But have you really thought about what you're doing? For example, what about your father? What about his business?"

David roared "That's not the issue. The issue is…"

Again Karen intererupted. "Whoa! There is <u>no issue</u>. There is only the fact. It's not up for discussion, dears. And by the way, what happened to my great liberal-cause-party-givers? Where are my oh so progressive parents? Am I to understand that you only talk a great game?"

That calmed David down considerably. After a moment he shrugged. "Listen, if it was Harry Belafonte maybe I could understand it. At least he's rich and famous!" Karen saw the familiar twinkle in the eye and the smirk, but she knew it was only on the outside and she suddenly saw her father in a whole new light.

To Karen's surprise, the following week Sara offered to be present at the City Hall adventure and since they knew they were going to need witnesses they welcomed her presence. Karen suspected that it was one of the few times in Sara's life that she opted to do something that David didn't necessarily go along with.

"Karen darling," she had said, "It's only that we don't want to see you suffer pain, and we know how hard it's going to be. But it's your life and we have to let you live it."

Conrad insisted that he didn't want his parents present. "It would just complicate things," he'd said. So he didn't tell them when they were actually going to perform the ceremony. But he asked one of his oldest friends, Al, to be his best man. Conrad and Al had been buddies since high school and Al was also an aspiring actor, although he made his living as a bank security guard.

As it turned out, the City Hall wedding was one of the funniest sketches any of them had ever seen much less participated in. The large sterile beige colored ante room containing only rows of straight backed wooden chairs was almost filled with couples waiting to be married and sitting stiffly with their relatives and friends. The first chuckle came as they looked around the room and Conrad said "What set are we on? Call the costume person!" There was every size and shape of human being, dozens of ethnicities. Eclectic was too narrow a word to describe the variety of choice of dress. Everything from jeans to tux and white gown were represented. Karen and Conrad had decided to come neat but not gaudy. Conrad wore a very elegant darkly patterned dashiki with dark trousers. He hated wearing shirts and ties and the dashiki was not only 'in' but comfortable, so he wore them quite frequently these days. Karen wore a simple but graceful beige silk dress with fitted empire waist that Conrad loved. He had given her a beautiful brown and green orchid which she'd pinned to her waist. They were a class act and Karen thought that, indeed, Conrad looked like a movie star who had wandered onto the wrong set.

When they were finally called into the 'marriage' room they had all they could do to keep from cracking up. The clerk standing behind the lectern who bade them approach had buck teeth, teacup handle ears and curly blonde hair like Harpo Marx. He looked like a cartoon. And when he spoke, he had such an obvious lisp "Do you take thith woman…" that Conrad's shoulders began to shake convulsively. He grabbed Karen's hand for control, but when she felt his shaking she could withhold her own impulse no longer and she too began to shake with laughter. The "I do's" erupted from the effort not to explode hysterically and soon none of them could contain themselves, so that when they finally completed the ceremony and were released, this wedding party burst forth from the room roaring so uncontrollably that the waiting crowd of couples-to-be froze with alarm.

"May the rest of your lives together be filled with as many laughs as we've had today," said Sara, as she hugged Karen and kissed Conrad on the cheek. And for months afterward, whenever some little thing reminded Karen and Conrad of that hour at City Hall, it triggered gales of laughter.

They headed straight for the Montecito when they arrived in Los Angeles. They had been advised by all their black actor friends that this was the least expensive and most welcoming apartment hotel. Because it was showbusiness oriented, the managers were accustomed to a multi-ethnic clientele and therefore not likely to give them any trouble. Located on Franklin Street in Hollywood, it was almost entirely populated by New Yorkers temporarily residing on the west coast in the quest for work. It was an old, slightly rundown building carrying the faded elegance that hinted of a more glorious past. It reminded Karen of West End Avenue in Manhattan. The lobby was large with big ornate green sofas that looked like they came off a movie set. A concierge desk was manned occasionally by an odd-looking middle aged man named Fred who wore a hairpiece and needed to go on a diet. He examined the entry and exit of every individual as though he were casting a film. The 'apartment' was a large studio like room with a small kitchenette attached. It was cream colored and completely furnished in what Karen liked to call 'contemporary Flatbush': serviceable but nondescript furniture of the type one sees at garage sales. The kitchenette provided dishes, pots and pans, silverware and anything the transient might require to cook a simple meal.

The big attraction was the convenience of its location at the heart of Holly-wood, and the big luxurious looking pool that nestled against the back of the building. This is where everyone congregated, exchanging bits of information about 'the business' and commiserating about the toughness of finding employment.

Conrad gazed out the window after they'd settled in and begun to unpack. "Well, at least we have a view of the pool." He grinned ruefully. "This is going to be very temporary. We need to go apartment hunting right away."

"I thought there were going to be palm trees everywhere, and lots of beach like Florida," sighed Karen. "It's not anything like I imagined it to be."

"We'll find a place where there's a palm tree." Conrad put his arms around her, patting her reassuringly and they kissed. "Let's baptize this funny looking bed." he whispered. Their lovemaking shut out the world and they forgot about their surroundings and the path that lay ahead.

The first thing they had to do was buy a second hand car. It became instantly clear that they could not function without wheels, and Karen informed Conrad that she was going to teach him how to drive.

"I thought I'd just get a bike," was his reply.

"Are you crazy? Everything is a hundred miles apart here," protested Karen. And so, at the advice of their new friends around the pool and with the help of one of them, they explored the used car lots in the valley and came home with a servicable white Valiant sedan.

Conrad decided that before they went to look for an apartment he should investigate the possibilities for getting some kind of a 'bread' job. He figured that if he had a local employer it might favorably impress a prospective land-lord. Around the pool he'd heard a mention of a possibility on the Twentieth Century Fox lot, so the next day they went off in the Valiant in search of Cen-tury City. It was a thrill to drive onto this famous lot and suddenly feel a part of a huge industry filled with glamor and excitement. Karen waited for Conrad in the parking area while he went to the personnel office. She was dying to drive around and get a closer look at the whole place, but you needed a pass to be able to get through the gate. That will come, she thought. When Conrad approached the car finally, he was grinning from ear to ear.

"What happened?" asked Karen. She knew by looking at him that it was something good.

"Got a job, baby!" Conrad said triumphantly.

"So fast? Doing what?"

"Security guard on the night shift. Eleven to seven. I start tomorrow night. I just walked in at the right moment."

"Oh Con. You really want to do that?" Karen felt apprehensive already. No wonder the job was available. It sounded dangerous. But when she saw the look on Conrad's face she quickly added "So fast! How did you get it so fast?"

"The guy in charge was a black dude from New York. Turns out we had a mutual friend. Small world, huh?"

Conrad explained that it would be an ideal situation. He'd have his days free to look for work in his field and meanwhile he could explore the Fox lot all night and learn more about the business of making films. And he could get a bus on Pico that would take him right to Highland Avenue so Karen wouldn't have to worry about calling for him. Karen's silence as they drove back to the Montecito spoke volumes.

"Look baby, it's all just temporary. Just until we get our bearings, you know. I've got to bring in some bread. I can't let you go on paying for everything," said Conrad.

"Will you step into the twentieth century? You're an actor. What's wrong with my paying the bills until you find work here?"

"Hey, there's Grauman's Chinese Theatre! That's the footprint place," Conrad chortled. "I've always wanted to see that place. Holly<u>wooood!</u> Here we are!"

Karen knew the subject had been dropped. She didn't sleep much the next night. In the first place she'd gotten used to having Conrad next to her. And then she was having all kinds of nightmares about his being attacked by gangs of thieves. She finally fell into fitful sleep as morning arrived and was awakened with a start by the sudden weight of Conrad's body as he dropped into bed beside her.

"Hi," he said weakly. He was exhausted.

Karen hugged him. "Oh, I'm so relieved. I worried all night." She looked into his face. "What's the matter? You look positively green."

Conrad giggled and then as they lay there with the morning sunlight streaming in, he recounted the night's events. The first thing they did, he told her, was hand him a small car and spell out his duties. He was expected to drive around the lot, which was miles wide, and check every building to see that it was locked and secure. He was to check all open sets to make sure there were no robbers and drive around the perimeter to make sure all the gates were locked.

"Drive? But Con, you don't know how to drive!"

"Well, I wasn't going to tell them that and blow the job."

"You mean to tell me you got in that car and drove?" asked Karen, horrified.

Conrad laughed. "It's funny in retrospect. But I have to admit I was shitting in my pants when the guy stood there and I had to drive away. It's a good thing I've been watching you."

"But they didn't ask you for a driver's license?"

"Nope. I guess they assume that everyone out here drives."

"I can't believe it. So how did you manage to not kill yourself?"

"Well, I went very slowly and I bumped into a few things. Once I stalled and I thought it was all over, but I finally got it started again. It's what you call jumping into the deep end of the pool. The lot is a little the worse for wear, but nobody caught on, I guess, 'cause the guy said see you tomorrow. But man, it was a strain. I'm exhausted. The real problem was the bus home. It never came and I'd still be standing there if someone hadn't given me a lift." Conrad yawned and turned over. "It was fun though, in a strange kind of way. It was pitch dark and empty like a ghost town. Eerie, kind of...." and he drifted off to sleep.

Karen stared at Conrad's beautiful chiseled jaw in repose and stifled the urge to kiss him. She would have to teach him to drive immediately, she thought, so he could get a driver's license. What guts it took to get through that night. Another man would have thrown up his hands and walked away from it but Conrad rose to the challenge. She was so proud of him.

As it happened, Conrad only had to stay at the job for two weeks. Karen got a call from one of the few friends in New York who knew and approved of the marriage. Kelly had heard that Paramount was being threatened with a discrimination suit because they had no black personnel. Times were changing and companies were scurrying to get their token minority person lined up to avoid being singled out by CORE or SNCC or the NAACP.

"Tell Conrad to get in touch with the president of the TV Division right away," she urged. "He would be perfect for them."

Karen knew exactly what Kelly meant. She meant acceptable because of his color. But she relayed the information to Conrad and he followed up on it. Before either of them knew what was happening, Conrad had a job, a title, and a studio car. It was luck and timing. He even had a parking space on the lot with his name on it.

Conrad was ecstatic. "How do you like that? I'm the Executive Assistant to the the President of the Television Division! Right from security guard. What a town!" And it was a good salary, although Conrad wasn't at all sure of what his duties were going to be. They gave him a good sized office, put his name on the door and introduced him to all the producers on the lot.

He told Karen about all the handshaking and executive trappings, adding "The only other black guy on the entire lot is in the mail room."

Karen immediately suggested they go shopping. "You need some clothes, Con. You're going to have to wear suits."

"No way." he protested. I'm the spook by the door, babe. Dashikis will do just fine. How else will they know I'm the spook?"

Karen wasn't so sure he was right about that, but she kept quiet.

They were anxious to get out of the Montecito and settle in a real home so they began to scour the classified ads for houses and apartments to rent. They soon discovered that Los Angeles was more like a myriad bunch of linked suburbs than a city. After several days of driving around and discovering how segregated each area was, they realized that one was expected to choose a neighborhood according to means, ethnicity and convenience of geographic location, probably in that order. But Conrad refused to play by the unwritten rules. He decided he wanted to live in Beverly Hills where the other men at the studio lived. So they began their hunt in the less expensive flat side, south of Wilshire Boulevard.

They got the local paper and selected the ads that sounded right. The first one was on a quiet, tree-lined street in the block between Wilshire and Gregory Way. Most of the buildings were two story white, peach and ochre colored stucco houses with well manicured lawns and flowering trees. The Manager who came to the front gate was a stocky middle-aged man with salt and pepper hair who wore thick lensed horn-rimmed glasses. He peered at them for a moment, looking them up and down. Then he announced that there were no vacancies.

"But it was in today's paper," protested Karen. "And I called and spoke to somebody. I think it was you…"

"Nope. Wasn't me. And that one in the paper is rented. Sorry." And he started to leave.

"But, see here…" said Karen.

Conrad took her by the arm "Let's go."

She resisted. "But…"

"I said let's go!" Conrad raised his voice slightly and guided her towards the car. "Don't you know what's going on?" he asked grimly when they had settled into the car. "He wasn't sure but he sure as hell wasn't going to take a chance. I shouldn't have spent time at the pool. Too bad I tan so fast."

"That son of a bitch. We ought to report him. It's against the law."

Conrad laughed and kissed her on the cheek. "You're cute when you're angry."

"I'm furious! How can you take it so calmly?" she raged.

"Years of experience."

Several hours later, after seeing a few really depressing places south of Olympic that smelled funny and having a few more repeats of their first experience, they were finally shown a lovely large apartment in a one story, two apartment building. Karen couldn't get over the fact that in Los Angeles apartments and houses were often supplied with wall to wall carpeting and drapes but no refrigerator or stove. But this one had everything and a fireplace as well. The living room was high-ceilinged and a crystal chandelier hung in its center. The windows looked out on a garden with a large lemon tree. The bedroom was good sized and the kitchen was lined with high old-fashioned closets with glass knobbed doors and tiled counters. The landlady was a scrawny white-haired wisp of a woman with a slight Germanic accent. She had beady blue eyes and a sharply pointed nose that gave her a birdlike look. She never took her eyes off them for a second.

"Zo, ver are you from?" she asked Conrad. She was clearly trying to make up her mind about him.

"New York," replied Conrad.

"Ah. De Big Epple. Vat part?"

"Manhattan." Karen jumped in. She really liked this place and she wanted them to get it.

"Ah, zo." She turned to Karen and focused her beady eyes on her face. "Rent iss nine hundred a month. First and last months' rent and one month security ven you sign der lease." It was delivered as a challenge.

"But that's $2700 up front!" gasped Karen. "That's not what the ad said…"

The landlady smiled as though she were enjoying sucking on one of her lemons.

Conrad put his arm around Karen's shoulders and said wearily "Let's go, Karen." As he steered her toward the door, she yelled at the woman "You're not going to get away with this!" and she stormed out.

Back in the car Karen pulled out the paper. "Look. The ad says the rent on that place is $300 a month. We've got to report her. It's clearly discrimination. It's outrageous!" As Conrad silently started the motor she steamed quietly, muttering "Damn. I really loved that place."

"This is a southern town, baby. You might as well get used to it," said Conrad. "Isn't it ironic that the New York theatre critics thought I was white and here everyone seems to know I'm black?"

"Well why don't we look in Watts or Compton?" she replied. When she saw the look on his face she added quickly "Just kidding."

After a few discouraging days they caught on to what needed to be done to get housing. They zeroed in on a sweet little one bedroom cottage with a big back yard, a peach tree and a huge garage which sat incongruously on a street lined with large expensive Beverly Hills type homes of every style and shape. Karen suspected that it was originally a guest house attached to the mansion next door. She went to look at it by herself, claiming that her husband hadn't arrived from New York yet but that he was due in a few days. It was perfect. The ubiquitous wall to wall carpeting was deep, luxurious and an easy to take shade of gold. The living room and bedroom were furnished tastefully in simple modern blond maple furniture with brown tweed upholstery and the drapes were of a light beige woven fabric that Karen actually liked. There was even a stove in the kitchen so, as the owner pointed out, they would only have to acquire a refrigerator and a washer dryer. Karen could imagine having picnics in the back yard under the peach tree. And the fireplace was large with a big mantle like the kind you see in movies about Christmas. It was light and airy and very California and Karen loved it. She charmed the owner of the house into giving her a lease and a key right away, saying she wanted it to be all ready for her husband when he arrived so that he could go right to work at the studio. She knew that naming Paramount as her husband's employer would impress the owner and that he would therefore never suspect any identity problem. It had all been choreographed by Conrad who had given her strict instructions on what to say, and when Karen came home triumphant with key in hand they hugged and kissed and congratulated each other on having outsmarted this bigoted town.

Gradually they adjusted to this strange new environment. It was odd not to be able to take a walk to the corner store for a box of Kleenex. Or not to see anyone walking on the street when one looked out of a window. It seemed as though every move involved getting into the car and driving somewhere.

Everything was beautiful, as perfect as a stage set. The sky was eternally blue, the carefully clipped faithfully watered grass in front of each home was just the right shade of green. Flowers flourished and trees offered not only shade but also occasionally fruit and sometimes even avocados. Instead of pedestrians there were cars of every size, color and make. Cars whizzing by, parked in front of garages, in garages, even parked on the street. They had never seen so many Rolls Royces, Jaguars and Cadillacs. And one could drive right up to wherever one was going. Karen really appreciated that part of this new suburban lifestyle, although it was difficult to adjust to spending so much time sitting in the car. She resolved to join a dance class to make up for the lack of exercise.

Conrad wasted no time learning the fine points of driving and becoming a newly licensed driver. He got a big kick out of the Grand Prix the Studio had given him and loved the feeling of being able to drive onto the Paramount lot with a wave of the hand to the guard at the kiosk as he slid into the parking space with his name on it. It gave him a new sense of importance. Being an executive was so entirely different from anything he'd ever done before and he was really digging it.

Karen spent her time connecting with relocated New York buddies. They helped her ferret out the whereabouts of places like a good hairdresser, the nearest bank, a convenient supermarket, the best Chinese restaurant and so on, all of which were spread out all over the area accessible only by car and able to be found only by the previously initiated.

Conrad's connection to the Studio also seemed to render them suddenly socially acceptable and friends who had ignored them in New York were now seeking them out. They were mostly Karen's friends, so they were mostly white. Although Karen urged Conrad to seek out some of his black actor pals who were just beginning to get work in television and a few exploitation films, suggesting he invite them over for dinner, he always changed the subject. Karen didn't know whether it was because of her, or because he didn't want them to see how comfortably they were living and how well he was doing.

Karen's New York friends, however, were doing very well and living quite lavishly. Most of them had big houses in Brentwood or Westwood with pools and all the storybook Hollywood trappings like bars and pooltables. Entertaining seemed to take the place of the more cultural pursuits offered in the east, so that when the weekend came around the question would not be <u>what</u> are we going to see but rather <u>who</u> are we going to see. Conrad, customarily impatient with obeying social conventions for the sake of acceptance, was surprisingly compliant when Karen suggested that they needed to socialize to make contacts and learn their way around this town.

"Okay baby," he grinned at her. "If I'm going to be a mogul we'll have to 'play the game' I guess."

Conrad studied the powerful men he was meeting at the Studio and came home with stories about their expensive habits, beautiful clothes, gold jewelry and eccentric behaviour. And Karen could see that he was enjoying being included in this upper echelon. She also knew that he longed to get a chance to do something creative, to be involved in the actual production of a show. Conrad knew he had a lot to learn about the politics of the place, so he did his best to swim with the tide and fit in while quietly watching and learning.

But Karen knew the social life was painful for him. He never felt comfortable or relaxed with these people and Karen, seeing the strain it placed on him, never felt comfortable either. Conrad was either welcomed too warmly by those who wanted to show off their liberalism, or eyed suspiciously by those who weren't sure who or what he was or how they felt about him.

One night they went to a party given by Karen's friends, the Diamonds. Karen and Marie had made rounds together as young struggling actresses and had kept up their friendship after Marie married Sam Diamond who was also a struggling actor. The couple moved to the west coast early on, and Sam discovered that he had a talent for writing comedy. Now he was a successful producer of TV sitcoms. They were among the few people who welcomed Conrad and Karen as a couple unquestioningly and didn't make them feel like an oddity.

They lived in a large French Chateau style house in the celebrity dotted neighborhood near the Beverly Hills Hotel. Karen loved the house because it was filled with paintings and sculpture and objets d'art. Every nook and cranny was a surprise. Marie was a compulsive collector and filled her days with roaming the city looking for things to buy. Karen suspected that she did it to fill a very large void since she had long since abandoned a career as an actress. Marie often talked about how boring it was in L.A. and how she longed to go home to New York for 'a fix'. But she had excellent taste and now also money to burn and she often called Karen to come with her on her shopping binges.

"Thank God you're finally out here, Karen." Marie had said one day over lunch. "All our so-called friends are Sam's business associates. I've been so lonely. There's no one I can talk to."

"Yes, it can be a very isolated life, can't it," replied Karen. "I've really got to start thinking about getting some work."

"Good idea, dear. You could never cut it just being a wife. Wives have absolutely no status here. They're just treated like appendages." Marie stabbed at her lettuce with her fork in a way that had made Karen suddenly aware that all was not fairy tale perfect in the Diamond house.

The Diamond parties were another form of distraction for Marie. The guest lists were always interesting and so was the food. Marie was given to trying out the hottest new caterer to the Beverly Hills crowd. Since this changed every few weeks, a frequent guest could always count on some new and strange cuisine to present itself.

On this particular night, Karen and Conrad sat on one of the huge velvet couches facing the glass wall that looked out on the pool area sipping champagne and munching on some weird little canapes that a cruising waiter had just offered them.

"What is this stuff?" asked Conrad.

"Some sort of shrimpy thing I think," replied Karen.

"You white folks sure eat funny. I'd give my left arm for some greens right now. Or even a sausage sandwich."

Karen giggled. "As soon as I find the place to buy the ingredients, I'll make you all your favorites."

"We'll have to go to Watts, I expect."

They watched the room filled with carefully groomed people dressed in studiously casual-to-kill clothes mix and mingle and drift toward the pool area. It was a large room filled with antique furniture and impressionist paintings that were totally at odds with brightly colored silk jumpsuits and gold chains. The cut glass crystal chandelier that hung over the gleaming dark mahogany dining table at one end of the room made patterns in the candlelight and gave the room an eerie glow. Karen couldn't help thinking that none of it matched the ultra modern sliding glass wall that led to the pool area. She looked at Conrad sitting next to her, looking beautiful in the black velvet dashiki she had made for him using one of his cotton ones as a pattern. Nothing fits in here, she thought. Including us.

Marie appeared suddenly and whispered that Barry Loomis had just arrived and that she was anxious for Conrad to meet him.

"Remind me. I've met so many people in the last few months," said Conrad.

"He's the agent I told you about. He knows everyone and he could be a great help to you. In this town you've gotta have an agent in your corner," said Marie solemnly. "Come on. I'm going to introduce you."

Conrad was reluctant but Karen nudged him. "Go on, hon. I'll wait here."

Marie led him to the other side of the room where a short, round, balding middle aged man sat on an embossed velvet two seater. He was surrounded by several younger people and was obviously holding court. Conrad smiled to himself when he saw the silk shirt, the ubiquitous gold chains and a large gold pinky ring. It's like a uniform, thought Conrad. When Marie introduced him, Loomis studied Conrad for a moment, then invited him to sit by his side as he continued his conversation and sipped his scotch.

"Yeh, so I just flew in from New York this morning. Had to cover a client opening in a Broadway play." He turned to Conrad. "Bitch! She's losing money hand over fist to do it."

Conrad noticed he had a very slight lisp. Then he felt the pressure of the man's thigh against his. Oh shit, he thought. A faggot. "What's the play?" he asked politely.

"A turkey called 'Butterflies Are Free'. Is that a title? A bomb, believe me. And I had the worst flight back!" Barry's voice rose in anger. "Now that the airlines are hiring those damn 'schvarzes', it's a nightmare!"

Conrad saw Marie stiffen in horror. "Tsk, tsk. Is that a fact?" he said calmly, grinning at Marie.

"They can't get anything right," continued Barry relentlessly. He appealed to Conrad, oblivious. "What are we coming to? Such stupidity. I made a simple request and this lame-brained Negro..."

Marie was having a fit. "Barry...! I need to talk to you about something."

"Just a minute, dear. I'm talking to Conrad here."

"Now, Barry. It's very urgent." Conrad tried to signal to Marie to forget it but she was insistent. "<u>Now</u>, Barry."

Barry rose with a sigh. She was his hostess, after all. "Excuse us. To be continued."

Conrad chuckled to himself. I doubt it, he thought. He casually lit a cigarette and wondered what the fuck he was doing here with these clowns.

Meanwhile, Karen had been nailed by a lanky redheaded screenwriter with a prominent nose and horn rimmed glasses who had been flirting with her from a distance and who moved in as soon as he spotted Conrad moving away. He was not good looking in the conventional sense of the word, but his charm and humor made him seem attractive. After the initial exchange of names and mini bios, which is the way all conversations in this town seemed to begin, he began giving Karen some pointers on survival in the industry from his perspective as a newly succesful TV writer.

"It's all in who you know and being in the right place at the right time," he told her.

"Well, I'm ready to start looking for a job, so I guess I'd better start meeting the so-called 'right people'," Karen replied.

"You should call me and pick my brain. It's musical chairs in this business. But I keep in touch with who's where. Say do you want to split this scene and go somewhere for a quiet drink? I'm getting tired of looking at the same old faces at every party."

"I don't think Marie would appreciate my leaving." Karen was amused at the pass and kind of enjoying it.

"Listen, I usually hear when something good opens up." He took out his wallet and fished out a card. "You can reach me here."

Karen glanced at the offered card which was embossed with raised lettering that said 'Arnold Lang, Screenwriter' with an address and phone number. Like a CEO, she thought. "Thanks" was all she said aloud and tucked it into her purse.

"Do you have one?" Arnold asked.

"Not yet. We've just recently settled into a house."

"We?"

Karen thought she saw his ears prick up like a dog's. "Yes, me and my husband."

"You're married? Is he here?"

Karen looked across the room. Conrad was still sitting on the couch but he'd been joined by a woman Karen hadn't seen before. "Yes, he's right over there. On that couch with the blond woman."

Arnold gave him a long look. "That's your husband?" He turned to Karen and snorted "Hah! I wish you both luck out here. You're going to need it!"

Karen stiffened. "Just what do you mean by that?"

Arnold shrugged. "Darling, he's much too good-looking. This is the land of ogres who eat happily married couples for breakfast. You two don't have a chance! I give it a year." His smile seemed like a sneer to Karen.

"What a bitchy thing to say. Excuse me." Karen swept across the room head held high and plunked herself down next to Conrad.

"What's wrong?" demanded Conrad immediately. He always knew.

"Nothing." She added under her breath, "Tell you later."

Conrad turned to the blond. "This is my wife Karen." He had forgotten the blond's name already.

She smiled at Karen. "Hi, I'm Nora." She rose. "It was nice talking to you. Nice to meet you Karen. I have to find my date." And she beat a hasty retreat.

Conrad laughed. "I think she thought I was a producer."

"Let's get out of here," pleaded Karen.

"My sentiments exactly." And hand in hand they strolled casually but determinedly toward the door.

Later, when they were getting undressed for bed they shared their experiences at the party. They agreed that while the living was easy, with the beach so accessible and cars able to drive and park everywhere, the social life had been an ordeal so far. But it seemed to be a necessary evil if they were to accomplish anything in this town. So they resolved to grin and bear it and 'play the game' as Conrad liked to call it, at least for a little while longer.

Karen crawled into bed and looked around the bedroom. She was beginning to get used to it. She had tried to make it more inviting with some brass framed posters, lemon colored throw pillows and burnt orange curtains on the windows. She'd wanted to replace some of the furniture with something more to their taste, but they'd decided not to spend too much until they were sure they wanted to stay. At the beginning it felt a little like being in a hotel. Everything was so strange and different. Even being able to walk out into the backyard or drive the car into the garage was a novelty for these two inveterate city dwellers. Conrad loved that part of it. They went to a huge bargain store called Akron and picked up some outdoor furniture. They had drinks outside when Conrad came home from work. Weekend mornings they would bring their breakfast out and lie in the sun. And they loved the fact that it only took them fifteen minutes to drive to the beach. Since they were both water and sun lovers, it felt like an extended vacation. They couldn't get over the size of the markets and the beautiful and bountiful fruit and vegetables which were so much cheaper than New York. And they wandered around the mega stores like Akron where you could get everything from a bag of cookies to a Spanish breakfront at discount prices. A lot of it was fun.

"I have to admit this socializing shit is getting to me," Conrad muttered as he sank into bed beside Karen. "It's bad enough I have to deal with those clowns at the Studio."

This was the first time he had said anything negative about the job, thought Karen. He hadn't told her much beyond amusing her with the day to day anecdotes. "We'll just have to be more selective," she said aloud. "I'm going to look for a job. Maybe we'll meet some new people. Problem is, there's not much else to do in this town."

Conrad threw his arm around her and they snuggled and kissed. "MMmm. You taste good," he whispered. Then, as he threw his leg over her body and drew her closer to him he muttered "I'm going to have to find some folks to spend time with." Karen knew that by 'folks' he meant black people.

CHAPTER 8

1968   Martin Luther King Assassinated

Karen did find a job at a small television production company with the help of Sam Diamond who knew an executive producer on one of the two network shows the company had currently running. The offices of TLT Productions were on Melrose Avenue in a two story brick building with an ornate iron gate at its front. They were located on the second floor, sharing the building with a talent agency which occupied the first floor. Waiting for her interview, Karen admired the plush carpeting, tasteful modern chairs and interesting small sculptures that were placed around the space. Someone has good taste, she thought. Although she was rapidly learning that out here the front was everything and often the front was all there was, the look of the place gave her hope that this was a company of some substance. The office she was ushered into was the epitome of Hollywood style luxury. Her feet literally sank into the carpet which was an autumn shade of rust. Huge, deep armchairs were upholstered in a tan suede-like material and somehow the Tiffany lamps didn't seem at all incongruous with the warm walnut tables and desk. The desk was also huge and Karen was impressed by its smooth surface which was uncluttered except for the phone console. He must keep everything in little cubicles behind the desk, she thought. I could never keep a desk that clean.

The man rising to greet her was both tall and wide. Karen thought he was probably in his mid forties, but he was already lined and jowly. The thick neck and overall size of the man made him look like a former football player gone to seed. As is the case with many large men, he spoke very softly. After offering her a seat and covering the amenities, he insisted Karen call him Chuck. Mr. Forrest was too formal, he protested, and this was an informal small company.

The job was as junior executive in the Development department. Karen's duties would involve reading submissions, taking pitches and writing reports.

Chuck looked at Karen's resume. "Your experience would certainly seem to qualify you for the job. We like the New York sensibility here. Of course, we'd have to see if we're on the same wavelength. Tastewise, I mean."

Karen replied with as much charm as possible. "Well if this decor is your taste, I think we're on the same wavelength. I love it."

"I'm really taking a stab in the dark here. But Harry said you were terrific. So why don't we try it out?"

It was that easy. Never mind that she'd never met Harry and that he was just paying off an i.o.u. It was all in who you knew, thought Karen as she flashed a grateful smile at Chuck.

In discussions with friends she had learned that 'development' meant not making a commitment to buy until there was a certainty of success. It was a long, slow gestation period in which many people put a finger in the creative pie as a project was forced into birth. The trick was in finding the project that was worthy of moving from the idea into the next stage. She was sure she could find out how to 'take a pitch'. She had learned that 'the pitch' was the term used for the process by which ideas and material for television were sold to prospective buyers. The writer and/or the producer had to sell the concept, sometimes even before a word of script was typed. Everything in this town was 'taken'. You took a meeting and you took a pitch. She imagined Chuck would soon 'take' lunch. They probably took a leak instead of going to the bathroom. Karen giggled aloud at this last thought which had crept in uninvited.

"What's funny?" demanded Chuck.

"Nothing," Karen added quickly. "I laugh when I'm happy and you've just made me very happy."

And so it was that Karen found herself in a nine to five job in an office behind a desk. Although she soon discovered that there wasn't much happening before ten a.m. and that everyone took at least two hours for lunch, factoring in driving time to a restaurant. A great deal of business was conducted at lunches which sometimes stretched to three hours. There were also business drinks and sometimes even business dinners. Karen could never get used to the idea of eating and doing business at the same time. And then there was the constant jumping in and out of the car that this new lifestyle dictated. The rest of the company personnel were pleasant enough but everyone seemed pretty wrapped up in themselves and left Karen to her own devices.

With Conrad based at a major Studio and Karen involved in TV producion, they were quickly thrown into the whirl of news, gossip, events and social life that were part and parcel of being bona-fide members of 'The Industry'. For Karen it was not that much of a culture shock. She had been in a showbusiness atmosphere, been around celebrities and gone to big benefits and award dinners in New York.

But for Conrad it was a revelation. He was like a kid in a candy store, seeing all kinds of possibilities opening up around him, possibilities that were unthinkable in his Harlem days. Although he was the only person of color in the executive building, he envisioned the opening of doors previously locked. Why shouldn't he become a producer eventually and have his own show? Drive a Rolls Royce? Live in a big house with a pool and servants? He was already driving a large luxury sedan and had his own parking space at Paramount. He had a good sized office with his name on the door in gold letters. He was cleared to go anywhere on the lot, to observe any filming, attend any screening. He was making a good salary which came in steadily every week. Look how far he had come and in such a short time!

Between the two of them he and Karen were invited to every major event and screening. What didn't come to his desk came to hers. Suddenly it became necessary to have good clothes, even a tux. He struck up a conversation with James Garner on one of the shoots and found out who made his suits. At Karen's urging, he finally got up the nerve to go to the tailor on Sunset Boulevard. He was apprehensive about it, confessing to Karen that if he was refused service he might lose it and punch the guy in the mouth.

"This is a southern town, you know," he warned her.

"You always say that, but things are changing. You'll see," she replied.

She was right. The tailor was crazy about Conrad, raved about his body and made him two beautiful pairs of slacks.

Conrad didn't know if things were indeed changing or if it was the old 'aren't you an Egyptian prince?' syndrome. But most people were treating him well. Almost bending over backward to be nice and hospitable. What he didn't take into account was that in this land of make believe if you were extremely beautiful or handsome you had a good chance of being welcomed. This was a world where one never knew who was going to be the next star or the next meal ticket. One covered one's bets by being nice to the beautiful people, because they were the ones who had the best chance of making it. And Conrad's appearance, as well as the way he carried himself and dressed, made him striking and different.

At the Studio he was greeted like an oddity, a special visitor from another country on some kind of diplomatic pass. True that to date he hadn't been given a single assignment involving any real responsibility, but Conrad knew he had to be patient, learn the ropes, feel his way around. So he spent his days reading the inter-office communications and the trade papers, DAILY VARIETY and THE HOLLYWOOD REPORTER. He read scripts that appeared on his desk and wrote his comments on them and visited sets to observe the directors and actors in action. Occasionally there would be a screening of dailies or a rough cut and at the end of every week there would be several screenings of finished features. After the first couple of weeks Conrad began to wonder what they were paying him for. But he was learning and he could be patient, he thought. If he could just lay low and keep his mouth shut, he could gradually work his way in.

On one of their increasingly rare evenings home Karen and Conrad sat in front of the fireplace sipping scotch on the rocks with their feet up on the big coffee table.

"This is so nice," sighed Karen. "We never have time to do this anymore. It seems like we're always running to some party or banquet or something. It's getting to be just like New York—always running."

Conrad nodded. "Yeh. We've gone from one extreme to the other. Hard to believe that just months ago I was a security guard driving a bumper car around Fox."

Karen squeezed his arm. "I'm so proud of you."

For the first time Conrad shared his growing frustration. "They're not giving me a damn thing to do, babe. I feel guilty about collecting my check."

"Give it time, darling. Why don't you show them some of your writing?"

Conrad shrugged. "I didn't want to say anything until I got a reaction, but I've been working on a treatment for a screenplay. God knows I've had plenty of time to write," he said wryly. "I left it for Biff to read today."

Biff McKee was President of the TV Division and Conrad's boss. Karen knew that this was a big step for Conrad. "Terrific. Do I get to see it?"

"I just happen to have a copy in my coat pocket," he grinned.

How like him, thought Karen. It's probably rolled up in a ball. She rose to go and get it.

"Don't read it now, babe. Wait 'til later."

Karen knew from past experience that he hated to have her read his stuff while he was around to watch her face. It made both of them nervous. "Okay," she said and sank back into the couch.

Later when she read it her heart sank. It was good, but it was about the Tuskegee Airmen, a little known black unit of World War II, and it was political. Black and political was an impossible sell, she knew. The only black shows they were interested in were the comedies with very funny stereotypical or caricature characters. She knew that Conrad hated them and that he hoped to use his position to pioneer the concept that black people were something other than cartoons. She feared that this treatment would be yet another source of anger and frustration for him. But she kept quiet, hoping against hope that she would be proven wrong.

One day Karen came home a little late and as she pulled her leased Dodge Dart into the driveway she was surprised to see Conrad's car already there. He was stretched out on a chair in the backyard, gazing up into the lemon tree.

"Hi honey. You're home early." She bent to kiss him.

"Yep."

Karen could feel the tension hanging over him like a veil. "You okay?"

"Sure."

Oh, oh, thought Karen. She knew the mood. He was furious about something. Best to wait until he was ready to spill it. No doubt it was something that happened at the Studio. Maybe they returned his treatment.

Conrad brooded and spoke in monosyllables for the better part of the evening. After dinner he turned on the ballgame loud enough to shut out the world, irritating Karen to the point where she finally burst out with a "Damn it, Conrad!"

He looked at her quizzically.

"Are you going to tell me what's eating you? Because this mood thing is driving me crazy."

Conrad sighed and turned off the TV. "What is it now?"

"What do you mean, what is it now? I'm asking you what's eating you. You're obviously upset. Does it have anything to do with me?" Karen persisted.

"Nope."

"What then?" She waited for a reply.

"Forget it. It's nothing," he shrugged.

"Okay then. Fine." Karen stormed out of the room, slamming the bedroom door behind her.

Conrad followed her a few moments later. Karen was lying face down on the bed with her head buried in the pillow on her side. He sat down beside her and gently massaged her neck. They were both beginnng to wear thin under the pressure of this enormous adjustment. The new environment, the new life style, the constant awareness of the need to be careful, discreet, political, all were beginning to tell on them. After all, they were still practically honeymooners, although it seemed as though they'd been married for years.

The best thing about this town so far was the built in isolation factor. Since there was no street life, it was possible for them to maintain a certain invisibity. They had their separate jobs, their separate cars, and the only time they were seen together was when they went shopping at the Supermarket or agreed to attend a selectively chosen party. Once in a great while they went to a play at the Ahmanson or the Mark Taper. More often they went to private screenings of new films. They were spending a lot more of their free time at home together now that it was too chilly for the beach. Though neither wanted to admit it, they were getting bored, missing the vitality, cultural stimulation, noise and activity they were so used to in New York.

"I'm sorry, baby. It's the fucking job. It's getting to me." said Conrad softly. And the story came out. He had been waiting patiently for an assignment, some indication that he wasn't just a token hired to avoid a discrimination suit. He had held his tongue, watching all the men around him—the leather jacketed, gold chained, fast talking white boys—move into every opening that presented itself since he'd started there. He'd been virtually ignored to the point where he found himself visiting Joe in the mail room, the only other Negro on the lot, to shoot the breeze about the Knicks and Lakers. He'd hung around the sets watching actors who were not as good as he knew he was louse up starring roles, watching directors who didn't know how to talk to actors or set up a shot make mistakes, watching producers who couldn't make an intelligent decision order everyone around. But he'd kept his mouth shut, trying not to overstep his bounds, politely agreeing with the jerks, only occasionally offering an opinion when asked, trying to 'play the game' by the 'white boys' rules'. Today they had finally given him an assignment and after all the waiting, Conrad's heart had jumped with joy when Biff called him in to tell him that they had something important to put him on.

"And what did the motherfuckers dream up for me?" he asked, his face contorted. "I'm to be 'dialogue director' on *Great Times*. That's the new show with Jim Johnson and Esther Robbins. Translated it means I'm the director's intrepreter for the Negroes on the show. I'm supposed to be able to talk to the black folk so they'll understand. And I'm supposed to make sure they behave and don't embarrass anybody when the press comes around."

"You can't be serious!" said Karen. "He actually said that?"

"He as good as said it. I think the exact words were 'look after them'. So that's what I get after all the waiting. Baby sitter for the folks. Shit! It's enough to make me say fuck it and go back to acting."

They talked for a long time. Karen understood what Conrad was feeling. She knew why he wanted to quit. Not only was he being demeaned by his boss, he was being put in a totally embarrassing position with the actors, some of whom might even be friends or aquaintances. He was locked into an inferior position when they both knew that his ability was so much greater than what he was being allowed to do. But Karen kept reminding Conrad that this whole thing was just a means to an end. That it was worth sticking it out for a little while longer because it could lead to something much better. At some point they were going to discover how valuable he could be. If he could just hang on, he might become the first black executive producer at a major Studio. At the very least, any day he might run into an important contact who could lead him to something better.

"Just think about it darling. You're meeting agents and managers and all sorts of wheelers and dealers. And so am I. Things change fast out here."

"Yeh, and it's a steady check. You've left that out. Don't think that doesn't mean a lot to me after what I've been through the past few years."

"I'm so proud of what you've accomplished since we got here. Really. And look where we are. A house in Beverly Hills, two cars, even a garbage disposal and washer-dryer." Karen giggled at the silliness of what she was saying. "We sip drinks in front of our fireplace and hobnob with the stars."

"Yeh, and pick lemons and peaches in the backyard." He put his arms around her. "It's not a bad life as long as you don't let your brain interfere." He buried his face in her neck. "Mmmm you smell good." He reached for her mouth with his and they kissed and made love and fell asleep like two spoons in a drawer.

During the weeks and months that followed Conrad's level of frustration and anger steadily increased. Every day he was forced to watch in silence while others, who he often felt were undeserving, were given the opportunities that he so desperately craved. He steamed quietly, keeping a low profile so as to try not to 'get into trouble'. The few times early on that he had expressed his opinions about anything it was apparent by the horrified looks he got that his perspective on things was totally different from that of the men who surrounded him. They came from privilege, he came from the street. They moved with the ease of belonging in a white world, he fought the daily battle of a rejected and repressed minority. They were accustomed to the pretense of upwardly mobile aspirants, he was accustomed to speaking his mind, bluntly and directly. He soon learned that speaking the truth was useless. They simply took it as a joke saying, "Oh, Conrad." So he took the cue and became the jokester when he was among them. They didn't take him seriously anyway, so what the hell, he thought. And the guys ate it up. Not only was Conrad good looking, he was funny, too. Although they never really took him in, never invited him to their homes, they liked having him around on the lot. He was amusing, he was an oddity and he served a purpose.

One day Biff stuck his head in Conrad's door. "How're ya doin?" he asked.

Conrad, startled because Biff never did this, replied "Great." He wondered what was up, but he seized the unexpected opportunity. "Say, I was just going to call you. I wondered if you'd had a chance to look at my treatment yet?"

"Uhhh…" Biff had been taken by surprise, but he recovered quickly. "It's on the top of my pile. Sorry, man, but I've been swamped, ya know. I'll get to it by the end of the week."

Conrad wanted to punch him. It had been months and he'd called Biff's secretary at least ten times to find out if he'd seen it yet.

Biff moved in quickly and leaned over Conrad's desk. "Listen, Conrad, will you do me a big favor?"

Oh, oh, thought Conrad. This is new. What's this going to be?

"The Studio wants us to give some guys from the NAACP the grand tour…You know, watch a shoot, see some stars, etc.etc. Handle it, will ya? Keep 'em happy. Oh, and there might be some press along, too."

So that was the reason for the visit from the boss. The lot was being given the once over and they needed to put on a good face. "Yeh, I'll take care of it," Conrad replied. "But I'd sure like to get your reaction to my material."

Biff practically leaped to the door. "I'll get to it, man. Just give me a few days." And he was gone.

Mother fucker, thought Conrad.

That afternoon was spent escorting two middle aged, slightly balding black men in suits and a well dressed light skinned younger woman with an impressive Afro from set to set on the lot. As they stood surrounded by a large 35mm camera, boom mikes and an array of lighting equipment, they plied Conrad with questions that had less to do with filmmaking and more to do with their immediate concerns.

"So how many brothers have executive positions at this Studio?" asked the woman whose name, Conrad learned, was Florence. She had been introduced initially as Miss Hemple.

"You're lookin' at 'em." replied Conrad.

"You're the only one?" chimed in Mr. Green, the more portly of the two men.

"There's me and a guy who works in the mail room."

Florence surveyed Conrad as though he were a piece of clothing she was about to try on. "How'd you get in?"

Conrad tapped his head with his forefinger. "Chutzpah." God, how he hated having to deal with this, he thought.

"I don't see anyone on this crew either," said the other guy. "Or in the cast, for that matter. And this show is supposed to be happening in New York."

"There's a story about Marlon Brando," said Conrad. "When he started to shoot ONE EYED JACKS which he directed, he discovered that there were no minorities on the lot. So he refused to start shooting until they hired a black crew member. And that was the historic breaking of the barrier at Paramount. This wasn't exactly a hotbed of liberal thinking. And not much has happened since."

Later, as they strolled toward the gate, Florence asked Conrad if he really participated in the decision making process.

"Process?" replied Conrad sweeping his hand across his hair. "I thought the 'Fro was in!"

Florence looked as though she had just sucked a lemon.

"Sorry. Just trying to inject a little humor into an otherwise sorry scene."

Florence must have quickly forgiven him; when they said their goodbyes she slipped Conrad her card with a whispered "Call me," followed by a dazzling smile.

Everyone is on the make here, thought Conrad as he hurried back to the relative shelter and peace of his office. But peace was not to be his that day, Conrad discovered. Minutes after he settled into his leather swivel chair with DAILY VARIETY the intercom buzzed. It was his secretary Miranda. Miranda was a sweet twenty six year old skinny southern belle who was marking time working while waiting for her wedding to an aspiring young agent. Although the date had not yet been set, she sported a good sized diamond on her engagement finger. She was expected to cover Conrad and two other lower echelon executives and while not exactly a candidate for Mensa, managed to get done what needed to be done. Conrad liked her because she was one of the few women who didn't come on to him in the aggressive way that seemed to be the modus operandi out here. She was always a pleasure to look at, neatly dressed and perfectly coifed and she like Conrad best because he treated her with more respect than the others did.

"The guard at the gate wants to know if he should pass in someone who wants to see you. Name is Carl Brown. He's not on any appointment list. But he's being insistent." Miranda's voice sounded tinny over the intercom.

"Carl Brown? I'll be damned! Sure, babe, let him in. Thanks."

Carl was an old buddy from the uptown days. They played basketball and joined their first scene class together. Later he was part of Conrad's theatre group. And then they lost touch. He remembered now that he'd heard on the vine that Carl had moved to L.A. How long had it been? At least a couple of years. He straightened the pile of scripts on his desk and looked around the office. Although it was medium sized there was a round glass coffee table surrounded by a two seater couch and two chairs in addition to his sleek wood desk. He knew Carl would be impressed. Conrad had tried to add a few personal touches. A couple of posters of plays he'd been in were mounted on the wall and flanked a hand carved wooden African mask he'd picked up from a push cart in Harlem years before. On one of the end tables alongside the couch was a small stereo system and a pile of LP's and tapes and on the other side was a small brown and white Mexican onyx chess set that Karen had found in an out of the way Mexican shop on Ventura Boulevard and given him for his birthday. Yeh, thought Conrad. He'll be impressed. It sure ain't Harlem.

The intercom buzzed again.

Conrad flipped the switch. "Yep."

Miranda voice crackled a bit. "Mr. Brown is here."

"Send him in, please." Conrad grabbed the script on top of the pile and placed it in front of him open.

Carl opened the door tentatively and stuck his head in. He was a very tall, very dark-skinned man with high cheek bones, large brown eyes and big white teeth that were revealed by a wide grin. He posed in the doorway for a minute, taking it all in.

"Hey, man, look at you!" He crossed to the desk as Conrad rose and they locked hands in the 'brotherhood' handshake.

"Hey, Carl, what's happenin'?"

"Samo, samo, man. But look at you."

Conrad crossed to the couch and motioned to Carl to sit with him.

Carl was wearing jeans, a T shirt and a black leather jacket. The leather thing must be the uniform of the day, thought Conrad. I'd better get me one. Conrad noticed the zippered leather portfolio he carried. Very out of character.

Aloud he said, "It's great to have a steady gig, man. But it's all bullshit. So what're you up to?"

"Hey, you're on the inside, man. Maybe you can make a difference."

Conrad shrugged. If he only knew. "We'll see."

"You think you'll miss the acting?"

"Nobody's been bangin' on my door. I'm hoping to get a chance to direct."

Carl sat up. "Hey, great. Quiet as it's kept, it's been real bad for actors. I've been out here a year and all I've been gettin' is crumbs. Extra work on Sidney's picture and shit. But it's startin' to pick up, and now that you're here I know you'll find stuff for us."

Yeh, sure, thought Conrad. I can't even find stuff for myself.

"We're all countin' on you, bro'. If anybody can do it, you can."

Conrad began to feel a little sick. It was starting already. Once the word was out on the vine, they'd be coming after him, expecting help. Why was it that the few that made it were expected to be responsible for the whole community?

Carl was still talking as he reached into his portfolio and pulled out a photograph. "Here's my new 8x10. Waddya think?"

Conrad pretended to study it, turning it over to look at the resumè on the back. He knew most of the credits Carl claimed as experience were lies, but he also knew that was what you had to do to get anyone to pay attention. The photo itself was okay, but poorly lit. Few people knew how to properly light black skin. He'd noticed that problem on the sets.

Aloud he said only "It's great," and handed it back to Carl.

"No, buddy, you keep it. You never know, right?"

Conrad checked his watch. It was now very clear as to why Carl had suddenly surfaced. Oh well, he thought. Can't really blame him. I probably would've done the same thing.

He stood up. "Listen man, I hate to cut this short, but I got this fuckin' meeting coming up. Why don't you come over to the house for dinner some night?"

"Hey, that'd be great! I'd like to meet your old lady. I heard you married a white chick. Can she cook fit to eat?"

"Come and find out."

Carl started for the door. "Thanks, man. I'll call you." He stopped suddenly. "Hey, I don't have your number."

Conrad moved to the desk and fished a card case out of a drawer. He extracted a card and handed it to Carl with a flourish. "Here you go."

"Whooeee! Impressive! Cards and all." He stood there for a moment shaking his head. "Mmm, mmm. You're lookin' good, Con. Great lookin' threads, man." He tipped an imaginary cap. "Later." and disappeared out the door.

Conrad sank into his desk chair with a sigh of relief.

It'd been hard to put on a front for this old friend. Yet he knew it was what Carl needed. Everyone was looking for a little bit of hope that things might get better. So he knew that he was in for it now that the word was out. He knew that there would soon be a long line of 'me-toos' and 'gimmees' and he'd better figure out a way to deal with it. He wondered if his stomach could stand it and for how long.

CHAPTER 9

As the weeks passed Karen could see Conrad getting more and more unhappy about his life at the Studio. For one thing, he'd stopped talking. No more funny anecdotes or gossip about stars. He came home from work looking exhausted and tense. His conversation was monosyllabic until he'd had a drink or gone out for a half hour to throw balls at the hoop he'd mounted on the garage door. She understood the difficulties he was facing daily, the frustrations and the feelings of impotence that constantly asaulted his self esteem. But short of urging him to quit, she didn't know what she could do about it.

She was doing well at her job. She'd been moved into casting which she liked more than development and which put her closer to actual production. She had nurtured a good relationship with Chuck whose skill at deal making and running a company she admired. And he seemed to have a healthy respect for her knowledge and abilities which he always referred to as 'New York smarts'. He had even invited her to a party at his house. Karen had quickly made up a reason to decline the invitation, knowing how difficult it would be for Conrad. Later, in the shelter of her car as she drove home from work, she wondered if she'd been protecting Conrad or herself and her position in the company. She really didn't know what the reaction would be to a mixed marriage. There had been so much flak about Lanny Davis and his white wife in gossip and in the press. It must have been very hard on the marriage. And on the children. No wonder it had broken up. Better to be on the safe side and keep a low profile when it comes to work, thought Karen. For both our sakes. It's not as though we're hiding. We've been to all the dinners and screenings together. Karen slammed on the brake at a light on Wilshire Boulevard. Oh, hell! she thought. Listen to me. This town and its talent for devious destructiveness is starting to get to me. I mustn't let that happen.

That night Karen made it home first and was in the kitchen seasoning a broiler for dinner when she heard the slamming of Conrad's car door. He was whistling a lilting tune when he came in the house. Karen's spirits lifted. Maybe something good had happened today.

"Hi honey," she called. "How're you doing?"

Conrad crept up behind her and nuzzled her neck. "Great." He put his arms around her waist and squeezed. "Put lots of garlic on it. Mmm, I'm starved."

Karen held up her spice covered hands so as not to dirty his shirt. "Tell me."

"Tell you what?" Conrad put on a poker face.

"Tell me what happened. You look like the cat that swallowed the canary."

Conrad went to the refrigerator and removed a bottle of water. He was always thirsty because he put so much salt on his food, so Karen kept a special bottle filled for him so he could get ice water at a moment's notice. He took a long swig.

"Well?" Karen demanded.

He loved to tease her. "Get that chicken in, woman. Then we'll talk."

She knew he was purposely dragging it out. This was such a change of mood from the past few weeks, Karen's spirits soared. Something really good must have happened.

"Well, what is it?" she demanded finally as she put down a tray of crackers and cheese on the coffee table.

"I made you a drink." Conrad pushed a generous Dewars on the rocks toward her.

"Thanks. So are you going to tell me?"

"We've been invited to a dinner party," he said solemnly.

"Is that all?" Karen couldn't understand all the gaiety. A dinner invitation was a pretty common occurrence out here.

"That's all." Conrad grinned at her and took a sip of his drink.

"You're being maddening! What's this all about?"

"Aren't you going to ask me where?"

"Okay. Where?"

Conrad answered with a question. "Guess who I ran into on the lot today?"

"Con, you're being exasperating. I don't know. Who?"

"Mr. Lanny Davis Jr. He's doing a guest shot on *Wild, Wild West*. We really hit it off. Actually, he said he'd heard about me. He pulled me into his trailer and we hung out while he was waiting for his shot. Now he's my new best friend. And we're invited to dinner and a screening tomorrow night. I hear he entertains and shows movies every night. We made it into the upper echelon, baby! Right up there with all the celebs!"

Karen laughed. If this is what it took to make him happy, she was all for it. She knew he was grasping at straws after the beating his ego had been taking. "Will we meet the rat pack?" she asked.

"Babe, we are going to meet everybody. That's what it's all about."

"Oh God. Wait a minute," Karen gasped.

"What's up?"

"I just remembered. We have a big casting session tomorrow. We probably won't get finished until six or seven. Oh, shit."

"He said around seven. You can leave from the office."

"But I don't want to meet you there. That's no good."

So they made a plan. Conrad would pick Karen up at the office. She would leave her car there and on the way home they would stop off and pick it up so she would be able to use it to get to work the next day. This was the kind of arrangement that had to be made constantly in this car dependent society. Everything had to be worked out according to transportation. Karen was beginning to find it a major source of irritation. Damn! I'm going to have to bring a change of clothes, she thought. But she said nothing. She didn't want to rain on Con's parade. He'd been so down and now for a moment he was happy.

It was another thing about this L.A. life that irritated her. Every day she found herself packing the trunk of her car as though it were a suitcase. Everything was so spread out in this town that if one wanted to do more than one thing in a day, like take a run on the beach after work, one had to pack the car for it. On any given day the weather could embrace at least three seasons: the mornings were spring, the afternoons mid-summer and the evenings sometimes as cool as late fall. She never knew what to wear. Or how to dress. When they first started going out to parties and dinners, Karen wore the clothes she brought from New York, and soon found she was always overdressed. Everyone was much more casual out here, and she quickly learned that pants and tops with some glittery earrings were sufficient for all but the most formal dinners and banquets. Then everyone went all out, wearing starlet formals and sometimes even fur coats, which looked kind of silly in that climate and were really only necessary during a rare cold snap.

It was easier for Conrad. He wore dashikis most of the time now. Not only did it relieve him of the necessity of wearing a tie, which he loathed, it gave him an exotic look and certainly helped him to stand out in a crowd of white people. Karen suspected that it was also an unspoken means to publicly reaffirm his ethnicity.

Aloud she said "I guess I'll have to dress at the office."

Conrad reached over and kissed her. "You'll look gorgeous in whatever you wear. With this body you'll put all those stars to shame."

Wow, thought Karen. He is really thrilled about this invitation. She hadn't seen him this elated since he first got the Studio job. All he needed was a little sign that he belonged to the club.

It was just 6:30 when Conrad pulled into the parking area in front of the low stucco building housing Karen's office. He turned off the Coltrane he'd been listening to on the car radio—he'd finally found some jazz on a university radio station after a long search for decent music—and wondered if he should wait in the car for Karen. Checking his watch again, he decided to go in and get her.

As he entered the reception area Conrad was startled by the tasteful decor. He remembered the often sleazy, sometimes even shabby rooms he'd sat in for hours, waiting for an audition in New York. There were four actors seated around this room. Conrad wondered if they were all reading for the same part. They were so different from one another. One was tall, rangy and redheaded. He tapped his foot impatiently and kept looking at his watch. Another was stocky and round, slightly overweight. He was reading a HOLLYWOOD REPORTER. The third man was coffee colored and when he rose, Conrad thought he must have had Watusi heritage. He was built like a skyscraper with long sharp bones. He walked over to the receptionist, a petite blonde who was sucking a Coke through a straw and thumbing through a magazine.

"Are you serving dinner? We've been here long enough to deserve it," said the Watusi.

The fourth actor, a short fellow who reminded Conrad of Lenny Bruce, joined the Watusi at the desk. "SAG oughta have a law about how long they can keeep us waiting," he said.

The receptionist shrugged. "Sorry. They're doing the best they can. Just take a seat. It won't be long now."

They took their seats again, glaring balefully at Conrad whom they assumed was more competition.

Conrad recalled the frustration with the waiting, waiting, waiting. Thank God I'm out of that, he thought. But he wondered how he was going to spring Karen loose from this in time to make Lanny's. He walked over to the reception desk.

The receptionist glared at him. "Do you have an appointment? I don't have anyone else on my list. We're not seeing anyone else today."

Conrad gave her his most charming smile. "Hi," he began.

"Sorry," she interrupted. "We're finished for today."

Conrad persisted. "I'm Conrad Taylor and I..."

"We're not seeing anyone else!" she raised her voice slightly.

"You know, I think you think I'm an actor." Conrad was determined not to lose his temper with this bitch.

"Please, it's late and I'm tired," she snapped.

Conrad wanted to punch her but he controlled himself. "Would you please tell Karen Stoner that her husband is here." Bad enough we're going to be late, now I have to deal with this little shit, he thought.

The little shit straightened up suddenly and peered intently at Conrad. Was it a tan or...He must be! If not, would he be dressed like that? Aloud she said "Oh, wow! Her husband! I mean, uh, I didn't know Karen was married."

Conrad clenched his teeth. "Well, would you please let her know I'm here?"

"Uh sure...." She picked up the intercom phone, still staring at Conrad as she punched in the extension. "You're husband is here," she said sweetly into the phone. "She said she'll be out in a minute," she announced to Conrad as she hung up. "Why don't you take a seat?" Wait'll I tell the gang about this one, she thought.

Conrad turned away and walked over to the standing ashtray. He lit a cigarette and took a deep drag, tossing the match in the tray. He'd read the bitch's mind as usual. This was a lousy idea. He'd deliberately laid in the sun to get darker and make his ethnicity recognizable. He was tired of the game of 'guess my color'. He'd wanted to shout yes! I am colored, I am a Negro, I am a black man. Now with a deep tan and a dashiki, he was more identifiable. But he'd obviously stepped into it here and maybe made it tough for Karen. There was always something raining on their parade. He'd been in such a good mood in anticipation of tonight. The expectation even helped him control himself on the lot in the face of the usual patronizing that had become his daily diet. It was as though they had let in a retarded person with whom they had to be very patient. It drove him mad.

Minutes later Karen appeared looking sleek and gorgeous in a black cocktail dress and glittery hanging earrings.

"Oh wow," said the receptionist. "You look fantastic."

"Thanks, Bridget. Eddie is taking over." Karen nodded in the direction of the waiting actors. "He'll be out in a second. Goodnight." Eddie, her assistant, was only too happy to stay late and relieve her. She knew he was dying to get her job. "Sorry honey." she grabbed Conrad's arm and headed them towards the door. "We've been backed up all day."

As they settled into the car and Conrad started the motor, Karen let out a sigh. "Whew! I'm whipped. We've been auditioning since ten this morning for the new pilot. And the director doesn't have a clue as to what he's looking for. How do these guys get these jobs I wonder?" Conrad was silent. "It's a good thing I brought everything to the office to change into. I had a feeling we'd be in trouble today." She watched Conrad for a moment. He was intent on his driving. "I wish this party had been tomorrow night. I'd rather be fresh and dazzling when I have to compete with the beautiful starlets who always hang onto you."

"You look great, babe." He made a right turn onto Doheny Drive heading toward Sunset Boulevard.

Karen studied his tightly set jaw for a moment. "Con, are you upset about something?"

"I may have cost you your job by showing up there."

"What are you talking about?"

"The chick at the desk nearly dropped her teeth when she saw me. They obviously didn't know you're married, and to a Nnnnegra! But they will now."

"I never discuss my personal life. I just do my job as well as possible. And you don't know Chuck. It won't make a damn bit of difference."

"Oh, is he one of these Beverly Hills liberals?" he said mockingly as they turned onto Sunset Boulevard and proceeded into that very neighborhood.

"Let's not spoil the evening, darling." She gazed out the window. "Look at that house!" she exclaimed, determined to change the subject. "What awful taste." The wide avenue was lined with huge fence enclosed estates surrounded by rolling grounds.

"That one's owned by an Arab sheik, I think." Conrad glanced at it as they went by. "I read something about it in the L.A. Times. They're trying to get rid of him." He turned right at the Beverly Hills Hotel and started up the hill. "What was that address again?"

Karen reached for the piece of paper on top of the dashboard. "1435 Skyline Drive. Say, I think it must be near Pickfair." She had heard about the Mary Pickford—Douglas Fairbanks estate. It was one of the must-see historic sights for anyone interested in the movie industry.

"Here's Skyline," said Conrad and they turned into a steep winding road that seemed to go on and up for miles. It was hard to see anything but the protective gates and trees and except for occasional signs on posts, impossible to identify numbers. The road became steeper and even more winding. "Jeez! We ought to be on top of the mountain by now."

Karen giggled. "I think this is a Beverly hill, not a mountain. Wow, look at that gorgeous jacamaranda tree!" She spotted something familiar. "There it is I bet. PicFair. I've seen pictures of it. I'm pretty sure that's it."

Conrad pulled over to the side of the road and stopped the car. They looked at the sprawling old fashioned white house. "We're going to be living up here some day," said Conrad. "In a great big house. With a jacamahoosis tree."

"No thanks. Think about cleaning it."

"The servants will take care of that."

"Well, it's a nice place to visit, but give me good old crowded, dirty, on foot New York anytime."

Conrad stared at her. "You're kidding."

"No, I'm dead serious. Imagine having to drive up and down this hill every time you needed a box of Kleenex? This life is not for me."

Conrad started the motor and proceeded up the hill. He knew Karen was just trying to distract him and change his mood, but everything seemed to be getting on his nerves.

"There it is. Over there on the left." Karen sang out. She had spotted the number on the edge of the curb. So that was why they couldn't find any numbers. Properties were marked on the ground.

They drove up to a huge wrought iron gate in front of which stood a very large black man holding a clipboard. He must have been about six feet five with a neck and chest befitting a football star. He wore a dark suit with a black turtle neck sweater. His large bald head held dark, piercing eyes, a flat nose and full lips. But when he spoke it was in a soft, almost whispy, voice. "Good evening," he said as he bent to the window on the driver's side. "May I have your name?"

"Taylor. Conrad and Karen." Conrad exchanged looks with Karen as the man checked his clipboard list. They had both seen the pistol in a holster at the man's side.

"Yes. Welcome." said the armed guard as he found the name on the list. "Just drive right in and park." He pressed a buzzer, and the gate swung back while he stood at attention like a soldier as they drove through.

Once inside they found themselves in a large circular driveway leading to a huge oval where many cars where parked. Further ahead was the mansion, a large two story sprawling white building, somewhat eclectic and unimpressive in its architecture, a sort of neo-Georgian.

A red vested attendant appeared and motioned them to join the parked Rolls Royces, Bentleys and Mercedes. Karen giggled as they slid into a space between a Maserati and an MG. "It's a good thing we didn't come in the Dodge Dart. We really should put a cover over this car. It looks so out of place here. Who are all these rich people?"

"Look at that one. That's a Maserati, I think."

"Are we among the last? Are we late?" Conrad asked the attendant as they got out of the car.

"Oh, no. Most of these cars are Mr. Davis'. He collects them, you know. Right this way, please." And he escorted them to the door of the mansion with a flourish.

On the huge door at about eye level was a brass plaque. Conrad read it out loud. "All those who believe in the brotherhood of man regardless of race, color or creed are welcome here." He whispered to Karen, grinning, "As long as you get past the dude with the gun."

The huge door swung open and waiting for them on the other side was another red-vested attendant, smiling and asking for their wraps. They found themselves in a lushly carpeted entrance hall lined with mirrors and paintings reflecting the prisms of light thrown off by the crystal chandelier hanging above the hall. As they took it all in, a small, wiry black man wearing dark glasses and dressed in a black leather jumpsuit suddenly sprang into view. It was Lanny. He had a cigarette and a fat glass of something amber in one hand and gave Conrad a vigorous brotherhood handshake with the other.

"Hey, baby! So glad you could make it. This the old lady?"

"This is my wife, Karen."

Karen flashed her best smile. "I'm so glad to meet you. I'm a great fan of yours."

Lanny surveyed Karen appreciatively. "Look out! What a body! She's a real fox, man." As though they were long lost friends, he put arms around both of them, steering them into what under ordinary circumstances would be called the living room. It was the size of a ballroom but so gracefully appointed that it had the appearance of a very elegant smoking room in something like the Harvard Club. Large, deep couches and chairs strategically placed next to fine exotic wood tables were all facing in the direction of the walk-in fireplace over which hung an abstract wall mural. One side of the room was a glass wall which looked out on the grounds beyond. To the rear was a long, very modern mirror-lined bar with a row of leather upholstered stools in front of it. It was to the bar that Lanny steered them first saying "Get yourselves a drink and then I'll introduce you around. After dinner I'll take you on the grand tour." And with that he skipped off to greet another arriving couple.

Yet another red-vested person served them each a scotch on the rocks in a beautiful fat crystal glass and they sat at the bar for a moment facing the room and munching on tiny pretzels.

"Wow," said Karen sotto voce. "So this is how the other half lives."

"Look. There's Freddie Prinz over there. And isn't that Raquel Welch with him?" whispered Conrad.

"Yeh, it is. I feel like I just stepped through the looking glass." Karen realized with a start that there were about fifteen people in the room. The place was so large that it had seemed empty when they entered. Everyone looked familiar, but Karen knew that it was because they were all performers of one kind or another. These were the beautiful people: beautifully dressed, beautifully coiffed, beautifully draped around the room. The funny thing was, Karen noticed, they were all ogling each other surreptitiously. They could all qualify as celebrities but they seemed to be just as star-struck as civilians.

"When did you get to be Lanny's best friend?" asked Karen.

"That's the way he is. Like a friendly puppy. How'd you like to live in a place like this?"

Karen could hear the envy in his voice and it made her strangely uneasy. "C'mon. Let's mingle. Let's pretend we're celebrities too," she answered.

"Yeh. James Garner's over there. Let's go talk to him."

A tall, slender black woman with a closely cropped Afro, dressed in a sleek, tight fitting and very decolletè black satin pantssuit suddenly appeared at Conrad's side. "Conrad darling!" she cried as she threw her arms around him. "It's so good to see you. Where have you been?"

"Wha's happenin' baby?" said Conrad as he extricated himself gently from her grip. Karen noticed the switch in his dialect whenever he ran into black people from his past. Conrad turned to her. "Honey, this is Lanny's wife, Rowena. Rowena, this is my wife, Karen."

"How do you do?" said Rowena politely giving Karen a once over that took in every detail.

"Rowena and I went to high school together," Conrad explained.

Karen felt anything but warmth in the woman's scrutiny. "I'm happy to meet you." There was an awkward pause. Karen tried again. "This is a beautiful house." Is it that I'm white or just that the woman doesn't like females, she wondered.

"Thanks. Lanny is very happy here." A gong sounded and its low tone reverberated throughout the room. "Oh, that's Oscar's signal that dinner is served." She squeezed Conrad's arm. "We'll talk later."

Karen watched her as she hurried off to the dining room, gathering guests as she went. "You never told me about Rowena," she said teasingly to Conrad.

Conrad shrugged. "It didn't seem very important. She was a dancer on one of Lanny's shows. One night his date didn't show up and he was so annoyed he grabbed Rowena and took her out instead. They wound up taking a week long yacht trip after which he proposed marriage. Or so the story goes. If it's true, that other chick must be kicking herself from here to New York." Conrad laughed. "Lanny's worth a lot of money."

"Obviously." snorted Karen. "Clever Rowena."

Lanny was already seated when they walked into the dining room. They were startled at the size, elegance and formality of the place. The walls were painted a pale mauve and were decorated with ornate sconces, the pattern of which was echoed in the candelabra in the center of the huge oval table. A crystal chandelier, similar to the one in the entrance foyer hung above the table. The dining chairs were of dark sculptured wood with high backs and upholstered seats that matched the wall shade. Each place was elaborately set with a full complement of shining silver and beautifully decorated china. Karen was surprised at the difference in style from the living room. They live modern and eat period, she thought. As they found their placecards she was relieved to find they were sitting together. Sometimes at these kinds of parties she was relegated to an opposite end with total strangers.

"Ain't this somethin?" Conrad muttered to Karen under his breath.

Karen waited until the white-vested waiter had finished serving her soup and moved on. "It's somethin' allright." she whispered back.

Conrad nudged her. "See that guy over there? Two seats to the left of Lanny. He's a heavyweight feature producer. Marty Ryan. His latest big one just wrapped at Universal last night. I hope I can get to talk to him later."

The dinner was magnificent. Roast lamb, tiny new potatoes, a melange of vegetables, salad, anything but the soul food Karen somehow expected. There were three people serving the food and a steady stream of wines with each course and the whole thing smacked of Le Cirque rather than Sylvia's. Karen for the first time became consciously aware that most of the people at the table were white. Karen wondered whether Lanny actually segregated his guests, serving one kind of dinner for his white friends and another for the black ones. But what black ones? Who among the black community would consider an invitation anything but charity? There were only two people Karen could think of who were on the same level: Sidney and Harry. There were a few TV stars coming up, like Red Foxx and Flip Wilson, but…. The train of thought was interrupted by a tapping sound.

"Announcement, announcement!" cried Lanny, tapping his glass with his fork. The babble in the room obediently subsided almost immediately. All turned towards Lanny expectantly. "Everyone here is invited as my guest at Caesar's Palace when I open in Vegas," he proclaimed loudly. He was beginning to sound as though his dinner was more wine than food. Rowena, who was at the other end of the table opposite Karen, had a stiff smile on her face. The little shit was always making these grand gestures, she was thinking. He's gonna drive us into bankruptcy.

There was a smattering of applause and shouts of "what a guy" and "That's great!"

"When is it?" asked one of the guests.

"November 2nd."

Conrad winked at Karen and whispered into her ear. "See? Next month, Las Vegas. Next year, the world!" He held his wine glass up to her and they clinked glasses solemnly before breaking into not-too-well controlled giggling.

It was during the Baked Alaska that Karen suddenly noticed it. "Oh my God, Con. Look at that," she whispered.

Looking in the direction of Karen's nod, Conrad saw what had shocked her. Marty Ryan had fallen into a deep sleep with his head lying smack in the middle of his lamb and potatoes. The waiters had discreetly left him to snore in his meat. And Lanny had just noticed it too.

"Hey everybody, look at Marty!" Voices dropped as heads turned to observe the phenomenon. Titters, laughter and gasps floated over the oblivious producer who was snoring as though drugged.

"Say, Lanny, what did Maria put in the soup?" asked one of the guests. Maria must be the cook, thought Karen. I've heard of falling asleep on a dime, but this is ridiculous.

Lanny was enjoying it immensely. "The poor bastard is exhausted! Sssh! Don't wake him. Let's all tiptoe out and leave him there."

Marty slept like a baby, head in plate, while they all finished their dessert and coffee and left the table. Karen and Conrad hovered in the doorway to see what Lanny was going to do about him.

"So this is how the celebs behave," said Karen.

"Honey, when you're rich and powerful, you can get away with anything and still be asked back."

Lanny, leaning over Marty, suddenly shouted in his ear. "Time to get up, Marty baby. Dinner's over!"

Marty sat up suddenly, potatoes dripping from his face. "Wun'erful, pal. Wun'erful. Great meal."

Lanny attempted to lift the big man out of his seat. "C'mon old man. I got a waker upper for you upstairs. Let's go." Spotting Conrad in the doorway, he said "Gimme a hand with this, will ya man?" Conrad joined him and helped raise the body to his feet. "Thanks," said Lanny. "Come upstairs with us? I got some great stuff."

"No thanks, not right now. We're doin' fine." Conrad waited for a moment to be sure Marty wasn't going to fall on Lanny.

"Well, anytime, bro. Upstairs, anytime. Ya dig?"

"Yeh, thanks. Later."

He rejoined Karen who had been watching the rescue. "Say, did I miss something? Wasn't he inviting us to see the rest of the house? Why'd you turn him down?" she asked.

"Upstairs is not our scene, baby. Believe me."

Karen stared at him for a minute, then realization dawned on her. "Oh! I get it. I'm really slow. All that food must have clogged my mind."

It was one of the many things about Conrad that never ceased to amaze her. Here was someone who had grown up in Harlem, been on the street, played ball, often hung out with jazz musicians and some of the toughest guys in the neighborhood. Yet whenever drugs were offered, as they were at almost every dinner, party, social gathering of any kind usually discreetly in the bathroom or some adjoining space, Conrad would politely decline, often saying "no thanks, I gave that up when I was ten." Karen had asked him how he managed to avoid getting hooked when he was a kid like most of his buddies did, and he shrugged and muttered something about wanting to be a great athlete. Once when they were at a large dinner party with many of the newly earning black film actors who had begun to emerge in exploit films like BLACULA and SUPERFLY and were making comparatively big money for the first time in their professional lives, the cocaine and marijuana were served with dessert and coffee like after dinner mints. Karen, afraid to seem square and acutely conscious as the only white person at the table that refusal might appear to be negative comment, took a few quick drags on the joint that was handed to her.

She caught Conrad staring at her from across the table and saw the impercepti-ble shake of his head. Later she asked him why he disapproved when everyone else was smoking.

"I'm afraid you'll get to like it, babe. And then we'll be in trouble!" was his tossed off reply. The more serious the issue, the lighter his tone, so Karen knew that there was more to it than what he was revealing. How many of his friends had been wasted by drugs when he was growing into manhood, she wondered. And what saved him? Was it that he was already inured to the lack of accep-tance because of his color and therefore immune to the prodding to belong, to which most adolescents fell victim? Or was it the strictness of his West Indian father and incongruously prim and straight-laced white mother?

As they wandered into the living room they were greeted by Rowena. "Let me show you the rest of the place" she purred. She gathered a couple of the other guests as she headed toward the glass wall which slid open at the touch of a button. They walked along a gravel path edged by flowering bushes and roll-ing lawn until they reached what Karen assumed was a pool house. It was indeed adjacent to a large kidney shaped pool, but she noticed in the dark that there was another small house at the other end.

"This is Lanny's playroom," announced Rowena as she ushered them in with a flourish. Noone was prepared for what greeted them: every known kind of pin-ball machine, carnival game and slot machine lined the walls. There was hardly room to move. It was the personification of a teenage boy's fantasy. "You can't exactly dance in here, but we have another space for that," Rowena giggled. "Follow me!" she sang gayly. And follow her they did around the pool, through the pool house which of course contained every amenity associated with swimming and sunning, then back into the main house to view the gun room. Lanny's collection was famous and the room contained enough weap-onry to accomodate a Civil War with guns mounted on the walls, resting on shelves, some against red velvet.

"It's like a museum," Karen whispered to Conrad.

"Let's hope he stays sane. I'm sure all this stuff works." Conrad whispered back.

After the gun room they went upstairs to view the jacuzzi, sauna and in the middle of the room, a totally glassed-in shower.

"Not much privacy," Conrad observed under his breath. Then there was the video room, filled with cameras, tapes, monitors, VCRs and other equipment.

"Lanny intends to make his own film when he gets some time," announced Rowena.

"Amazing what you can get with a few bucks," Conrad hissed into Karen's ear. "Lanny in Wonderland".

Just then a voice called from downstairs. "We're starting! He's here."

What now? Karen wondered. It was indeed like a trip to some sort of eerie Playland. As they descended the stairs they saw the huge mural above the fireplace slowly lift to reveal an equally huge movie screen. They were ushered to deep brown suede armchairs facing the screen and for the first time Karen realized that there was a projection booth in the wall adjacent to the bar. The 'he' that had been referred to was the projectionist, a greying short pudgy and generally nondescript little man who shook a few hands in recognition and shuffled towards the booth.

All the guests settled into couches and armchairs as the lights dimmed just as they do in a movie house. The bartender came around and took drink orders which he discreetly served as the picture credits began to roll. Conrad and Karen later learned that this was a routine that happened every night starting at about eleven o'clock and continued until Lanny thought he'd had enough. He sometimes watched films all night, drinking and sometimes snorting coke, and guests would peel off as their stamina waned. Lanny was like a little kid, clapping, laughing, making comments at the screen out loud. He seemed to be having a marvelous time and his joy was infectious, although Karen suspected that it was partly the result of a cocaine-aided high shared by some present.

They stayed through the picture, which had just been released and which they had wanted to see anyway.

"This is the way to see a film," yawned Conrad when it was over, stretching his legs. "C'mon, let's split, I've had enough of the high life."

As they said their goodbyes, Lanny protested. "Hey, man, we're just gettin' started. Stick around!"

"Thanks, Lanny. It was great. But I have to go to work in the a.m," replied Conrad giving him the current black handshake.

"Well, come by again soon so we can hang out, bro. And bring this delectable ole' lady with you!" Karen could feel Lanny's teasing eyes on her body even through the darkened, smoky haze.

Conrad was very silent as he guided the car's descent down the curving hills towards Sunset Boulevard. It was very late and they were both exhausted, but Karen sensed that something disturbed Conrad and she wasn't quite sure what that was. She had thought he would continue to be elated at having been included in one of the top echelon 'Hollywood' parties. But here he was in a blue funk. He was doing that more and more lately: throwing her off with his unexpected changes of mood. It made her feel off-balance and nervous.

"It was fun, wasn't it?" She turned to look at him.

"Yep."

"Are you in a bad mood all of a sudden?"

"Nope. Just tired."

"Do you think we ought to go to that Vegas opening he talked about?" Karen persisted.

"Yeh, Maybe. We'll see."

He said very little more. They stopped to pick up Karen's car and she followed behind Conrad to their driveway. In a matter of minutes he had tossed off his clothes, visited the bathroom and fallen into bed.

And though Karen was keyed up, jumpy and wide awake Conrad seemed to fall asleep the minute his head hit the pillow.

CHAPTER 10

1971   L.H. Sullivan first Black to Head U.S. Auto Co.

During the weeks and months that followed Conrad became increasingly withdrawn and moody. Karen tried to break through his silences only to be met with irritation and abrupt retreat. He would come home from work, shoot baskets in the yard until the light faded, eat dinner, then bury himself in a script or watch TV. Weekends were spent playing basketball with 'the guys' at the Poinsietta Place court or watching 'the game' on TV.

In retrospect, it seemed almost as if the party at Lanny's had started him on a downward slide into depression. Karen was at a loss as to how to handle the situation. It was just the opposite of what she had expected. Much to her surprise Conrad finally refused Lanny's invitation to Vegas, making up some excuse about a weekend story conference. Although she knew how he felt about the "talentless white turkeys" as he called the men he had to deal with every day at the studio, resenting their success and the patronizing way they treated him, she also knew he had an enormous respect for Lanny's talent and thought he was a great performer. Why then would he reject Lanny's invitation?

Once in a great while he would relax and agree to go to a Saturday night gathering at the home of one of his new friends. A clique was developing as the second tier of black star actors emerged. They were not as wealthy as Poitier or Davis but newly successful and affluent as the studios discovered there was an audience for black adventure films and TV producers discovered the possibilities for caricature in the black sitcom. Karen would encourage this even though she was always made uncomfortable by the tension her presence as the only white person created. She thought perhaps what was bothering Conrad, in addition to the frustration, was the loss of a connection to a community, the feeling of always being the outsider. She was beginning to understand that viscerally as she never had before. It was what she felt when she was with the new friends he seemed to be making. It seemed as though everyone was on to an inside joke that she couldn't quite comprehend.

Karen had tried to get Conrad to invite some of his struggling relocated New York actor friends to their house, but he had resisted. He didn't want to confront them with his middle class comfort in an all-white community. But this other group had money. They were living well and Conrad didn't have to feel apologetic about his Beverly Hills address or his job at Paramount. It somehow didn't seem to be an accident that most of the people in this group were beautiful and almost as light skinned as Conrad, with the exception of a few comedians and non-visible black writers. They were not exactly welcomed into the Hollywood community at large, but they were acknowledged to the extent of being invited to the big Awards events and Benefit galas. They hung together protectively in much the same way as their less fortunate brothers and sisters in Watts and Compton.

One night Conrad took Karen to a dinner party at Ron Deal's home up a winding hill off Laurel Canyon Boulevard. It was a typical hill house, perched high with a gorgeous view but tucked away from the road so as to be almost impossible to find if you didn't know where it was. Conrad found it like a homing pigeon, even though it was late enough to be completely dark.

"You seem to have been here before," remarked Karen.

"Yeh, drove Ron home from the set one night when his battery went dead. Stopped in for a drink," replied Conrad.

"Oh. You never mentioned it."

Conrad shrugged. "Didn't think it was that important."

Karen let it drop. This was happening more and more. He seemed to need to have a separate existence, one which didn't include her but did include his black friends. It was as though some magnet was pulling him towards them, away from her.

It was an odd, charming little house with one big windowed studio room, a bathroom and a kitchen on the ground level, and two small bedrooms upstairs with another bath. Everything was done in shades of brown and beige, with the generous couch accented with large bright pillows of African design. The walls were covered with large and small oil paintings which Karen later discovered were all done by Ron's wife Carol, who was an interior designer. The couch and arm chairs were upholstered in soft, velvety fabrics and everything sank deeply when sat on. Errol Garner's piano and soft humming wafted through the air along with sweet pungent smells from the kitchen. One Chinese hanging rice paper lamp in the center of the room, together with many chunky candles placed strategically, provided a soft glow over everything.

There were two other couples lounging about the room, laughing, sipping drinks and utterly relaxed. That is, until Karen came into the room. She sensed it immediately. Carol welcomed them sweetly as they entered and everyone greeted them warmly. But Karen saw, or perhaps felt, the imperceptible stiffening of the shoulders, and hooding of the eyes that she had come to recognize. She was introduced to Wes Little and his wife Jackie. He was one of the leads in a new 'revolutionary' series about a cop and his sidekick. It was considered an historic effort at integrating series TV by casting one lead of each color. Then there was Lou Cook and his current lady Angela Adams. Lou had just played the heavy in the film Ron had starred in which had wrapped the day before. Angela was tall and bony with a beautifully coiffed afro and much silver jewelry. Karen learned that this party was a celebration of the completion of the film.

The food was spectacular. Everything was served buffet style and seemed to be a mix of southern, Creole and good wholesome American cooking.

"Carol, you're a genius!" exclaimed Karen as they scraped dinner plates and stacked them in the dishwasher. "How do you make that fantastic sweet potato dish?"

"Oh, it's easy. You mash up some yams with a half a stick of butter, add some sugar, nutmeg, a couple of egg yolks, about a teaspoon of rum, a bit of vanilla, oh, and some evaporated milk. Then you toss it into the blender and bake it in a casserole dish at about three fifty. And I like to put marshmallows on top, but you don't have to." Carol smiled. "Got it?"

"Got it." Of course Karen hadn't gotten it. Carol went so fast, all she retained of the recipe was the teaspoon of rum, which was a surprise. She didn't know if it was a deliberate effort to be polite but not really surrender the specifics, but she had gotten the gist of it so she wasn't going to press the issue. Karen had been doing a lot of experimenting with 'soul food' lately, in the hopes of cheering Conrad up, and this would probably be another one of the experiments. She could always call Carol up and get her to repeat it.

They sat around talking after dinner, enjoying the fullness of their stomachs and the warm feeling of contentment that envelops one after a really good meal. Ron replenished the wine glasses and offered the men some choice cigars. They were exchanging battle stories about the film industry and who was doing what to whom when suddenly the doorbell rang.

"Are you expecting anyone else?" asked Carol.

"Nope," replied Ron as he went to open the door.

Two white men, one tall and well built, the other shorter and chunky, stood in the doorway. "Hi," said the tall one.

"Hello." Ron faced the two men as they seemed to peer inside.

"How're ya all doin?" asked the tall one. He seemed to expect to be invited in.

Ron's body stiffened as the two men inched forward into the room.

"We're doin' fine. Can I help you?" Ron replied politely. The living room got vey quiet as everyone felt that danger had suddenly entered the room.

"Is Alan here? He said he'd be here," asked the chunky one, looking around, checking out the room.

"Sorry. There's no Alan here. I think you have the wrong house." Ron was keeping his cool but slowly edging them back out the door.

Lou arose, stretching to his full six feet three and joined Ron at the door. "Wha's up?"

"No problem," grinned tall one. "I guess we stumbled into the wrong house. Sorry." He and his buddy backed slowly out. "Have a great evening."

Chunky giggled. "Yeh...heh, heh...sorry to butt in. Must have mixed up the numbers." They retreated into the darkness as Ron carefully closed and locked the door.

Ron stood there with his hand on Lou's arm for a couple of minutes listening as the rest of the group, now alerted, watched them. "Do you hear a car motor? I don't hear a damn thing." he muttered to Lou finally.

"They must be walking." replied Lou.

"Who walks in these hills? Alan my ass. Those mother fuckers are looking for trouble." Lou nodded in agreement.

As they came back to the group Conrad tried to lighten things up. "Here come de fuzz. See man, that's what happens when you're a big star. Now that you've made it you're red meat!"

Ron was not amused. Fists clenched he growled, "Those bastards had better not fuck with me!"

Karen whispered to Conrad. "I don't get it. What just happened here?"

"Those guys were probably plain clothes. They were hoping to find something to pin on Ron. Someone probably tipped them that he was having people in tonight. They were hoping to catch him with drugs or weed so they could take him down. The minute one of us looks like we're going to make it they go after us."

"Oh Con. Aren't you being a little paranoid?" asked Karen. She regretted it as soon as it was out of her mouth.

Conrad's nostrils flared, but he controlled the urge to shout at her. He didn't want any of them to hear this exchange. "Damn it Karen," he said between clenched teeth. "How many times do I have to remind you that this is a southern town?" He got up abruptly and went into the kitchen for another drink.

Karen had to admit that he was right. She hadn't even told Conrad about the thing that had happened to her the week before because she knew how it would enrage him and make his mood even worse than it had been. One of her old girlfriends from New York had a part in a workshop production out in Santa Monica and she'd wanted to see it but her car was in the shop getting a tuneup. Conrad coincidentally had a meeting about a project with someone in Pacific Palisades. So he'd arranged to drop Karen at the play and have their new friend Brian, who was also in the play and who lived near them, drive her home. Brian was a lightskinned black actor and screenwriter who had come from a wealthy family, been a Rhodes Scholar and talked with an ever so slight British accent. He was very bright and Conrad got a kick out of him, so he was one of the very few that had been to the Taylor home.

After the show Karen and Brian met at the stage entrance of the one hundred seat theatre and Brian led her to his elegant little MG convertible. Karen remarked about what a cute car it was and Brian, a bit pompously, explained that he'd bought it in England and had it sent over. They hadn't driven more than ten minutes when they were pulled over by an L.A. P.D. squad car. Karen, in her innocence, thought perhaps Brian had been speeding and she hadn't noticed or perhaps one of his lights had blown out. There were two cops, one of whom went to the driver's side, one to the passenger side. Karen noticed that the one approaching her had steely blue eyes and blond hair and, to her horror, that his right hand rested on his very large revolver.

"Would you get out of the car, please?" said blue eyes in a low monotone.

Karen was beginning to panic. "Oh, what's the matter?"

"Just get out of the car, ma'am."

As she got out she saw the other cop had Brian doing the same. He was taken to the back of the car as this cop stationed himself in front of her and obstructed her view. With shaking fingers Karen extricated her driver's license from her purse when asked for ID. Wild thoughts flew through her mind. Was

Brian in trouble? Was he wanted for something? Had someone been hurt? She kept asking for an explanation but was greeted with silence as the cop stepped away. Hand still on gun and eyes never leaving her, he walked back to the squad car and called in the information on her license. Meanwhile the other cop had Brian spread eagled against the car as he patted him up and down. Then he came back and seemed to be searching the car.

"This is outrageous!" she yelled. "Isn't anyone going to tell us what's going on?"

Just as the blue-eyed cop moved towards her, a voice called out on the radio and he quickly turned back to respond. He said a few words to the other cop that Karen couldn't hear and then returned to her, handing her the driver's license.

"Okay, you're free to go." He was on his way back to the squad car before Karen could exhale.

"Hey, wait a minute," she protested with all the righteous indignation of a clear conscience, following him. "What was this all about? I demand to know!"

Blue eyes shrugged, mumbling something about having received an APB on a woman who fitted Karen's description. He leaped into the car alongside the other cop and, red light whirling, they gunned the motor and raced down the avenue towards whatever they'd just been called to do.

Brian sat tensely clutching the wheel, a grim look on his face. "Saved by the bell" he muttered. "They must have gotten a real call."

"Whew!" Karen couldn't stop trembling, but now it was more fury than nerves. "What the hell was that?"

"That was the L.A.P.D. going after a black man together with a white woman in an expensive car," replied Brian grimly. "They were probably bored and thought they might score a drug bust or at the very least find something to hassle us with."

"But it was me. They said there was an APB on someone who looked like me."

"Total bullshit, my dear."

Yes, this was a southern town, thought Karen. But only the people with the wrong skin tones knew the dangers that lurked beneath the serene surface of sunlight, warmth, peach trees and white sand beaches. This constant awareness, coupled with the accompanying tension that it produced, was only a partial explanation for Conrad's growing emotional distress. The pressures from the black community in this town had to be factored in as well. He was being compelled to choose sides, to select an identity. In this carefully segregated, sharply fragmented town one had to make a choice. There was the entertainment industry, and there were the service industries and the business industries. There were the valley people, the Beverly Hills people, the Malibu people, the West Hollywood types and the Hollywood types. There was the clique of upscale and highy successful entertainment industry moguls, the clique of star film actors, of star television actors, second tier industry people who were moderately successful and of the techie and crafts people. Everything and everyone fell into categories and cliques.

And the same was true for the black community. There was the suddenly successful new breed which started with a few comedians and was developing into a larger group. Then there were the up and coming and the wannabees. There were those who were beginning to venture into the white communities for residences and those lower on the scale who confined themselves to the eastern sections, closer to Watts and Compton. There were those who came from New York and Chicago and some who were native Californians. And then there was always that ever present intra-community self determining division of light skinned and dark skinned. The country, asleep for ages under a patchwork quilt of bigotry, was now awakened by leaders, marches and even legal and government action which challenged these cliques and attempted to force more interaction. But forced interaction in its very compliance breeds hostility and resentment. And this is where they were and where Conrad was. Caught in the middle of a maelstrom not of his own making, made worse by the accident of his birth which now and always left him planted right in between; useful as a tool of compliance, acceptable to a rare few on either side but more often resented by both.

"Earth to Karen." Conrad nudged her. "Where did you go?"

Karen realized with a start that she had totally blocked out the room. "Sorry. I kindof got lost in thought." She hoped she hadn't been rude. She had no idea what the rest of those present had been talking about. "But, you know, Con, I have to say you're right, finally. This is a southern town in the most hateful sense."

They went home shortly after that.

"They're very nice people," said Karen as the car descended the hill. "I like them."

"Well, you'd never know it," responded Conrad. You certainly didn't join in the conversation much. Unusual for you." He turned to grin at her.

"Well, I was busy listening and learning."

"Oh yeah? I think they got the impression you were aloof."

"Aloof?" sputtered Karen. "You don't know what you're talking about. If anything, I was the one making the effort."

"What do you mean 'making the effort'? Is being with my friends so hard? I put up with your little gold-chained Jewish boys all week long. Surely…."

"Whoa!" cried Karen. "<u>My</u> little Jewish boys? Where did that come from?"

This was a first. Alarm bells went off in her head. She knew that the time had come for them to have a long heart to heart talk but she also sensed that this was not the right time so she let it drop and remained silent as they glided through the deserted streets of Beverly Hills. Gazing out the window at the oddly shaped buildings on Wilshire Boulevard she nursed her anxiety about what seemed to be happening to their relationship. She didn't know exactly what was causing it, but Conrad was beginning to change and Karen was sure it had something to do with the job.

Or perhaps it was some new influence on him that was pulling him away from her. She knew less and less about what he did and who he saw when they weren't together. He used to give her a blow by blow description of his day when he came home from work, making funny observations, acting out the characters and often sending her into hysterics. But lately he'd been silent with the apology that he was tired, or that the day's events were so negative he just wanted to forget about it. Karen knew that most of the problem lay in his frustration. He wasn't being allowed to do anything creative and he was made to feel like a door stop. But she didn't have a clue as to how to help the situation, how to make things better for him. Perhaps she should quit her job and spend more time developing some project with him, she thought. Maybe they could produce a play for him to direct.

"Are you pissed off about something?" asked Conrad as they rolled into the dark driveway and he switched of the headlights.

"No. Why?" Karen got out and slammed the car door.

"You haven't said a word in ten minutes. Very atypical." He walked towards her studying her face in the reflection of the the full moon that hovered over them.

"Oh Con," Karen threw her arms around him and pressed her body against his. "I love you."

"I love you too, baby." He held her tightly for a moment. "Look at those stars. Isn't it a beautiful night?" It was one of those perfect skies, cloudless and dotted with stars that shone brightly in the surrounding darkness and seemed to blanket the earth.

"And look at the full moon." The nightblooming jasmine hung in the air with a sweet, heady perfume and the air swirled gently around them nudging them with a soft breeze. Karen wanted him to hold her like this and never let go, as if somehow their closeness would protect them from the world outside.

He sighed and whispered softly. "If only we could just enjoy the place and not have to deal with the people in it."

They made love that night for the first time in a couple of weeks. It was passionate and demanding lovemaking and Karen felt a sense of desperation in the intensity of Conrad's caresses. He kissed the length and breadth of her body, lingering over her breasts as she ran her hands over the taut smooth skin that covered the hard mounds of his muscle. She could feel the pulsing of his veins and the beating of his heart against her which seemed to be in time with hers.

"Don't let them pull us apart," she whispered into his neck.

He entered her like a nomad seeking an oasis and she welcomed him with a gasp of pleasure. This was the moment she lived for, the time when she felt complete. They lay still for a moment joined and throbbing together.

"Oh, darling, don't let them hurt us," she whispered holding his face in her hands.

"I won't, I won't, I won't" he breathed with the slow rhythmic thrusting of himself deeper and deeper inside her. They didn't want it to ever end, but finally surrendered and climaxed together. Panting and exhausted, neither moved and they fell asleep holding each other. A little while later, Karen awoke and slid out from under Conrad carefully so as not to wake him.

"Stay," he muttered and threw his arm over her drawing her close.

The next morning when Karen awoke, Conrad was already up and dressed in shorts and tee shirt.

"What time is it?" croaked Karen hoarsely.

"Go back to sleep. It's only nine thirty." Conrad was putting on heavy white socks over ankles thick with ace bandages. He never wore fewer than three pairs of socks when he wore sneakers. He said they protected his ankles.

"But it's Sunday, honey. Where are you running to?"

"I'm going to play some ball with the guys." He reached for his huge heavy duty Addida sneakers.

"So early? Can't we at least have some breakfast together first?"

Conrad carefully laced up his sneakers and patiently explained that he didn't want to play ball on a full stomach. He would just grab some juice and coffee. When he saw her turn over and bury her head in her pillow he added that if she wanted to, she could meet him at the Poinsietta court in a couple of hours and they would go somewhere for brunch.

"Okay, great." Karen hated Sunday brunch in the restaurants because the decent ones were always packed and noisy, but this was the first time he'd suggested including her. She didn't want to miss the chance to see what he was doing when he wasn't at work or with her, and meet whomever he was doing it with. "What time?"

"Make it noon. Meet me at the court."

"Okay, darling. Have a good time." Karen turned over and closed her eyes. Another hour of sleep would be nice, she thought. She wasn't exactly sure where the court was, but they'd driven past the park many times and she was sure she'd find it if she went east on Santa Monica Boulevard. She suddenly realized that they would be stuck with both cars and silently cursed the town which made driving everywhere a necessity.

Conrad eased the Grand Prix out of the driveway, relieved that Karen's Dodge Dart had come in first and he wouldn't have to go through the business of musical cars that usually drove him nuts. That was one of the things his New York psyche could never get used to. The car was the substitute for legs. He resented the fact that he was deprived of the use of his legs. In New York he used to walk everywhere and when he didn't have time to walk he rode his bike all around the city.

The other evening just for the hell of it he took a stroll down Maple Drive towards Olympic Boulevard, not with any destination in mind, just to stretch. Within minutes a patrol car glided alongside and a cop got out and asked to see his I.D. The cop had, as usual, given him the 'are you one of them?' stare and seemed quite stunned when he saw the Beverly Hills address and the Paramount Gate Pass. Yeh, thought Conrad. What's a nice nigger like you doing in a place like this? Just taking a stroll, mother fucker. But he'd learned to keep his mouth shut. The officer had muttered something about not seeing many people on the street in this neighborhood by way of lame apology and had regretfully retreated to his car reminding Conrad to take it easy which Conrad knew meant 'watch your step'. Sorry to disappoint you, asshole. He wondered if he would have been stopped if Karen had been with him. He hadn't told her about the incident, hadn't wanted to provoke a whole discussion which he knew would be inevitable once he brought it up. It is what it is, he thought. Step over the shit or clean it up. And I don't have the shovel yet.

It was so much easier in New York, easier to maintain a certain anonymity as just a couple of drops in a sea of humanity. Here it seemed as though they were living in a small town composed of isolated but warring factions. Conrad wondered if they'd made a huge mistake coming here. Yes, they were living well, he was making a good salary, doing far better than he ever had in the east. But he'd had stomach cramps for months from the effort of holding himself in, reigning in his temper. He was constantly juggling the pulls and pressures from the black community, from the jokers at Paramount, from Karen and her friends.

If he could only get into a position of some power so he could manage it all, maybe even bring them all together. He was sure he could think of a way if they would just let him function. Ha!, he thought grimly. Like tongue exploring sore tooth, he let himself recall the meeting he'd been called to at the end of the day on Friday. Biff had sent word that he wanted him to attend a story meeting in his office at four o'clock. Conrad's heart had jumped, thinking that perhaps, after all this time, Biff had actually read the treatment he'd given him ages ago. The day had gone by agonizingly slowly while Conrad roamed the lot, looked in on his mail room pal to exchange a few current jokes, and checked out the working sets. Finally maybe I'll have something to do, he thought. Promptly at four he appeared at Biff's half opened door.

"Hey Con, c'mon in," called Biff. He was sprawled in his big highbacked brown leather swivel chair, positioned so he could see not only the door, but everyone seated in front of him.

It seemed mandatory in Hollywood that an executive's office reflect his level in the pecking order and Biff's clearly reflected his top position. The room was huge with deep piled moss green carpeting and antique oak furniture. Two walls of glass overlooked the studio streets and the remaining walls were lined with bookcases filled with scripts, tapes and even the occasional book. Biff's desk was carved oak and looked like something out of a Victorian period film. The top was smooth and empty, completely devoid of ordinary distractions like papers or phones but Conrad knew they must be hidden somewhere behind that massive piece of furniture; he heard a faint buzz from time to time which Biff studiously ignored. The armchairs circled in front of the desk were equally plush, upholstered in a rich green, beige and brown print material and in the center was a magnificent brown and white marble coffee table mounted on gilt rococo legs. There were two large couches at the other end of the room covered in a gold satiny fabric. Conrad counted at least four differently colored Tiffany lamps strategically placed around the room.

Conrad was startled to see three other men there. One of them he recognized because he'd seen him on the set of "*Great Times*." He was touted as one of the currently busiest and most successful sitcom writers in the business. The other two were strangers.

Biff rose to make the introductions. "I think you know Rich Wink. You've already worked together haven't you?"

Conrad shook hands with the tall, slim man with the long loose jaw who gave him a wide toothy grin and a big paw. "How're ya doin'?" drawled Wink. Conrad couldn't take his eyes off the huge silver and turquoise ring on the paw and the matching belt buckle that circled black suede jeans. Conrad surrendered to the urge to look at his shoes. Yep. There they were. Lizard skin cowboy boots. The other two men turned out to be producers. Sid Jaffe, who Conrad had heard of but never met, was a chubby, middle aged balding guy with the usual black leather jacket, jeans and gold chains. Stan Kimmer was fortyish, nondescript, wearing buff colored Daks trousers and a plaid sport shirt under a cardigan sweater with an alligator on it. This one looked like he'd just come from playing golf. Squares and a half, thought Conrad.

Why did Biff call me in? Each of them nodded with a polite "Hi" as they were introduced, then quickly turned their attention to Biff. It was clear to Conrad that he'd already been discussed with those present and that their response to him was more obligatory than welcoming.

"Conrad," Biff was saying, "I'm putting you on this project. You'll be part of the team. Especially the writing. We're very excited about it. I think it's gonna be a winner."

For a moment Conrad's heart leaped. Finally a real assignment on a real project. Something to do. Maybe even something to write. Possibly a credit that would help him move forward. His joy was short lived. Biff went on to explain that the show was a sitcom about black family life, with the head of the house played by that 'new little black comic', Floyd Flann. Conrad's heart sank. He knew Flann's work. He knew exactly where they were going. Another cartoon. Another minstrel show for the white folks. Biff was talking fast now, extolling the virtues of the work done so far by the team, adding that they also had the great Mabel Moss to play the mother.

"Oh yes," nodded Conrad. "The 250 pounder. That figures."

The men eyed him warily. Biff jumped in with "Can't you see them together? What a sight gag, before they even say anything!"

Conrad began to feel very sick to his stomach. He wiped the sweat off the top of his lip. "So what do you want me to do?"

He knew that this was the moment of truth. He was either going to keep a tight lid on himself, or tell them what he thought of them and walk out. He wanted desperately to walk out, but he knew that it would be the end of the possible dream. This was a small town and word would spread around faster than the wildfires that plagued L.A. in the dry season. Were they thinking that he could write it? No way. "What's my assignment?" he repeated.

"Well, we've got the pilot and three half hours." Wink was on his feet now, pacing back and forth. "And we think they're right on the money. But Biff thinks…." he paused for a moment, trying to make it clear that it was Biff's idea and not his own.

Biff jumped in. "We need you to look at the scripts and check them out. You know, make sure the dialogue's authentic, know what I mean?"

Conrad couldn't help himself. Everyone looked so uncomfortable he had to laugh. "You mean make sure they all talk that ni…black talk?" he chuckled. He'd almost said it but caught himself knowing that it would be pushing it too far. I wish I could take a picture of this, he thought. They all look like they just ate shit. The fucking clowns! Next they'll be giving me an apron and a tray. The now familiar pain in the pit of his stomach was getting more persistent.

As Conrad pulled into the Plummer Park area he tried to put the memory of Friday's events behind him. He hated himself for not having had the guts to tell that bunch what he thought of the project, of them, of the whole damn scene. He knew that Biff hadn't yet looked at the treatment that had been sitting on his desk for what seemed like months. The asshole didn't even know if Conrad was an able writer. He was just trying to protect himself from making some critical error and winding up with pickets or something. It had happened at some other studio. Now that the discovery of a minority market had been made, everyone was jumping on the bandwagon to get those numbers. But they didn't have a clue as to how to go about it and these were tricky times. The networks were very jumpy about controversy.

Conrad made his way along the path adjoining the tennis courts, anxious to play some ball. He knew that the physical release would help dissipate some of the rage that welled up in his gut whenver he thought about the job. He was delighted to see three brothers already on the court, practicing. Carl Brown was shooting jump shots and J.T. and Ed were playing a short one on one game. J.T. was a tall light-skinned black man with a goatee and a neat Afro who Conrad had met recently through Carl. Conrad liked him; he was bright, articulate and political. He seemed to be one of the leaders in the community. Ed was a writer, a strong, very dark, chunky guy who didn't say much but played his ass off. Conrad was usually matched against him and they often locked horns. Probably because they were both mad as hell and taking it out on the game, thought Conrad. Carl, the actor, was always the moderator, the politi-cian.

It was strange playing here. Such a difference from the gritty, pockmarked asphalt street courts of New York City. Here the court was surrounded by neat lawns, trees and lots of white people in white tennis clothes or jazzy leisure suits. We look like we were dropped here from another planet, mused Conrad as he looked as this small group of sweaty tee shirts and ragged shorts.

They played two on two competing as though it were the playoffs, as though their manhood depended on winning. Elbows flying and bodies shoving they grunted and groaned, seeming to revel in the pain inflicted on self and others. It was a rite of venting, of the exorcism of suppressed emotion. It was finally, a release. Conrad drove in for a lay-up and was rammed by Ed just as he reached the basket.

"Hey, mother fucker. You fouled me." Conrad had had enough of Ed's macho crap.

"Watcha talkin' about? It's called deefense," Ed shrugged.

"You know fuckin' well what I'm talkin' about!"

"Okay, c'mon. Let's play ball," said Carl. These two had a conflagration every time they played. It was getting boring.

"Listen, I'm tired of taking shit from this mother…" Conrad fumed.

"Who're you callin' a mother, mother fucker?"

J.T. put himself between the two men. "You're acting like two year olds. Let's just finish the damn game."

Later, as Conrad and J.T. sat on a nearby bench, toweling themselves down and removing the ace bandages from their ankles, they talked about the con-stant eruptions that had invaded their playing of late.

"I can't stand Ed, man. He's out of control. Waddya say we call somebody else next time?" muttered Conrad.

"You know, man, it takes two. What's up your ass lately?" J.T. looked him square in the eye.

Conrad shook his head. "I don't know. I've had shits like Ed go after me all my life, but lately I have no tolerance for it."

"Save it for the honkies, man. That's who you're really mad at."

Conrad shoved his towel into his bag. "Lately I don't know who's worse, the honkies or the folks."

"Life would be a lot easier for you if you'd just decide where you belong," said J.T. softly.

"Now what the fuck does that mean?"

J.T. fell silent for a moment. He studied the zipper on his bag and then stared at the ground.

"Well??" demanded Conrad. It was clearly a challenge.

"Well, this is probably the worst time to tell you this, but you're going to hear about it pretty soon anyway...." J.T. paused.

"Wha's up, man?" Conrad was losing patience.

And the story unfolded. It seemed that Farrakhan was in town. He was the new and rapidly rising Muslim leader that everyone was so excited about. And J.T. and his wife Nancy had invited the whole crowd to a party at their house to meet Farrakhan and hear him speak. Everyone was thrilled about the opportunity to get together and hear what he had to say.

"That's funny," said Conrad. "Karen hasn't said a word about it."

"That's what I'm trying to tell you, man. We couldn't ask you." J.T. was examining the ground again.

"Why the hell not?"

"Well, Nancy and I feel like shit about it, but you know Farrakhan. He won't be in the same room with a white Jewish woman."

Conrad just stared at him.

"Sorry, man."

"So that's where you were going with that 'where I belong' crap. Why would I want to belong to anything that ignorant bastard was a part of?" Conrad tried to keep his cool. J.T. was one of the few people in this lousy town that he felt any kind of connection with and he didn't want to lose that. But he felt betrayed. Excluded, deceived and ultimately betrayed. They had chosen this so-called leader and his narrowminded bigotry over him and that hurt. Sure, they flocked to him when they thought he might give them work or be instrumental in helping advance their careers. But when the chips were down, whose side were they on? Certainly not his.

"So that's how it is, man. Of course, it would be great if you could come by yourself." J.T. had collected his stuff and was getting ready to split. "We want you to be there."

Conrad had so many conflicting emotions at that moment he found it impossible to speak, so he just nodded.

"Later, man." J.T. hurried away.

Conrad checked his watch. Five to twelve. Karen would be here any minute, and he was grateful that the game was over and everyone had left. He certainly wasn't in the mood for all the negative vibes her arrival would have produced. He admitted to himself that he had subconsciously planned it this way, deliberately giving her a later time than he thought the game would take. He thought about what J.T. had said. Where do I belong? he wondered. How should I handle this snub? Why am I always the man in the middle?

When Karen arrived Conrad was sitting on the bench, gym bag beside him, gazing at the empty basketball court. She knew immediately that something was amiss. "Where is everybody? I was hoping to meet the guys." It was obvious that he had planned it this way and it hurt. "Game over already? Is something wrong? Did you get it in the hip again?" The last time he played he had fallen on his side and it had bothered him for days.

"Nah. Just twisted my ankle a little." He grinned at her.

She grinned back. "Well, it wouldn't be a good morning if you didn't come away with a little injury, right?" Karen suspected that whatever was eating him was more than physical. "Listen, darling. We don't need to go to a restaurant. What do you say we go back to the house and I make you some pancakes and bacon and..."

"Got any bagels?" Conrad put on his idea of a Jewish accent. "How can ve hef a brunch mitout a bagel?"

"We'll stop and pick some up on the way. And don't get anti-semitic with me or I'll poison your bacon."

"Who's anti-semitic? I love bagels." He put his arm around her as they walked out of the park. "I'm sorry I dragged you all the way over here."

Karen smiled. "No sweat." She was glad of the chance to get him alone and all to herself at home. It was time for that talk.

CHAPTER 11

※

They were comfortably full and entwined on the couch with the Sunday NEW YORK TIMES which they'd found right near the bagel place on Pico, much to their delight. After a time and because Conrad seemed a little more relaxed, Karen gently suggested that this would be a good time to have their often promised talk.

"Talk, talk, talk. That's all I do all week. Why do Jews love to talk so much?" said Conrad impatiently.

"Con, don't start that. You know it bothers me. Whenever you hang out with the folks you come home sounding like one of those Black Muslims." Conrad snorted and turned to the Sports section.

But Karen persisted. She was determined not to let this opportunity slip by. And finally by prodding until she was in danger of nagging, she got him to open up to her. Gradually all the details of the events of the last few days came out along with the built up anger and frustration. At first he avoided the most recent issue and talked about work.

"So you know who they got to produce and write the new black sitcom?" he went on. "Three snotty white assholes who are making it into a fucking nigger-shit cartoon. And what is Mr. Token doing? I'm checking the fucking dialogue to make sure it's <u>authentic!</u>" Conrad rose and went to the cabinet where the scotch was stored. He poured himself a good sized drink and went into the kitchen to get some ice.

"Isn't it a little early for that?" called Karen.

"No, it's not. You want one?"

"No thanks," Karen replied. She'd better keep a clear head, she thought. This is not going to be easy.

Conrad reappeared, flopped onto the couch and put his feet up on the coffee table, ice tinkling in the glass. As he sipped the amber liquid he began to unwind and talking seemed to come more easily. He revealed what he had experienced the first time they went to visit Lanny, how he felt like they were the poor relatives being allowed to see how the other half lived. All that ever so visible money and success made his teeth ache with the desire to get some of that. He knew that on another level that's how his newly acquired friends who lived in places like Compton and Watts would feel if they came to visit Conrad and Karen in their comfortable upper middle class Beverly Hills surroundings. They were still viewing him with a bit of distrust because of his light skin and good hair. So he never felt comfortable about inviting anyone to his home.

And he felt like an oddity when he socialized with Karen's white friends. They were always a bit too polite, too curious about his heritage. Was he white, black or Egyptian? The question inevitably arose in one form or another. And everyone was always so damn careful. Including himself. Nobody wanted to get caught saying the wrong thing, the hurtful thing, in the presence of the potential 'enemy'.

"Oh Con," Karen protested. "Aren't you exaggerating? My friends are crazy about you and you know it."

Conrad assured her that she couldn't possibly know what it was like, or feel the vibes the way he did. He confessed that he'd been thinking about leaving L.A. and going back to New York, but everytime he thought about it he remembered the struggle to stay afloat there. At least here he was making a good living, even though it meant being emasculated most of the time and developing stomach ulcers. He just had to learn to bear seeing all the white boys catching the brass ring just beyond his fingertips. There was always the lure of the possibility that he might score with something. And then there was the weight of responsibility that went with being another 'first', being the only black man in an executive studio position. Conrad jumped up to pour himself more scotch.

"You know how many black folks come to see me every week pleading for help? Actors, directors, writers, you name it. They act like I'm the Pope. I'm supposed to be their saviour. We all want a piece of the pie and I'm supposed to be the one who can get it for them. Little do they know!" he said bitterly as he sat down again.

Karen put her hand on his knee and said softly, "It seems to me the 'folks' only know you're one of them when they want something from you."

"Oh, I'm one of them alright. It's not me that's the problem." Conrad regretted saying it the minute it escaped his lips.

"What does that mean?" demanded Karen.

It was as though he'd dropped a curtain. "Forget it."

They were silent for what seemed to be a very long time. Then Conrad rose.

"Please don't go. We're not finished," said Karen.

"I've got to pee. Okay?" He headed for the bathroom.

Karen suspected she was treading on dangerous ground by forcing him to air the problems that seemed to be eating at his innards. Perhaps the more he voiced them the more depressed he would get. But she knew they hadn't covered it all, that there was more. Perhaps his emotional state also had to do with the fact that she was doing well career wise, making progress, new contacts, a new circle of friends. The comparison must constantly be highlighting his frustration with the stasis thrust upon him. Did she dare to press on? Karen's instinct told her that if they didn't confront the issues, didn't face the devils and deal with them together, their marriage would be in deep jeopardy. She flashed for a moment on that horrible screenwriter at Marie's party and his dire prediction about them. That was ages ago, or so it seemed, and she was beginning to understand what he meant about a town full of ogres waiting to pounce.

As Conrad emerged from the bathroom she took the plunge. "What else has happened Conrad? she called to him. "What's going on? You haven't told me everything, have you?"

He came back into the living room and retrieved his drink. "No, I haven't. And I think it's better that way."

"Why?" she demanded.

"Because it's only going to upset you, and it's something I have to decide how to deal with. It's my problem." He went into the kitchen for more ice.

Karen followed him and stood in the doorway. "I thought this was a partnership. I thought we were going to share everything."

Conrad banged the ice tray against the sink to loosen the cubes. "Okay, you win. It's no big thing. J.T. and Nancy are having a party to which we are not invited."

"What? Why not? Why aren't we being invited?" Karen was shocked. They had been the one couple from Conrad's recently met group of friends who had seemed the most welcoming and with whom they got along the best.

Conrad pushed past her into the living room.

"How come?" Karen repeated, following him. "How come we're not invited?"

"Does it matter?" sighed Conrad as he poured an inch more of scotch into his glass.

"Damn well it matters! What's the story? I thought we were friends. At least that's how it seemed."

Conrad took her hand and sat her down next to him on the couch. He knew this was going to be hard so he took a sip of the biting liquid to fortify himself against the reaction he expected. "Karen, do you know who Farrakhan is?"

"Yes, I've read a little about him. He's one of those militant Muslims, isn't he? Kind of a scary guy, full of hate."

"He's rapidly becoming one of the big leaders and very respected among certain members of the black community. You might say he's a rising star."

"I'm sorry to hear it," said Karen grimly.

Conrad put his drink down carefully and faced her. "The party is for him. He's a kind of celebrity, you see. and everyone wants to meet him, see what he's about. So J.T. and Nancy have invited everybody who is anybody. It's kinda the event of the season."

Karen stared at him. "So?"

"So that's why <u>we</u> are not invited." He was hoping she'd get it, hoping he wouldn't have to say it.

"I don't understand. Aren't we anybody?"

Conrad sighed. She wasn't going to make it easy for him. "Karen, <u>I</u> am invited. <u>We</u> are not."

Her jaw dropped. "You're kidding."

"I wish I were. Farrakhan has this thing about Jews. J.T. just told me about the whole thing this morning. It's said he walks out if a Jew walks in. They're afraid they'll lose the guest of honor if you appear."

"The ignorant s.o.b.! I can't believe Nancy and J.T. are going along with this. Why would they want to buy into that kind of bull shit?" Karen rose and began to pace.

"You don't understand. It's very complicated." said Conrad patiently. How well he understood her hurt, the hurt of exclusion. He wished to God they hadn't been confronted with this, especially now when all the promise of coming to this town seemed to be turning to shit.

Karen sank into the couch. Nancy and J.T. had seemed so intelligent, so rational, so politically together. And they had welcomed her in a way that none of the others had. She was so disappointed in them. Apparently it was all an act. You couldn't trust anyone or believe anyone in this town, she thought bitterly. Everyone's wearing some kind of mask. "What're you going to do?" she asked.

"What do you mean?" Conrad rose and went to the HiFi to put on an LP.

"Don't you want to be there?" Karen knew the record would be Willie Bobo. He always played that one when he was particularly upset about something.

"Of course I want to be there. My absence will be noticed, you can bet on it. And it will be taken as desertion. Another nail in the coffin as far as the folks are concerned."

There it is again, thought Karen. The folks. The folks who are succeeding in their effort to form a flying wedge between us. "Well, what're you going to do?" she repeated. Conrad remained silent, apparently lost in the rhythm of the jazz drumming. "I know what I'd like to do," Karen snorted. "I'd like to just appear and force them to throw me out!"

"We're not going, Karen. And I'm not going. We're going to ignore the whole fucking thing. Let them all find out that this Farrakhan is just another loud mouthed bigoted turkey. I don't want to have anythng to do with it and I don't want to talk about it anymore."

But Karen knew that he was torn betwen his loyalty to her and his desire for acceptance by that community. She ached for him and cursed the lot that caused him pain.

Conrad drank a lot that afternoon, more than Karen had ever seen him drink before. Under the guise of having to work on scripts, he withdrew to the chair under the tree in the backyard and later tossed his long frame onto their bed, falling into a stupor so deep that he slept right through dinner and on to the next morning.

The start of a new week threw them both back into the whirl of constant activity. Conrad had to attend meetings on the new series that sometimes lasted well into the evenings. Karen's work load escalated to accomodate the rush of pilot season. It seemed as though everyone who could spell had a series or a movie they were trying to get on the network schedule and Karen's company was one of the most active producers. The stronger the casting the better the chance, although Karen knew that most of the network executives couldn't tell a good actor from a bad one.

They were both tired at night, and found themselves conforming to the routine of the company town. During the week everything seemed to fold up at ten o'clock, probably because it was an early town, catering to the needs of the film industry. Actors reported to makeup at six or seven a.m. and gaffers and grips were busily readying the day's sets before daylight. It was so different from New York which stayed open all night long and, particularly for theatre people, was a late town. Conrad and Karen often passed each other like ships in the night, with a quick kiss or a "how's it going?" as they went their separate ways.

Although they both harbored the tension about it, the subject of the Farrakhan party didn't surfaced again until some weeks after the party. They were finally having dinner together at the Chinese restuarant on Pico near Robertson. It was one of the few places in L.A. where waiters didn't serve ketchup and the food tasted like real New York Chinese food. Although the sign on the street was neon, the inside was a modest, quiet decor with luncheonette-like tables and straight-back wooden chairs. There were even a few booths, one of which they were lucky enough to get that night. Most places in L.A. seemed to survive on word of mouth and some came and went with the speed of light, but *Hoi Ping* was always packed and seemed to have been there forever.

"How did the Farrakhan party turn out? Heard anything?" asked Karen casually as she negotiated a slippery dumpling with her chopsticks.

Conrad shrugged. "Okay I guess. I haven't talked to J.T. but the word was that a lot of people showed up and he only stayed a short time. Damn!" The last was in response to his struggle with a shrimp which eluded his chopsticks. He discarded them and grabbed a fork. "I have no patience for these things. How's the chicken?"

Karen knew he was dismissing the topic and didn't push it. But she got the message that his relationship with J.T. had changed. J.T. had been in the habit of calling every day to keep up with the 'happenins' at the Studio and the fact that they hadn't spoken in a couple of weeks was disturbing. Karen had the uneasy feeling that, whether he was aware of it or it was purely subconscious, Conrad would blame her if he lost one of the few friends he'd made out here.

The activity of the restaurant swirled around them. The three waiters who took care of the whole room carried large round trays full of exotic smelling dishes and hurried back and forth between the kitchen in the rear and the tables. The hum of dinner conversation was a steady background drone, pierced occasionally with raucous laughter from a table for eight in the rear. Karen grappled with a decision. Something had come up at work that she needed to talk to Conrad about and she wondered whether this would be a good time. He seemed relaxed and in a better mood than usual and God knows when she would get another opportunity to get him alone and have his attention for more than a few minutes.

She took a deep breath. "Con, there's something I need to get your advice about. Something that's come up at work."

Conrad had just shoveled in a forkload of pork fried rice. He knew that sound in Karen's voice so he waited until he'd chewed and swallowed carefully and put down his fork. "What's up?"

Karen giggled. "Well, you don't have to look so serious. It's nothing bad. In fact, it might be something good." *For me, that is,* she thought silently.

"Are you going to tease me or tell me?" he demanded.

"Well, you know that new sitcom the company's been developing for NBC…The one with Ed Saner?"

"Yeah…?

"Well, I've been working with the producers and the director pretty closely. He's a great guy, by the way. Bill Cooper, one of the best. We really get along."

"Who's a great guy? The producer or the director?" *What is she leading up to,* thought Conrad. *Is she having an affair with this guy?*

"The director."

"Oh. So…?"

"Well, they've offered me associate producer on the show. If it gets picked up, that is." She watched Conrad's face for his reaction.

"Hey, baby that's terrific! I'm proud of you." Conrad reached over and patted her hand. "Way to go." He was truly happy for her. So why did he feel as though someone had just stabbed him in the heart?

"Look, Con. Don't make light of this. We need to talk about it." She had caught the pain in his eyes in the second before the mask appeared.

"What's there to talk about, baby? It's a big career move. If I know you, you'll be producing your own show before you know it."

He shoved his plate aside and lit a cigarette. He wasn't going to let her see his envy and frustration. She'd had enough of that. She deserved whatever she could get. It wasn't her fault that he'd been sitting on his ass ignored for months and months, watching all the short, fat white morons get the chances he wanted, and then watching them screw up. His inner eye flashed back to the last meeting they'd had late Friday. Conrad's hopes had risen for a moment because they'd decided to have the meeting in his office. They were checking the final draft of the pilot script, a so-called fine-tuning. Conrad had prepared a list of suggestions about dialogue and behaviour that he thought might contribute to the authenticity of the characters and, incidentally, help minimize some of the caricature stuff the comedy writers seemed to love. They had listened patiently, laughed at some of the ideas, interjected an occasional 'far out' in the interest of sounding 'hip', thanked him for his effort and proceeded as though he had never spoken. It was all done very politely which made it even more humiliating. Clearly the only thing that interested them where Conrad was concerned was getting the current black slang vocabulary. Conrad had left the meeting wanting desperately to hit someone or something very hard.

Karen's urgent low tone snapped him back to the present. "Con…? Listen, Con, let's be honest about this. I know how tough it's been for you. And now I'm getting a crack at being just where you should be. It's not fair!"

Conrad chuckled. "This is an unfair 'fair' world, baby. Don't sweat it. It's not your fault. Any more than the Farrakhan thing was my fault." He stared into her eyes intently as if trying to communicate what he couldn't express with words, what he hadn't been able to say about that whole issue.

Karen didn't want to go back to that. "Help me decide, Con," she pleaded. "I don't know what to do. If the show is picked up, it'll mean a much rougher schedule for me. Long days in the studio, and possibly some days on location. You know, associate producer is often glorified gofer."

"Are you telling me you don't want the job?" asked Conrad.

"I'm trying to say that I love you and that we come first. If taking this job meant driving us further apart, I'd say no in a hot minute."

The waiter arrived to clear the table and deposit the lichee nuts that always ended the meal. Conrad waited until he'd gone. "Further apart?"

"You know as well as I do what's been happening to us. We've been like roommates these past few weeks."

"Karen, I love you, but if you had any idea what I go through in the course of a typical day…"

"I know, I know, I'm not blaming you. I don't think it's happening because of us, I think it's happening to us."

Conrad took both her hands in his. "Look, we've always known it would be us against them. We can't let them win. And if we're going to survive here, we've got to play their game and beat them at it. That means that sometimes we might each have to go our own way, don't you see? And if you're constantly worried about where I am and I'm thinking about where you are, that prevents us from doing what we have to do. Then they're winning."

"Oh, Con." Karen's eyes welled up with tears. "I'm scared. I don't want anything to happen to us. L.A. terrifies me."

"Don't baby. Remember we're in charge. It's up to us to beat this town. And we're not going to let anyone stand in our way. You're going to take that job and give 'em hell. And then you can hire me!" He got up and reached for his wallet. "C'mon let's split and go home and shut out the world."

Conrad tried very hard to be his old charming self for the rest of the evening, entertaining Karen with the new jokes he'd heard on the lot that week, and relating some of the gossip about who was making it with whom, as he used to do in the early days. With the help of a few scotches he managed to keep his inner devils at bay, but Karen knew that he was hurting and she ached for him. Their lovemaking that night was a desperate attempt to reclaim what they both feared they were losing.

The work weeks that followed were busy and full of tension for both of them. Everybody in town seemed to be standing with one foot in the air waiting for the networks to plan their seasons. Karen was actually relieved when NBC stalled on its decision as to whether to pick up the new show. It meant that she could buy more time to think things through.

A new challenge presented itself, however, when Chuck asked her to accompany him to a casting session in New York. He said that he and the director really appreciated her eye for talent and she could be of enormous assistance to them. Agents in New York had lined up a whole bunch of up and coming young people for the producers in the hope of filling the growing need for the new shows coming in, many of which were designed to appeal to the eighteen to twenty five year old market. They would need to spend at least three days covering all the appointments so they would all be put up at the Park Lane on Central Park South which was centrally located. Chuck's suite would double as the audition space.

The thought of coming back to New York, the place in which she'd lived all her life, and staying at one of the luxury hotels like a wealthy tourist, tickled Karen. But she was concerned about leaving Conrad, especially now when things were not going so well. They really hadn't been apart since their relationship began and Karen worried that this would be yet another log on the fire that had been smoldering in Conrad's gut of late. Perhaps, she thought, I could persuade him to come with me. I'm sure there'd be plenty of room in a swank place like the Park Lane, probably two big double beds. She knew as soon as the thought entered her mind that he wouldn't go for it. Being brought along on her job would be an assault on Conrad's ever-so-male ego. And even if he consented to go, how would he get off from his job? But she was dying to get back to New York, to see her parents and maybe even one or two friends. And career wise it was important to be in on everything with Chuck and flattering to be included. Turning down the request would not be politic.

Conrad actually urged Karen to make the trip. Pointing out that it was only for a couple of days and that he was going to be very busy anyway, he seemed genuinely pleased that she would have this opportunity to go home.

"It'll do you good, babe, give you a shot in the arm. I wish I could find an excuse to go back sometime soon," he said wistfully.

"Come with me darling. Can't you sneak away?" Karen pounced on the opening.

"No way." It was flat and final. End of discussion.

Actually, the trip turned out to be both great fun and strangely disconcerting. It was certainly odd coming into her own city feeling like a visitor. They had flown first class which in itself was a thoroughly enjoyable novelty for Karen. The room they had reserved for her at the Park Lane was spacious enough to be a suite and overlooked the south end of her beloved Central Park. She got a great kick out of having her parents come to the hotel and see her accomodation. Then she took them to dinner at the posh St. Moritz down the street and insisted on picking up the check. They were duly impressed, especially since Karen knew they'd expected the marriage to Conrad-the-black-actor (what could be worse?) to doom her to a life of slum squalor. The evening was a huge success from Karen's point of view. She knew that Mother and Dad had gone home happy and visibly relieved when they both hastened to say "love to Conrad" as they departed.

The few days in New York flew by filled with meetings, agents and auditioning actors. Chuck and Bill, the director, had various production people to see in the evenings, so Karen did manage to squeeze in dinner with her old friend Amy who insisted that they celebrate their reunion at Sardi's. Karen hopped into a cab in front of the Park Lane and peered out the window as they sped toward Fifth Avenue past Bergdorf Goodman's sleek, chic mannequins, then down Fifth amidst the rush hour traffic. Crowds of people rushed by on the streets, toward the subway, the bus stops, the next block. This was what she had been missing. The pace, the vitality, the edgeiness of her native environment was so markedly different from their current Los Angeles life. L.A. was a bunch of neatly manicured, rather sterile, non-integrated little suburbias, carefully parceled and all strung together by strands of freeways. But this was a city seething with humanity, with a rhythm and a pulse and a drive. It was like getting a mainline shot of adrenaline.

As they pulled up to Sardi's, the same tall, thick-necked doorman in burgundy uniform and captain's hat opened the cab door and smiled, pretending to recognize her. Karen thanked him and sailed in to the famous and pricey showbiz hangout feeling once again as though she had come home. This was the community in which she grew up and to which she belonged. She gazed around the room at the familiar sight of the hundreds of caricatured drawings of performers lining the walls and spotted Amy at one of the small tables in the front. The maitre de insisted on escorting her and holding her chair for her. He waited patiently as Amy and Karen hugged and squealed and checked each other out as women do when they haven't seen one another in a very long time.

"You look great!" gasped Amy as they finally sat down and stared at each other. "Whatever you're doing out there certainly agrees with you. And I love your hair that way."

Just before she left for New York, Karen had visited one of the hairdressers-to-the-stars she'd heard so much about and splurged. "So do you," she replied quickly. Actually, she thought Amy had aged noticeably. She was starting to look matronly and there were dark circles under her eyes. I guess the stress of New York can do that to you, sighed Karen inwardly. In L.A. everyone looks good, even if they're wasting away of emphysema internally.

They both ordered scotch sours and the canneloni, a Sardi's special, and chewed on little brown rolls as they sipped their drinks, exchanging news and gossip and bringing each other up to date. Amy now worked for a large ad agency as a copywriter and was doing very well.

"But look at you." She grinned at Karen. "You're fast on your way to becoming a movie mogul."

"Well, hardly." Karen chuckled. "I'm in t.v. not films. There's a big distinction out there you know. And I'm still one of the worker bees. Though I am moving up the ladder."

"You mark my words. You're going to have your own show before you know it. I'll make you a bet."

"From your mouth to God's ear!" laughed Karen. "Although…." She stopped abruptly. The sudden thought of Conrad gave her pause.

"Although what?" demanded Amy.

Karen was rescued from explanation by the arrival of the food which they both, being hard working women, fell on.

The dinner was excellent and Karen ate with relish, again reminded of the differences between New York and L.A. Although there were a few good high priced restaurants, for the most part the food in the west was provincial. It might be another ten years before they caught up to the sophistication of the east.

As soon as they'd finished the gooey Boccone Dolce that Amy insisted they order and lit cigarettes, Amy returned like a dog with a bone to where they'd left off. "So what's going on, Karen? What's the 'although'?"

"You always could read me like a book."

"Oh, yeah," nodded Amy. "Ever since high school."

Karen took a deep drag on her cigarette and blew out the smoke slowly, buying time. She wasn't at all sure she wanted to discuss Conrad with Amy. She was well aware of how her friend had reacted to the relationship. And she was one of the people who'd tried to talk her out of marrying him. But she needed desperately to vent to someone outside of the situation, someone close with no axe to grind. And she knew Amy cared about her and had her best interests at heart.

"It's Conrad, isn't it? You haven't said a word about him," urged Amy.

"It's hard to talk about it," said Karen slowly. "I'm not even sure what's happening. But it feels like we're falling apart. The marriage I mean. And I don't know what to do about it." To her own amazement, Karen felt her eyes welling up with tears.

Amy took her hands in hers. "Keep going," she said softly.

"There's something so destructive about that place! I can't understand it, but everybody seems to be competing with and trying to shaft everybody else. And it's so bigoted and segregated. They're trying to get at us and I don't know how to fight them...and the fact that I'm doing well makes it worse......" Karen stopped for breath and took a gulp of coffee.

"Well, which is more important, your career or your marriage?" asked Amy.

"You know the answer to that one. I love him."

"Then why the hell don't you come home? At least here you can count on anonymity."

"I'm dying to come home." Karen heard herself admit it for the first time out loud. "Career be damned. What good is success if you're unhappy? But Conrad wouldn't dream of it. Even though he's miserable at work. He sees so many less talented, less able guys getting chances and making piles of money and they just ignore him. He wants his turn and he's determined to get it. I don't think he can be persuaded to leave until that happens. And besides, he loves the climate." She added the last with a wry smile. "It's very seductive."

"Things do seem to be opening up for blacks more than ever before."

"Oh yeah," said Karen. "But not for him. For the actors, mostly. And specifically for those who fit the white image of what black looks like. It's the same old story. Con isn't entirely trusted by his so-called brothers who think he's too white. And the establishment is afraid of him because they know he's black." Karen added ruefully. "He makes sure they know. Sometimes I think he bends over backwards."

"Would you rather he didn't?"

"No, of coure not. But…"

"But what?"

"Oh, I don't know. I don't know what I'd rather anymore. The truth is, although he never says anything, I think he's blaming a lot of his troubles on our marriage. It's difficult enough without having to deal with the anti-semitism."

"What?" Amy almost choked on the last mouthful of dessert. "Wait a minute. You've obviously left something out."

Karen related the whole Farrakhan episode to her and watched her horrified reaction. It was a relief to be able to tell someone, to air some of the anger and hurt she'd been harboring the past few months. In L.A. there was noone she could trust, noone she could confide in and know for a certainty that it wouldn't go any further. Amy had her faults. She was a middle class princess with a slightly skewed set of values and a touch of bigotry, but she was as loyal, honest and true a person as one could hope for and Karen was grateful for her friendship. It was reassuring to know that they could go for a year sometimes without seeing each other and then get together and easily pick up where they left off.

"My God!" exclaimed Amy. "Karen, you've got to get him out of there!"

"Do you really think it would be any easier here?" asked Karen as she felt the tears welling up again. "Isn't it just that we picked the worst possible time? Everyone's becoming militant, choosing sides, preaching separatism, judging allies by their color, by their look, not by who they are or what they think."

"But look at that woman…what's her name…Angela Davis. She was certainly one of the louder leaders. After a summer in Easthampton, I look darker than she does," Amy giggled. "And it costs me a fortune to get that look."

"That's another part of the picture. So many of the leaders are light skinned. Davis, Malcolm, Cleaver…It almost seems as though the lighter the skin the more militant they have to be to make up for their color," Karen replied.

The restaurant was thinning out, the dinner customers having either left for the theatre or gone on their way. There would be a lull and then the after theatre crowd would begin to file in filling the room with noise and laughter and smoke. Karen felt suddenly weary and longed for the comfort of the Park Lane bed and the reassurance of Conrad's voice on the phone. She wanted desperately to get back to the hotel to call him.

"I'm so glad we had this chance to get together Amy darling," she said aloud. "I wish we could spend more time, but I have to get up at dawn and I'm beginning to fade. It's been a long day."

Amy reached for Karen's hand and held it in both of her own. "Listen, please remember that I'm always just a phone call away. If you need someone to talk to, or just to hear yourself talk…"

"I know. And I'm grateful for that."

"Maybe you should just chuck it all for a week or two and come to a spa with me. Let everybody find out how much they miss you. What do you say?"

Karen laughed. "Oh, Amy, what a lousy idea. You know I hate spas!"

When she got back to the hotel she placed the call and let it ring for a long time. Figuring the three hour time difference, she thought Conrad might have just come home from work before going out for something to eat or to a screening. But no such luck. By the time he got home, she would hopefully be asleep. And in the morning it would be too early, he'd be annoyed at being awakened at dawn. Oh well, she sighed, I'll be seeing him tomorrow night. She turned on the TV and let the drone of voices lull her into a fitful sleep.

CHAPTER 12

1973   Bradley   First Black Mayor of Los Angeles

Conrad didn't want to admit it to himself but Karen's absence, even though it was just for a couple of days, was a relief of sorts. Lately he'd been in a constant state of tension about anything and everything related to her. The black community in L.A. blatantly rejected her. He had to edit his thoughts and dialogue for fear they would offend her. And he was often put in the position of having to choose between their relationship and something he really wanted to do. It was bad enough having to contend with the honkies at the studio and the frustration with the lack of career progress. The additional burden of this other load was becoming more than he could bear. He did love Karen and missed her physical presence, but couldn't deny that this momentary freedom was welcome. He could stop in at Fatburger's on La Cienega for a grease laden lunch or drive out to Compton after work to grab some soul food for dinner.

He also began to hang out at the Inner City Cultural Center down near Watts in the evenings. He'd been tipped off by some of the black actors who came to see him at the studio that this was where new black projects were being developed and that it was wide open and sorely in need of a strong leader. It was started by an actor, Gregory Peck and a writer, Budd Schulberg, They'd managed to get some grant money from the government after the Watts riots shocked everyone into realizing there was a big problem that needed addressing. But there was the usual resentment on the part of the black community at being controlled by a couple of benevolent white men and now there was an urgent need to find a capable artistic director to replace the figurehead black administrator currently fronting the organization. Or so the story went. Conrad went down to check it out.

The large grey building was located on one of the seamier south side downtown blocks and looked like an old movie house. It had been renovated inside to produce a fairly good sized theatre and on adjoining floors there were a couple of small rehearsal rooms, a black box for readings and several offices.

The first time he showed up Conrad was greeted like a movie star. The grapevine in the community was one of the most efficient in the world and everyone knew, or thought they knew, Conrad's history. He was the New York director from Harlem who'd landed an executive job at Paramount and Messiah-like, would somehow turn them all into working members of the television and film industry. The young writers and actors, of all sizes and both sexes, flocked around him hungry for information about New York theatre and job opportunities within the L.A. establishment. The women in particular were struck by Conrad's good looks and charm and instantly offered their charms in return. It was more than flattering. It was salve to Conrad's tattered ego, a restorative sorely needed.

The mainstage was running a production of GLASS MENAGERIE with an interracial cast, integration in the arts being one of the primary aims of the original Board. The 'Laura' was white, the 'Gentleman Caller' was a black actor who had begun to achieve recognition on television. As Conrad had long fought for the idea that black actors could and should participate in the classic literature of the theatre, he was excited about the possibilities of getting involved with this group. But like all efforts of this kind at this period in time, the path toward development was slow and rocky, rutted with the protests of various factions each with its own ideology.

Before he actually saw the show, Conrad heard varying reactions from amongst his new friends, many of whom felt the theatre should be devoted entirely to black plays by black writers, preferably with lots of parts for black actors.

"Shit, man," growled Clifford, a dark skinned wiry young man in his twenties wearing large horn rimmed glasses. "The cat playing the Caller, y'know? They made him put on white face makeup! And that ain't all. He's using green contact lenses to make him look more white. Ain't that a bitch?"

"What we need around here is a director who's one of the folks," said Russell, joining the circle around Conrad. Russell was a short round teddy bear of a man with an almost bald head. "We need to get those honkies out of here and get Conrad involved."

"Thanks, man. That's a real compliment. But I've got a job." Conrad smiled at the group.

Russell snorted. "Yeh, yeh. Slaving on the plantation, man. How long will your gut be able to take that? You belong here with your own. Shit, you can take over, be in charge. Quiet as it's kept, they'd be happy to have you. Then they wouldn't have to come down to this dangerous place any more." Russell did his bogey man thing on this last remark.

"Yeh, well I just got here, remember? Let me look around a little bit, see what's happenin'." Conrad's blood pulsed. The thought of having a theatre to run sent his brain spinning. He could choose the plays, direct, start a training program, get his message out. Whoa, he thought. They probably can't pay more than two cents and who knows what political machinations might be necessary to worm his way in. But it was worth looking into. In addition to the creative part of it, it would be so good to be amongst the folks again, to be where he was respected and his talent acknowledged. They were looking for a leader and willing to accept him unquestioningly because of his New York background and his ability to straddle the gap between the black community and the establishment. It was true. He was perfect for the job.

Aloud he said only "We'll see. Give me a little time to check out the situation."

He went to see the play and confirmed his suspicions. However well intentioned, the result was weak and the play suffered from poor direction and a muddled concept. The actor playing the Gentleman Caller, Paul Winston, struggled valiantly, but seemed uncomfortable and stiff in his green eyes and white face. It was as though he felt dishonest and that feeling was an obstacle to finding the truth of the character. Although, thought Conrad, it's been known to work. Frank Silvera, a very light-skinned black character actor successfully played a white father in HATFUL OF RAIN on Broadway. So maybe it's the uncomfortable contact lenses that are doing him in. Conrad sighed inwardly. It's always about color, he thought. It's always so fucking complex because of the eye of the beholder.

He came back every night while Karen was away. It was as though he'd found his oasis, his private club away from the world that he'd built with Karen and away from the world of the studio and the industry. He hung out with the group of young actors who looked up to him and lapped up his every word.

A curvaceous coffee colored young woman with a trim afro sidled up to him on one of those nights. She wore shiny black peddle-pushers that clung to her legs like a second skin and a flower print chiffon see-through blouse that revealed an ample bosom. She flashed a wide smile at Conrad.

"Hi," smiled Conrad.

"Hi. Man, you are fine! I'm Gladys," whispered the woman. "You married, ain't you?" Gladys' grin got wider.

"Yup." Conrad grinned back.

"Yeh, I heard. You married to Miss Anne, huh?"

Conrad's smile disappeared.

"Hey, that's cool baby. I can dig what you're about. She can get you in there, right? But don't you just die for a piece of luscious black ass once in a while?" Gladys rubbed up against Conrad's side.

Conrad frowned at her with distaste as he moved away from contact with her. "Listen to me, babe," he lectured. "Don't you know you're just embarrassing yourself when you behave this way? You're a nice looking woman, so let's see you act with some dignity and respect for yourself."

Gladys shrank from him. "Fuck you," she muttered and walked away.

I might be able to do some good here, he thought. And he went back to Beverly Hills that night with all kinds of ideas whirling around in his head.

The next night he had dinner with an old friend from New York, an actor who had moved out to Los Angeles in the early days of the east to west exodus and become a star character actor. Roger Brown was older and much wiser than most of Conrad's circle. He also had a lot more education having once been a professor at Howard University, as well as a lot more class in Conrad's estimation. He was revered for his talent, his taste and his open door to any and all who sought advice and counsel.

Since Roger lived in the Hollywood Hills, they met at Musso Frank's on Hollywood Boulevard for dinner. It was a huge old style barn of a place reminiscent of the glamour of old Hollywood, with dark wood decor, sparkling white tablecloths, intimate booths and waiters who seemed to match the age of the place. Conrad got a kick out of watching Roger order the choicest wine and carefully consider the specials of the day asking pertinent questions as to their preparation. "This is on me, dear boy," he interjected as he caught Conrad's exression.

"Oh, no," protested Conrad but he was quickly silenced with a look.

They had a wonderful dinner accompanied by Roger's gossip about anyone and everyone in the film industry and it wasn't until coffee was served that Roger sat back, lit his cigarette and Conrad's with a gold Dunhill lighter and said "So what's the problem my friend?"

Conrad always marveled at the sensitivity of the man. He seemed to read people's minds. "I'm having great difficulty deciding who I am and who I want to be," sighed Conrad. "And this town isn't making it any easier."

"Come now. Is it the town? Wouldn't this be true wherever you were?" Roger's dark eyes were piercing.

"I'm not sure." Conrad plunged in to the heart of the matter. His voice dropped to a whisper as though he were afraid he might be overheard. "I see certain opportunities here, but I feel that the marriage stands in the way. The community isn't ready to accept it and therefore they can't accept me. They can't figure out where I'm at or whether they can trust me."

"They who?"

"The people I want to work with. Our community."

"And you think it's the marriage that's the problem?"

"Well, yeah, I do." He sat silent for a moment. "Well, I don't know. Maybe it's not. Maybe it's me. Maybe it's the genes of my white mother." He laughed with embarrassment. It sounded so ludicrous.

"Do you love Karen?" Roger leaned forward as if to emphasize the importance of this question.

"Yes, yes…of course I do. But…."

"But what?"

Conrad hesitated for a minute. "I think the pressures are getting to us. And I'm not sure I'm strong enough to withstand them."

"Then maybe you should leave. Go back to New York."

"But I don't want to leave. I want to stay and stand my ground. I think I can do something here. Leaving would be admitting defeat. Then I would know what I was. I'd know I was a coward."

"So what about the marriage?"

"I want the marriage. I love Karen…but…" He ground his cigarette into the ashtray with unecessary force. "I want to prove myself!"

"You keep talking about what you want. What about Karen? What does she want?"

Conrad stared at him blankly.

"And everytime you talk about how you feel about her there's a 'but'. Are you being fair to her?"

"What do you mean?" asked Conrad.

"I mean," said Roger slowly and patiently, "if you have all these doubts and there are always 'buts, consider what is inevitable in the future. Are you taking up the best part of Karen's life to serve your quest for identity? What if you choose another path down the road? Then where is she?"

Conrad sipped his coffee silently, absorbing Roger's words. Roger beckoned to the waiter and ordered two brandies. When they arrived he held up his glass in a toast. "To your happiness," he said and added with a meaningful stare "…and to Karen's."

Conrad met Karen at the airport and on the drive home there were a lot of news bits and anecdotes to exchange. But Karen left out the Sardi's visit with Amy and Conrad left out the dinner with Roger, just mentioning the Inner City visits briefly without going into too much detail. Karen expressed interest in the theatre company and immediately suggested that she visit it with him.

Conrad stiffened slightly. "I don't think you'd enjoy it," he said. "It's pretty primitive."

"Why are you putting it down?" asked Karen.

"I'm not putting it down. It's just that it seems to be in an early stage of development."

"All the more interesting for me," replied Karen. But she didn't press it and Conrad devoted himself to the rush hour traffic on the freeway.

As Karen unpacked in the bedroom Conrad came in with two drinks, solemnly handed her one and clinked glasses with her.

"Welcome home, baby," he said taking a gulp of scotch. Then he put down his drink and put his arms around her. "I missed you," he murmured into her neck.

"Oh, I missed you too darling," whispered Karen as she pressed her body hard against his. He lifted her up and she wrapped her legs around him as he carried her to their bed. There was no need or desire to talk, just to be close. They made love for a long time, intensely, as if to make up for something lost.

During the next few weeks both their schedules again kept them so busy that they barely had time to see one another or even have dinner together because both were working late. What Conrad neglected to tell Karen was that he was running down to the Inner City Center after work to continue making contacts and establishing himself as a member of that community. He felt a bit guilty about not including Karen, but he knew she would want to get involved along with him. He also knew that because of the political separatist stance of most of the group, her presence would kill any chance he might have at landing some kind of paying position there.

Karen sensed that Conrad was tightening up and withdrawing from her again, but she attributed it to his continuing frustration with work, and the demands of her own job kept her from doing more than thinking about it. The days passed quickly. With little sign of a change in season in this climate, the sameness of the bright sunny days lured them into a passive acceptance of the routine and the passage of time was rarely noted.

Until the night the phone call came. It was quite late by L.A. standards, around eleven o'clock. They were in bed watching the small TV on top of the dresser and waiting for the late news. That was another thing about L.A. that was hard for Karen and Conrad to get used to: the sidewalks folded up around ten, especially during the week. One couldn't even think of getting a late night snack at a restaurant and the few clubs that stayed open late were carefully hidden to the naked eye. One had to be in the know to find them. They figured that it was because it was pretty much a company town, and film workers started at five or six a.m. in the morning so they had to go to bed early for their beauty sleep. No wonder actors cut looose when they weren't working. Nobody outside the industry realized what a grueling schedule the making of a film involved. So the insistent jangling of the bell at that hour was startling. Karen, fearing that it might be bad news from New York perhaps about one of her parents, instinctively hung back and didn't rush to answer it as she usually did. Conrad hated talking on the phone so he usually waited for Karen to pick up, but when he saw her hesitate he grabbed the receiver and answered with his usual monosyllable.

"Yep?" His voice was low and guarded. Karen looked at him questioningly and watched his attitude change and his face relax into a smile. "Oh, hi, how're ya doin'? What's happenin'?" Karen relaxed. She knew it had to be a friend, someone he liked. Probably one of his basketball buddies. "No kiddin'!" he was saying. "That's great. He'll knock 'em dead."

He listened for what seemed like a long time eyes darting in Karen's direction and then away. Then he got out of bed and began to pace playing out the extra long phone cord, back turned to Karen. Now her curiosity was fully aroused.

"Yeh, yeh, sure…I'm hip. What's the date?" he said grabbing a pencil from the top of the dresser where the contents of his trousers had been dumped. Karen handed him the pad that lay on the nighttable next to the bed and he scribbled something on it. "You're sure there's no way…?" He listened for a moment frowning, then seemed to interrupt the talker. "No, no, of course I will. It's fantastic and I'm really flattered." Another moment, then he chuckled. "I'll bet you say that to all the cats," he purred.

Karen was getting a funny feeling in her gut. This had to be a female caller.

"Black tie?" Conrad was saying. "Sure, I'll wear one with my dashiki!…Right…Talk to you then. Later, baby." He hung up the receiver slowly and carefully, as if buying time before he faced the inevitable questioning from Karen. Saying nothing, he climbed back into bed.

"So what's up?" asked Karen impatiently.

Conrad was silent.

"C'mon, give. What just happened?" persisted Karen.

"You're not going to believe this."

"Try me,"

"That was Rowena. Lanny's going to be the emcee at the Academy Awards. They're all excited about it. It seems he's a last minute replacement for somebody who was going to do it and chickened out or got sick or something."

Karen's jaw dropped. "Don't tell me she invited us! Oh God, I've dreamt all my life of going to one of those things!"

Conrad was silent.

"What?" demanded Karen. "What is going on?"

"Rowena needs an escort. Lanny's going to be on stage or backstage for the whole thing and Rowena needs to come in with an escort. She'll be in the audience for the whole show." Conrad, who had been looking straight ahead until now, turned to face her eye to eye. "She chose me."

"Well, that's great, darling! Oh, I'm so excited! When do we go? I'll have to get a dress."

"That's the hard part, Karen. I'm the escort but there's no extra ticket."

Karen stared at him for a moment, letting it sink in. "You mean I'm not invited?"

Conrad took her hands in his. "Listen baby, try to understand. They were only given a few tickets and they had a long list of obligations. Rowena explained that she tried to get an extra ticket for you but there was no way."

Karen snorted. "Bull shit. I disliked that female the minute I laid eyes on her. She wants you all to herself is all. Or is it that the white wife would be an embarrassment?"

"Karen, please…"

Karen got out of bed and started to pace. "I'm furious! How dare she?" She screwed up her face and raised her voice pitch in an imitation of Rowena. "Can I borrow your husband to be my boyfriend for a night while you get lost?"

"Karen…."

"How dare she put you in this position? You want me to believe that with her husband the emcee, she can't get her hands on another ticket?" Karen was shouting now. "That bitch!"

"Karen, I told you. It was a last minute replacement. All the tickets had been given out, she said."

"I don't believe her for a minute! She's had her eyes on you ever since that first party. I saw it then. That fucking bitch! Why couldn't she ask one of her single men friends to escort her? I'm sure she's got plenty of them!"

"She's doing me a big favor," said Conrad softly, spelling it out as though talking to a child. "Being seen at the Academy Awards, meeting everyone, sitting with the stars…It's a fantastic opportunity. I was hoping you'd be happy for me."

"But Con, don't you see what they're trying to do to us? You go to the most visible event of the year without your wife, then the gossip starts and the predators move in. And that's the way they do it." She stopped for a moment and stared at him. "You said you'd go, didn't you? Without even asking me how I felt?"

"She needed to know right away. And you're overreacting. It's just one lousy event."

"Yeh, one lousy event. Just something I've longed to go to all my life." Tears sprang to Karen's eyes. "What really hurts is how easy it is for you to play along with this shit. I didn't even hear you press the issue." She couldn't control it and the sobs erupted.

"Karen, sit down for a minute." The tone of his voice prompted her to sit on the edge of the bed. She blew her nose into a kleenex as Conrad put his arm around her. "We've always known there would be special challenges in this town that we'd have to cope with. If we want to succeed, we have to play it smart. Now look at Sidney and Jo. He's about as big a star as anyone can be. But he's still a black man. And noone sees the two of them together in public. Jo just seems to be willing to cool it and stay out of sight. Sidney is always a single at events and command appearances. I don't think it's because she's that shy. They're just playing it smart and waiting for the time to come when they don't have to worry anymore."

"What about Harry? He's got a white wife. They go everywhere together."

"What about Harry. A: He's in New York. And B: Julie bakes herself in Aruba to keep herself looking so dark she can pass for a black woman."

"So you're saying I ought to get a better tan or hide? And you go along with this? You're afraid to be seen with me?" Karen's voice rose again.

"No, that's not what I'm saying……"

"And what happened to the loyalty of a husband to his wife? What hurts the most is how willing you seem to be dust me off. What would have happened if you'd said you didn't want to go without me?"

"What did you expect me to do?" Conrad's nostrils were flaring. "Tell Rowena to fuck off? Run the risk of antagonizing a valuable friend? What happened to the wife who wants her husband to succeed?"

"How can you say something like that to me? Everything I've done has been for you and your 'career'! Whose idea was it to come out here in the first place? I turned my life upside down for you, and this is the thanks I get." Karen's tears were coming thick and fast now. "I guess I'll have to make my own opportunities to get invited to the Academy Awards. I'll have to choose who I want to go with!" She got up and ran into the bathroom, slamming the door behind her.

Conrad called out to her. "Karen, this is childish. You're making a big deal out of nothing."

"Go to hell!" she shouted from within.

Conrad stood there for a moment wrestling with the conflict. She was probably sitting on the toilet and crying. He wanted to go to her and comfort her. He knew how she felt. He'd dealt with rejection and exclusion all his life. The torment of constantly being pulled in opposite directions was beginning to be more than he could bear. It was making him physically sick. This was not a situation of his making and she knew that. Mounting rage made him tremble. It was hard enough just to make one's way in this lousy world without having bricks thrown at you from opposite sides while you stand flailing in the middle. Conrad felt himself getting flushed and feverish. He needed air. He pulled on his jeans and grabbed a tee shirt and his wallet and car keys. He had to get out, drive somewhere, breathe some fresh air.

Karen heard the car motor start. At first she thought it must be the neighbor's car. Still crying, she opened the door to the bathroom. "Conrad?" she called. She walked around the house sobbing, knowing he'd gone and full of regret. In shock and hurting, she'd reacted like a child. Christmas had suddenly come and she didn't get her present. But it wasn't really about something as small and ephemeral as the Awards event, and they both knew it. She poured herself a straight inch of scotch, gulped it down and went back to the bedroom. Curling herself up into a miserable knot in bed, she cried herself to sleep.

Conrad climbed back into bed in the middle of the night. He'd driven all the way to Venice and sat on the beach staring at the ocean, thinking. The beach was deserted and the sand stretched before him like a vast desert in the dark. A steady breeze made the trees along the avenue that ran next to the beach seem to whisper. The Pacific ocean was dark and calm except for one ray of light sent down by the moon. It was eerily quiet as he sat there gazing out at the horizon and listening to the water hit the shore. He sat there for a long time, until he saw a prowl car coming down the avenue and he got back into his car and drove home.

Karen awoke momentarily when he climbed into bed. "Sorry," she murmured in her sleep.

Conrad put his arms around her. "Me too," he whispered.

Like so many things that were happening these days, they didn't dare discuss it again. Conrad did go to the Awards with Rowena while Karen suffered through the evening watching it on television in her bathrobe. At first she just felt sorry for herself and the tears began to flow, but the self pity soon turned into anger when they took a reaction shot of Lanny's wife in the audience and Conrad was included in the shot. I'll show them, she thought. I'll get there under my own steam. I don't need him or anybody else. Things are opening up for women in the business. I'll show them. I'll produce an award winning film! Then fuck them all!

There was a party at Lanny's house after the show and Conrad came home to pursuade Karen to go with him. At first she refused, but finally she gave in. She put on her sexiest body-clinging dress and derived some small satisfaction out of watching Rowena seethe when Lanny came on to her openly and noisily. Everybody was roaring drunk by the time they got there and pretty boring, so Karen and Conrad stayed for a very short time and drove silently home.

CHAPTER 13

1974 Frank Black First Black to Manage in Major League

Conrad spent more time away from home running between the studio and Inner City. Karen, to compensate for his absence and with renewed resolve to build her own career, devoted more time to her job, putting in long days, scheduling business dinners and sometimes getting home just in time to go to bed. Although it was never discussed, there seemed to be a tacit agreement that perhaps they each needed some space in which to work things out, a little distance from one another.

Conrad announced one night as they were getting ready for bed that he'd been asked by the Inner City group to direct a play. "It's one I'm dying to do," he said thoughtfully.

"What is it?" asked Karen from the bathroom. She rinsed her mouth of toothpaste and came into the bedroom. "It's by a writer named William Hanley. It's called SLOW DANCE ON THE KILLING GROUND. Three characters, one set. Just right for a first time out on that stage."

Karen plumped up the pillows and climbed into bed. "Oh, I saw that on Broadway. It was wonderful. Can you cast it here?"

Conrad grinned at her. "You going to work for me already?"

Karen knew what he was thinking. If he did it he would want it to be all his own; he would want her to stay out of it. "Don't be silly," she said aloud pulling her knees up under her chin. "But how will you manage to do it with your job in the way?"

"Rehearse at night. And the weekends. Everyone down there works at a day job. How else would they survive?" It was Conrad's turn to brush his teeth. "We'll have four weeks," he said with his mouth full of toothpaste.

Karen knew that if he did this they would have no time together for at least a month. But she also knew how much he needed it. "Tell them you'll do it," she called to him.

Conrad came out of the bathroom, turned off all the lights and crawled into bed next to Karen with the relieved sigh of a tired body. He turned to her, kissed her lightly on the nose and pulled the covers up. "I already have," he said and turned away, falling asleep almost instantly.

Karen lay staring at the ceiling, eyes wide open, for a long time. She tried to sort out her feelings. So it was a done deal. They used to discuss every thing at length before either one of them made a move. Now he seemed to have another life completely separate from theirs. Or was it simply that she was jealous, envious of his opportunity to get back to the theatre, to work on a play. She'd been missing the theatre so much lately. The taste of New York lingered on and made her all the more aware of what she was missing in this new life.

She knew that she would have to be very careful to stay out of it, to not intrude herself on his work, much as she'd like to be a part of it. It would be difficult for her. They'd shared so much together and now there was yet another thing to distance them from one another. What was happening to them? Were they really falling apart? Would this be another nail in the coffin? Karen was at a loss as to what to do. Should she keep quiet and bide her time? It was as though they were sledding down a slippery hill and couldn't be stopped. Will we hit a tree? she wondered as she fell into a fitful sleep and dreamed about Central Park in the wintertime.

The tree that lay in their path loomed suddenly and from an unexpected source. During the weeks that followed Conrad's decision to accept the directorial assignment, he spent even more time at the Inner City theatre, ostensibly concerned with casting and other preproduction details. Actually, he thrived on the attention he got there. The black women flocked to his side hanging on his every word and the black men, particularly the younger ones, saw him as their new mentor and saviour. Conrad, sore from the ache of the perceived daily humiliation and frustration provided by the establishment, welcomed the balm of their admiration. The need worked both ways and Conrad began to take on more of the prevailing political attitude. Their distinctly nationalist and separatist stance was pervasive, and gradually he became more like them than they like him. At first he played the game to win their trust but as time went on it was the liberating force of their adulation that seemed to turn him around. He could afford to take risks finally, say what he thought, blow the lid kept so firmly in place at the studio.

This new found freedom was such a relief that it began to inform his behaviour in general. He no longer kept his guard up at the studio. His comments, while still couched in humor became more caustic and barbed. He began to be more vocal about the lack of minority hiring, particularly in the producing and directing areas. No longer was he the quiet beige person of indeterminate origin lurking quietly in the background. Now he was the militant black man making demands. No longer a benign follower, now he was a threat. These changes did not go unnoticed and it wasn't too long before the inevitable request for a meeting with his boss occurred.

Conrad came in late that morning. He'd been at Inner City half the night before and had trouble getting the day started. As he passed Miranda on the way to his office she stopped him.

"Uh, Conrad?"

"Good morning beautiful," he waved as he kept going.

"Uh, good morning." She flashed him a pearly smile. "Listen, Biff's secretary told me to tell you that he wanted to see you as soon as you came in."

Conrad frowned. Biff was the last person he wanted to see at this moment in time. He had a bitch of a headache, probably from the reefer he smoked with those kids last night. Just to be sociable, he told himself. It was a dumb ass thing to do. He usually told people no thanks, he'd outgrown dope when he was twelve. But he didn't want to put the cats down. And now Biff had remembered he was alive on the one day he came in late. Aloud he said, "Okay, babe. Thank you."

The pearls appeared again. "You're welcome," she drawled.

Biff was sitting behind his huge desk when Conrad knocked and then peered in through the half open door to his office. He waved Conrad in with a "Hi, how're you doin'?"

"You wanted to see me?" Conrad looked for signs on the desk that maybe this was about his script. Nothing in sight but a coffee carafe, mug and a plate of doughnuts.

"Yeh. Sit down. Take a load off." Biff smiled ingratiatingly.

Oh, oh, thought Conrad. What's this going to be?

"Listen man, I've been wanting to talk to you about something." Biff hesitated.

Conrad's guard went up. This was unusual. "Yes?"

"Well…it's a difficult situation…" Biff was actually squirming. "But I've been getting some complaints so I thought it would be a good idea to air the problem with you…" He paused for a moment. "Say, would you like a dough-nut? These are really good." He held out the plate.

"No thanks. What's the problem?"

"Well, you know, the guys like you, y'know. You're very well liked."

Conrad tried not to laugh. "That's nice," he replied. He didn't know what else to say.

"Yeh, but sometimes they can't figure you out. I mean they say they think you don't like them. And sometimes they don't know what to make of your suggestions, they're so far out. You're sort of out of sync if you know what I mean."

"Do I have to sound like them to work with them?" Conrad asked.

"Well, no, that's not what I mean exactly…" Biff reached for a doughnut and took a huge bite out of it. "The guys feel you're not making a constructive contribution," he said with his mouth full of sugar and dough.

"That's really funny, Biff." Conrad knew he had to contain his anger so he smiled sweetly. "Because most of the time they don't even know I'm there. I rarely get a word in. After all, I'm just the resident spook proofreader."

"There, you see. That's just what I mean." Biff searched for something to wipe his sticky fingers on. "You say these things, and we never know when you're kidding and when you're serious. It's nervous-making."

Conrad handed him a kleenex from the box on the side table. "Which part makes you nervous? Resident spook or proofreader?" God, he thought. If I just had the balls to quit right now.

"Now Conrad…" Biff could feel himself losing it. This Negro drove him nuts. "Conrad…" Just then the intercom buzzed urgently. "Yes!" he barked as he flipped the switch. "I told you I didn't want to be interrupted!"

"Would you pick up the phone Mr. McKee? It's an emergency." His secretary's voice sounded shrill.

Biff stared at Conrad for a moment. "Excuse me," he said gruffly. He picked up the phone. "McKee here, what's going on?" he said anxiously.

Conrad could tell from Biff's expression that something serious was happening.

"Oh my God," whispered Biff. "What the fuck…? How did he get….?" He listened for a moment, then glanced at Conrad. "Hang on, I'll be right over." He slammed down the receiver and headed for the door. "C'mon. We've got to get over to the *Atlanta* set right away. I need you. Some maniac's going beserk."

Conrad didn't quite get what was happening. Why was he needed? What could he do about a maniac going beserk? Why didn't they call a doctor or a psychiatrist? But he trotted alongside the boss, grateful that at least for the time being their discussion had been aborted. He sensed that Biff was trying to work up the courage to fire him. Although Conrad had about had it, he wanted to split on his terms, and after he'd had a chance to regroup and develop other options. On the other hand, he thought grimly, if he fired me I could collect unemployment insurance and buy time that way.

They ran through the rectangle of greenery surrounded by low brick office buildings, cutting through one of the narrow alley ways to the center road which led to the sound stages. Biff was breathing heavily now as they continued past the large ecru colored hangar-like buildings and sped towards the north end of the studio. Conrad couldn't help thinking that it was a lovely day for a run. The sky was cloudless and a brilliant blue and the ever present and seemingly relentless sun was beginning to heat up the ground. Apparently the word had gone out because Conrad noticed several guards running in the same direction, and actors in costume together with grips and gaffers emerged from the buildings, all gazing towards the north. Biff shouted at one of the guards running by.

"Tell Security NO SHOOTING! That's an order!" he panted.

"What the hell's going on?" yelled Conrad as the trot became a sprint.

"Some guy on stage 21's got a huge knife and he's gone nuts. It'll be all over the fucking press," gasped Biff.

As they raced toward the soundstage Conrad tried to figure out why he, in particular, was needed. He grabbed Biff's arm, slowing him for a moment. "Is he black?"

"Yeh."

"Oh."

They went through the heavy metal door to the stage and onto the cavernous floor which was cluttered with the equipment of filmmaking. Cameras, dollies, a huge crane, set pieces, flats, lighting apparatus of various shapes and sizes, made the space an obstacle course for anyone attempting to reach the center. Coming out of the bright sunlight, eyes had to adjust to the darkness as only the worklights were on. It was an almost circus-like scene. A large ring of security people, hands on holsters, surrounded a figure in the center who was heard before he could be seen. Anguished roars interspersed with curses and howls of pain filled the echoing space. Members of cast and crew huddled outside the ring and in corners or behind flats watching a real drama unfold, frightened but mesmerized. Conrad noted in the midst of the melee that one individual, a young scrawny boy-man was actually shooting the event with a video camera. As they approached the center they saw the source of the noise. He was a huge, dark-skinned, burly black man dressed in the costume of a plantation slave and wielding a huge bolo knife. Eyes wild and sweating like a stoker, he stabbed and jabbed at the air with the lethal looking weapon.

"Lying mother fuckers!" he roared in a penetrating bass voice, "You think you gonna kill me? C'mon, c'mon…come and get me cock suckers!"

Biff and Conrad joined the circle of uniformed guards. One of them, a beefy red-cheeked man, whispered to Biff. "Hey, I can take him out right now. Piece of cake."

"No!" screeched Biff. Then dropping his voice he added, "No shooting, understand?"

"Yes sir, but he's out of control. No telling…"

"How the hell did he get in here?" interrupted Biff.

"He's one of the extras on the show. They say he just suddenly went nuts."

Conrad had been listening. "What's his name?" he asked.

The guard shrugged. "Don't know," he replied.

"The bastard's obviously cracked up. He's psycho." Biff was trembling with fear. "Where the hell's the ambulance? I thought the medics were called."

"I'll go check," said the guard, welcoming the chance to get away from the scene.

"Gonna make me disappear?" the man was yelling. "Huh?? C'mon, c,mon…wanna see me crawl, huh? Wanna make me beg?" He threatened an imaginary adversary with the knife, continually stabbing at the air, spinning around, jabbing at anything or anyone that seemed to be in his line of vision.

Another older guard, with greying hair and stripes on his uniform apparently implying some kind of seniority, approached the two men. "Excuse me, sir."

"What?" snapped Biff.

The guard whispered into Biff's ear. "If someone could occupy his attention for a minute, we could come around behind him."

"I don't know." whispered Biff. "That fucking knife is dangerous."

The man's hysteria seemed to mount. "Say one thing and mean another!" he shouted. "Wanna make me crawl? Yassa massa, yassa massa…kiss my assa massa!"

"Where the hell is Springer?" Biff scanned the faces of the observers loking for the producer of the show.

"Think he went to get help, sir," replied the guard.

Conrad had been standing quietly, watching and assessing the situation. His heart went out to the poor anguished soul who had snapped and was spilling his guts for all the world to see. He could relate to the cat. He often felt pushed to the edge himself these days. The necessity of holding himself in, of censoring his every reflex sometimes made him feel as though he would burst if he didn't scream. That's how they get us, he thought. They de-ball us and drive us nuts, to the point where we do outrageous things, and then point their fingers at the crazy nigger who has to be removed because he's dangerous.

"C'mon Mr. Charlie, c'mon you sons o' bitches," the man continued to rant, moving in his space like a caged animal. "Waddya want, huh? You want my skin? You want my bones? You want my blood?" He tore at his shirt, ripping it off. "You want my soul? Oh, nooo…you can't have my soul, mother fuckers…no, no, no, no…" The shrieks began to die as he repeated this last again and again until it became a muttering chant.

"Biff, I'm going to try to talk to him. He seems to be running out of steam," said Conrad. Maybe I can keep them from offing the poor bastard, he thought.

"For Christ sake man, be careful."

Conrad noted with wry amusement that Biff made no attempt to stop him from putting himself in jeopardy. He moved forward slowly, a step at a time, never taking his eyes off the man. The crowd that had gathered grew so still that one could actually hear the heavy breathing of the two men facing each other.

"Hey bro. What's happenin' here?" said Conrad in a low, intimate tone, as though these two shared a secret that noone else was in on.

The man stopped in his tracks, knife dropping to his side. The wild eyes focused on Conrad, then stared, trying to figure him out. "What you doin' here?"

Conrad kept advancing, very slowly. "I'm Conrad. I work here, man. Just like you."

The man laughed hysterically. "Not like me, man. You're them, ain't you?" He pointed the knife at Conrad accusingly. "You one of those oreo cookies, huh?"

"That's not me. I'm with you, man. What do I call you?"

The man stared at him for a second then pulled himself up to his full height. "You call me mister Brown!"

"Mr. Brown, I dig what you're saying." Conrad edged a bit closer. "We got to stick together, man."

The man suddenly burst into tears. "They treat you like shit, man. Walk all over your soul."

"I'm hip."

"I'm human damn it!" He was calming down now.

Conrad stood right in front of him, eyes not leaving the man's face, but periphally watching the knife. "Tell me what happened."

"They want me to crawl on my knees. Up theirs!"

"Right on."

Conrad extended his arm offering the brotherhood handshake. If I can get him, to transfer the knife to his left hand, he thought, that would be a step. Intently fixing Brown's eyes with his stare while concentrating on the possible movement of the knife, Conrad was unaware that one of the security guards was stealthily creeping up directly behind the man. Just as Conrad reached toward him, the guard lunged. Brown, reacting, lunged forward with the arm holding the knife extended.

Blood spurted from Conrad's mid section as the knife pierced the skin. Was it he that gasped or someone in the crowd? He felt the pain, the sudden dizziness, heard a rushing sound in his ears something like the sea in a storm and then he must have fainted because when he awoke he was in an ambulance on his way to the hospital.

As Karen sped towards the hospital, fighting the traffic on Beverly Boulevard and edging around the creeping cars on Vermont to get to the Kaiser Permanente Hospital on Sunset, images flashed through her mind: Conrad bleeding, Conrad on a guerney being wheeled into an O.R. Conrad lying in a white bed looking pale and waxen. When his secretary called her with the news, she didn't wait for details. She had simply said "Where is he?" and made a dash for her car. She pulled into the visitor parking area and sprinted towards the Emergency entrance. Karen loathed hospitals. They always made her feel queasy. The smell, the atmosphere, the general implication of illness, disease, impending death, always frightened her and made her want to escape. She was out of breath when she reached the nurse's station.

"Can you tell me where I can find a patient named Conrad Taylor?" she gasped.

"Are you a member of the family?" asked the nurse, barely looking up.

Oh God, thought Karen. What's happened? "I'm his wife," she said, her voice choked.

The nurse took her time. Karen tried desperately not to look around, not to see the the sick and maimed in the waiting room, not to inhale too deeply.

"He's on the third floor. Room 10A."

"Thanks." Karen tried to figure out which way to point. So many corridors. No sign of an elevator. "How do I get there?" She could have gladly strangled this uncaring female behind the glass.

"Go through those double doors to the end of the corridor and turn right. You'll see the elevators at the end. When you get to the third floor the nurse will direct you." The nurse finally looked at Karen. "Calm down. It says here he's stable."

"Oh…thanks." Well, so you are human, she thought as she ran towards the big white double doors.

Room 10A was a small semi-private room with two beds, two nightstands, a bathroom and a window. Everything was that once white color that becomes cream with age, including the bedsheets. Conrad was lying in the bed closest to the window, his head partially raised but the rest of his body prone. He had an I.V. in his arm and when Karen entered the room, his face broke into a pained grin.

"Hi baby," he said.

Karen ran to his side and leaned over to kiss him.

"Careful," he warned. "The s.o.b. really got me."

"How do you feel, darling?" aske Karen anxiously. What a relief it was to see him awake and sounding almost like himself.

"Great. Just great." Conrad eyed the I.V.

"Can you talk a little bit?"

"Sure, sure."

"So what the hell happened?"

Karen tried not to look at the contents of the I.V. She was getting that old queasy feeling again. She looked at the bare walls and the empty cot like bed across from Conrad's. It was tightly made with sheets, pillow and cotton coverlet, standing at the ready for its next occupant.

Conrad briefly described what had taken place at the sound stage.

"Did you have to be such a hero?" asked Karen. "You scared the shit out of me!"

Conrad closed his eyes for a moment. Adjusting his position carefully he muttered "Poor bastard."

"You or the other guy?"

"Both of us."

Karen tried another tack. "So how bad is this?"

Conrad shrugged and immediately regretted the motion. "Ow," he winced. "It's nothing. I should be out in a couple of days. Luckily it didn't go in too deep." He grinned at her. "Wanna see my stitches?"

"No thanks!" Karen quickly responded. She knew Conrad was teasing her, and that was a good sign. He was well aware of her weak stomach. "I don't understand why they dragged you into it," she added.

"Guess they thought the resident spook would know how to deal with the cuckoo spook," Conrad chuckled and then gasped in pain. "Ouch! Don't make me laugh for God's sake."

"It's not the least bit funny." Karen reached for Conrad's hand and held it tightly.

"What is funny is that I think I was about to be fired when it hit the fan."

"Good. I hope you <u>are</u> fired. Then we can go home where we belong. We've got to get out of this town, darling. Before it kills us."

Conrad stared at the ceiling. "It's not the town, baby. The town's okay. It's the world."

Those words echoed in Karen's mind as she drove home from the hospital that night and again during the weeks that followed.

Conrad's recovery was amazingly swift. He was a strong man physically and his athletic past had inured him to pain. He was used to functioning with injuries and this time was no exception. He couldn't wait to get back on his feet and regain his self sufficiency. Whenever Karen attempted to wait on him she was met with "I'll do it" and forced to watch Conrad wince his way through whatever task had to be accomplished. She knew better by now than to fight him on matters like this. She knew he had to recover in his own way and wisely kept her mouth shut.

The most difficult part was not the healing of Conrad's body. The event had affected him psychologically and emotionally. He told Karen he'd spent a lot of time in the hospital thinking about the present and the future. but he hadn't shared his thoughts and she felt it would be best not to push him until he was ready. There were long periods of silence during the days he spent at home recuperating. He read a lot, took walks, slept. There were whole days when Conrad didn't speak at all and Karen decided ruefully that she might as well go back to work.

Calls from the studio were ignored. Of course they told him to take all the time he wanted. The individual who caused the whole event was resting comfortably in the psychiatric ward. They had asked Conrad if he would press charges and he had refused, saying it was an accident precipitated by poor judgment on the part of the security guards. Biff was happy because they had managed to avoid any bad press. There was just one small article in the L.A. TIMES about an extra having a nervous breakdown in the middle of filming a movie-of-the-week.

Every time Karen tried to get close to Conrad she was rebuffed. He had built some kind of protective shell around him that seemed to be all but impenetrable. She knew it wasn't just the accident, that many things were conspiring to bring matters to a head. She also knew it was best to wait it out. But it was maddening. Like waiting interminably for the other shoe to drop. She buried herself in work to keep from blowing up and saying something she might regret.

As it happened, the sitcom had been picked up and they'd gotten an order for thirteen shows. As associate producer she'd been up to her ears in work, usually getting assigned all the tasks the line producers wanted to avoid. But it was a great credit, a real stepping stone and Karen was grateful for the fact that it made her so tired by the end of the day that she could barely manage to eat dinner, much less solve the problems of this marriage.

CHAPTER 14

✻

At the end of two weeks Conrad returned to the Studio. Several days later he came home even later than Karen with a grin on his face and scotch on his breath.

"I'm fired, baby. Free at last! Let's celebrate!" He hugged Karen and danced her around the kitchen. "Ow," he said slowing down. "Still a little sore."

"What happened?" Karen made him sit down at the dining table and pulled up a chair alongside him. "Tell me."

Conrad described how he had gone into Biff's office, demanded the return of the screenplay that Biff had been sitting on all these months, announcing that he would like to spend his time developing it and therefore was giving two weeks notice. Biff had laughed and complimented him on his timing. It seems that Biff's contract was up and he was leaving Paramount to form his own company.

"So you weren't fired. That's bad. No unemployment insurance," interrupted Karen.

Conrad put his finger to her lips. "Patience," he said. "Wait 'til you hear the rest."

Karen's heart leaped. He was in such a good mood. Maybe this was a turning point. Whatever had taken place, he was like his old self. She listened attentively as Conrad went on. They were 'very appreciative of his contribution' so they were going to give him six weeks severance pay and a housekeeping deal.

"What's that?" Karen asked.

"They give me an office on the lot, a secretary, and the use of the phones, etc., in return for first look at whatever I develop. I'm free to do whatever I want. I'm a producer, baby! Thank God for white guilt."

Karen didn't want to bust his bubble, he was so happy. But she knew how hard it was to get a project off the ground and how long it could take. Everyone in the business called it 'development hell'. She hoped he wasn't going through one of those typical revolving doors. She wasn't worried about the rent, her job would take care of that. But she feared they were setting him up for another cruel fall by getting his hopes up and then letting him sit in an office and rot. Aloud she said only "Oh, Con, that's wonderful!"

Once again Conrad had a schedule that took up all day and all night. By day he sat in his office on the lot writing, seeing the never ending line of minority actors, writers and directors looking for work, and trying to get at least one project developed. By night he was at Inner City, rehearsing the play which had been postponed until his recuperation. He also spent entire weekends at the theatre, so that Karen was forced to go to the screenings and must-attend A list parties by herself. Once or twice when she caught Conrad in the morning as she was getting ready to go to work, she asked about visiting Inner City to watch a rehearsal. But she could tell by his response that her presence was the last thing he wanted at this point.

Karen, determined to survive this difficult period, began to create a separate life for herself filled with work and social contacts that derived from the work. She went to dinner often with her new friends, all of whom were bright, ambitious white workaholics whose main aspiration was success in the industry. Most of them didn't know anything about Conrad and didn't ask questions, simply accepting the fact that he was as busy as they were. Her days and nights were filled but Karen felt lonelier than ever. It was clear that for Conrad their marriage had taken a back seat to everything else, that she was unnecessary. It was as though the accident and the hospital stay had given him a jolt that changed his whole direction.

Karen deliberately waited up for him one night long past her usual bedtime. It was almost one a.m. when she finally heard his car pull into the driveway.

"Hi darling," she said softly as he entered the bedroom.

"Oh, hi." He was clearly surprised to see her still up.

"How's it going?"

"Great." He pulled off his jeans. Now that he was his own boss he wore jeans and a dashiki to work everyday. "We had the tech dress tonight." He lifted the dashiki over his head and draped it over the chair. "I'm beat." He went into the bathroom.

"Con, when am I going to see it?" called Karen.

There was silence in the bathroom followed by the sound of the flushing toilet.

"Con??" She could hear the water splashing as he washed.

He came to the door of the bathroom toweling hands and face. "Come to the opening," he said behind the towel and disappeared again.

Karen waited until he climbed into bed and leaned over to give her a goodnight peck on the cheek. "So when is it?"

"When is what?"

"The opening of SLOW DANCE. Wow, you <u>are</u> out of it!"

"Oh. Sorry. This Friday. I'll leave you a ticket at the box office. Eight o'clock."

Conrad rolled away from her and seemed to fall asleep immediately.

Thanks a lot, thought Karen. An overwhelming wave of sadness swept over her and tears welled up as she turned over and edged towards her side of the bed. But she wouldn't allow herself to surrender to them. This too shall pass, she thought grimly. It was the mantra she used to get her through the rough spots. He's tired and tense about the show and going through some big adjustments. Be patient! This too shall pass.

Conrad pretended to sleep so he wouldn't have to talk. He knew Karen was upset but he felt powerless to do anything about it. He loved her so much and it pained him to have to reject her. At this moment he wanted to take her in his arms, bury himself in the smell of her and the softness of her body. He needed her warmth and caring and he needed her intelligence and critical eye with this play. But he couldn't risk it. He had to prove himself, this was his chance and he couldn't risk doing anything to louse it up.

It was all getting to be too much to deal with. Like the steady stream of old friends and new aquaintances visiting him at the studio, thinking because they saw the outward trappings of success that he could do something for them. His stomach contracted when he recalled how impressed they were when they saw his name on the door of the wood paneled office and the tough, middle aged redheaded secretary who was assigned to him from the studio pool. If they only knew how truly impotent he was in that setting. It was all just for show. Noone had given him the time of day so far, much less entertained getting a project off the ground. He was still the 'spook sitting by the door'. Thank God for Inner City and the chance to direct this show. At least there he was undisputedly the man in charge.

His stomach lurched again when he thought about the opening. The show seemed to be going pretty well, although his young black actor had been a handful. He had had to work his balls off to win him over. There was still a lot of tension between Scott and the two white actors. And he didn't know how he was going to deal with Karen on opening night. One look at her and he'd lose the trust of half the young niggers in the group. They were so full of blind hate and rage. He had worked so hard to get them to see that he was on their side, to get them to accept him as one of them. He knew Karen was hurt at being so excluded and he felt guilty as hell about the way he was dealing with it, but what could he do? God, he felt as though he were being torn in half. Playing white man during the day and black man at night—he was so sick of it.

Maybe if the show's a big success it'll lead to something more and I can get enough clout to be my own man and call my own shots, he thought. He wondered if the stage manager got to the lighting man about that fade in the last scene. He reviewed the notes on the night's rehearsal in his mind until he finally fell into a fitful sleep.

Karen hadn't known what to expect as she drove to the Inner City theatre on opening night, but was unprepared for the size and faded grandeur of the old greying brick building. The old movie house still looked like one on the outside, though the marquee and the large glass panels where posters had been were gapingly empty. There was an adjoining parking lot in the back but no valet parking. Conrad had warned her that he would be busy back stage and that he would look for her during intermission or after the show, so she picked up her comp. at the box office. Since there was hardly anyone standing on the street outside the theatre as one would expect to see in New York, she went inside to take her seat even though it was a bit early.

Once inside she felt as though she were in an old Loew's house. Although signs of neglect were everywhere, in the slightly tattered seats, the fading gilt trims, the chipped paint, the chandelier's missing crystals, it was obvious that it had once been an impressive hall. It reminded Karen of those stately old buildings lining upper West End Avenue. Faded Elegance Row, she used to call them. It was certainly too large a house for a straight play. Okay for a musical, maybe. There was no curtain and the proscenium size had been cut down by a frame so that the audience would have the impression of looking through a huge window. The set, which appeared to be the inside of a store, was more suggestive than realistic but there was a real juke box on stage left near a small table with two chairs. Three stools lined a small soda fountain, stage center. The walls of the set were shelves filled with various articles one might find in some kind of seven-eleven store. Wow! thought Karen. What a load of props. Conrad must have a big crew.

She examined the program she'd been handed by a young black woman as she entered the theatre. All the information had been squeezed onto one page so the print was pretty small, but 'directed by Conrad Taylor' stood out in bold black letters. Karen didn't recognize any of the names of cast or crew, and there were a lot of them. For the first time she realized the scope of what he'd been doing and the difficulty of mounting this project. And, she realized, it was important that it be all his own, that he prove himself with this. That's why he kept me out of it, she thought. He wanted to surprise me with the finished work, something special and wonderful. Her spirits soared and she settled back in her seat in happy anticipation.

She watched the audience file in. Most of the people were black. Some were accompanied by children. Probably friends of the staff, thought Karen. There was a handful of white people, probably friends of the cast members. There had been no advertising that Karen knew of, unless they spread the word in this area only. Probably didn't have the money for it, thought Karen, but it's a shame. The audience barely filled three quarters of the sprawling orchestra section.

As the play unfolded Karen found herself crying, not so much because of the content of the play, but because of her awareness that Conrad's talent was so impressive and that until now he had not been allowed to use it. The work was wonderful, his directorial ideas were creative and effective and the play held. She was so proud of him and joined the demonstrative audience in cheering at the end. They even gave Conrad a curtain call when the actor playing Randall ran into the wings, grabbed him by the arm and pulled him out on stage. This is what he should be doing, thought Karen. The whole Hollywood thing was a snare and a delusion, fraught with frustration and disappointment. This was where he belonged.

Karen waited for what seemed like an eternity for Conrad to come out front from backstage. A good portion of the audience also waited for their friends or family connected with the show. When Conrad finally appeared he was immediately surrounded by a crowd of fans and Karen had to wait some more until Conrad broke through and came toward her.

"Darling, it was terrific," Karen hissed into his ear as she threw her arms around him, as much to claim him as hers for the assembled onlookers as to greet him.

"It went well, didn't it?" asked Conrad, gently unhooking her from his neck.

"Understatement! You did a great job. I'm so proud."

Conrad took Karen by the arm and guided her toward the door. "Let's get out of here," he muttered. Once outside he steered Karen towards the parking lot.

"Hey, am I getting a bum's rush or something? Don't I get to meet the cast?" asked Karen.

"There's a party at this restaurant nearby. We'll go in my car and then we'll come back and pick up yours on the way home," replied Conrad.

When they settled into the car he turned to Karen. "So you really liked it? You're not just bullshitting?"

"Con, this is me you're talking to, not one of those lay people in there. Your work was wonderful. It was so good it made me cry." Karen reached over and kissed him. "My multi-talented man. This is what you should be doing."

Conrad stared straight ahead. "Yep. I know, but…"

"But what?"

Conrad started the motor. "We'll see."

They talked a little about the play and the cast on the way to the restaurant, but it was obvious to Karen that Conrad was exhausted and making an effort to answer her questions.

"You're beat aren't you?" she said finally.

"Yeah. I hope you don't mind if we don't stay too long at this thing. I'm dead on my feet. Just got to put in an appearance."

Karen hid her disappointment. She was looking forward to this chance to know more about the people Conrad had been so involved with lately. "Whatever you say, darling. This is your night," was all she said.

Conrad felt a pang of guilt when he heard her bravely cheery response. He knew she'd been looking forward to this as much as he'd been dreading it. Most of the folks at the theatre knew he was married, but he'd kept it an abstract idea and deliberately avoided confronting them with the fact of his white Jewish wife. He knew what a problem it would create, what conflicts would arise with some of the more militant, bigoted members. He hated what they stood for,.but he'd been working very hard to turn them around. Tonight's success was just one step forward. He also knew that he couldn't spirit Karen away and then return to this party. She would be horribly hurt and he couldn't bear to do that to her. Again torn in half!

Aloud he said only "Your opinion means everything to me, baby. I'm so glad you thought the show was good."

"It was better than good. Are the critics going to come?"

Conrad shrugged. "Don't know. This whole Inner City Theatre is a pretty new idea. I hope so, but they don't usually come this far downtown except to cover the Ahmanson and the Mark Taper."

Karen was about to suggest some ways to get the attention of the papers, but Conrad cut her short. "We're here," he announced as he pulled alongside a low stucco building whose facade proudly proclaimed in bright red and yellow neon that it was the *Star Cafe.* Sounds of a rock beat drifted out to the street. As they emerged from the car Conrad took Karen's arm.

"Brace yourself. It's going to be noisy as hell," he said.

"And dark," added Karen. "Have you ever noticed how much darker L.A. restaurants are? Probably because the sun is so blinding."

Conrad knew she was nervous. She always chattered inconsequentially when she was tense about meeting new people.

As it turned out her fears were not groundless. The minute they entered the small, dark, packed room Conrad was swept along by several young men who shouted "Here he is" over the din of the persistent drum beat and a cacaphony of shrieks, laughter and brass notes. He turned back to reach for Karen but realized it was hopeless in the density of the crowd. Karen pasted a determined grin on her face and pushed forward to get to him, noting even in the darkness and the closeness of the bodies that she might be one of the few, if not the only white person in the room. As she fought her way to Conrad's side one of the young men handed Conrad a drink and started yelling a toast to the 'best director in L.A. if not the world'.

Conrad handed Karen his drink with a sheepish grin and shouted into her ear "they're all stoned arcady" as he responded to the toast and then attempted to push his and Karen's bodies toward the back of the room out of the crush. Amazingly, in about four feet of space, several couples were dancing.

"Who are all these people?" shouted Karen.

"Cast, crew, staff and all their friends," shouted Conrad back. "Wait here. I need a drink."

Before Karen could protest being left to her own devices, he was pushing his way back to the bar.

Karen looked around the room. The tables had been pushed to the sides of the room and sported checkered tablecloths, candle bowls and bud vases filled with something that looked fake. The walls were covered with black framed photographs under glass, presumably of celebrities although it was too dark to see. The four musicans making all the noise seemed to be improvising both the music and their positions in the room; all but the drummer seemed to keep moving. The crowd was getting thicker by the minute and Karen could see Conrad trapped once again near the bar by an adoring cadre of young black women. She sipped her drink and tried to look pleasant and casual, although judging by the way people around her were reacting to her presence, she suspected she might be invisible. At best she was ignored until a young couple, visibly drunk and trying to dance, staggered into her causing her to spill her drink down the front of her dress.

"Shit!" she exclaimed. She hastily searched for a kleenex in her purse to soak up the damage.

The young woman giggled when she realized what they'd done to this white woman.

Karen didn't see the joke. She glared at her. "Not funny, sister. I just had this dress cleaned."

This seemed to ignite a spark in the dancing girl. "Sister? You ain't my sister, bitch. What the hell you doin' here anyway?"

Karen knew the girl was drunk but her temper got the better of her. She straightened up, stood tall and shouted "I'm <u>Mrs.</u> Conrad Taylor…bitch!"

It was one of those classic moments when one thinks one has to shout to be heard over noise and suddenly everything goes dead quiet. Or so it seemed to Karen. Heads turned and the room's decibel level dropped suddenly.

The girl's partner froze. He pulled her away and they lost themselves in the crowd, which seemed to revert to its previous state, except that now small groups were forming. There was an undertone of buzzing and Conrad was making his way towards Karen.

"What the hell just happened? Can't I leave you alone for a minute?" he demanded.

"That female knocked my drink onto my dress, asked me what I was doing here and called me a bitch," replied Karen through clenched teeth. "Aren't you going to introduce me to anybody?" she challenged.

"I think you already accomplished that. Everyone heard you." Conrad laughed, trying to make light of it. "I'm sorry, babe. They wouldn't let me get away. This is a zoo. Maybe we should split."

They hovered for a bit longer and Conrad sought out the members of the cast and a few of the staff, making a show of introducing Karen as his 'old lady'. They were stiffly polite, barely able to conceal their surprise and disdain. Karen felt Conrad's discomfort and a huge knot began to grow in the pit of her stomach, until it was she who urged that they head for home.

Karen watched the stores and trees and houses rush by in a blur through the window of the car. Conrad had immediately put on a local radio station that played Aretha loud enough to preclude any in-depth conversation. Karen's thoughts raced through her head in pace with the scenery. She understood so much more now. Suddenly the reason for the distance and separation she had felt from Conrad had a framework. She had no place in this other world. She was an intrusion. And if she tried to remove him from it she would be harming him, because he needed what it gave him so desperately. The discovery made her sick to her stomach. She felt utterly helpless because her adversary was this behemoth of a complex societal condition rather than one individual she might get her hands on. It would've been easier if it had been one mistress or one anti-semitic friend. But how do you fight attitudes born of a century of mistreatment and the anger it engendered? Conrad was being forced to make choices based on....

"...Wasn't it?" repeated Conrad.

"I'm sorry. I didn't hear you. Wasn't what?" His voice had snapped her out of the train of thought.

"Wasn't it a nice party?" Conrad repeated raising his voice.

"Yeh, sure."

"Okay, so let's have it. What did you really think of the show and what mistakes did I make?"

Karen knew he was trying to distract her. "Con, I told you I thought your work was wonderful and I meant it. But if you want to talk in detail I'd rather wait until tomorrow when my head is clear and I don't have to fight Aretha Franklin. Okay?"

"Okay, babe," he shrugged. He knew damn well she was upset and he had no intention of igniting an explosion. Not tonight.

Please, he thought, let me have just one night of feeling a little bit good about what I'm doing. Karen was no fool and he knew she had picked up on exactly what had been eating him for the past few months. Trying to bring her into his new life downtown was just not going to work and he'd known it from the start. He shouldn't have to live down the fact that he had a white Jewish wife. But how could he turn his back on this opportunity now? God knows nothing was happening in any other part of his life. The white world had all but slammed the door on him, although he was still unwilling to admit that there wasn't a crack somewhere that would enable him to break through. If he could only come up with something they couldn't resist.

He hadn't told Karen about how completely they had ignored him once he moved into his little Paramount lot office. Or how he'd spent his days seeing one black actor or writer after another and listened to them tell him how they were counting on him to 'turn things around'. And how he knew he couldn't do shit for anybody and it was all a lie but he had to face them and pat them on the back and mutter "keep the faith baby, we'll see what we can do" or some other equally inane cliche. Inner City was a way to stay sane. He didn't want to have to give it up. But he could see what might lay ahead for this marriage if he didn't and he was sick about it.

They were both pretty quiet for the remainder of the trip and when they spoke it was small talk about the weather, the car, anything but what was on their minds. When they got home and began to undress Karen went to Conrad and put her arms around him.

"I was awfully proud of you tonight darling," she murmured into his neck.

"That's good. I wanted you to be," he replied.

"Oh! I almost forgot. I put some champagne in the refrigerator." Karen ran to get it and quickly returned with two glasses and the damp cold bottle of Moet. "I thought we'd want to have our own little celebration." She grinned at him.

Conrad felt like crying. He knew what she was doing, that she wanted him to know she understood and he loved her for it. And he loved her for not insisting that they talk about it. They toasted and drank and got ready for bed and made love. But they never said a word about what had happened that night and what they both feared might happen next.

CHAPTER 15

Karen often thought of the opening night of SLOW DANCE as the turning point date when she allowed herself to think about it at all. It was like having a bad black and blue mark. Don't touch it and you won't feel it. So she tried not to touch it in the hope that by some miracle it would heal of its own volition. Her responsibilities as associate producer had escalated and since the series had been picked up there was more than enough reason to throw herself into the work. Karen wondered if one of those nubile young black women she'd seen fawning over Conrad at the party had managed to get her hooks into him. An affair? she wondered. She dared not raise the question even as a joke, almost not wanting to know the answer. And anyway she knew what the attraction really was. They made him feel important and valuable. It was an antidote to everything he'd had to put up with since they came out here. She knew that unless she could think of a substitute, wild horses wouldn't drag him away. So she opted for silence and letting time take its course.

Conrad felt his sense of desperation mounting. He seemed always to be on the verge of something. At the Studio they kept jerking him around, making him feel that any minute they would okay one of his projects but never making a definitive move. At Inner City the promise of the leadership position of artistic director continued to be dangled before him. So he had to keep playing their game, buying into their militant stance, because he knew only with their trust could he make constructive changes. This meant hiding Karen, risking their relationship which he felt was also on the verge—of destruction. He walked around with a chronic bellyache and carried every known over-the-counter cure for indigestion available at Thrifty's. He told Karen it was the aftermath of the stabbing, but he knew better. I can't go on like this much longer, he thought grimly as he headed for his office. Something's gotta give. He decided he had to make a move of some kind to break through this suffocating web.

Karen was amazed when Conrad appeared on the set suddenly one early afternoon. She'd been standing in front of one of the monitors with the lighting designer. They were in the middle of rehearsal of a scene in one of the standing sets on the other side of the studio. The director was in a huddle with the writers as the actors remained in the set going over their lines. The cameramen were standing patiently behind their cameras experimenting with the framing of shots. The production assistants were standing by, chatting as they waited for the next order.

"Something is off," she muttered to the man standing alongside of her as they both stared into the monitor. "I can't put my finger on it."

"Of course it's off, damn it," replied the designer. "I can't light the star and that new black actor the same way. Black skin needs a whole different thing. And they never give me enough time to solve it when they're in a shot together."

Yeh, thought Karen. You mean you've had very little experience with it up to now. It was as she turned away that she saw Conrad approaching, picking his way through the maze of wires and cables that snaked along the floor. He was dressed in jeans, sweatshirt and sneakers and needed a shave. A warning bell went off in her head. He never visited her at work. He hated sitting around while she was busy working.

"Hi, darling. Come to watch rehearsal?" she smiled, trying to sound casual. She wondered how he'd managed to get past the gate without her having put his name on the list. The CBS gatekeepers were notoriously tough.

"I need to talk to you. Think you can take a minute away from your chores?" There was just a slight edge of sarcasm in Conrad's tone.

Karen stared at him. He looked awful. Tired, drawn, almost seedy in fact. It was all totally out of character and her heart sank. Something terrible must have happened. She took his arm and led him up the stairs toward the dressing rooms. "Come with me," was all she said.

Conrad followed her up the narrow iron stairs to the balcony which surrounded and overlooked the studio and housed the dressing rooms and green room. She pulled him into one of the empty rooms and closed the door. The room held a serviceable dark brown couch, a dressing table and dark wood chair and a large mirror. She caught a glimpse of her own face in the mirror and was shocked to see how pale it looked. She collapsed onto the couch.

"Lord, my feet hurt," she sighed. "Come sit down, Con. What's up?"

Conrad remained standing. "Karen, I'm going away for a few days and I didn't want you to come home and just find a note."

Karen's jaw dropped. "Going away? Where?" She could feel her heart pounding very hard suddenly.

"I'm going up to the high desert for a while to work."

"But what about the office at the Studio and Inner City?"

Conrad shrugged. "I'll never be missed at the Studio. Most of the time they don't know I'm there. And Inner City knows I'm going to work on our project."

"Yours and who elses?"

"It's the one I've been working on with Jay Hairston. We're so close to getting it right." He was pacing back and forth.

Karen had never met this Jay fellow but she remembered that he was one of the black writers that Conrad had mentioned over the past few months. "What the hell's in the high desert?"

"Jay has a cabin up there. It's quiet. No distractions."

"You mean no dancing girls?"

"Come on, Karen. I'm desperate. This script is the only thing I've got going for me and they're now saying one more draft will do it. If I can just get Jay to focus and concentrate. And even if they pass on it, there's a rumor about a new black production company starting at Universal..."

"Couldn't this wait until tonight?" Karen interrupted, aware that they were probably looking for her on the set.

Conrad checked his watch. "We're leaving in an hour."

"Oh! Well, thanks for all the advance notice. How long will you be gone?"

"I told you. A few days. I dunno. As long as it takes."

Karen fought back the tears. "Thanks so much for your support."

"What the hell does that mean?"

Karen jumped up and confronted him, tears flowing now. "You know damn well what that means. I'm working on a new show with enormous pressure and you barge in here in the middle of everything and lay this on me. Isn't this some sort of punishment because I'm doing what you think you should be doing?"

"Karen, I don't have time for this. Talk about not being supportive...."

"Why can't you wait a day until we've had a chance to talk? Can't you wait until the taping is over at least? Do you have to do this to me now? Of all the destructive...."

Now it was Conrad's turn to explode. "Waiting is all I ever do! Waiting for your folks to notice me. Waiting for them to decide my fate…"

'DON'T GIVE ME THAT 'YOUR FOLKS' SHIT! I'M SICK OF HEARING IT!! Karen was screaming into his face now.

"You know what? You're right. This was a bad idea. I should've just left you a note. Later." Conrad turned on his heel and stormed out, slamming the door behind him.

Karen got through the day somehow and was grateful for the numerous crises that occupied her physically and mentally as the rehearsal progressed. The script was going through constant revision to satisfy the director and answer the questions and concerns of the actors. Each change meant new pages in different colors and distribution to crew, cameras, production personnel, the a.d., the p.a., etc. By the end of the day Karen was too exhausted to feel much of anything and she couldn't wait to get home.

It wasn't until she'd left Studio City and was sitting in her car at Mulholland on top of Laurel Canyon waiting for the traffic to curl its way down towards Sunset Boulevard that she allowed herself to think about Conrad and their fight. Perhaps she'd been unfair, she thought. She'd been so involved with work that that she'd left their marriage waiting in the wings. She understood the daily culture shock to which Conrad was subjected and the toll that it took. They hadn't even made love in quite a while.

As she pulled into their driveway her heart leapt at the sight of Conrad's car. Maybe he didn't go, she thought. Then she remembered that he was meeting Jay and that they probably went in Jay's car. The house seemed strangely quiet and empty as Karen kicked off her shoes and began to shed her clothing. She'd often arrived home before Conrad, but tonight it felt different somehow. Strange what the mind is capable of doing. Karen poured herself a generous gulp of scotch and went into the bedroom. It wasn't until she saw how much of his stuff was missing from the bathroom that the tears started. She checked and found one of the suitcases was gone. She hurried to the closet. The dashikis and jeans were missing but the suit and good jacket were still there. She downed the rest of the scotch before she threw open the dresser drawers and confirmed her fear that Conrad had packed for an extended absence. She hurled herself onto their bed and sobbed until exhaustion and alcohol sent her to sleep without any supper.

She lay in bed the next morning halfway between sleep and awakeness, thinking. In the cold light of day, Karen decided she had made much too much of Conrad's departure. She'd been totally unreasonable. Of course he would have wanted to get some space. She was wrapped up in her job and he was trying to get a career going and reclaim his self respect and why shoudn't they be able to spend some time apart without damaging their marriage? After all, she'd gone to New York without him and he hadn't made a scene. She'd been unthinking and unreasonable and now she was full of remorse and wishing she could apologize to him. She realized with a start that she had no idea where he was or how to reach him. She wondered if he'd left any information for her. She got up and padded barefoot into the kitchen for some juice and coffee. As she reached for the refrigerator handle she saw the note taped on the door: "I'll be at 805 323 5472. Be a good girl. Love."

Karen forced herself to wait until she'd finished her coffee before she dialed the number.

"Hello?" It was a soft female voice. Karen's throat closed for a moment. Did she have the wrong number?

"Uhhh…is this 323 5472?"

"Yes it is." There was a trace of laughter in the response.

"Is Conrad there?" All sorts of thoughts raced through Karen's mind as she heard the other voice calling Conrad's name.

"Yep." It was Conrad's familiar greeting.

"Hi" said Karen tentatively. "How are you?" That was dumb, she thought grimly. "I just wanted to tell you how sorry I am about yesterday," she added hastily as though afraid he might hang up.

"Yeh. Me too."

Karen waited for him to say more but nothing came so she plunged on. "Who was that?"

"What?"

"Who answered the phone?"

"Oh." He paused. "Jay's woman. Gloria. She's a terrific cook." He paused again. "Checking up?"

"No, Con, just curious. You didn't mention a cook." This wasn't going well. She was sorry she'd made the call. "I miss you and I'm sorry we didn't have more time to talk."

Conrad seemed to lower his voice as though not to be overheard. "Yeh. I miss you too. We'll talk when I get back, okay? I gotta go. Take care."

"When are you coming home, Con?" Karen persisted. She knew it was a mistake but she couldn't help herself.

"As soon as we finish. Later." He hung up.

Karen tried not to think about the phone call as she showered, dressed and got ready to drive to the studio. But sitting behind the wheel waiting for the ribbon of cars on Crescent Heights to cross Sunset Boulevard and wend their way north up Laurel Canyon, her thoughts turned to it like tongue to sore tooth. Who was the woman who answered the phone? Was Conrad having an affair and using Jay as a front? Or was it a foursome with Jay and his woman and Conrad and his? Karen cursed the fact that her eyes were welling up again. Damn, she thought. Why am I so suspicious? Is it that I don't trust Con and his feelings for me, or is it this town and its insidious aura of infidelity and amorality? And if he is having an affair, whose fault is it?

Karen started as a blaring horn alerted her that the line of cars was moving. She thought about doing some detective work to find out if Jay was indeed up at this cabin or still in town. Then she shuddered at the ugliness of what she was even contemplating. Look at this, she thought. Here I am planning to spy on my husband. What is happening to me? I'm not going to call him again, she resolved. The less she knew about what he was doing the better. She was going to wait for him to call her.

It was hard to focus on the show that day and in the days to follow. Karen went through all the usual motions but she felt as though she were carrying a load of coal in the pit of her stomach.

Conrad sat on the steps of the cabin and gazed at the cactus growing not far from his feet. It was such an odd looking bluish green plant with its thorny spikes growing every which way. He had never seen terrain like this or experienced this kind of heat and aridity. It didn't look like any desert he'd ever seen in the movies. No graceful rolling hills of soft sand. The ground was more like dried yellow clay. The vista extended for miles and the dwellings were few and far between. He couldn't understand why anyone would want a get-away place here. Although he had to admit there was a certain sterile beauty to the clear blue of the sky and the beigeness of the land. Beige is my color, he snickered to himself. I blend right in. And it certainly was quiet. In fact, the quiet was deafening. Tossing and turning in the suddenly cool night as he tried to fall asleep, his ear had seemed to reach out for some kind of sound.

He took periodic gulps from the water bottle at his side although its contents had grown tepid and less than satisfying as it sat on the wooden step. Four days had passed and they'd gotten very little accomplished. Conrad knew when Gloria turned up that he was going to have a hard time getting Jay to focus on the work. Conrad had been shocked when he saw the wood cabin.

The tiny living room and two small bedrooms were even more rustic than what Jay had described, but what was worse, it looked as though it hadn't been cleaned in a year. There was no washing machine and Conrad discovered that the laundry was in the tiny town some miles away. So the first day was shot making that trip to do the sheets and towels and stock up on groceries.

They tried to make the place temporarily liveable and Jay had brought several bottles of booze to, as he put it, 'court the muse'. This turned out to be pure fantasy because once Jay started drinking he was virtually useless to Conrad as a writer. So they had really only managed five or six hours of concentrated work on the script in these four days, especially since Jay had blabbed about their plans to the adorable little brown skinned twenty something from Inner City who had such a crush on Conrad. Tanya had suddenly appeared yesterday in her little red VW to make it a foursome. Conrad suspected it had been part of a plot that Gloria and Jay cooked up to make it a fun time.

Or was it a plot to break up his marriage to the detested white Jewish woman? He'd been as charming as possible, but he had no desire to sleep with Tanya even though he knew that was what she expected. He'd used a migraine as an excuse and she'd left this morning. He was sure that she'd report back to the group that he was a faggot. He was furious with Jay. He'd come here to work, not screw around, and now he'd put him in an impossible position. And for all they'd accomplished so far he might as well do all the writing himself.

Conrad lit a cigarette and thought about trying to rent a car and return home right away. Then he would have to deal with Karen and the inevitable questions and tears. He'd felt so guilty about Karen. He knew he couldn't be the kind of partner she needed now that she was moving in the more heavy-weight professional circles and coming up the ladder. Her people tolerated him but their discomfort was obvious. He was as much a liability for her as she was a liability for him at Inner City where there was an equal amount of ignorance and prejudice.

He had hoped to be the force that would bring everyone together. He was sure that it was what he was meant to do. But it would take time and careful maneuvering and Inner City was where he belonged right now. His effort to break into the establishment with this bull shit housekeeping deal at Paramount was all smoke. They weren't ready to accept his kind of project or his kind of script. One major black role per show was what they considered 'progress' and it was about as much as they could handle. Unless it was a cartoon with a group of ludicrous stereotypes. For the sake of the marriage he'd tried to play their game and failed miserably at it.

Conrad stood up suddenly and tossed the butt. Who am I kidding? he snorted. He knew he wanted to be one of them. He wanted the Mercedes and the house with the pool and the designer clothes. He'd seen what the white boys had and he'd wanted some. He'd thought he had the talent and smarts to get it. What he hadn't realized was that they weren't going to let him get it. Not yet, at least.

He had to find another way in. Perhaps become a star in his own community, find the black money, start a black production company. Be the 'first to…' again. But could he do it in this town with Karen as his wife? Could he get Karen to play the invisible role like Sidney did? Those two never went anywhere together, were never seen together in public. Would it be fair to ask that of Karen? What kind of life would that be for her? Much as he loved her and needed her, he knew he had to face the reality. Their marriage would have to be put on hold, for both their sakes.

As he started to pace, his sneakers leaving prints in the dusty ground, Conrad decided to give Jay another two days to finish the work of the script. Together they'd already improved the delineation of the two main characters. Now all they had to do was fill in a couple of the story line holes. If we can get that much done it won't have been a total loss, he thought. Once this is off my chest, I'll be able to think more clearly about Karen and what to do next.

As it turned out, they got quite a bit done in the next couple of days and Conrad's spirits began to lift. As he read the screenplay through at the end of the week he was certain they had finally gotten the draft they needed. This one would make them take notice, he was sure. The script was about a very light-skinned black man named Bert Williams who was actually one of the stars of the Ziegfeld Follies. He was a Negro performer forced to work in blackface, and the story was full of racial signifigance neatly tucked into a package of humor and showbiz history. Conrad knew that if they bought it his chances of directing the film were slim to none. But maybe they would let him play the lead. After all, how many black performers were there who were so light they could only get acceptance by blacking up like Jolson?

"Hey, man, let's celebrate! Have a taste," hooped Jay when Conrad told him how pleased he was. "Gloria! C'mon out here!"

"Break out the scotch, man. I am ready to party!" exulted Conrad. And party they did for the rest of the day. Conrad was so drunk by the time the little red VW containing the adorable Tanya showed up, he didn't even question her second sudden appearance. And that night she wasn't disappointed.

CHAPTER 16

✿

It had been difficult for both of them after Conrad's return. He'd decided not to tell Karen anything beyond the work on the script. After all, he'd reasoned to himself on the drive home, what she didn't know wouldn't hurt her, and the whole Tanya thing was totally meaningless anyway. He was so bombed he couldn't remember much about it anyway. Tanya had blessedly had to leave early the next morning to get back for an audition and he was pretty sure he could rely on her discretion. As he sat quietly in the back seat of Jay's old Pontiac pretending to be asleep, he silently kicked himself for letting himself be compromised by the folks he knew had a sneaky agenda. Or am I looking for a way out? he thought suddenly. When he arrived home he played it cool, concentrating on what they had accomplished with the script and what a constructive trip it had been.

Karen allowed herself to be swept along by Conrad's enthusiasm. Although she'd gone through many phases during his absence, from anger to hurt to despair, when he finally appeared she was so relieved and happy to see him that she was determined to be as warm and welcoming as possible. He hadn't called and she'd resolved not to call him, but fantasized constantly about what was really going on. Then she'd upbraided herself for dramatizing the whole thing and making it much more serious than it was. So it was a happy reunion. They hugged, kissed and joked and finally ate a great dinner that Karen cooked in celebration of Conrad's return.

They'd both been actors and now they were each giving a great performance. They walked on eggs, careful of every word, saying anything but the truth, anything that would prevent opening the can of worms. They were sweet and caring with one another whenever they were together. They became sociable roommates more than husband and wife. Since neither wanted to confront the issues that were driving them apart for fear of an irretrievable explosion, they went on this way as the weeks flipped by and turned into months.

Since Conrad was always busy at Inner City in the evenings, Karen continued to go to screenings and plays at night by herself or with one of her New York friends or someone from the show. Conrad, relieved to have the pressure taken off, would apologize and assure Karen that the situation was temporary and that once he was firmly ensconced as head of Inner City, he could adjust his schedule more conveniently. But Karen knew that if he did get the job he'd probably be putting in fourteen hours a day.

Their separate worlds did not allow for crossing paths or interaction of any kind. The isolation caused by auto transport eliminated the possibility of running into somebody on the street or on a bus or subway as would so often happen in New York. The sprawling chain of suburbs that is Los Angeles made it unlikely that one would meet an acquaintance in a restuarant or bar unless they'd planned to do so. East, west, north and south each had their own hangout. So what happened one night when Karen went to see one of the actresses on the sitcom in a workshop production of a new play was even more of a shock. She'd called Marie Diamond to go with her to the tiny theatre in the valley since they hadn't had a chance to visit in a long time and the thirty or forty minute ride to and from the theatre would give them time to talk.

"Let's take Ventura Boulevard instead of the freeway," Marie suggested. "You won't have to concentrate on driving and we'll be able to talk."

"You're a very smart friend," said Karen. "You know when I've got a lot to unload."

"Well darling, it doesn't take a psychiatrist to see that you haven't been the happiest of campers lately. What's going on?"

Karen recounted some of the events of the last few months, carefully edited and with just enough specifics to convey her anxiety about the marriage. She tried to avoid getting emotional, but tears filled her eyes when she admitted how lonely she was and how at a loss she was about what to do next.

"Look, Karen. You've got to face something. It's not just about race and the black and white thing. Remember, I warned you when you first got here. We're all lonely out here. All the wives. That's the nature of this company town. We're supposed to be invisible, stay home and make nice when our weary hunter returns from pillaging and burning in the jungle."

Karen laughed in spite of herself. "Talk about mixed metaphors!"

"It's true that things are twice as hard for you because of who Conrad is," continued Marie. "I do think you guys might have had an easier time of it in New York," she added thoughtfully.

"But there was no work for Con there," objected Karen. "Although, they're not letting him do much of anything here either."

"Well, if I were you, I'd get him out of here as fast as possible. Go home. Go back to the city and the theatre. That's what I'd do."

"I doubt if I'd be able to tear him away now. It would probably seem to him as though he were admitting defeat," said Karen softly. But she knew Marie was right.

The theatre was located in one of those block long malls so common in the valley. It was flanked on one side by a PIP copy shop and on the other by a beauty supply shop. The advantage of these places was that in addition to street parking there was always parking in the back. Karen was startled to discover that this theatre only had about fifty seats and that the stage couldn't have been more than about fourteen feet wide. The walls were painted black and there was no curtain separating the stage from the audience area. A large table at the back of the house held a portable switchboard from which the handful of stage lights were controlled. I hope it doesn't have more than three in the cast, Karen giggled to herself. It's amazing how they find these tiny spaces to feed their theatre Jones. That was one of the expressions Con had taught her. A 'Jones' was an addiction.

It seemed that no matter how much money actors made, or how successful they seemed to be, they still lusted after a live theatre experience and were willing to work for no money, stretch themselves thin time-wise and take big artistic risks. It was clear that the theatre satisfied something in the actor that TV and film couldn't reach. Of course, it must be the audience…the immediate audience response. Most of the sitcoms had live audiences for just that reason. It was a high wire act. But in TV there was a net. They could always do a retake. No net in the theatre. That must be it, she thought. The tremendous thrill of taking that big risk must be the lure that keeps bringing them back.

Here the audience was in such close proximity it was as if they were all in the play. Unfortunately, the seats were hard wood that was intensely uncomfortable and there wasn't much in the way of ventilation. And although Sherry, the actress that Karen had come to see, was more than capable, the play was talky and lacking in any real story line. Intermission was a welcome relief and the forty or so people made a bee line for the cool breeze outside.

"Sorry I dragged you to this, Marie." Karen had to see it, but she felt guilty about subjecting her friend to this bore.

"Hey, it's not your fault that the guy can't write," protested Marie. "You never know with these little workshop things. Sometimes you find a little gem and sometimes it's 'who do I have to kill to get out of here?' Are you planning to go back to see your friend?"

"Yeah, I have to. She's a regular on the show and she's the one who got me the tickets."

"Well, actually, she's not bad. What are you going to say?"

"I'll let you know when it's over. Maybe it'll get better."

But it didn't get better, although Sherry had a big emotional scene towads the end of the act that was quite moving. The applause at the end of the play was enthusiastic and sounded suspiciously like an audience composed mostly of friends and relatives, many of whom remained in the theatre waiting for the members of the cast to emerge.

"I doubt if there's a stage door here. They'll probably come through the theatre. We can wait out front if you like," said Karen.

"I do like. I'm dying for a cigarette," Marie responded.

As they stood in front of the theatre in the cool night air watching the audience file out and the cars drive by on the adjoining avenue, Karen felt as though she were standing on a street in a very small town. There wasn't much light in the tiny mall and the sky overhead although dotted with stars was an inky black. The surrounding buildings were only one story high and except for the low humming of motors when the nearby traffic light turned red, it was startlingly quiet. I'm still an alien in another country, thought Karen suddenly.

Sherry didn't take long to dress and emerge. The intimacy of the theatre eliminated the need for much makeup and noone wanted to linger in the close quarters of the miniscule unisex dressing room with its thin curtain hanging down the middle of the room. She was a petite coffee colored woman in her thirties and Marie was surprised to discover that she'd been wearing a straight long haired brown wig in the show. Her close cropped Afro made her look even tinier. Her beige pants suit had been carefully tailored to reveal a stunning figure which had been totally obscured by the dumpy housedress she wore in her role.

She greeted Karen effusively with a hug, exclaiming "Karen, I'm sooo glad you came! You're the only one from the show so far."

"I'm glad I came too. You were great. Sherry, this is my friend Marie Diamond."

Marie tried to be charming. "I enjoyed your work. Thanks for the evening."

"Thank you. What did you think of the play? Do you think it has any potential?" Sherry seemed to be addressing the question to both of them. She didn't know who this other woman was, and she might be someone of importance in the industry.

Karen came to the rescue, jumping in quickly. "Well, I think it needs a lot of work. But who knows? I'm sure the writer is learning a lot from this run and the basic idea is good." When she saw Sherry's face falling she hastened to add, "And your last scene is beautiful. I hope you get a lot of people in to see you."

"I'm trying, I'm trying. But you know how it is. You can't get these film people out here to go to the theatre for love or money. God, I hope it has a life. There are so few parts for black actors. It may be years before I get another part like this." Sherry brooded over that for a second, then suddenly her tone changed and became conspiratorial. "But listen to me, only thinking about myself." She patted Karen on the arm and her voice dropped to a whisper. "How are you doing?"

"I'm fine Sherry. Just fine," replied Karen, slightly mystified. Did she think I've been sick or something, she wondered.

"I was sooo sorry to hear about you and Conrad," Sherry cooed into Karen's ear. Marie heard it and her eyes opened wide but she said nothing.

Karen stiffened. "What do you mean?"

"Well, you know. The vine says that you and Conrad have split up."

Karen's heart began to pound. She knew all about the 'vine'. It had always been amazing how the word got around in the black community, both in L.A. and in New York. It seemed as though any time there was relevant news pertaining to the 'folks' it would travel their grapevine with the speed of light. But what was this about? Who had put this word out?

"I'm sorry," Sherry hastened to add. "From the look on your face I guess I just stepped in it."

"It's not true, Sherry. I don't know how such a rumor could have gotten started."

"Well, honey, it must have been that bitchy Tanya. Word is she's been hangin' on Conrad wherever he's gone this past month. Someone must have gotten the wrong idea."

"Who's this Tanya?"

"Oh, she's just one of the kids in that group down at Inner City. We all go down and hang out there from time to time, you know. But listen, honey, I'm sooo sorry I even brought it up. Me and my big mouth."

You're not the least bit sorry, thought Karen. You knew exactly what you were doing. Should I be grateful for the 'heads up'?

"Anyway, I'm sooo glad it's not true. And I thank you for coming all the way out here to see me." Sherry turned to include Marie. "Both of you."

Marie managed a wry smile and nod of the head.

"Well, we'd better be on our way before Conrad starts to worry," said Karen with a wink at Marie behind Sherry's back.

"Gee, I wish he could have come to see this," said Sherry. "He's such a good director."

"He's been awfully busy lately, what with two offices. He'll probably be getting home just about now," replied Karen sweetly. "But I'll tell him about it and maybe he'll be able to catch it before you close."

"Oh, I hope. See you on the set." And Sherry beat a rather hasty retreat.

"Talk about bitches!" Marie fairly spat it out as they walked toward the car.

The fist that lay in Karen's chest turned into a knot that started moving up her oesophogus and into her throat making it difficult for her to talk for a moment. It wasn't until they were both settled in their seats and she had started the motor that she found her voice.

"Maybe." Karen said thoughtfuly. "It was bitchy, but I think she thought she was doing me a favor."

"This lousy town!" snorted Marie. "Everyone's so bored they have to create excitement by ruining people's lives."

"It's not just the town, Marie. If there weren't some holes in our relationship, these worms wouldn't be able to crawl through and make them larger."

"Well, if I were you, I wouldn't ignore this. I'd look into this Tanya thing. There are a lot of predatory females roaming around these parts. And if you want to hold onto your man you've got to let your claws grow."

"Yeah. I guess I've been postponng the inevitable. Con and I have to decide what it is we really want. And maybe going back to New York is the answer. Maybe that is our only hope."

As Karen pulled up in front of the Diamond house on Coldwater Canyon Marie turned to her and said "Honey, I'll tell you a secret. Sam and I have a pact. The minute he decides to retire we're moving back. And I am counting the days!" She reached over and kissed Karen's cheek. "Hang in there, honey."

It wsn't until Karen had seen the door close behind Marie that she allowed herself to let go and she cried all the way home.

Conrad knew something was up and that they probably had reached crisis point. Karen had made herself very scarce all week, saying only that she urgently needed to talk to him on the weekend and that he should be sure and designate time in his busy schedule because it was of extreme importance. It was the way her jaw was set and the fact that she looked everywhere but at him that tipped him off. He knew her so well that he could feel the pain emanating from her body like darting rays piercing his own skin. He was filled with disgust at the way he was behaving and it made him sick to his stomach. But his ego wouldn't let him change the path he'd chosen. He knew how much he was hurting Karen but hadn't the strength of will to stop so they continued rolling ever faster down the hill towards the inevitable. He was glad she'd made the first move toward getting it out in the open.

It was almost as though they had both played out the scene in their heads independently prior to that Saturday. So when they sat together in the living room after a late breakfast, each nursing a second mug of coffee, it was anticlimatic. It was as though they'd had a silent on-going dialogue and therefore could start somewhere in the middle of the topic. This ability to get inside of each others' heads without verbal communication, was one of the things that had drawn them together initially. It was one of the things that would never change.

Karen drew her white terrycloth bathrobe around her and curled up in a ball on the sofa. Conrad had thrown on his old Knicks tee shirt and ratty green shorts. He stretched out in the big chair propping his long bare legs up on the coffee table opposite her. Karen suddenly flashed on how they used to joke about how much each enjoyed looking at the others' legs because they were two such beautiful pairs.

"The rumor is that we've separated," began Karen.

"Oh yeah? Where'd you hear that?"

Well, according to Sherry, it's 'on the vine.'"

Conrad sipped his coffee. "Who's Sherry?"

"Sherry Jones. She's the black actress on the show. I went to see her in that showcase she's in and she commiserated with me over my loss."

"Well, that was sweet of her."

"How do you suppose that rumor got started, Con?"

"Shit, Karen, you know this town. Breaking people up is one of the parlor games. You gonna fall for that?"

Karen was silent for a moment. Then she put her mug on the table and stared at Conrad. "So who's Tanya?"

He was taken by surprise. "What?"

"Who's this Tanya who's always with you?"

Amazing, thought Conrad. In a sprawling town of this size, every move... "She's a student in my class."

"Class? What class?"

"Well, I haven't had a chance to tell you about it, but I've started an acting class at Inner City. Now that the folks are getting parts once in a while, they desperately need training. I'm trying to build a school specifically for black actors."

Karen's eyes opened wide. "You've started a school and you didn't even bother to mention it to me?"

"Well babe, you've been pretty busy lately and so have I...and it's in a very early stage. I was going to tell you when I thought we were really underway."

"And this Tanya who goes everywhere with you is an actress and one of your new students?"

"Karen, cut it out," growled Conrad.

"Cut it out? I was so humiliated!" Karen was desperately trying not to lose control. "It seems as though everyone in the world knows what's going on but me!"

"There's nothing going on. This girl is following me around because I'm from New York and she thinks I might be able to help her career. You of all people should understand that. I haven't done anything wrong, regardless of what you've heard. What happened to trust?"

"Oh, Con." The tears were coming now in spite of her efforts. "We've got to get out of here. Please, please let's go home."

"We are home."

"I mean New York."

"Out of the question. I'm just beginning to see the possibility of getting something started here."

"Con, don't you see?" pleaded Karen. "This place is destroying us. We're not together anymore. You're in your world and I'm in mine. And the gap is getting wider and wider. I love you and I don't want to lose you!"

"I love you too, Karen. But what makes you think it would be any better in New York? The problem has nothing to do with the place. There are things I have to do that I can't do with you. And it's the same for you. We're in each other's way, can't you see that? If you really love me, you'll understand what I need to do to crack the barriers. It's because I love you that I back off and leave you to your world. I'm a fucking liability for you. Can't you see that?" He was shouting now and he jumped up and started to pace.

"That's not true!"

"You know damn well it's true!"

"So what does this mean?" Karen jumped off the couch to confront him. "Are we going to let them tear us apart? Are we going to let them win?"

Conrad grabbed Karen by the shoulders. "I don't know who 'them' is anymore. I only know that we both need some space right now." His eyes began to glisten with tears. "Karen, don't you see? I can't be any good to you or myself until I feel like a man again. Let me do what I have to do to get back who I am." He grimaced suddenly as a pain shot through his innards. "I have to get some aspirin." He headed toward the bathroom.

"Are you going to play ball today?" Karen called out. She knew that the chances of continuing this talk now were slim. As soon as the issues were confronted and the going got tough, Conrad found a way to withdraw. She heard the door of the medicine cabinet slam shut.

"Nah," he replied. "I'm not feeling so good. I'm going to lie in the sun in the back for a while and read a script."

After she cleaned up the kitchen Karen put on some shorts and a tee shirt and joined Conrad in the backyard. It was a classic California sun day with a cloudless bright blue sky making the green of the trees and grass even more intense. The air was still and the sun hot on the skin. Karen tried to make Conrad talk about what was happening with his screenplay project and what he planned to do at Inner City with the acting class he'd started, but when all she got were monosyllabic replies to her questions, she gave up. So Conrad pretended to read his script and Karen to read the week's copies of Daily Variety which she'd saved to get to when she had time.

After an hour of silence Conrad jumped up and stretched. "This is dumb," he said. "Why don't we go to the beach? It's a beautiful day and it's getting too hot here."

"Great." said Karen. At least they'd be together for the day. That hadn't happened in quite a while.

It was a twenty minute drive to the stretch of beach between Santa Monica and Venice that they liked to go to because it was the least populated. The big parking lot was right at the edge of the beach and skaters and bikers sped alongside on the adjoining thin cement path.The soft cream colored sand burned the bottoms of ones feet but the cool breeze blowing gently from the sapphire ocean acted as a soothing salve.

"You can't get this in New York City," Conrad murmured as they stretched out on their blanket.

"No, and you can't pick a peach off a tree in your backyard either," retorted Karen. "I never said there weren't good things about this life. But at what price?"

"Let's just enjoy the afternoon, Karen."

They lathered themselves with sun tan lotion and dozed in the sun. After a while Karen got up and took a walk along the edge of the ocean letting the cold foamy water lap at her ankles. The breeze was even stronger there and the waves were gentle but big enough to discourage a non swimmer from going in, especially Karen who didn't really like ocean swimming. Conrad, still the city street kid, hardly ever did any serious swimming even in the many pools belonging to their local friends and aquaintances. When she finally returned to their blanket, Conrad had turned over on his stomach and chin resting on hands was gazing at two teen agers playing frisbee behind them.

Karen lowered herself onto the blanket and stretched out on her side, facing Conrad. "Con?" she said gently.

"Hmm?" He continued to stare ahead, not looking at her.

"I've thought it over and I've decided what I'm going to do."

Conrad was silent.

"The show has three more weeks of shooting and then it's finished, unless they get a pick-up which is anyone's guess. Then I'm going to go to New York whether you come with me or not. Maybe it'll give us both a chance to decide what we want to do. Or should I say what we really want."

Karen waited for a reply hoping to get some kind of reaction, or argument or protest, but Conrad remained silent. "Of course, I hope you'll come with me. But if you decide to stay here, maybe it'll help give us both the space you seem to think we need." Again she paused waiting for a response but all she heard was a sigh as Conrad put his head face down on the blanket.

"If you don't come with me I guess I'll stay with my parents," she continued. "You think about it, okay darling?"

"Okay." With his face buried in the blanket the response was muffled but from his tone it was clear to Karen that he wasn't going to discuss it further that afternoon on the beach.

As the days sped by and the date of Karen's departure got closer Conrad agonized over what to do about her. He knew damn well he was not going to leave L.A. just when things were on the brink. He'd worked hard on the new screenplay and an answer from the studio might come in any day. The Inner

City people were crazy about him and that situation had all kinds of potential. It was true that there were no training programs and that Frank Silvera was the only acting teacher of any worth in the area and he was getting on in years. So the opportunity to head a school was there for the taking. No, it would be insane to leave now after struggling so long to find his place here. But he also knew that if they separated geographically it might be the beginning of the end for them. And he knew how much it would hurt Karen. He loved her deeply and would miss her terribly, but he was used to pain and deprivation. Denying himself his wonderful white wife would be just one more sacrifice to add to a long list of survival tactics he'd employed in his life thus far.

But for Karen it would be harder. This was her second marriage and if they split up, it would be her second failure. But she needed someone who could devote his life to taking care of her, a whole man not someone divided into two pieces only able to give her half, a professional man of substance who had already arrived financially and career wise. She deserves that, he thought. And she's still young enough and attractive enough to find it. Conrad had found a way to paint himself as the good guy, the one thinking more about Karen's well being than his own. He had to do something to be able to face himself.

Karen sat quietly as Conrad carefully explained why he couldn't come with her. She didn't try to argue or plead with him. It was clear that he'd made his choice and no amount of rationalization on his part would make it easier to take. It was the way it had to be and she was going to have to accept it. They were coming to the end of what had been for her a remarkable and often thrilling journey. She had hoped that their marriage would last forever but somehow in her heart of hearts she had always known that the odds were stacked against that. Although Conrad attempted to assure her that they were just going to be apart for a while, she knew that from this point forward their lives were going to move in opposite directions and that getting back together would grow increasingly more difficult with each passing day.

Their parting, weeks later, was gentle and subdued as though there had been a death in the family. Conrad drove Karen to the airport and waited with her until it was time to board. They both pretended that it would be a brief separation, like a short vacation.

"Be a good girl," Conrad murmured in her ear as they hugged. "And take care of yourself."

"I love you Con." Karen's eyes were filling with tears in spite of her best efforts to contain them.

"I love you too baby. Have a good trip."

Conrad watched Karen move toward the AA personnel at the gate who were taking tickets. She turned to wave at him and as he waved back she disappeared into the terminal.

As Conrad headed for the crowded parking lot blocks away, he felt strangely weak and empty. "What are we doing?" he muttered. "How did we get to this?" He finally located his car and when he got in and turned the ignition key both the motor and the jazz sounds from the radio turned on simultaneously. Karen would remind me not to run down the battery, he thought. I'm even going to miss her nagging about silly little things. But his mood began to change as he drove onto the San Diego Freeway facing north. He realized he would no longer have to worry about checking in with her or letting her know his where-abouts. There was something to be said for complete freedom, even though loneliness was a by product.

CHAPTER 17

1979 KKK stages 50 Mile March from Selma to Alabama

Once back in New York it was only a matter of time before Karen resumed her old life. She knew she'd missed it but hadn't realized how much until she began to hook up with many of her former friends who'd made themselves scarce during her marriage to Conrad. Although she'd resented the apparent subconscious bigotry that had kept them distanced, she knew she needed to reconnect, needed to use them for support in this very difficult period.

At first she cried herself to sleep every night but gradually the pain wore off and she managed to keep herself sufficiently occupied with meetings, lunches and dinners to keep from calling Conrad more than once every few days. It became more difficult to make contact, what with the time difference and their individual schedules. And they found they had less and less to talk about. Or perhaps it was that there was too much to talk about or to go into over the phone. Their conversations became discussions of the latest films and plays and the relating of the latest gossip and industry jokes. Occasionally Conrad would ask about Karen's plans for returning to L.A. or Karen would tell him about a project in New York that might interest him enough to consider returning.

Karen was offered a job as managing director of an off-Broadway theatre company. Shortly after Karen left, Conrad did get hired as artistic director of Inner City and immediately initiated a full-blown theatre training program primarily for black actors, directors and writers. Time passed quickly as they each became more deeply involved with their individual pursuits and began to adjust to the reality of the physical and emotional distance that lay between them. Although every conversation ended with the mantra "I miss you" and "I love you", they both knew that they were coming to the end of the road. It had become a marriage in name only and the pain of that knowledge had to be confronted and anesthetized through work or play or any distraction that would serve the purpose.

One day on the number 10 bus going down Central Park West towards the theatre section Karen ran into Louise Warren, the character actress who had been in the production in which Conrad and Karen had first met. They made a date to meet at Sardi's for lunch the next day to 'catch up' as they hadn't seen one another since Louise had come to L.A. the year before to do a film job.

As Karen was ushered to the corner booth by the welcoming maitre d' and slid into the generously upholstered maroon leather seat, she took in the familiar room, the quiet bustle of well trained and discreet waiters, the gleaming white table cloths and the caricature faces of theatre notables grinning down at her from the walls. There it is again, she thought, that feeling of coming home, of belonging. If only Conrad were here, I'd be completely content. And then she smiled wryly to herself. Who am I kidding? Con hated this place. It made him uncomfortable. Never any black people. Of course, things were slowly changing. The 'folks' were coming downtown more often. Karen found herself looking around the room to see if there were any folks and then stopped suddenly when she realized what she was doing and how much her perspective had become Conrad's over these past years.

Louise appeared in her line of vision and snapped her out of her reverie. She was wearing a startlingly yellow pantssuit and some stunning primitive African jewelry. "Darling!" She swooped down upon Karen and planted a kiss on her cheek. "It's so good to have you back in town. I'm so glad we ran into each other. How long are you here for?"

"I'm back in New York for good, Louise," Karen heard herself saying.

"Hurray! This calls for a drink." Louise motioned the waiter over and ordered a perfect Rob Roy straight up. Karen ordered a Bloody Mary. They exchanged theatre gossip and nibbled on rolls while they waited for their drinks. When the cocktails arrived Louise raised her glass. "Here's a welcome home to you and that gorgeous hunk of yours."

"Thanks, Lou. But it's just me. Conrad and I are separated." It was the first time she'd said it out loud.

"No, really?" Louise was caught off guard but recovered quickly. "Well, I guess I'm not really surprised. It was inevitable, darling."

Karen stiffened. She was surprised at this reaction from a woman who was known to be at the forefront of all the current liberal causes.

"I mean it's hard enough to keep a relationship going in our industry, but what with what's going on in the world…" Louise hastened to add.

"He needs to stay in L.A. and I couldn't stand it another minute. I needed to be here."

"No explanations necessary, darling. And you know that I've got the best shoulder in the business to cry on."

"I think I'm past the crying stage. It's just that now that I know where I want to be I've got to figure out who I want to be. But thanks for the offer."

"He was one of the most attractive men I've ever met. And such good taste. Well, he found you, didn't he? He would've loved this jewelry. I think I subconsciously chose to wear it today because I was thinking about him," chattered Louise.

"My God, he's not dead, Louise, he's just living in L.A."

"Well," protested Louise, eyes twinkling, "Isn't that the same thing?" She got Karen to laugh a bit, anyway.

Weeks grew into months and Conrad became deeply ensconced in the black community. They'd been waiting for someone like him; someone who was acceptable to the white establishment so he could make inroads for them, but who was hip to their needs and concerns because he was one of them. They wanted him to lead them to the money, to the glory road of the white upper echelon of Hollywood. When it became clear that Karen was not returning, Conrad gave up the Beverly Hills house and moved to a small studio apartment in the Rossmore dostrict which was half way between the eastern section where Inner City was located and the Hollywood and western section where the studios and industry offices were.

At first he was flattered at the attentions paid to him by the students and seduced into believing that he could indeed show the young wannabees the way. He made suggestions about how to dress, corrected their speech insisting they say 'ask' instead of 'axt', etc., talked about dignity and respect for each other and themselves, demanded that they abandon the habit of 'c.p. time' (colored peoples' time) and arrive at sessions ten minutes early instead of thirty minutes late. In addition to Leroi Jones' DUTCHMAN and Douglas Turner Ward's DAY OF ABSENCE he introduced them to the classic literature of the theatre: Shakespeare, Arthur Miller, Tennessee Williams for a start. He insisted that the casting of VIEW FROM THE BRIDGE could just as easily be a black family as an Italian one. He gave them an awareness of acting as a craft to be learned. They hung on his every word and the young women in particular treated him like a guru. It was tonic to his damaged ego. Discovering this propensity for leadership, for a time he even toyed with the idea of entering into politics and running for some kind of office.

Tanya fought hard to remain his main woman. She'd claimed the space left by Karen as soon as she discovered the opportunity and Conrad, taking the course of least resistance, submitted to her constant ministrations. He missed Karen terribly but he kept reminding himself that their separation was for the greater good. It was as much for her fulfillment as for his that this breakup had occurred. He still had dreams and fantasies about becoming the first black head of a studio and returning to New York in triumph to reclaim her as his partner. Or becoming the first black feature film director and offering her a part in his picture. He knew they were adolescent dreams and he mocked himself for indulging in them. The screenplay he'd tried so hard to sell as a project went from hand to hand with a never ending stream of development executives offering just enough hope to keep him waiting.

As time wore on the burden of responsibility for everyone's journey to success began to wear thin. But he persisted in the hope that some miracle would occur, some contact made, some stroke of good fortune would turn his luck around. However, he soon realized that without Karen's presence as a link, the lines into the white community were growing frayed and disappearing. He knew if he wasn't careful he'd become a victim of the crab syndrome: those at the bottom of the barrel struggle to pull the ones at the top, about to get out, back down to the bottom with them.

Karen found a small apartment on Bleeker Street in the west Village. It was a very old six story building in the midst of a block filled with what she used to call 'artsy crafty' stores. She'd always dreamt of living in the Village with its antique charm and cast of unique characters. And it was very near the theatre where she and Conrad began their relationship so it made her feel closer to him. As time passed and communication between them became less frequent she'd faced the reality. Her marriage was over. Three strikes and you're out, she'd thought grimly. What's next? Was she destined to live out her life alone?

It was time to move on although she still missed Conrad terribly. She began to go to parties and eventually to date an occasional interesting man. They would go to concerts, the theatre, peoples' homes for dinner. The few black friends that were still in New York kept in touch at first but gradually became more distant. Karen found herself searching among the guests at parties for a black face or some brown skin, but there was none. The polarization that was happening in the country was now reflected in her life and Karen found herself once again surrounded almost exclusively by white people.

The no-fault, no alimony divorce a year later was more expeditious than Karen would have thought possible. She flew into L.A., stayed overnight at a downtown hotel, met Conrad at the big white stone County Court building on Grand Street and together they appeared in a small courtroom before a rotund, balding judge. There was hardly time to say 'hello how are you' to each other. The judge took one look at the papers and the couple standing before him, nodded knowingly and the whole thing was over. It was as though he'd said 'how could you ever expect this to work?' The detached nature of it reminded Karen of their City Hall wedding ceremony, without the laughs. As they walked outside they couldn't bear to look at each other, so with a murmured 'take care of yourself' and 'good luck' they went their separate ways outwardly appearing like two strangers who had just completed a business deal but inwardly feeling as though a limb had been lost.

The periodic phone conversations continued. When they weren't in touch with one another directly they kept contact through the relayed gossip of mutual friends. Both were loathe to completely surrender the relationship. Each had experienced a change in the perception of life as a result of exposure to the other and whatever had drawn them together other than sheer chemistry seemed destined to endure forever.

Much later, it was made abundantly clear to Karen that part of her would reflexively continue to think and react like a black man's woman when she went to see a play with the man who would eventually become her live-in lover and companion. David Sillman, an architect in his early forties, was just the kind of comfortable, sensitive and caring professional man that every Jewish mother hopes her daughter will find and marry. He was tall, and attractive with craggy features, a square jaw and a full head of curly brown hair. The best part about the relationship as far as Karen was concerned was his complete lack of any connection to the entertainment industry. He was an avid theatregoer however, and in addition to getting tickets to everything on Broadway, was a more than willing escort to any and every little off-Broadway and experimental theatre production Karen felt like seeing. Karen looked forward to his comments and reactions to plays as, even as a layman, they were always intelligent and inciteful.

As they emerged from the Houseman theatre on west 42nd Street, David stopped to light his pipe.

"Let's wait a minute 'til the crowd thins. We'll have a better chance of getting a cab," said David between puffs as he drew on the pipe creating a small cloud of smoke. It was his only flaw as far as Karen was concerned. She didn't much like the smell of the tobacco. "Wasn't that a wonderful play!" he exclaimed. It wasn't a question.

"Did you think so?" asked Karen.

"I thought it was brilliant. The characters were so beautifully drawn. I was very moved by it. Weren't you?" There was a note of surprise in his tone. How could anybody not love it?

"I thought the actors were good," responded Karen quietly.

"They were excellent. And so was the play."

"Another piece of Uncle Tom bullshit," Karen muttered.

"What did you say?"

"Nothing. Forget it."

"No, tell me. I want to hear your opinion," David persisted.

"Well, no wonder it's such a success." Karen blurted it out. "It'll probably get a prize. And why not? It perpetuates the myth of the obedient old black servant who tends faithfully and forever to the needs of the rich white lady. How many black people did you see in the audience? And how many of those were applauding and yelling bravo?"

David stared at her thoughtfully. "That never occurred to me for a moment. It's interesting that you should see it that way. But I couldn't disagree more…."

Karen interrupted. "Forget it, David. Don't pay any attention to me. I'm glad you enjoyed it. I'm just coming from a different place, okay?" She raised her arm towards the lighted yellow cab coasting east on the avenue. "Taxi!" she called. David was smart enough to know when to drop a subject. It was one of the things that made him so likeable.

As she slid into the cab and leaned back against the hard vinyl cushion Karen sighed inwardly. Conrad's voice would always and forever lurk inside the recesses of her gut making it impossible to return to her former perception of the world around her. What existed pre-Conrad was no more. Now there was this strangely schizophrenic ability to see both sides of the issue. Perhaps that was a good thing. Perhaps what the world needed now was more like her, she thought.

EPILOGUE

Conrad sat at the tiny outdoor table in front of the Saloon Restaurant on Broadway and watched the steady stream of pedestrians passing in front of him. It was a wonderful show. All this humanity. Every shape, size and color of human being. It was so damn good to be back in New York, he wanted to shout with the joy of it. How had he stayed away so long? It must have been the lack of change in the seasons that made the years slip by unnoticed. The fall breeze had just enough bite in it to promise the eventual coming of winter. Even the air was more stimulating. His mind felt clearer than it had in a long time. He looked across the avenue at the buildings that made up Lincoln Center and at the cascading fountain that stood in the middle and was the meeting place for so many concert, opera and theatre goers and thought how busy and beautiful and full of vitality everything seemed.

He'd called Karen as soon as he'd arrived. He couldn't wait to see her. It had been so long since they'd had as much as a satisfactory phone conversation. And he still missed her and needed her, even after all these years. Conrad looked at his watch and sipped the tea the waiter had placed in front of him. She ought to be here any minute, he thought. She was always on time, or at least, used to be. He wondered if she'd changed as much as he thought he had. Well, they were both older and wiser, certainly. And the world around them was changing, although in almost invisible increments. Miscegenation was no longer against the law except for a few holdout states who hadn't gotten around to it.

He spotted Karen getting off the 104 bus that stopped a block south of the restaurant. It was the same softly curved body, the same curly brown hair although trimmed shorter, the same rhythm to her walk. She was wearing a brown suede jacket and beige corduroy pants and had a large tote bag slung over her shoulder. Everyone in this city seemed to be carrying a bag or a back pack. Perhaps because everyone moved on foot instead of tossing stuff into a car, he thought. God, listen to me. I'm thinking like a tourist!

Now Karen had seen him and she hurried towards the table, startled at how her heart had started to pound. She'd been so looking forward to this moment, perhaps for years, and now that it was here, she was suddenly afraid. It had been so long. And she knew she had changed, grown older, more mature and part of a very different world now. But then, she was sure it was the same for him. As she drew closer he rose to greet her and she saw with relief the familiar blue jeans, sweat shirt and METS baseball jacket. I can't believe he still has that jacket, she thought. And he looks older but just as gorgeous as ever, except there's a little grey in his hair and flecks in the start of a beard. He's wearing dark glasses. A Hollywood affectation? Or are they prescription, she wondered.

They hugged like relatives who had been parted for a long time. Then Conrad held Karen at arms length and they stared at each other, simultaneously laughing with relief as they read each other's minds. They had each aged a bit of course, but nothing essential had changed, except for Conrad's beard. He'd grown one once while they were married because he'd said it might change his luck, but he'd gotten tired of trimming it after about two weeks and shaved it off. Conrad held Karen's chair for her as she sat and had she seen his face as he looked down at her head it would have told her volumes. They sat and grinned at each other saying nothing for a while, until the waiter who looked like an actor glided up and asked if they'd decided to order. Conrad said he was fine with his tea and Karen ordered a cappucino. And then they just sat and looked at each other some more because neither wanted to spoil the specialness of the moment with words.

It was Karen who broke the silence. "Finally. You're here."

"Yep."

"I'm so glad you called."

"Been thinking about you a lot."

Karen didn't know how she wanted to reply to that, so she let it go. "How long are you staying?"

"I'm not sure. I'm here seeing about a job." He paused for a moment. "I might move back permanently."

Karen looked into his eyes. "How are you really? Are you okay?"

Conrad showed his surprise. "Of course. I'm great. Why? Don't I look okay?"

"You look handsome as ever," Karen teased. "A little older, perhaps, but nonetheless handsome. Although I'm not sure about the beard. Are you changing your luck?"

Conrad noted that she'd remembered that detail and took it as a sign. "It's supposed to make me look dignified. I'm a professor now."

"Oh Con, that's wonderful! Where?"

"At Marymount. But I've pretty much had it with L.A. I'm hoping to get something here and maybe just spend two months a year out there in a summer session or something."

"That would be perfect."

They fell silent again and both watched the traffic go by as they searched for words. Conrad studied Karen for a moment. Her large brown eyes had the same intelligent depth but her face was fuller and more mature now, matching the voluptuousness of her body. "You look fantastic Karen."

"Thanks."

Conrad hesitated. "Still with that guy?"

"You mean David? Uhhuh."

"Married?"

"Nope."

"How come?"

Karen made a wry face. "Three strikes and you're out. He's wanted to but I don't."

"What does he do?"

Karen shrugged. She didn't really want to talk about David. "He's an architect."

"Impressive. At least to this underpaid schoolteacher."

"Is your wife with you?" asked Karen.

"That's over. We split up."

Oh. I see, thought Karen. "I'm sorry," she said aloud.

This time Conrad shrugged. "It was a dumb move. I guess I wasn't ready to go it alone so I jumped into something convenient without thinking much." They both fell silent for a few moments then Conrad spat out the words. "We should never have left New York! God, what was I thinking? Temporary insanity."

Karen was surprised to see the tears in his eyes. "Don't, Con. Don't look back. It doesn't do any good." She was determined not to give in to the need to cry.

"I've missed you, Karen."

"I've missed you too. I never stopped caring about you. You know that. That'll never change," she added quickly. So he'd been unhappy too.

"We certainly let them fuck us up," said Conrad ruefully.

"It wasn't 'them', it was us. We fucked ourselves up. We weren't strong enough to fight for what we had. And you were so desperate for more."

Conrad nodded and sipped the tea which had now grown cold. There was so much he wanted to say but he found himself at a loss as to how to begin. "I thought the world was changing…" he said slowly. "I thought the so-called mountain top was in sight and that we could get there together. We were all so full of hope. Then the reality set in and the slide began. Now it seems as if we've come full circle. All this backlash, alienation, that's going on now. Racism is a disease that seems to have no cure. It looks like there will always be two separate worlds. You'll be in yours, I'll be in mine and never the twain shall meet."

"No!" protested Karen. "I refuse to believe that. What happened to us was a result of who we were. We handled it badly. We let ourselves be beached on the shore by a wave of ignorant opinion and our own weakness. But we're stronger and wiser now and there are many more like us. I'm damned if I'm going to surrender to ignorance and give up hope that's it's all going to come together."

Conrad grinned at her. "Would you like a box to stand on?"

"Don't make fun of me. I'm dead serious."

"So am I." Conrad stared at her intently for a moment, then took her hands in his. "Can we come together, Karen?" he said softly. "Can we try again?"

A huge lump collected in Karen's throat, making it impossible for her to speak for a moment. She had played out this moment in her dreams so many times when they first split up. But as the hurt and anger had dissipated and she'd adjusted to this new life, she'd finally accepted the idea of reconciliation as impossible. Now here he was playing out the scene as she originally conceived it and all sorts of warning bells were going off in her head. Just the touch of his hands sent tiny coils of heat through her bloodstream. The chemistry was still there. But so were the problems.

Conrad let go of her hands. "I guess your silence is my answer."

"I don't know, Con," she whispered. She saw the pain in his eyes. "I know we can't go back. We have to go forward if it's ever going to come together. And you have to be very sure of who you are and what and with whom you want to be."

"Yeh, sure. That's it. It always comes down to having to make a choice, doesn't it?" Conrad stared out at the steady stream of humanity passing before them. It was rush hour now and even pedestrian traffic was heavy. "Who was it that called the city a 'gorgeous mosaic'?" He turned back to Karen. "You know, when I was a kid I wrote a poem that I never showed to anyone. But I never forgot it. It went: 'I am forever a twilight man

suspended between day and night

hung in the middle, a twilight man

belonging to neither black nor white...' Will it come together in time for me? I wonder."

Karen reached for his hands again and they sat there together silent and touching and watching the passing parade.

N.Y. TIMES JULY 1999
Wrongful Arrest of Black Actor is Blamed on Bias

THE END

0-595-30009-X